BOUND BY SHADOWS

McAllister Justice Series
Book Two
by
Reily Garrett

Thank you for reading
Bound By Shadows

For information on updates,
new releases, deals, bonus content,
and other great books, sign up for
Reily's newsletter at
reilygarrett.com.[1]

---

1. http://www.reilygarrett.com/

Acknowledgments

This book is dedicated to Darius, Leyna, and Raptor, the incredible trio, loyal, kind, and energetic. Three incredible beings who don't understand the words "give up." To Faith, whose love and compassion changed my life.

Special thanks to beta readers Graham from Fading Street Publishing, Siobhan Caughey, Lori Sickles, and Daphne Stanley. I appreciate your time and insights. To my readers, each one of you who selects and reads one of my books, thank you for the opportunity to share my work.

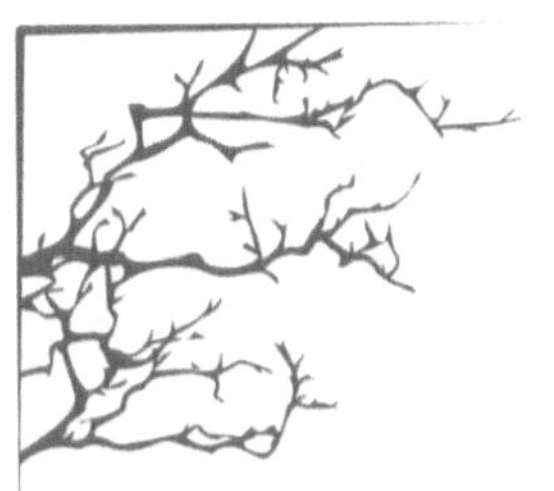

Chapter One

Confusion and pain intertwined to delay Kaylee's escape from the depths of a nightmare. Her subconscious' attempt to alert her to some horror or another had been common the past two years, but this time the warning came with physical characteristics she couldn't ignore.

The pain was an unwelcome element for which she could not account.

Cozy flannel sheets had never felt so rough under her cheek, nor had her head ached from a glass of wine. Despite the tomboy tag since adolescence, she appreciated certain creature comforts. The rough material scratching her face didn't number among them.

A quiet foreboding swelled within that fuzzy twilight between the dream state and the hazy stages of surfing to consciousness. Sleep would be welcome if not for the musty odor and an undefined menace crowding her mind. Her brow furrowed as her pulse increased, awareness mounting with each painful throb.

Why is dirt in my bed—and what the hell is wrong with this mattress?

With each erratic contraction of her heart, the tension in her head increased, ratcheting like the shell around a drumhead until pain reverberated along every nerve. In grim anticipation, she reached to touch her temple. A crusty line of fibrous, threadlike strands crumbled in her brow line and snaked down to her ear.

Blood? What the hell?

Moving back to Portland had entailed a certain degree of compromise, yet shouldn't include a cotton-mouth morning. This was too much. A light finger-comb revealed a large tangled knot and a painful lump over her ear.

Did I fall off the mattress and hit my head?

"Hey, kid. Wake up, damn it. Hurry."

The harsh whisper embodied urgency and desperation that replicated and swelled within her chest.

What the hell? The voice in her head wasn't her own. Enlightenment would come after punching through the suffocating fog and fully emerging in the suddenly hostile world. Stabbing pain accompanied the dingy light spearing her eyes after cautiously lifting one lid.

A blur of flashbacks included sitting in an outdoor riverfront café enjoying the sunset with her favorite camera nestled in her lap. Snapping the riot of colors slipping into the ocean had equaled the day's highpoint, nature's way of assuring her she'd made the right decision in moving to Portland.

Now, for reasons evading memory, her gaze soft-focused on a scene defying logic.

"Kid, open your eyes before it's too late. Grab the small rock by your head. Hide it behind you."

Okaaay, evil mini me is crazy, and I will never drink wine again.

Five minutes of silence would help her collect her thoughts and allow time to search her virtual portfolio for whatever was causing the nausea-producing pests in her brain and stomach. Each vied for the position of top party host. Intuition whispered taking that time would be her undoing.

Instead of the distant hustle and bustle of city life swarming her senses, Kaylee found the intense quiet more disturbing than the harsh whisper. "Wait...what rock?"

Fragments of her surroundings wavered in and out of focus. Brick walls smeared with dirt were partially visible through the horizontal bars.

Horizontal bars?

She reached with shaking fingers to touch the rusted metal cylinders then tried to rattle them. They didn't budge. A cramp in her thigh from resting in a semi-fetal position grew in intensity while her feet crowded against hard, cylindrical surfaces and prevented her from stretching out.

More bars.

She didn't have the strength to yell.

The quick, indrawn breath was also not her own. "C'mon you stupid kid. Knock that off, or we're both dead."

A shower of dirt sprinkling her face and hair made her cough, the resultant sandy inhalation perpetuating the cycle.

The collaborative dream, having taken a southern turn into hell, brought another wave of anxiety along with nausea. Each of her senses plunged deeper into a dark abyss, taking logic and rational thought through a twisted, interactive roller-coaster ride.

Disorientation, chaos, and the first stirrings of panic took root like a well-fertilized seed that sent its growing tendrils sliding deep within the earth.

Loose dirt and small rocks covered the hard base and abraded her shoulder as she moved to a cramped position on her back. The changed perspective brought enlightenment.

That's why the bars were horizontal.

"Damn." Details assimilated sluggishly. Dirt-covered metal comprised a bed, but it wasn't in her apartment. Walls of brick as seen through her cage, lack of windows, and stale, dank air, pointed to an underground zip code.

Micro currents ferried a thick, putrid scent and muffled the faint, eerie groans of venting tunnels.

"What's your name?" Again, a whisper twisted with annoyance and despair saturated the air.

Halting breaths and extreme concentration staved off the blind terror threatening her sanity.

"Kaylee. My name is Kaylee." Slowly, she searched for the irritating heckler.

"Listen up, Kaylee. The bastard who took you is gonna be back soon, probably looking for a bit of afternoon delight. And he won't be asking. He kidnapped you, too. I don't know why."

Kaylee's befuddled mind took in more of her surroundings, low ceiling, dirt floor, cramped, cave-like room, and the caged, bedraggled woman three feet away. Purple and black surrounded her right eye and busted lip. Her shirt front hung in tatters, the ripped flannel exposing a large bruise above her breast.

"How long have we been here?" A torch along the wall cast flickering shadows over the adjoining cage, just short of her own.

Flickering—indicates an air current.

"The last thing I remember is shopping." Tears trailed down the petite blonde's mud-streaked alabaster cheeks which sharply contrasted the bruises marring her face.

"There's a slight breeze coming from—that way." Kaylee strained to see where the tunnel led. Pitch black. Some apparitional entity scuttled in the darkness beyond the seedy illumination and left the impression of ghostly stalkers. Stalkers that chittered in the dark. *I'd rather see the boogeyman than rats.* "We seem to be in an underground room?"

"Yeah. I think so. I woke up just like you, but the bastard tied my hands before my head cleared." A sob choked further words as the victim's wide gaze flickered around the room.

A cursory exploration of the small perimeter marked the filthy, tight confines, then the small, sharp-edged rock which fit in her palm. Instinct saw her sliding it behind her. Mud covered her jeans and colored her T-shirt and jacket. Bathing was the least of her worries.

"Someone slipped us a roofie." Bruises, tattered flannel, and bound wrists conveyed the woman's recent past.

Kaylee's continued scrutiny yielded no clues of how to escape her dilemma. Even if she could squeeze her hand and arm through the bars' two-inch gaps, she didn't have the strength or leverage to break the heavy-duty padlock securing her prison.

"Yes. Yes. But at least you're not tied up, yet." The girl lifted her hands to reveal a double loop, plastic cuff. "See if you can break out."

Kaylee studied the thick, padlock and then the small rock. "Shit." Stomach acid threatened to revolt if she moved too fast. "I don't think—"

Low, rumbling conversation in the distance indicated a quarrel. A man complained of "damaged merchandise" while another argued something about perks of the business.

The few words discerned, argued the merits and risks of something important, judging by the intermittent expletives and plaintive appeals. A third person had entered the dispute.

A female?

Thick foreign accents hindered clarification.

"Shhh, someone's coming. Lie down and pretend you're still unconscious."

The battered victim huddled back, trembling, eyes wider as she sought shelter in her prison.

Instinct guided Kaylee into fetal position with feet facing the door and her scrunched body hiding the crude weapon. Closing her eyes heightened other senses and expanded her knowledge of the impossible scenario coming to life.

Rambling steps. The soft rustle of denim.

A shuffle step skidded dirt in her face, filling her thoughts with images of a monster able to snap her neck with a flick of his wrist. Rustling sounds in the next cage testified to the other woman's movements.

"Let me go, please. My family has money. They're rich, and they'll pay for my return." A sob choked off as the beaten woman continued. "I won't tell anyone where I've been or—what you've done."

"Money, huh? You're dressed no better than a junkie. Though you did smell nice." The nasal whine and broken English was followed by a sleazy chuckle. "I doubt anyone even knows you're missing."

"You guys have a new girl for your entertainment. Please, let me go." Desperate words ended in a choked mewling.

"Dunno how *entertaining* she'll be. So damned skinny. I like to grab hold of some meat. At least she has nice hair and tits."

Kaylee kept her eyes closed while listening, unable to condemn the woman after having suffered obvious atrocities. Would she have done the same if the circumstances were reversed?

"You're worth a lot of money. Why would I chance losing it for a lie? If you were a rich bitch, you wouldn't be dressed in rags. Stupid puss. Be quiet while I sample the new sweetmeat or I'll stuff your mouth with my cock."

Kaylee still couldn't place the accent.

Dull metallic clinking marked the shifting of chain between bars before tumbling to the cell floor.

"Wakee, wakee, doll face. Time for some sexercise." A new gruffness in his voice stoked Kaylee's fear.

The metal door shrieked in protest before a meaty fist grabbed her right ankle and yanked. The painful grip encircling her leg spawned a tsunami-force horror to swell within her chest, then gush outward to seize every nerve ending. She'd never experienced man-handling.

Kaylee's eyes snapped open. Evil incarnate crouched in front of the open door. Grinning. Almost drooling.

Her photographer's eye cataloged nuances of his appearance while her scrambled thoughts tried to formulate a plan. Long, greasy hair, tied in the back. A gap between crooked, chaw-stained teeth. Sagging jowls. His thickened nose suggested a prior break.

Barbarian, I hope it was at the hands of a woman.

A low whistle hissed out in appreciation while black eyes glittered with menace, intensified by the jagged scar running from temple to chin. An artist's stroke of malice. The bastard outweighed her by at least a hundred pounds.

I'm a fly caught on sticky tape.

The abrasions earned from him dragging her through the cage paled in comparison to the bands of shock and repulsion seizing her lungs. A painful wrench scraped her into a new position—on her back.

A muffled voice grumbled from the far side where the tunnels hid their dangerous secrets, its owner still concealed in the depths of the new hell.

The split-second diversion would either save her life or delay an inevitable fate. Regardless of the garbled warning, another presence spelled trouble.

Kaylee's explosive response took advantage of her assailant's distraction. Terror aimed her left foot at her kidnapper's crotch with all the strength of a desperate hostage. Regardless of the outcome, she'd go down fighting.

The dirtball toppled on his back with both hands cradling his junk amid a long groan, dry-heaves, and growls. His slight rocking motion and tightly clenched eyes gave her little satisfaction.

He deserves so much more.

With mere seconds to escape, she glanced at the caged woman. Widened eyes and dropped jaw bared a soul beseeching help. Hope was premature.

"I'm sorry."

The thug opened his eyes. "Ahh, bitch. You'll pay for that." Hissed through tightly clenched teeth, the threat carried a vomit-provoking promise. Curling to a sit, his bulky frame still blocked the exit while labored breathing punctuated his groans. His expression declared her already dead.

Physically, she was no match for the brute. A sloping forehead engendered hope that his mental processes equaled dull wits. Time was not on her side. Before she could crab-walk out to kick him again, his malevolent smile flagged a hatred she wouldn't survive.

The decayed leer, like his gaze, never wavered but extended a new and foul determination. This time, he kneeled up, and his two-handed reach secured both lower legs in a matter of seconds. Vicious yanks pulled her from the cage. Pain stabbed her back as her body twisted and jerked in a bid to loosen his grip. Instinctively, her hands reached for the bars on either side. Something sharp jabbed her arm.

The rock.

Releasing the bar on one side allowed her to palm the stone. The movement gained a weapon but cost another layer of skin on her back. Nausea and the remnants of drugs threatened her effort while revulsion and encroaching blackness warred for dominance.

When her head cleared the opening, she curled her upper body in a disjointed sit-up. A new light-headedness chiseled away at hope, her head swirling in a foggy mist between consciousness and bloodcurdling fear. Unable to focus, she prayed her upward momentum and continued arc proved true, and bashed his head with the crude weapon. A sickening thud asserted her triumph, if only temporarily.

The sight of a crimson gush pouring down his temple gave her strength. His hands went lax as he slumped sideways to the ground. Blood flowed freely over his forehead while his eyelids fluttered then closed.

If she crawled closer to hit him again and he roused, she'd be dead. Despite the circumstances, she couldn't murder an unconscious man. Killing another human had never made her to-do list. However, making sure he remained out cold for a while longer would grant her time to help the other captive.

"Quick. Get me out of here!" A frantic rattling of the cage accompanied the harsh whisper.

Clumsy movements gained Kaylee an upright advantage on shaky legs before anger and adrenaline supplemented her power. A well-aimed but weakened kick rocked his head. The crunch of nasal bone granted small satisfaction.

"Kaylee, he's down. Free me."

Four steps in the other victim's direction and Kaylee stopped short. The bloody rock in her hand was no match for the thick padlock. The key she needed rested harmlessly in the lock to her own cage. Retrieving it would mean stepping between the dirtball and prison, thereby blocking her exit. She shuffled one step.

The bastard groaned then cursed.

She scrutinized his sluggish movements.

Blood flowed around thick fingers pressed to his temple and nose. "Hell. I'm gonna kill you slow, peel the skin from every inch of your body."

The kidnapper's awkward movements wouldn't stay clumsy for long. Kaylee glanced helplessly at the woman's tear-streaked face. To delay would mean death. With each wild heartbeat, the bastard regained his senses.

She had no choice.

"I'll send help." The minuscule blink linking one heartbeat to the next rifled myriad images of cosmic lunacy through the dark reaches of her mind.

She tried to use me as a bargaining chip. The realization didn't justify leaving her behind.

"No, don't leave me here. He'll kill me. Grab the key. Just toss it to me!"

There were no good options. The kidnapper rolled to a sitting position.

The chamber had two exits. Two choices held equally dark and dismal hope. Two echoes that defied origin. She figured it came from the farthest black yawning mouth. Fear and disorientation hampered her certainty, a fifty-fifty shot of running toward death. Each led into a dark unknown, each a question mark for escape and survival.

She fled through the closest shaft, blindly reaching forward, urged faster by the string of curses trailing her.

Should have taken the light. Yet that would have given the kidnapper something to track.

Do they know which way I went? She prayed the other victim would use misdirection in hopes of eventually gaining her own freedom.

Small rocks dotted the sandy ground and threatened her balance with each step. *Please let them be rocks.* At least they didn't squirm underfoot. Above, the ceiling's height outdistanced her reach. With one hand stretched in front and the other slightly overhead, she rushed forward, stumbling into the walls each time the maze curved.

Curses and shuffling sounds floated from behind. Each shunted her faster in a blind scramble to find an exit. *These tunnels can go for miles.* At any second, she expected someone to fist her hair in a punishing grip or fire blindly, the bite of a bullet piercing her back.

What felt like hours probably passed in minutes. After several turns, she no longer detected sounds of pursuit. Nothing eclipsed the rush of blood in her ears.

Musty air choked her lungs, the dampness making each heavy breath the equivalent of sucking air through a dirty, wet filter. The darkness was a blessing and a curse. Surely her pursuers would use some form of light. A quick glance over her shoulder ensured no flickering shadows drifted through the maze.

Time measured itself in each faltering step, each erratic thrust of her heart against its cage, and each smothering gag she suppressed. Without knowledge of her location, she couldn't guess what lay ahead. Each time the tunnel branched in front of her, she kept to the left. Always left. She'd already gone too far and made too many turns to track her route, not that she wanted to return.

The police will search for the other woman. They'll use tracking dogs.

No light and with nothing to mark her trail meant she'd have to rely on her wits, frazzled and twisted into a mindless, instinctual creature now acting on intuition.

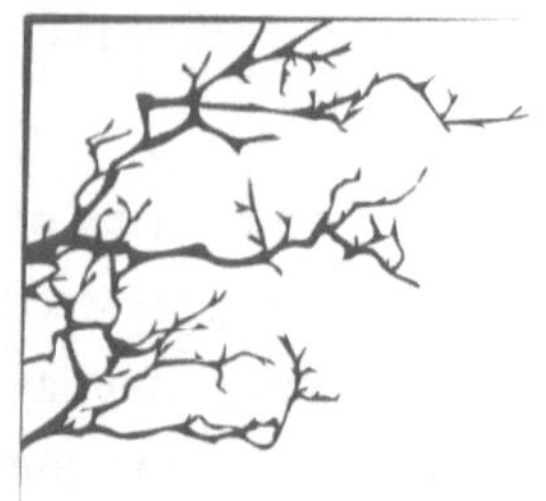

Chapter Two

Time held little meaning as every harsh exhale returned a mini echo, the cadence a reassurance of continued life. Phantom talons plunged from the void every time her outstretched hand collided with solid wall while the conjured images of a flesh and blood nightmare spurred her desperation. Each time, a gasp threatened exposure to the fiendish rapist located in the bowels of the catacombs.

She imagined small recesses to either side, filled with skeletons of those unable to escape. Empty sockets stared, silently jeering her onward. The musky scent of the past both followed her and foreshadowed the future.

The fact she couldn't hear her kidnapper in pursuit didn't mean he wasn't close. The dirt floor and mazelike configuration muted sound while ominous dark tunnels held tight to their secrets. She existed in a black void, a rat caught in a maze but lacking any positive stimulus as a guide.

As if fear gave rise to action, a scream stopped her cold. Begging and pleading tones echoed off brick walls, then suddenly cut short.

Would they kill her? Stomach acid boiled up at the back of her throat.

Surely one of the kidnappers was searching the tunnels in hopes of catching their escapee. She wondered to what lengths they would go. Listening to the overwhelming silence, she could hear no telltale shuffling or curses delineating her remaining life.

An odd thought made her reach for the wallet she always kept in her back pocket when working. It was gone.

They have my driver's license, which hasn't been renewed since moving.

The bastard wouldn't know where she lived *if* she made it back to civilization. The thought pushed her forward.

Shock and pain reshaped her focus after her nose struck jagged rock. Instinct forced her to crouch and collect her wits.

A narrow wedge of wall scraping her left hand outlined the partition of the tunnel's split. If someone tried to track her and used enough light, they'd see a fresh, bloody smear on the edge.

Wiping her lip covered her fingers in the slick, coppery fluid and reminded her of when a childhood crush had rescued the neighborhood twins from the school bullies. Caden McAllister had stood between her and the future hoodlums. He'd become her hero, worshiped from afar and glimpsed sporadically with his older brothers. She could use a hero in her life.

She couldn't spare the seconds to apply pressure to her nose when she needed both hands in front to detect where the passage split. Every second differentiated the gossamer thread between life and death. Sticky moisture dribbled down her chin and would cement her long hair in spiky patches.

Trembling fingers defined the tunnel's split into what she guessed was only two shafts. Without visual confirmation, she realized she may have missed many partitions.

Left, always left.

Again, the jagged surface removed a layer from her finger pads as she felt her way forward.

Oregon's underground tunnels were partly the reason for her return to the Pacific Northwest, a young photographer's dream.

She'd wanted to recapture the security of prior years and reconnect with old friends. Ironic to find herself trapped in what she assumed was the very system she'd wanted to explore as a child.

Darting farther into the black void, she prayed she wouldn't fall down a vertical shaft. Being mindful of the miles of gnarled paths ahead didn't help her frantic heart rate or help her come up with a better plan. She could die down here with no one the wiser, her parents unaware and unable to mourn her passing.

Shaking legs forced her to brace herself against the wall at intervals to catch her breath and keep nausea at bay. At some point, her nose stopped bleeding. Pitch-blackness and an overactive imagination skewed her time perception. The only goal, escape.

High-pitched squeaking in the dark forced her onward as her cunning dark side fashioned beady red eyes in mutant monsters hungering for the taste of flesh.

I hate rats.

She realized the kidnapper might have no choice other than to kill the other woman now, even if it wasn't the original plan. They would also hunt any witnesses. They had a name, birth date, and driver's license number. With that information and the right connections, anyone could track her down.

Time shifted images of a woman's dead body through her mental folders. There was nothing she could do except pray and send help.

Narrowing her focus to each step led to structure and order as her thoughts swirled in a drug-hazed mist. Assuming she survived, the police would use dogs to search, but what would they find? Even a dim-witted criminal would try to cover his trail.

Claustrophobia had never resided among her shortcomings. The subterranean maze now crushed her hopes with its seemingly endless branches lacking a discernable pattern. The path curved and twisted in defiance of her attempt at developing a mental template.

Both cell phone and wallet were gone, along with her keys always attached to her belt carrier when working. The only remaining piece of her existence lay cold against her neck. An SD card inside the locket she wore would yield some information about what happened before she woke up in a cage. The lost camera was her prized possession.

Nothing compared to a woman's life.

Light mist coated her forehead despite the coolness of the musty air, possibly the last moisture she'd ever feel. It was a sobering thought.

At intervals, queasiness forced her to stop for slow, controlled breaths, time she spent listening for muffled curses and searching the distant recesses for torch light.

When exhaustion botched her step and it ended with a face-plant, she considered yielding to fate. The memories of her loving family who had bolstered her lagging spirit whenever darkness encroached, threatened her composure. Giving up had never been in her vocabulary, but she'd never been bombarded by so much evil and so many insurmountable problems.

If she survived, she'd make sure her parents knew their worth. It seemed life brought her greatest epiphanies during the bleakest moments. In the back of her mind, her father's voice drifted to her as unconsciousness dragged her into oblivion. 'You can't prevail if you don't try.'

"I'm sorry, Dad."

A nightmare woke then followed her into the waking world as a not-so-distant chittering compelled her clumsily to her feet. With no idea of whether moments or hours had passed, she forged ahead, one foot in front of the other. She had no other choice.

At one point, the heavy thump of music overhead throbbed in her chest. Perhaps it defined a deadfall through which someone might have dragged an inert body. Stretching up, she couldn't reach the ceiling. Even if she had a light *and* could find a trapdoor, the occupants on the other side might be her enemy.

Without light or specific stimuli to guide her other than the stone scraping her fingers, she shuffled forward as precious memories of her family filled her thoughts. Gradually, she detected the low buzz of voices, growing louder with each turn in her maze. Lack of discernable words kept her hidden in the shadows.

Freedom was too close to risk stumbling into more thugs. After hearing the bloodcurdling scream cut short—what felt like hours ago—it wasn't worth the chance.

A sudden loud crack coincided with her turning another corner in the pitch-black maze. Instinctively, she ducked at the sound of solid impact. Perhaps someone had dropped a barrel on a dock. She knew many of the tunnels led to the river. Her traitorous imagination created images of bound and gagged women dropped on the decking, waiting to be led through whatever horrific chain of events others had endured.

Cautiously, she eased forward around another jagged curve that like the others, branched out into places unknown. The air became sharper with a saltwater tang, making her want to take large gulping breaths. She savored them slowly, quietly.

Dim light.

Just around the corner, the blessed luminous energy she'd spent years studying in perfecting her craft, sent dingy spindles that stopped short about twenty feet from the opening. She strained to gather the gist of the conversation.

"Careful with that merchandise. We don't get paid for damaged goods." The deep, harsh tone would have frozen any demon in hell. The voice gave no indication as to the nature of his *merchandise.* At any moment, she expected to hear a thin wail or a pleading cry.

If they were unloading stock to bring through the tunnels, fate had swung its pendulum against her. As quietly as on approach, she backed to where the tunnel branched and felt her way along the other shaft, not knowing if she'd taken their intended route or slipped out of their path. When something soft underfoot squirmed and screeched, her own squeal pierced the musty air before she could clamp a hand over her mouth.

"Hey, you hear that?" The speaker's voice sounded reedy, younger.

It seemed unlikely that bootleggers would hire teenagers for extra help but it wasn't worth the risk of discovery to find out. She retreated several more steps.

"Yeah, sounds like your mama when I stroke deep." Several gravelly chuckles followed the admonition. "Now pick up the barrel and ignore the tunnel rats. I'd like to skin whoever's putting poison down here. Makes the air fouler than necessary."

Nasty air becomes tolerable when consumed by a free individual.

Quiet tears washed her face. She wanted desperately to bolt toward civilization, but without knowing where she'd exit, she had no clue which route led to the city. She wasn't even sure of the date. After spending time wandering underground and exhausted, she couldn't outrun a small child, much less a grown man. If she waited until night, perhaps the city's lights would act as a beacon to safety.

Sounds of shuffling feet with occasional grunts and crude comments followed the men's passage down the other shaft as Kaylee made her way farther into her branch of purgatory. This time, with the hope of eventual escape guiding her, she mentally noted the turns taken. Hunger clawed at her belly, yet overwhelming thirst pushed her further in hopes of finding an aquifer or underground spring. Without a time frame since daylight last caressed her skin, either dehydration or the drug's aftereffects dulled her senses.

Exhaustion and fear jumbled the map she'd tried to form while a sense of self-preservation curtailed her search for water. Banking her reserves for the bolt to freedom led her to sit in silence while waiting.

It wasn't until she'd leaned against the wall she realized craggy dirt had again replaced brick. Along her tortuous route, she vaguely recalled varying changes under her fingertips and wondered if that was how others defined their path.

The horror of what she'd just escaped evoked a fresh accumulation of tears and a lump in her throat. A slow, muted breath helped steady her nerves. In a cursory assessment, she felt the scrapes and bruises on her face and head, along with the congealed strings from her nosebleed. Over her right ear, she found a tangled mess matted with blood.

Time passed in a jumbled blur of fear—punctuated randomly by distant voices and occasional guffaws. Were they devising methods of torture? As much as she wanted to close her eyes and sleep, she stayed vigilant, wary of furry, red-eyed critters and the chance someone would stumble her way. In her mind, she reviewed her rusty memories of the area. She could be miles from civilization with nothing but forest between.

Why would these men transfer their goods during the day if the merchandise was illegal? If they were legit, why use the tunnels at all?

Limited external stimuli offered no help in gauging time's passage and compelled her thoughts inward. The dull awareness of so much quiet wrapped in thickened layers of moist air reminded her of the caverns she and Reese explored in Pennsylvania. They'd planned to move back here at the same time. Her parents saw her moving to Oregon alone as her way of honoring her brother's dream, but it'd been her dream, too.

A single tear traced down her cheek, soon followed by others, left to add their moisture to her damp shirt and jacket. She hadn't cried when Reese died, shock numbing that part of her which connected with her twin. If she ran into the goon squad, she'd likely see him in spirit and have no more need of tears.

When a drop in temperature suggested evening's approach, she crawled to the next split where she could taste the salty tang of the ocean on the slightest of air currents. Faint lapping sounds of water lulled her into a false sense of security while the screams of sea gulls reminded her of a last cry for help. The dichotomy snarled her nerves into knots.

Faint shafts of light stealing along the dirt floor dimmed, receding with the sun's descent. Again, she sat against the rough wall, waiting, biding her time, and fighting panic as the darkness threatened her sanity.

When pitch darkness consumed her once again, she palmed the wall to gain her feet. It was time to move.

In preparation for her bid for freedom, she shoved the bulk of her sticky, matted hair down the back of her shirt. Eliminating the perfect handhold made sense.

The last of the male voices had drifted off earlier, followed by the sounds of a motor rambling away. That didn't eliminate other threats.

Waiting for her.

There was only one way to find out. Cautious steps in the blackness yielded more of the same. Panic seized her with the realization she may not have retraced her steps but instead headed back into Hades. Nervous energy hummed through her head while faceless monsters again took shape in her mind. *I stayed left.*

Around the next bend, faint shafts of moonlight offered a promise of freedom, capture, or death. While a lighter shade of murkiness outlined the exit, she took her first unfettered breath. Another one followed. Each pace brought her a stronger tang of fresh air until she stood on the edge of a precipice, both literally and figuratively.

The steep incline would have been dangerous to travel even during the day. A sharp, downward slant represented the merging of two worlds where a bad decision equaled degradation, pain, and a return trip to the netherworld. Careless forward movement would see her injured and unable to outrun the morning sunrise. Over her shoulder, the yawning mouth of oblivion pushed her out into the unknown.

The last night she'd spent in her rental house, the rising full moon allowed her to sit on the patio to enjoy a comfortable and relaxing evening. Now, light, salty fog coated her skin with moisture, the welcome coolness accompanied by a slight breeze. Behind her, the misshapen entrance of jagged rock approximately six feet in circumference urged her forward.

She kept to the side and peered through the darker shadows, making out a dock at the bottom of a rocky slope. Twenty yards of craggy boulders and outcroppings would take her to the water's edge where moonbeams pearled the water gently sliding to the sandy shoreline as far as she could see. To her left, someone had carved the stone into crude, narrow stairs to the dock, not a direction to venture. The boat which had brought the unknown merchandise was gone.

One stealthy step. Quiet. Forward. She listened for soft footfalls. Uneven footing meant a slow descent over large, slime-covered stones. Each measured tread a test when lichens coated rock surfaces and clefts. Once again, her stomach threatened revolt when she needed all her senses aligned and geared for escape.

Scrub brush yards from the shoreline was too low to offer camouflage and usually harbored snakes and other creatures she'd prefer not to meet since a startled gasp could pinpoint her location. To see better, she'd have to expose herself. Her current view offered no evidence of another presence, no telltale furtive footsteps, quiet breathing, or mumbled threats.

It's now or never. If I move fast and there's someone around, they'll spot the movement and give chase.

On the other hand, she'd never held aspirations of ninja skills. If she crept slowly and someone remained near the entrance, she still wouldn't have a chance to escape. Without specific knowledge of the tunnels, she had no idea how many other entry points existed, much less their location.

In the end, depletion of energy relegated the choice to slow and stealthy. She sent up a prayer she'd live to see her parents and brag about her adventure. Twice, she slipped on the craggy boulders in her bid for freedom. Behind and above, a grassy incline sloped upward to a small crest extending fifty yards parallel to the shoreline. Once away from the entrance, she dared to glance back at the wretchedness she'd escaped.

The gaping black mouth watched her, mocked her efforts, and waited for her return. Night concealed its menaces within the shadows, but the tunnel cloaked bloodcurdling stalkers that devoured all hope while spewing desperation and hopelessness. It breathed terror as easily as she took in quiet gasps of oxygen. The tunnel's entrance looked like a snake's mouth with outcroppings for fangs, the whole ready to swallow its prey.

Forward. Never backward.

When she'd scrambled to the slope's gentler angle, she maneuvered upward until reaching the top yet kept her body low to present a smaller target. The breeze was a little stronger at the ridge, its tug pulling at the snarled disarray of bloody hair. In the distance, a tree line offered concealment while sheltering its own murky secrets. Above that shadowy refuge, the soft glow of city lights beckoned her to move, and she prayed they originated from Portland.

Slow deep breaths purged nausea. After surveying her surroundings again and finding nothing more threatening than a few gulls, she set out across tall grasses toward presumed safety.

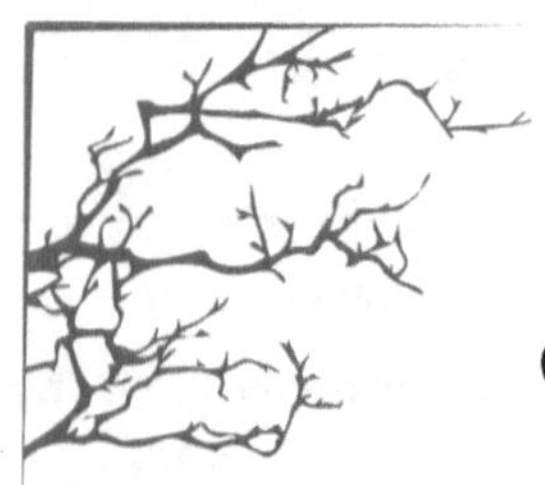

Chapter Three

"Hey, cabbage counter. Thought I'd call and give you an update on your girl. Things got a bit out of hand." The ensuing, entangled conversation would decide the number of people destined to die. Not that it mattered, Hale had plenty of time and enjoyed his naughty pleasures.

"What the hell? You've held her for twenty-four hours? Why is she still in the country?"

"Hold onto your shorts. My contact docked a few hours ago. The rich bitch won't be seen again." Hale softened his tone, amused as much by temporarily accepting a subordinate position as keeping the third and silent partner nameless.

"Then what's the problem, roadrunner?"

The newly adopted moniker fit, suiting his expanding business. Profits had increased exponentially since trading girls for cash. Losing one was intolerable, not to mention costly. It seemed he needed to hire better help.

"Our newest acquisition turned out to be a feisty bit of fluff. We took her 'cuz she's a fresh arrival from across country. A little shutterbug that'll fetch a fine sum. Unfortunately, she escaped, but we did get her camera with the pics she inadvertently snapped of my team."

Still so much better than my day job.

"Does anything trace back to you or just the tunnel?"

The unspoken *back to me* irritated more than losing the merchandise. "Just to the tunnel. They're cleaning up and scouting new locations as we speak." Hale shook his head, deciding on a new course of action. Leading a damning trail to his partner held a wonderful irony but came with inherent risks. Cabbage counter was anything but stupid and might share the wealth when confronted by police.

"Good. Clean up your mess and our business together is finished. I'm anxious to move on."

"We'll get the photographer. Since society dames aren't Ning's stereotypical choice for selection, he's a bit nervous. She smells of power and refinement. Both he and the Asian want to dump her body and forget the money."

"No! I didn't sign up to have her murdered, just humiliated and used for *service*."

Hale rolled his eyes at the arrogant prick's attitude. Cabbage counter had little respect for the operation's scope, comically thinking himself master manipulator in a private scheme. "You'll benefit either way. She's out of circulation."

"I draw the line with killing."

"After what you've done to her? Really? I heard stories..."

"No. And that's my final demand."

One fatal decision decided, Hale had tested the waters to dictate survival rates of others involved. *Sometimes you have to remove the Hydra's head to allow for new growth.*

"And Hale? Don't call my office again."

"All right, but I need information. You have contacts in the right places. Use them and find out if the bitch who escaped us surfaces. Her name is Kaylee Tate. She's from Pennsylvania. *We* can pick her up if she heads back to her rental, but I want to know if she makes it to the cops or hospital first."

"Yeah, yeah. Tell my girl I said bon voyage and she won't be missed. Give her a black eye for traveling."

"Actually, I've got a nice video for your viewing pleasure." Hale grinned with the thought of the socialite's upcoming shock. His would be the last face the society bitch saw.

"You can drop the DVD off at my home. After that, we'll have no further contact."

"As you wish. Pleasure doing business with you."

"Just make sure you clean up your mess. I don't want a convoluted trail leading back to me. Oh, and one of her ex's is a private dick by the name of Caden McAllister. I've wanted to stick it to that bastard for a long time. Use him if you can."

"Damn, you really are a sick prick. I like the way you think."

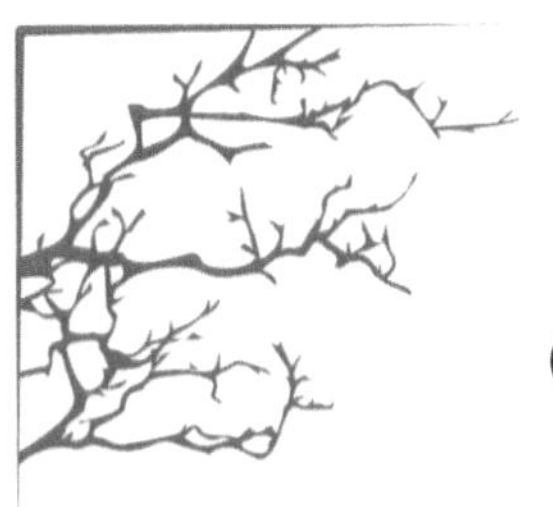

Chapter Four

"Hey, Caden. Who pulled you out of the gutter?" Matt dropped his dog's leash to allow the familiar meet and greet, filling the police station's wide lobby with the animal's low *woofing* while observing the welcome exchange of affection.

"Your girlfriend. She says hi, by the way. Oh, and she's too tired to see you tonight. She should be less sore in about, um, a week." Caden smirked at his brother, their familiar comradery drawing chuckles from the desk sergeant trying to look busy behind the glass partition.

"Cute. I see becoming a private dick hasn't helped your attitude in the least. Still the man-whore."

"Seriously? I'll have you know I've turned—"

The opening of the lobby's heavy glass door ushered in a shot of cool, brisk air along with a battered and bloody urchin sporting a ripped shirt, jacket, and jeans, the latter soaked to the knee. Despite the bulk of hair pulled back, loose strands clumped with blood stuck to a filthy face.

Squishy steps carried the disheveled ragamuffin forward while a jaw already turning reddish-purple and streaked with blood opened and closed several times. No sound issued forth. Crimson smeared the victim's outstretched hands and streaked the filthy, blonde hair hanging in tangles before disappearing under the shirt collar.

"Help. He's gonna kill her. Oh God, He's probably already done it."

"Whoa there, young man. What kind of squabble did you find?" Caden lunged forward to steady the stumbling youth while Matt grabbed the dog's leash.

An audible sob camouflaged the shudder as Caden steadied the victim with a hand at each elbow. The delicate bone structure within his grasp confirmed his first mistake.

"I'm not a man." Anger and disgust dropped the speaker's pitch to a husky growl.

"Sorry. Obviously not, hon. Tell us what's going on. Here, let's get you back to where you can sit." Caden helped the slim girl navigate the path to his brother's office. Nodding to one of the officers en route, he asked, "Johnson, can you grab us a blanket?"

"You wanna take her straight to the ER?" One of the three detectives in the squad room stood to help but backed off at the victim's raised hand.

"No. No hospital. We have to go find her. I promised."

"Let's start at the beginning. What's your name?" Once in the office, Caden guided her to a chair opposite the large desk before taking the nearby seat. "Jeez. You're shaking. You need some carbs in your system to counteract shock."

Matt closed the door before taking his seat, his dog whining but remaining by his side. "I'll have someone bring something in while we talk." Murmured words issued the directive over the phone before he settled back in his chair.

A momentary pause. The haunted gaze took in her surroundings before locking onto Caden's face. "Caden? Caden McAllister?" Her expression was a picture of open-mouthed confusion.

Caden leaned back to take in the bundle before him. Despite the dirty face, crystal clear eyes reminded him of sea glass washed up after a storm, just as they had years ago.

"Kaylee? What the hell's going on?"

"Kidnapped. Held underground in a tunnel." Shaking fingers supplemented her plea in meaningless gestures.

"Hell, I didn't know you'd moved back." Caden wanted to wrap her in his arms but wouldn't initiate contact until knowing the extent of her ordeal. "All right, hon. Let's start at the beginning." As Caden listened to the twisted tale of horror, a glance at his sibling, an unspoken offer to help, was accepted. Four years of police work along with two as a private investigator gave him a variety of contacts and informants from which to draw.

Disjointed words tumbled from a mind caught in a nightmare with her descriptive descent into a labyrinthine horror. Minutes later, an officer brought in a blanket and protein bar. The latter, her uncoordinated fingers failed to unwrap.

Caden removed the wrapper and eased the confection into her grip before draping the blanket around her shoulders. Having something to do with her hands added purpose and seemed to help order her thoughts.

"I was sitting at a café drinking hot chocolate and watching the sunset. Suddenly, my head felt funny, and my tongue felt—thick. I don't remember anything after that until I woke up in an underground cage." Repetitious motion of her free hand became the outlet for a mind unable to cope.

When words degraded to sobs with the reasoning behind leaving the other woman behind, Caden offered a tissue from Matt's desk and shifted his chair closer. Careful not to force contact, he offered his hand. Years ago, he'd helped her out of a scrape. This time, he was too late.

Her grip betrayed a desperation barely held in check. "I couldn't fight him. He was too big, and the drugs made me fuzzy." Wide-set eyes pleaded for amnesty.

"Listen, Kaylee, you did the right thing. The only course you could've taken and survived. But we need to take you to the hospital and get you checked out. They'll—" The grip on his hand clutched tighter before she cut him off, willing him to understand.

"No. We have to go find her first." Her other hand, also covered in scrapes and dirt, fisted around her snack.

Matt's grimace signaled what Caden already knew, but Kaylee hadn't yet processed. The other girl was already dead or moved to another location.

After a recent near-death experience, Caden understood how Kaylee was feeling. Time would help her process and adjust. "Hon, you need to catch a mental breath, let your mind catch up with events."

"I'm fine. Clear headed, and ready to go."

Not likely. Caden watched as she released his hand, folded her candy wrapper and placed it neatly inside the pencil holder on Matt's desk. *Mental shock.*

"Yes, we clearly see that," Matt offered sympathetically.

After dampening his handkerchief from Matt's water bottle, Caden gently wiped some of the crusted bloody streaks from her face before placing the cloth in an evidence bag provided by Matt. A small gash on her scalp and a bloody nose were minor injuries compared to what she'd suffered.

"We'll search for her, but we first have to make sure the drugs in your system don't need to be flushed or counteracted." Confirming she hadn't been sexually assaulted meant Caden felt more comfortable circling her shoulders to impart whatever strength she'd accept.

"I—I know I have to file a report, but I want to find her first. I think she was a runaway."

"We can talk on the way to County Memorial. I'll stay with you and wait while they collect evidence. Once you're cleaned up, you'll feel better prepared to face the rest." Depending on the specifics of her trauma, merely giving a statement would deplete her reserves and leave her exhausted or unconscious.

Dealing with victims had never been Caden's forte but flashbacks of his childhood friend, scrawny yet fortified with the determination of a salmon swimming upstream, forced him into a protector's role. She hadn't yet mentioned her twin, Reese, or her parents.

Conviction twinned with vulnerability in her tight yet battered frame, an oil and water mix that compelled him to delve deeper into the mystery of Kaylee Tate.

"You said you hit him with a rock, so some of that—you might have his DNA mixed with your blood. We need to collect evidence to sort this out." Matt suggested.

Dawning struck as she plucked at her shirt. "Oh shit. Gross."

"Kaylee, is there anyone we can call for you? Reese or your parents? You'll need to stay with someone for a bit." Ten year's absence had changed her physical appearance, but her eyes, her eyes still held the same conviction.

"Reese died last March. My parents are still in Pennsylvania, and I don't want them to know yet. The bastards got my keys and wallet, but my driver's license is outdated so they won't know where I'm staying now."

"Okay, all right." Caden remembered being fresh out of college, wanting a new start, and determined to take on the world. It seemed they had much in common.

Matt shuffled his notes together and swiveled to face his computer. "I'll have the desk sergeant check missing reports. We'll start on this end while you take Kaylee to the hospital." Brisk efficiency in organization stemmed from years in the detective and K-9 divisions. The plan was already in action.

"Kaylee, do you think once you're cleared by the doc you can get us close to the tunnel where you came out? That maze runs for miles underground with many access points. Since your pant legs are wet from trudging through tall grass and weeds—well, a trail through wet terrain is more difficult for dogs to track." Caden helped her from the chair, steadying her with a hand at her elbow.

"No. Maybe. I'm not sure. I waited till dark to leave, afraid they'd spot me."

"I know things have changed since you moved away, but what's the first thing that looked familiar to you?" A starting point away from the city smells and all the foot traffic might help his brother's dog pick up her scent.

"I'd used city lights for my initial direction then just stumbled through the woods. The first thing I remember other than trees and briars was an ice cream shop. There was a big waffle cone advertisement attached to the storefront. I was so hungry, but it was closed."

"Fletch's Cream Dream down on Wooton Avenue, I know the place. It's not far," Caden advised.

When Caden met her gaze, Kaylee's anguish equaled a punch to the gut. Despite the misery etched in her hunched shoulders and the shifting of her wary eyes, she held an honest beauty mingled with pain that wouldn't let him look away. "Okay, we have a place to start."

"Figures you'd know it. Take her out the side exit so we don't cross her scents. I'm gonna see if Damien can track her from the station. Maybe we'll run across someone who saw something useful." Matt collected his K-9's leash.

She'd stumbled over the words when replaying events of how a bastard had dragged her from a metal crate, but her gaze was steady and strong. Her grip on his hand had been unbreakable, and she'd never flinched from his proximity. The shock and violence of her responses manifested as he'd expected.

Outside, the deep breath she took reminded him of a distance swimmer breaking the surface. With any luck, her subconscious would connect the traumatic event with the reaction and allow her to begin processing the ordeal, perhaps recalling other details. Shaking legs threatened her stance until he helped support her.

"I can't stop shaking. I think it's finally sinking in that I've escaped." Tremulous lips betrayed her vulnerability in a weak smile. "Can I hold onto you for a minute, Ca?"

Without hesitation, she stepped close and wrapped her arms around his waist, holding tight.

"It's just your body releasing all the pent-up energy from your ordeal. Reminds me of when you and Reese went up against the school hoodlums." Four years older, he'd been impressed with how the two had stood side by side, just as his four brothers did when confronted by any threat.

"Those three would have pulverized us if you hadn't come along."

"Nah, I think you might have gotten banged up a bit, but you both were scrappers. You'd have gotten the better of them."

"And then you taught me the easiest way to break someone's nose. It came in handy, though I used my foot instead."

"Hey, use whatever you've got, remember?"

"May have saved my life. The creep said he'd peel my skin off." She shuddered violently.

Minutes passed as she took slow deep breaths and her body calmed. He waited until she stepped back, steady on her feet, before guiding her forward.

"C'mon. Let's get you settled and to the hospital." Surely, they'd keep her overnight with the remnants of drugs in her system and obvious head trauma. A considerable amount of blood coated her scalp and hair.

Though he tried to keep her talking for the short drive, Kaylee withdrew into her own world, filled with pain, terror, and thugs raping women. He'd had little experience in dealing with the aftermath of a friend's trauma.

"You were taking pictures? Do you work for a magazine or a newspaper?"

"Freelance. I was sitting in an outdoor café. Can't remember the name, but I *can* find it again."

"Had you spoken to anyone, perhaps told someone you've just returned to town?" As disturbing as the thought was, he had to concede the possibility of new crimps starting a sex-slave trade. It wouldn't be the first time the tunnels had been used for such a despicable purpose. He might have a better direction to investigate once they identified the other victim and any common denominators.

"Um, yeah, several people, though I'm usually a decent judge of character. I sure as hell didn't see this coming." Anger, determination, and strength of will infused her voice. "I'm gonna put that bastard's face on the front of every newspaper and social media page in the state."

"Yep, I expect you will." *The question is—how do we keep you safe while you're doing it?*

"They're gonna be looking for me." Her thoughts were already forging ahead. "I'll have to find them first."

So, you'll be wary. Not a temporary state, based on personal experience. Fisted hands and bared teeth gave her a look of gritty tenacity she'd need in the coming months. "Yes, but you won't be alone. I'll help."

"I can sketch the son of a bitch while waiting in the ER if you can get me pencil and paper."

"I can do you one better if one of my brothers can pick up my laptop."

"Composite sketching software?"

"Yep. State of the art." He figured her aggressive mental stance a natural reaction and may have helped her through her brother's death. Her depth of conviction and grit surpassed anyone he'd known.

"You said you're a private investigator now."

"Yeah, comes in handy. I was on the job four years before I decided to go private."

"Rebel? Just like old times."

"Let's just say there are times when laws don't protect people the way they should, and I have a bit of a temper."

"Uh-huh. Okay. So, what's the game plan?"

"First, we get you cleared by the doctors."

It was rare to meet someone so resilient and with such backbone. A half hour ago, she'd been crying; now she wanted revenge, yet the human body couldn't sustain an energy surge over an extended period. He needed to obtain any details her subconscious mind brought to the surface while they were still fresh.

Matt had called ahead to advise the ER of their coming. Upon arrival, they were greeted at the emergency entrance and a nurse led Kaylee to a stretcher in one of the trauma rooms. With experience in triaging various crises, professionals approached calmly and asked questions in soothing tones while taking vital signs and notes. She'd asked him to stay, not realizing he would never leave his childhood friend in the hands of strangers and at such odds.

Two nurses had collected fingernail scrapings and samples of dried blood from her hands, careful to explain their intentions before approaching. Kaylee understood the basics of the proceedings, explaining her father was a cop. After the brisk efficiency of required tests gave way to the quiet murmurs and assurances of impending results, he sat beside her stretcher in contemplative silence, waiting for her to continue processing the chaotic flurry of events. Baggy sweats, given by a group helping assault victims, soon replaced the tattered clothes bagged for evidence.

When his older brother dropped off his laptop, they shared information. Billy worked in the criminal division of PPD and was combing through records and recent reports for missing women.

Time warps and modifies all within its domain. Ten years ago, he'd come to appreciate the cute kid bearing her first crush who struck out with sarcasm to cover her feelings. If not for her brother revealing the truth, he might've thought himself a monster in her eyes with the way she'd gone the extra mile to taunt him.

With time, belligerence had given way to a begrudging truce, then eventually, friendship. When her father had retired from the military, he pulled stakes and hauled his pre-teens cross-country to become a cop.

When the initial flurry of activity subsided, and they waited to see the doctor again, Kaylee's insistence on a proactive stance exchanged a victim's mantle and frame of mind for anger and an invisible coat of armor. The transformation entailed a combination of avenging angel and warrior woman.

Unfortunately, he didn't think her thin shield would bear up under a slight breeze.

"Well, boot up the computer and let's get started. I'm familiar with photo editing software, so this should be easy enough to pick up."

"Yes, ma'am." Only too happy to oblige, Caden tentatively took a seat beside her on the stretcher.

"It's okay. I don't bite."

Liking her grit, he added with a wink. "And I remember you having a good right hook."

It was her first tentative smile, warm if a bit shaky and shy. He liked it. A lot. Now that her face was clean, he liked that, too.

Residual mats of blood caked in her hair reminded him to proceed slowly.

"You know, don't you?" Kaylee's question was more of a statement.

"What?"

"What it's like to be a victim of something."

"What makes you say that?" Too late, he remembered her uncanny ability to delve underneath his even façade.

"Good judge of character, remember?"

"Yeah, I ran into a bit of a fuzzy situation recently. It taught me a new meaning of how some people apply the phrase *friends close, enemies closer.*"

"What happened?"

"Someone I'd called friend turned out to be a serial killer. He wanted to teach me a twisted lesson."

"No shit. Guess *I* got off easy."

Narrowed eyes and a head tilt lasered her attention on his face before accepting his laptop.

She wants to ask more.

After explaining the different aspects of the facial sketching program and how to manipulate the images, he watched as her kidnapper's face took rough shape on the screen, one feature at a time. Her assimilation of the new medium in rendering a two-dimensional image from memory evolved with a frown and her lips nibbled between even, white teeth. Her fingers shook slightly when tracing the line of his jaw before clenching in a fist. Resilient, yes. Determined, absolutely. Yet she had neither the resources nor strength to confront the monster.

Doesn't look like that's going to stop her.

"I think this is the best I can do."

"I don't recognize him, but I'll shoot this over to Matt."

"I remember two other voices. One was barely above a whisper, but they were arguing over something. I couldn't determine the *what*. I'm pretty sure one was female."

With little to offer in the way of encouragement, he didn't want her dwelling on something beyond her control. Obsession taking root would forge an iron mask and permit sight in only one direction, a tsunami to wash away all other thought and aspirations. Once the threat was neutralized, an empty husk would remain. Again, he culled the reasoning from personal experience and didn't want her following in his footsteps.

"Do you own a firearm?" He'd known her as a girl who wouldn't take any crap. Now, she'd be considering her options. Her expression disclosed more conviction than her words.

"Yes."

"Got a CHL to carry?" His question provoked a stronger response with thinning lips and a near-silent snarl as her gaze slid away.

"No." Belligerent, bold, and loaded with animosity. "My father's a cop. I'm safe with a gun. I'm also a good shot."

"Yeah, and your father is trained and licensed to carry."

"I'm not giving up my gun."

"I'm not asking you to. It's just that killing your kidnapper is a short-term patch, not a long-term fix."

"How would you know?" Her gaze sharpened to excise the truth from the darkest reaches of his heart.

"Been there, done that."

"The *fuzzy* situation?"

"Yeah. It came down to him or me. He was a serial killer, psychosis at its best."

"So—you regret his death?"

"Oh, hell no. Never. It's just that it didn't fix anything. You still have to deal with the crap in your head."

"Damn." Kaylee twisted her lips in a grimace. The need to discern details was written in her gaze, tempered by respect for his privacy. When the silence lingered for another minute, she continued. "I saw three crates where they kept us yet only one other woman. The bastards were arguing. I wish I could've heard their voices better."

"Forensics will sweep the entire area once we find it. If there was another woman down there, we'll find her. As for the voices, you said one mentioned money, which could mean either ransom or sale."

"Everything's kind of a blur."

"Give it time. They gave you some kind of roofie, so the aftereffects can take up to forty-eight hours to wear off. The trauma alone means nothing will make sense for a while."

"Known from past experience?"

"Kinda. I was poisoned." It struck him in that instant, their silent comradery equaled an unspoken bond, a connection formed from similar realities of terror. Friendship with a woman had never made it to his know-how list, but the challenge invigorated and breathed new life in his future.

"That's why everyone's giving you these looks. You've spent a good bit of time here and have gotten to know the nurses."

"What?"

"Well, my nurse looks like she wants to *examine* you. The one at the desk has visually undressed you—repeatedly. Back in your senior year of high school, you became known as the muff rider."

"Hmm, that was a long time ago. It's just the chemicals in your system." Caden hadn't missed the lingering looks or the interest in the women's gazes. He'd had intimate knowledge of more than one. He just no longer returned the interest.

"Soon as I'm clear, I want to find the other woman. I'm not sitting on my ass while she's out there."

"Didn't expect you would. But it's not a time to be alone either. The bastards will undoubtedly be searching for you. I'll stick with you until you're thinking clearly." *And for a while afterward, to make sure you're safe.*

"Jesus, I wonder where she is. Let me take a crack at drawing her composite. If I can get close enough, we'll have a starting point."

Opening up the program again, Kaylee considered the initial facial shapes and selected one, then rejected it in favor of a slimmer one. With the adeptness of youth comfortable in the digital world, she began plugging in features. Her fingers proved less clumsy and her gaze clearer with time's passage and the IV rehydrating her thin form.

"Do you have anyone to stay with tonight? A friend in the city, perhaps?"

"No. I've only been here a few days. I arrived cold turkey, so to speak, without contacting any old friends. I don't even know who's still around."

"They took your wallet."

"Yes, but they won't know where I live." A slight tightening of her shoulders accompanied the thinness of her voice.

"You can stay at my place for a few days if you like. Your virtue will remain intact, I promise."

A guppy confronted by a school of piranhas displayed less shock. Either Kaylee remembered his reputation, or her intuitive nature zeroed in on the nurses' lingering gazes and knowing smiles.

"Um, thanks anyway, but I'll be fine."

"Stubborn. The doc has already warned you about a probable concussion and wanted you to take it easy for the next twenty-four hours. They're going to either want you to stay overnight or have a friend stay with you. Tomorrow, I'll help you call your bank, credit card companies, and all that."

"I'm not staying here tonight. I'll sign myself out AMA."

"You sure you're ready to go?" As much as he didn't want to shake her flagging self-confidence, being alone wasn't smart either. What if the thugs were watching the hospital for her to show up? *It's not like I haven't done a stakeout before.*

Caden watched as her attention returned to the task at hand. Fragments and lines came together to form a refined face of elegance. Quick, short movements defined high cheekbones and molded the "stock" jaw to a slim and fine-boned beauty.

Oh, God. When Kaylee had first described the other victim, it never occurred that it would be someone he knew. Now, as the face came to life before him, a sour wad rose in his throat. Blood drained from his face.

"Kaylee, I'm gonna step out for a sec to make a call, okay? I'll be right outside the door, so nobody other than medical professionals can enter." He knew the woman's identity and had known her as intimately as any man could.

"Who is she?" Kaylee's voice rose in volume and pitch, a type of panic understood by any prey.

"She's a blue blood, not a runaway. Darling of the city type. Someone who should've been missed right away."

Cool air brushed his brow when he stepped out, the door's quiet snick reminiscent of how he'd abandoned an ex-girlfriend expected to become his wife. It took three tries to hit the correct buttons to ring Matt. Explaining the situation wouldn't be as easy.

"Hey, the missing woman is Ciera Kirpatzel."

"Jesus, man. Her husband warned you to stay away from her."

"Hey, she wasn't married at the time. He was just an abusive ex-boyfriend."

"That's one of the things you find out *before* you take a woman to bed."

"Yeah, yeah. Shit. Where are you?"

"At the ice cream shop. I'm waiting for Lucas to bring my gear so we can head into the woods. How's your girl."

"She's fine. Just waiting for labs and X-ray results. She refuses to stay the night."

"Oh, so you met your match in the obstinance department? Good. Keep an eye on her."

"Cute. I will. Listen, she's already said she wants to see the underground room where she was held. We'll be heading that way in a bit."

"You want to *immediately* bring a victim back to the scene of her attack? Are you nuts?"

"Hey, if I don't, she'll just come on her own, and she owns a gun. It's not like I can disable it and leave her defenseless."

"Shit, shit, shit. Why does she have a gun?"

"Her dad joined the force after moving across country."

"Of course he's on the job. All right. I'll send you our location and findings once we finish tracking. Just buy us some time, okay?"

"Yeah."

"Look, I don't remember much about her. She was closer to you in age. Stick tight until we catch these bastards. They'll either want her back or try to shut her up."

"Like I hadn't already planned on it?"

The connection went dead in Matt's usual abrupt manner to leave Caden in the *déjà vu* nightmare of protecting a friend. Two months ago, he'd not only failed but almost died in the process. The disfigurement marring his hands and arms didn't compare to the mangled remains of his self-confidence. His supportive family reinforced the fact that all men must confront their own mortality and reconcile their perceptions accordingly.

He wondered if Reese's death equaled Kaylee's reckoning.

He'd promised to stay by her side and always kept his word, which meant an excursion through the tunnels. Fear of the dark or any two-legged critters wasn't an issue. Facing the smaller demons would force a confrontation with a twisted horror he wasn't sure he could contemplate, much less endure. He needed more time to adjust. Rubbing a hand over his eyes didn't negate the terrifying images flitting through his thoughts. An injection of poison. Enraged rats with microchips, trained to attack and kill.

When Caden stepped back into the room, Kaylee's tight grimace signaled a temporary fortification of reserves. Experience dictated her fiendish specters would return when least expected.

She stared at the composite drawing as if making a silent promise, a look he remembered seeing on Lexi's face. It was only luck and his friend's persistence that he survived his ordeal.

"Kaylee, I've met a lot of people, few as determined as you." Her steadfast resolve was admirable, but was it wise to jump back on the horse before dusting off? Everyone dealt with grief and extreme situations in their own way and time. Initially, he deemed her determination to move forward far better than relegating the nightmare to a dark corner of her mind and never challenging its fragments, thereby delaying recovery. He hadn't seen her in ten years and had only the traumatic events spanning recent hours to gauge her strength and reserves.

"My dad always said the sooner you face your fear, the sooner you can move on with your life. I chose this place for my fresh start. No dirtball is going to take it away."

Fresh start after Reese's death.

The compulsion to protect demanded he know more, yet the freshness of her trauma and the fragility she'd demonstrated at the station silenced his questions.

Their quiet reflection ceased when the ER doctor, a portly gentleman known to all the McAllisters professionally and personally, strode in and settled a hand on her shoulder. Caden understood his expression and the words to come.

"Well, Kaylee, we won't have labs back for a bit. Meanwhile, I'm going to close this small laceration on your head and give you instructions." After a frown directed at Caden, he added, "As I said earlier, it would be a good idea to stay overnight at the very least. Clearly, you've been drugged, and it looks like you have a concussion. A situation I've seen a time or two before." A wry grin directed at Caden indicated a long history of dealing with stubborn patients.

"Thanks, but I need to be on my feet and out of here ASAP. A woman's life is at stake."

"Whom you can't help if you get dizzy, fall, and knock yourself unconscious." Caden relocated to the chair in the corner. "Does she need any prescriptions?"

"She's up to date on tetanus, so I'd recommend ten cc of relaxation and fun. No overexertion."

"I can help her with that, Doc."

"I'd listen to this young man if I were you." Further details and cautions rolled off the doctor's tongue as if already knowing the outcome, a preordained speech doomed from the start.

The scalp laceration received several stitches and the rest of her scrapes treated before release into Caden's care. If she experienced any warning signs mentioned, she'd probably ignore them. He had more respect for parenthood every day.

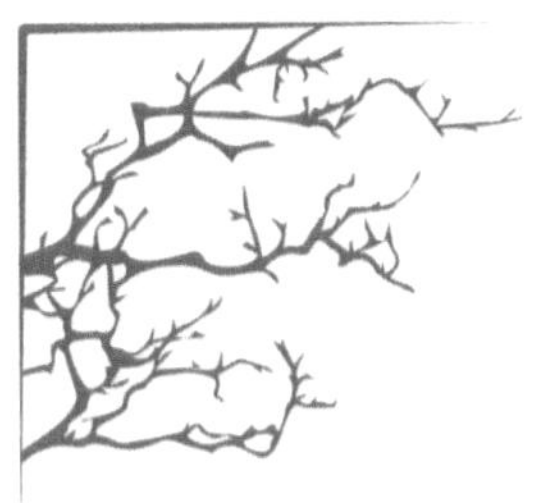

Chapter Five

Two hours later, with dry clothes and a full stomach after a fast-food burger and fries, Kaylee sat in the passenger seat of Caden's SUV. In her mind's eye, a loop of past events leading to her abduction repeated on an endless reel in hopes of picking out the one detail needed to narrow the hunt for the kidnappers. Each pass shored up her resolve to find her abductor and rescue the woman she'd abandoned.

"He could've followed me for some time, and I wouldn't have known it—not with so many people around and all of them strangers. Everything's changed so much. When did that mall go up?"

"About three years ago. The entire west side saw a boom."

"If I could hone in on the initial point where he picked me out..."

"You're thinking too narrow spectrum, and your memory of prior events is still too fuzzy. I think it's better to work backward until your head clears a bit."

"You seem to know a lot about these tunnels. How is that? Heck, Reese and I knew about them as kids, but Dad wouldn't let us explore. He said we'd only find kids partying or looking for trouble. It wasn't until we ventured through the caverns in Pennsylvania that we developed the driving fascination for them."

"Once we learned about them as kids, naturally, a mysterious underground maze provided five brothers with endless hours of exploration and pirate games."

"I wish we'd been closer in age."

"Yeah, the only reason they took me along was to keep me from blabbing. 'Sides, your dad's kind of a scary guy. Taking his kids into questionable areas didn't rank high on our agenda."

"Did you ever run into trouble down there?"

"No. We heard voices on occasion but took alternate routes to avoid them. Are you sure you want to go back down there?" A small fry fell as he scooped the last of them into his mouth. The slight fumble added a boyish charm and confirmed his mortal status.

A sliver of uncertainty appeared to slice beneath his surface concern. Her dad had taught her to *read* people, and she'd become adept. Just as in the ER when he'd hesitated before asking questions relating to the physical attack, he now rubbed his jaw and shifted his weight.

"Yes." It was the second time she'd answered that question. "Are *you* sure you want to go down there? Perhaps someone modified your system. I sure as shit don't want to get lost down there." A compulsion to slip beneath his invisible shield and discover what strained his self-assurance regulated her questions. Her mother called it strength of character, her father referred to it as her personal *man go away* trait.

"Don't worry. We'll be fine. We mapped and marked them as kids. It's been a while, but I'm betting our system is still present. Matt and Damien are already down there, along with forensics."

A soft glow from the dash highlighted the slight tightening around his eyes and mouth that had coincided with a heartbeat's hesitation.

For someone who spent so much time down there, why does the thought of returning cause anxiety?

The strength of Caden's quiet words painted a colorful picture of his life to date. Buried deep beneath his disciplined armor, she sensed a wealth of humor and a repressed frisky demeanor spoiling to enjoy life to its fullest just as when they were kids.

City lights blurred in the window, dwindling to small businesses including a barbershop, a putt-putt golf center, and a deli advertising their special of the day. The new enterprises and operations gave way to affluent suburbs.

"This looks more familiar. I remember a couple of these houses but was too scared to knock on some stranger's door. The ice cream shop was closed when I passed."

"At least you made it to the police station."

"I guess with the way I looked, nobody wanted to mess with me."

Colonial revival architecture featured larger footprints with the classical columns framing front doors and perfectly symmetrical sides. Craftsman homes with gable roofs and decorative brackets under the eaves showcased natural materials and finishes with handcrafted workmanship. Each home boasted artfully sculpted hedges and living privacy barriers. She'd photographed dozens of homes for the pure pleasure of studying the nuances of their structures. Something Reese would have also enjoyed.

"Ahead, there's a small side road that winds around the state park and overlooks the river." His tone adopted the smoky quality of someone mentally rewinding old experiences.

"And you'd know about this because..." She couldn't keep the smile out of her voice. With inky-black hair curling at his collar and the darkest blue eyes she'd ever seen, no doubt, he knew every resource available for a young man to woo his girl. Innocent smiles shouldn't warm her from the inside, nor should his presence lend such comfort, but remnants of the old infatuation doled out a comfort she'd cling to for now.

"That's the first honest smile I've seen. As I was saying, I'm thinking you came out of one of the tunnels near there."

He's skilled in the art of conversation and evasion.

The *road* equaled an eroded path cutting through the reserve. Each pothole and deep rut jolting her against the door reminded her of why she'd come. Find the other captive and put an end to the kidnapper's zeal for rape and humiliation.

Glossing over particular details of a misspent youth or perhaps something to do with his recent trauma added to Caden's difficulty with the present task. His hands tightened their grip on the steering wheel as he fought his own demons. Either way, he'd agreed to escort her back to her own Byzantine saga, and she remained grateful for the support.

A popular dog-themed jingle marked an incoming call with Caden's brisk efficient movements and speech so contrary to his demeanor in dealing with her.

"Yeah, we're on our way." Caden glanced over after a brief pause, his narrowed gaze assessing her resolve. "Yep, I remember. Meet you at the lopsided mouth in about twenty." His lips thinned in a slight grimace, the resulting silence filled with uncertainty.

What happened to him in the tunnels?

"Lopsided mouth? Is that where you got your jaw broken or something?" Images of Caden fighting over a girl flashed through her mind, only he'd be the victor and not the one nursing a black eye and bloody lip.

A grin hitched up one corner of his mouth. "Named for the shape of the opening. You seem to have a pretty low opinion of me. Or is it men in general?" His sudden intake of breath coincided with the dawning in his gaze. "Sorry. After what you've been through, I should be more careful with what I say."

"Don't be." Pondering his unvoiced assumption, she added, "I just figured with your looks, well, you'd know all the places like this."

"Don't assume anything. I've changed." As if wanting to draw the words back, he reached out and lightly touched her hand.

Warmth from a caring human being seeped through her chilly skeletal frame to cocoon her flesh and bone while smoothing the jagged edges from her soul.

"Sorry, Kaylee, I see things a bit differently nowadays."

The sharpness of his words had taken her back. In life, she'd found a no-nonsense approach kept her in good standing with her friends. She wanted very much to count him at the top of that list. "No, my fault." *Recent events?* "You mean the *fuzzy* experience?"

"Yeah, that." He paused a beat. "Listen, Matt's dog has traced your steps back through the tunnel and found the room where they kept you. There's nothing there now, but it's been twenty-four hours, and they've had plenty of time to clear things out. The forensics team is still down there so we can only go so far, but you can see the site, and maybe that'll jar a memory loose, a name, or some other detail."

"They took the cages?"

"Yeah. And you must have bashed your kidnapper's head pretty good unless what they're finding is your blood. Matt said there was a fair amount."

"My head wasn't bleeding by the time I woke up. It was already caked. So, most of it probably belongs to the prick who grabbed me—or it could be *her* blood."

The river's tang, a scent she'd loved days ago, strengthened as the road opened into a large, flat, scrubby land. Moonlight silvering the midget waves would have drawn her out for a late-night photo op less than a week ago. She wondered if there'd ever be a normal night again.

A gray SUV sat beside a late-model pickup a short distance from the shoreline. Two men, one she recognized as an older version of Caden, stood in deep conversation when they pulled to a stop.

Several others wearing gray coveralls loaded boxes in the Mobile Crime Lab parked behind Matt's vehicle.

"You don't have to go down there, Kaylee." Worry furrowed Caden's brow.

"Yes, I do. I *need* to do this." *While there's plenty of reinforcements and I can see it for what it is. Empty space.*

Off to her left, the slope of the land rose in graduated degrees of outcroppings and jagged, sawtooth formations while masking the river's path. The tip of a dock, visible beyond a craggy protrusion, brought back her initial fear of running into her abductors. She didn't remember scrambling over the rocky incline, only the silent repetition of her mantra. *Move forward. Find civilization.*

Irrational fear slowed her movements in exiting the vehicle. Nothing here would bring her harm, only shadows of the past breathed volume and life into her dawdling. Caden rounded the vehicle's front and strode beside her, his strength a much-needed boost to her battered ego. She'd moved across the country for a fresh start, free of her college sweetheart who'd wanted to see how many women he could screw behind her back. Now, she'd fallen victim to a kidnapper during her first week.

It was time to move forward.

She hated that word, victim. It equated helplessness, powerlessness, weakness. Only one other time in her life had she ever felt weak and didn't intend to go there again.

"Kaylee, you're looking like you feel a little better. You remember my brother, Lucas." Matt loosened Damien's leash to allow greeting of the newcomers.

Kaylee knelt with the K-9's approach, glad to have the opportunity to take a deep breath and clear her head. As much as she'd always wanted a dog, circumstances had never been right. *Maybe it's time to rethink that.*

"You're an officer, too?" She had to look up to meet Lucas' gaze. Like both his siblings, the man stood a head above her.

Lucas offered his hand, a slight shifting of his jaw denoting an ongoing assessment even as his relaxed stance assured confidence. "Hey, it's what we do. I guess Caden forgot to mention that during your catch-up."

"Yeah, but don't hold that against him. He just hasn't learned any better, yet." Matt nodded to his brothers before turning toward the rising slope of land she'd scrambled down hours ago.

"Is there any way to track the kidnappers?" Without specific forensic knowledge, she felt like a lost ball in high weeds.

"We parked farther back initially to search for fresh tracks. We found yours, but no others outside, which means they used a deadfall or different exit. Also, there are so many tracks, all the hell over the place, they could have multiple exits. There's no way for Damien to *date* a trail." Matt re-clipped the leash. "Damien and I will lead you through the tunnels. We have extra lights, in case Caden has forgotten the basics. Plus, there are lights set up periodically by the forensic techs already inside."

"Damien led you all the way here?" The idea of having a dog appealed more by the minute.

"And through the tunnel. To enter the room, well, they must've carried you, because Damien drew a dead end. There's tons of other tracks, and we don't have an article of the kidnapper's clothing for him to scent." Nodding to Caden, Matt hesitated, as if unsure how to approach a difficult subject. "Listen, you don't have to go inside. Lucas and I can take her."

"I'm doing this, Matt. Let's move it."

Caden's growled words through clenched teeth eased her back a step until he shook his head and forced a false nonchalance.

"All right. Our symbols and designations are still legible." Matt pinched the bridge of his nose the same way she did when trying to head off a migraine.

"Figured they would be." Caden's gaze slid away, his hesitation in following Lucas and Matt marginal and overshadowed by pure grit.

"Caden, I don't mind going in with Matt."

"C'mon kiddo. Let's do this." Again, the smile didn't reach his eyes when he shrugged off her comment and took her by the hand. He kept pace beside her up the steady incline, steadying her when her still damp sneakers slipped on loose sand.

"Kaylee, if you'd like, I can sleep on your couch tonight, in case you have aftereffects of the drugs." Caden murmured hesitantly.

He's redirecting.

"Thanks, but I'll be fine. I'm feeling a lot better."

Trusting Caden didn't equate with wanting him in her home. The infernal experience had already changed her, multiplying the growing need to prove her independence. An imagined conversation with her dad explaining the situation flowed through her thoughts.

That won't be pleasant.

A steady hand at her back when navigating the slick rocks kept her from further injury, but flashbacks of stumbling out of the tunnel and sliding down the incline stopped her in her tracks.

"Remembering something?" Caden lightly touched her shoulder, his warmth keeping her grounded.

"Yeah. Just fumbling my way out and slipping every other step." When changing clothes in the ER, she'd noticed multiple bruises blooming on her lower legs, but the technicolor changes occurring didn't rate when compared to the other victim's suffering.

The gaping black mouth framed by stony outcroppings seemed bigger regardless of the three men with her. Caden kept an even pace beside her, following Matt through a twisted path of craggy rocks. Lucas' soft steps behind them added a feeling of extra security.

"The first section includes parts we haven't navigated, Caden, so we've marked it with our old system. You'll see where it branches off." Matt held Damien's leash snug as the dog became more excited. "All etched arrows point to the exit, with the number of off-shoots marked accordingly."

Entering the somber and macabre maze, she swallowed hard to keep her food down. Each step replaced another degree of the sea's tang with the hopeless, dank reminder of her horror. Intermittent portable lanterns lit large swaths of her path while monstrous shadows cavorted between, waiting to swallow the unwary trespasser. What she saw coincided with bits of memory surging forward, rough brick walls giving way to stone and dirt. Flashbacks churned the burger in her stomach.

When they came to the next split, Caden cast his light on the upper wall to show her the markings. "All signs are on your left going in and your right coming out."

Not-so-distant squeaks and hissing brought her attention to a darkened offshoot of the maze. She couldn't stop her body from trembling. "When I rushed through here before, I knew there were rats. I sensed their movements and think I stepped on one. But seeing all these droppings. Jeez, I'm glad my colon had its affairs in order. Why would there be so many?"

"Dunno. Maybe kids come down here for picnics while telling ghost stories." The strained smile indicated prior experiences he wouldn't repeat.

Various gradients of shadows lined the walls where the flux and glow of radiance mimicked her life in general. Her attempt to settle into a once-familiar city had been degraded by dark forces out of her control, yet she'd found a staunch supporter when least expecting it.

Upon arrival, she'd been determined to get squared away before seeking out old friends. Some would have moved, married, or even died. There'd be plenty of time to catch up once she detangled the snarled web woven from brutality and carnal malice.

With further explanations of the numbers underneath each arrow, she understood the navigational system and breathed the dead air a little easier. "Damn, that's quite some *club* you guys had as kids."

Lucas thumped Caden on the back from behind. "Yeah. Lucky we were smart enough to avoid people. 'Sides, being the youngest and a tag along, Caden found enough trouble all on his own." With a chuckle, he added, "You okay, bro?"

"Peachy." The mounting tension in Caden's tone paralleled the tighter ratcheting of a drumhead, changing the pitch and volume the deeper they traveled.

Each step toward her monstrous event augmented her legs' tremble. When she stumbled over loose rocks, Caden caught and supported her against his body.

Damn, he's as solid as the walls.

"Hold up a minute, guys. She needs a breather. Drugged, remember?" Caden slanted a perturbed look at his elder siblings before bending to murmur near her ear. "I know how it feels, but you can do this. *We* can do this."

Again, a parallel past underscored the warmth and easy alliance allowing her to accept help without feeling weak. He *did* understand. In slow strokes of his fingers kneading her shoulders then brushing down her spine, she felt the heady rush of a longing never experienced, a new assault on her battered senses. The extent of how his proximity and effortless charm affected her grew exponentially.

"Thanks. I needed to hear that." Her options included withdraw from his support and moving forward or becoming lost in the comfort of his presence.

"My pleasure." The rough timbre conveyed sincerity while his warm, spicy scent countered the dank atmosphere.

Monumental effort afforded her two steps back and away from his warmth before forging ahead toward the nightmare she thought she wouldn't survive. Still a distinct possibility if the bastards found her. Damp air grew mustier with each step. A darkened stain on the wall, probably her blood, reminded her to focus on the task while tiny fragments and details of her captivity fluttered across her mental landscape. The way the rock walls replaced brick in places, the abrasions of her fingers that would take time to heal, and the enveloping hopelessness that had surrounded her came rushing back.

Sudden scurrying from a darkened branch off their path tightened Caden's hand at her waist. Through that connection, she felt the shudders coursing through his body.

"Damn I hate rats." Revulsion hissed through Caden's clenched jaw.

At the same time, Matt stopped and turned to his younger sibling. "You all right?" He stood near the entrance to her *room* but focused on Caden.

"Yeah, fine." Telescopic, portable work lights illuminated the sweat beading Caden's brow along with the room ahead. His upper body tightened, and his shoulders curled slightly while he avoided eye contact with his brother.

"Here." Matt thrust Damien's leash at Lucas. "You and Caden take the dog out. I don't want him fouling the crime scene. I'll bring Kaylee out in a few minutes."

"No. I've got her." The circling of Caden's arm around her waist didn't include pulling her closer this time, merely an increased show of solidarity. A fine tremor coursed up her back.

"Come on, C. Let's go. Matt's got lead on the investigation." Lucas' hand on Caden's shoulder pulled him back, more of a stumble-step than shuffling.

An immediate coolness enveloped her body, the loss of consoling heat sending a sliver of dread spiraling through her psyche. Each heartbeat widened the distance between them.

"I'll be back in a minute, Kaylee." Another round of squeaking from the dark and Caden's face blanched. With his brother's arm slung over Caden's shoulder, their murmured words merged, their voices tangling in the tunnel's echo. Lucas shifted Caden, urging him through the maze. Damien's whine drifted back.

Caden's sudden spin and retching took her by surprise. She'd underestimated his revulsion at entering her concept of bedlam. His muted groan that followed encompassed a world of emotional pain.

Furry experience. Rats are furry.

She'd inadvertently brought him back into his own living torment.

"He'll be fine. Must've caught some kind of bug." Matt directed her attention back to the crime scene.

Everything looked different, from the way the lighting cast unwavering and implacable shadows across the floor to the *feel* of the environment. Present still, was the cold, clinical atmosphere of evil, its foundation etched in the clumps of bloody sand the crime scene techs scooped into evidence bags. To top that mountain of burden—the bastard had raped a woman whose likeness turned Caden milk white.

"I heard two other male voices plus a female. One man had an accent, Asian, I think, but I'm not sure. The other was—different." When she moved to step forward, Matt's hand on her shoulder held her in check.

"We can't go in yet. Not until they're finished." To punctuate his words, the photographer's flash near the far exit temporarily blinded her.

"I see where the crates were laid. Mine was closest to that side." She pointed to a place near the opposite wall. "The other woman was next to me."

"Clear fluid clumps," one of the techs uttered apologetically as he glanced in her direction.

"That's where she was confined. She pleaded with me to open her cage." Kaylee's voice broke into a sob.

"You had no choice. If you'd tried to free her, you'd still be with the kidnappers, and her plight wouldn't have changed. At least now we have a starting point in our search." Matt turned her to face him, the light hands on her upper arms lending little comfort.

"A starting point, yes, but not for her." By now, the battered woman probably considered her life over, if she still drew breath. Kaylee's new start had brought nothing but pain to everyone her life touched.

Worry over Caden's sudden change in demeanor cast her glance backward. Such a strong personality—he'd feel humiliated over leaving the tunnel.

"He's fine, Kaylee. Really. Let's focus on this then get you out of here."

"Okay. The other woman didn't know how long she'd been down here, just that she'd been drugged and woke up in a dirty cage, just like me." Once she started talking, words spewed forth in a clutter of disjointed sentences. "Do you think they're bringing girls down here regularly for...?"

"Don't know, hon. We just don't know yet." Matt's solemn murmur filled the tunnel. "You're trembling. It's time for us to scoot." His voice roughened as if sensing her fear and rising panic.

With gentle authority, he led her back through the tunnels, each step a reminder of how she'd abandoned a desperate woman who could end up dead—or worse—facing a life of rape and degradation.

"We'll find her, Kaylee. We'll find her." The cold edge of conviction couldn't promise they'd find her alive.

When they reached the mouth of the entrance, Matt helped her over the rocks and down to the sandy beach where his brothers waited. Caden avoided eye contact with her, instead choosing to ask Matt questions about the crime scene. Moonlight caught the slight flush of his cheeks, whether from embarrassment or frustration, she couldn't tell. His ensuing silence seemed wrong somehow to a man she'd only seen as confident and easygoing.

"You all right?" She'd witnessed PTSD's devastating and abrupt symptoms in a college friend who'd survived sexual assault. Though the circumstances differed, some physical reactions remained the same. She wanted to be more direct but didn't know Caden well enough to be so forward.

"Yeah." Small lines etched the corners of his mouth and eyes.

The rats' chatter had spooked him in the tunnels, visibly tightening his frame. Outside, its grip had loosened enough to allow normal breaths, but his grin hadn't slid sideways and lacked his usual cockiness.

Lucas shifted and blocked her sight line. "I'd forgotten how claustrophobic it is down there, Kaylee. Sorry to skip out on you, sweetheart. You holding up okay?" His gentle reassurance came with a consoling squeeze of her shoulders. "If you're still a bit wired, we could go into town and get some coffee."

Caden's growled response altered Lucas' approach yet didn't stop the arched brow or smirk. Matt's chuckle and head shake confirmed her suspicion.

"She's gonna think we're a damned pack of hound dogs." Matt reclaimed Damien's leash.

"Hey, she's an old neighbor moved back to town. Just wanted to catch up, that's all." Lucas' wry grin belied his words.

To listen to Caden's brother cover for him reminded her of how Reese had distracted her father when she'd crossed paths with a large black snake. Her dad had smiled and twined the harmless reptile about his fingers. It always came back to the cohesiveness of family.

"I don't think I need coffee at this point."

The throb of her earlier headache morphed into an entire drumline auditioning snare, bass, and tenor drums with a side order of pit and mallet percussion to reinforce the pain. It didn't take a genius to know her discomfort would increase with the stress of going home alone. Recent events made a good case for a glass or three of wine.

"C'mon Kaylee. I'll take you home." Caden shoulder-bumped Lucas aside before offering his hand. They easily fell into step, Caden's grip a little tighter until they reached his SUV. When he slid into the driver's seat, she watched him take his first easy breath since arrival. A long, quiet exhale seemed to relax his entire six-foot-three-inch frame.

"I'm exhausted to the point of feeling punch drunk but don't think I can sleep. Does that make sense?" She folded her hands in her lap to keep their shaking hidden.

Apprehension over a surprise visit from the thugs would keep her awake until they were caught. Every settling groan of her house, the wind's sigh under the eaves, even the quiet chiding of tires thrumming down her residential street would keep her in hyper-alert mode.

"Yeah, sometimes the mind just won't quit." His commiseration appeared soul deep. "However—it does get better with time."

After her twin's death, her dad cautioned her about layering on thickening shields of veiled defenses and closing herself off from the world. It wasn't until spending countless hours alone in the foreboding tunnels contemplating the likelihood of death that she realized the depth of the shield she'd developed. Protecting the heart meant keeping everyone at arm's length. A fact her ex-boyfriend had thrown in her face before walking out of her life.

"Good night for playing solitaire or sitcom reruns." She hadn't taken the time to set up her DVR yet.

"I'd ask you if you'd like to go get a drink, but that wouldn't be a good idea with the remnants of drugs in your system. How about some decaf?"

"Thanks, but I need to go home and process this mess. I should be able to settle a bit since it's not like the creeps know where I live." The sooner she faced her fears, the sooner she could move forward in her life.

"True." He looked like he wanted to say more but instead worried his lip between his teeth as if trying to keep from blurting some type of rebuttal.

The smooth resonance of ensuing conversation detailed five boys' adolescent years, antics rife with adventure, daring, and a camaraderie rivaling the tightest-knit family she'd ever met.

A balm for a wounded spirit.

It wasn't the first time she longed for the simple affection of friendship, but the cost of baring her soul exacted a high tariff, a risk of reigniting the infatuation of years gone by.

Since her name was stricken from statements issued to the press, anonymity cloaked her from investigative reporters, soon to be snooping for any tidbits, however ruthlessly obtained. Still, small details niggled at the back of her mind, not fully processed, masked by vestiges of drugs and stress. The hope of shaking them loose by returning to the scene had failed, allowing them to fester and cultivate a new harbinger of evil looming in her future.

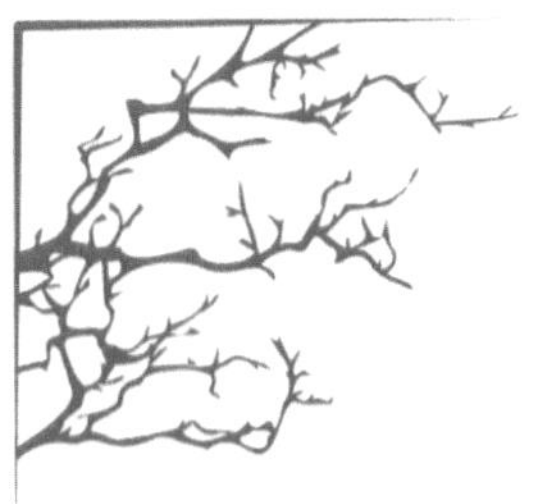

Chapter Six

Kaylee followed Caden's progress in checking each window, closet, and under the bed, before returning to the small foyer. The combination of open floor plan and tiny cottage shortened the task. The insecure part of her wanted him to stay, if for no other reason than having his comforting scent nearby to focus on throughout the night. Plan B included waiting for the nightmares to come, if sleep came, and appealed less by the minute.

Exhaustion fogged her ambition and hindered her coordination, but her need to exercise control silenced any concerns becoming vocal.

"All clear, Kaylee. We're alone here." As if just realizing the implications of his words, he narrowed his focus on her eyes, searching for signs of—fear? "The doc said you might have a concussion." Concern and the warmth of friendship filled his gaze and softened his tone. He stood close, assessing, as he tucked a strand of hair behind her ear, a brotherly gesture.

"It doesn't look like anything's been rifled through or moved." Unable to reconcile the intended expression with the new warmth invading her chest, she padded to the kitchen counter and fingered her backup camera to refocus her attention. "I lost my favorite rig. My brother helped my parents pick it out last year." She sighed then blinked quickly to stem the flow of tears.

"How about we hang out for a bit." Stepping close behind her, he smoothed his hands up and down her arms. "I watch a lot of late-night TV and could probably recite some of your favorite shows verbatim."

Pride kept her from leaning back into his strength and security, the promise of safety. She'd never been one to accept a crutch and wouldn't start now.

"Nah, I'm gonna take a long, hot shower then snuggle in a nice warm bed." She wondered if fatigue would overwhelm her subconscious and prevent replaying the ordeal throughout the night.

I doubt I'll even lie down.

"I expect you'll have some nightmares." His frown indicated a flip through his mental album of bad dreams. Reaching into his back pocket, he retrieved a business card before extracting a phone from his jacket pocket. "Here, if you remember anything tonight or just want to talk, call me. Lately, I'm a light sleeper."

The unspoken, *I know what you're feeling,* failed to break the thoughtful silence. As a man, he couldn't understand a woman's viewpoint of kidnapping and narrowly escaping rape. Yet he'd been a victim recently and still didn't hesitate to reach out to help others. That character trait shot him into the category of phenomenal friend material. Unfortunately, her body seemed to have different ideas since his presence revitalized the underused section of her brain containing her libido.

"Thanks. What's the number on the back?"

"Oh, um, it's the number to the rape crisis center." Settling his hands on her shoulders, he turned her to meet his gaze with a solemnness born of concern. "I know he didn't succeed, but you knew his intentions. That alone is worth a few nightmares. You can call them or talk to me. Either way, you'll need to talk about it with somebody at some point."

Memory of the other victim's bruised and bloody face derailed her concentration; the halting words, unarticulated terror, and helplessness encompassing a woman who'd experienced too much to cope.

Though Caden had a five-year advantage in dealing with life's peaks and troughs, his demeanor spoke of a wisdom surpassing his age.

"Thanks. I'll sleep on it."

Cupping her cheek in one large palm again reminded her of something Reese would do when he'd wanted to ensure she'd listen. "Lock the door when I leave, and I'll call you tomorrow. Try to get some rest. Your gaze looks a little fuzzy."

"My teeth *feel* a little fuzzy. I think they've grown a winter's coat since the last time I brushed."

Discharge instructions had advised keeping her stitches dry for the first forty-eight hours. *Yeah, right. If that bastard didn't best me, no infection will.* Dedication to ridding herself of caked blood took precedence over caution.

For the second time in her life, fate had clubbed her between the eyes, changing her in some fundamental way. Yet in the bathroom mirror, no visual evidence presented itself to her trained eye.

Each piece of clothing removed uncovered more scrapes and bruises. Her father would call them badges of courage. Her ex would point out her cowardice over leaving another behind. An inner voice whispered, *you survived.*

Pain stabbed her fingers when she tried to remove her book-locket necklace containing the flash drive. The jewelry had been a present from her parents on obtaining her bachelor's degree last year. They'd been so proud of her success. Reese had delighted in revealing the hidden compartment, sized for a backup flash.

Minor injuries like the one on her scalp would heal. The deeper wounds etched in her subconscious would hover with the rest among the darker wavelengths of self-recriminations until erupting at inopportune moments, like during her dash through the woods. A mental flash of Reese referencing her lack of grace during a hike had temporarily calmed her panic.

Her *older* brother by twelve minutes had always known what to say to ease her tension. Her mom promised that one day she'd form another close connection if she kept her heart open. The fragile bond with Caden intended as friendship was born of separate but equal circumstances and something she'd heartily accept. Maybe that's what her mom had meant.

Warm water stung her forehead and sluiced down her body to wash away the dirt, blood, and horrid images of how she'd become embroiled in abductions and failed rescue attempts. Rejuvenation during the simple pleasure strengthened her resolve even as the blood-caked dirt trickled down the drain. She hadn't realized it had turned cold until her body shivered.

Comfort came in the form of the thick terry cloth robe covering the tank top and boy shorts she normally wore as sleepwear. Contradicting the re-emerging sense of self was the chill invading her bones, the same penetrating bleakness endured in the tunnel.

The kidnapper had her keys, yet no identifying markings would lead him to her bed. Tomorrow would be a long day of canceling her credit card, obtaining a new driver's license, cell phone, and lock for each door. The older landlords were on holiday for the next two months but surely wouldn't mind the upgrade.

When she called her parents, they'd panic and insist she return home, which she'd refuse while assuring them of taking proper precautions. She'd expect a visit from her dad as soon as he recovered from the bout of pneumonia. Meanwhile, he'd make frequent calls to the officer leading the investigation.

Poor Matt.

Even the shuffle of her footsteps to the kitchen intimated a foolhardy campaign for independence that ended with her alone and wary. Per routine, she steeled herself for the long night ahead. Her best thinking generally occurred amid the white noise of television and conversations with Reese, something she'd never again enjoy.

Hot cocoa provided aromatherapy and warmed her hands while she sat on the sofa in silent contemplation. Despite the weariness, anxiety tightened the hold on her mug. If only she could extract some fractional detail, a small thread Caden and Matt could unravel that would lead to her kidnappers. That elusive fiber circled yet stayed one step ahead of her sievelike grasp.

It was times like these she missed her brother most. Quiet moments of desperation still crept up to invade her normally calm demeanor and forced her to seek a substitute. A poor replacement for meaningful conversation with Reese, the television mocked her isolation.

Apparently the kidnappers had disposed of her phone to avoid being tracked. Caden had said they couldn't *ping* it. Otherwise, she'd worry they might call her folks in a ruse to gain information. Since the rental didn't have a landline and she didn't want to burn up Caden's minutes, the call to her parents could wait until morning. Not to mention the fact that waking them would create instant panic.

Since Caden's number was programmed as the first contact and he'd sworn to be a light sleeper, she decided to take him up on his offer of late-night conversation.

He answered before the first dialing tone ended. "Kaylee? You all right?"

"Um, yeah, I'm fine." Getting right to the point might spare his patience. "I just keep thinking I'm missing something." Odd, instead of TV sitcoms in the background, she heard soulful crooning arias amid the backdrop of droning crickets.

Reese would have identified each anthem in the dusk-to-dawn soundtrack while identifying respective outdoor critters.

"We got his face. We have his DNA. If he's in the system, Matt will let us know. Either way, we'll find him."

"I appreciate all you've done."

"What aren't you telling me?" I hear the hesitation." Concern twinned with frustration before the silence stretched out. He could wait her out.

"Investigator's instincts?"

"Kaylee..."

"I keep getting the feeling that I'm being watched. Did you feel like that after your ordeal?"

"Still do, sometimes. I try to face a little of it each day."

She imagined him sitting on his patio drinking a beer with his feet propped up.

A slight hesitation suggested he held something back. "If not for your eye for detail and experience in photography, we wouldn't have as much as we do. We *will* find them."

Their conversation wended through old times despite few shared experiences. No amount of chocolate or wine could calm a restless soul, yet an hour talking with Caden settled her fidgeting demons. Similar experiences in white-water rafting and sketching phenomenal views on long hikes colored their conversation. Melding into that, brotherly high jinks described the McAllisters' close relationships in a way that made her long for a large family. When her clock chimed in the background, she realized how long they'd been talking.

"You sure you don't want me to come over?"

"No, and I think I'll let you get to bed. Maybe whatever is bothering me will come to me in my sleep."

"All right. I'll see you in the morning."

The soft disconnect sucked out all the warmth she'd begun to feel, replaced with a cold and calculating foreboding. Maybe she should take his suggestion and get a dog. It wasn't like she had to report to an office. The companionship would be great as well as lend a certain amount of security. A big German shepherd would be great.

Her sight line to the kitchen and both bedroom doors verified no one lurked in the near shadows, which left the depths of the bedrooms Caden had already inspected—so why did she feel so edgy?

After rinsing her cup in the sink, she trudged to the bedroom and debated on how many lights to leave burning during the night. Before slipping under the covers, she checked her Ruger with its seven-round, single stack magazine, full and properly seated. As much as she wanted to put it under her pillow, her father would have a cow at the thought. *'Either sleep and leave it in the nightstand or stay awake and search out your threat. You're never helpless.'* But that was how she felt.

Ten years in Pennsylvania law enforcement failed to chip away at his black and white approach to life despite losing his son. What the tragedy had cost him in pain, reformed into controlling concern in each aspect of *her* life. The circumstances of Reese's death had taken a toll no parent should face.

She expected to toss and turn until dawn, but exhaustion claimed its due while the full moon sank toward the horizon through the narrow gap in her curtains. The small swath of light cut across the floorboards and reminded her of the bars she'd seen that last time she woke.

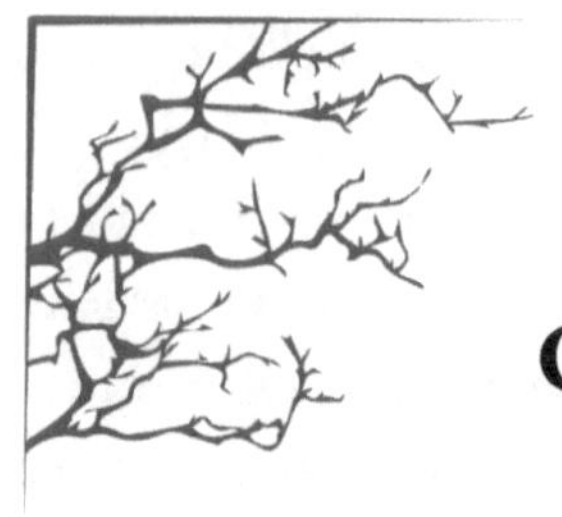

Chapter Seven

Minutes or hours could have spanned the distance between closing her eyes and fear filling her soul. Wispy webs of a nightmare cleared quickly when a low squeak jarred her awake. Either the back door opened or her subconscious was being a bitch.

Either way, the cold comfort of her handgun would lend strength.

She'd followed her normal routine of leaving the bedroom door open to hear any unusual noises around the house. Whether her imagination was making a sick joke or her kidnappers had found her, she'd face either demon.

Her heart pounded. Goose bumps prickled her nape. She'd have the upper hand since she was a good shot.

The bilious acid scalding her throat reminded her of waking up in the cage, not a memory or place she wanted to revisit. Lifting the covers and quickly scooting to the bedside, she reached for the nightstand drawer and her pistol.

The stillness in the air didn't preclude her from picking up the unseen malevolence which quickened her breath. Instincts had always served her well. Now they screamed a warning to run.

Sudden movement in the doorway.

Large.

The living room backlit the thug lunging for her hand. Her fingers closed around the pistol as the bastard slammed the drawer shut on her wrist. Pain spearing up her forearm forced a reflexive yank that freed her hand, but the gun wouldn't fit through the narrowed opening.

Breath seized in her lungs with the agony shooting up her arm. Did she imagine the crunching sound before the prick's satisfied grin filled her mind?

"Oh, no, bitch. We're gonna finish what we started. Love your case of shocked shitless, by the way. I've been anticipating it all day." He slammed the drawer shut.

Breath reminiscent of pigs and tobacco assaulted her senses at the same time it whispered terror in her ear.

Face to face, he sneered his superiority. "Can't say I mind the wait. Now we'll have a comfy bed instead of a dirt floor. Hope it's a pillow top." His moment of gloating coincided with his other hand's vicelike grip on her breast.

He squeezed.

She screamed.

His gloating equaled her window of opportunity. The advantage came in the form of a self-defense move a police officer taught his kids as youngsters in defense of bully tactics. With all her strength, she aimed her kick at his nuts.

An enraged howl filled the small bedroom as one hand cradled his groin, and the other supported his weight on the mattress. A slow-motion roll ended with him lying on his side.

"Screw the big plan." Hissed through clenched teeth. "I'm changing the program just for you." His swipe to grab her ended in a near miss that sent the lamp on her end table crashing to the hardwood. Terror bred speed as she scooted to the other side and dodged another lunge.

Outside, she heard a door slam. "Huh, you brought one of your partners? Man or a woman?"

The prick kneeled up between her and the nightstand. She was no physical match for the crazed brute, which left running as her only option. Ambient light glinted off ceramic shards on the floor while a hobble-step facilitated a sliver's removal embedded in her foot. Most likely, the second thug approached from the back, which would leave her running down the street and praying for some late-night traffic.

Weakness and a bloody foot caused her to slip on the hardwood floor, necessitating athletic contortions to stay upright. Grabbing the bedroom's doorframe steadied her flight. In the living room, a quick glance around revealed no other presence. *Yet.* The back door hung open.

If she made it to the street, she could lose him in the shadows then weave a twisted path toward the city. Dressed in skimpy clothes, it wasn't an ideal plan, but the best she could devise. She searched her memory for the closest sanctuary.

Booted steps thundered behind her as she thumbed the deadbolt to the front door. Just as she pulled on the handle, a meaty fist thrust over her shoulder and slammed it shut. A bulging forearm slammed her head against the adjoining drywall. With her right hand useless, she had no leverage but flipped the light switch in scrabbling for purchase.

Her garbled scream echoed in the room.

"Kaylee?" Caden yelled.

The bastard caging her stumbled off balance as the door opened slightly under a greater force. Unmitigated rage radiated from the air surrounding them.

"Prick. I'll have her yet, and in a way you'll never see coming." The intruder used his weight to close the door while crushing her against the wall.

She didn't have time to gather her wits before the assailant fisted her hair and stepped to the side. Using his other hand in the small of her back, he shoved her into the oncoming freight train of Caden McAllister.

"Ahh." Air left her lungs in a painful explosion.

"Later, bitch. I know everything about you." His sneered threat promised pain.

The thug's words trailed her slow-motion free fall in space.

"Oh God." The tangle of limbs saw Kaylee thrown back with flailing arms in a worthless effort to regain her balance. Her left hand snagged something soft over a hard frame, the intruder's mask. Tightening her fingers pulled the knit cover off. A flash of stained teeth and white sclera materialized into her kidnapper's face, filled with rage.

Caden growled a curse but couldn't stop his forward momentum.

Tunnel vision narrowed her focus to Caden's face, then his eyes, the depths of which she'd never fathom. The altered time perception allowed her to glimpse the violet striations around storm-darkened pupils. Sounds became white noise, elongated syllables without meaning. Each slight nuance of her body's position change registered as if recorded in a daily journal.

The detonation of pain in the back of her head chronicled the last page.

Vaguely, she accredited the elephant-worthy burden landing on top of her as Caden. The weight squeezed her lungs, and the last things she heard included Caden's curses while the intruder's boots drummed toward the back door.

Confusion. Darkness.

Distant voices grew in volume yet made no sense. Her eyes refused to open. Taking mental stock of her body, she realized everything hurt and couldn't stop the groan rumbling from her chest. Something pricked the inside of her right elbow before a streak of cold slithered up her arm.

"Kaylee? Can you hear me?" Caden's voice. Worried.

Not now, I hurt.

Cool air brushed her arms and legs, the resultant shiver a reminder she wore a tank top and skimpy boy shorts. *In Caden's presence.*

"Cold." As if conjured by wishful thinking, a scratchy blanket stretched from her feet to cover her waist.

Someone lifted her eyelid and flashed a bright light in her eye.

Prick.

"She's starting to come around." A vaguely familiar voice.

"Hmmm, Caden?" This time her eyes opened on command. Shapes blurred into indistinct outlines of bodies. "Fuzzy." She lay on something soft, a type of foam, but not her mattress.

"Yeah, we've always thought so. Damn, bro, you're right. She is a good judge of character." The cajoling tone, smooth and kind, sounded more distant. Lucas, one of the older brothers, slapped Caden on the back.

Cutting her gaze to the other side, Matt stood behind the paramedic taking her blood pressure. Someone examined her front door, another officer headed toward her bedroom.

"What happened?" The last thing she remembered was talking to Caden on the phone before going to bed. Now there was a small army in her living room.

"You sounded so—wary on the phone, I figured I'd hang around down the street."

"At restraining order distance." Matt snorted.

Caden ground his teeth. "She's proven to have good instincts. I trust them. Turns out they were right."

"You were outside in your car?" The thought brought a warm rush of comfort, but confusion hindered her ability to smile.

"Yeah, no biggy. In my line of work, well, I do a lot of stakeouts."

"You have the ultimate stalker, Kaylee, but he's harmless. Kinda like a cat." Lucas grinned at his younger sibling.

"Hmm, a two-hundred-pound blind cheetah," Matt grimaced as he looked around.

"More like an ocelot, sought after for its appearance," Lucas added under Caden's narrowed gaze. "We loosen his leash occasionally to humor his human delusion."

"I remember waking up and hearing a noise. I knew someone was in the house."

"No sign of forced entry. Either he picked the lock or had your keys. He probably trailed you before the kidnapping." Lucas glanced at his younger brother. "Then, Caden knocked you down and unconscious." The quip earned him a shoulder punch. "After which—he invited your intruder to leave—without bothering to look at his face after you were kind enough to remove the mask."

Caden glared at his older brother. "Asswipe, what do you want to come back as—in your next life? At least we have something to use in tracking."

"No. That's not..." Pain in her right wrist fogged her mind. "I—I don't remember."

"Rest now, Kaylee. You're safe." Caden took her left hand in his, linking their fingers. Glancing over his shoulder, he asked, "I'd just called it in. How'd you guys get here so quick?"

"Matt asked the uniforms to do a frequent drive by. One called in the fact a car door was hanging open down the street, the vehicle abandoned. We ran the plates and figured you were in trouble—again. Lucas returned his attention to her. "How're you feeling, Kaylee?" His brows knitted in concern, scrutinizing her face.

"My wrist hurts. I was trying to get away. I opened the door and—'

"Caden happened. In all his glory and suaveness," Matt murmured.

"Yeah, Caden. Looks like the only way you can get a woman under you is to bowl her over. Good move." Lucas' quip was answered with Caden's snarl.

"Leave it, Luc. She's had a hard go of it." Caden smoothed the back of her hand with his thumb. "We're going to take you to the hospital. Two head traumas in quick succession means you're gonna stay for observation this time. I'll stay with you."

"At least her warranty is still good, despite the perp's transfer of ownership." Lucas winked at Kaylee.

"Caden—a perp? Never thought of him like that. Maybe you should maintain a small barrier, bro, for her safety. Say like...legal stalking distance?" Another voice, unknown, joined in the brotherly banter. "Considering that you, you know, are the *cause* of her injury this time."

"Billy, knock it off." Caden hissed as a paramedic briefly urged him aside.

"Hmm, wish I had a big family of pain-in-the-ass brothers." She smiled to take the sting out of her words, squeezing Caden's hand to convey her gratitude for his presence. Raising her right arm, the movement revealed a splint on her wrist.

A strap tightening across her waist and restricting her movements caused a momentary struggle.

"Easy, sweetheart. It's just the paramedic securing you so you don't roll off the gurney. I'm really sorry." Caden shook his head. Self-disgust etched lines in the shadows under his eyes.

"Caden, did you at least pick up *anything* about the bastard?" Matt opened the door so emergency personnel could wheel the stretcher outside.

Once over the threshold, red strobe lights flashed on the vehicle. She shivered in the cool night air with only the thin blanket covering her.

"He fit the description and sketch of her kidnapper." Caden scrubbed a hand across his jaw's bristle as he kept pace beside her.

"I think I saw his face, just for a second." Kaylee closed her eyes in trying to recreate the memory. The outline of a head shimmered in her mind, the edges vibrating with each jolt of the stretcher's journey across the yard. She couldn't grasp the boundaries long enough to force them into a distinct shape.

Predawn light spilled over the treetops to lighten the atmosphere as the ambulance doors closed. It was going to be a long day.

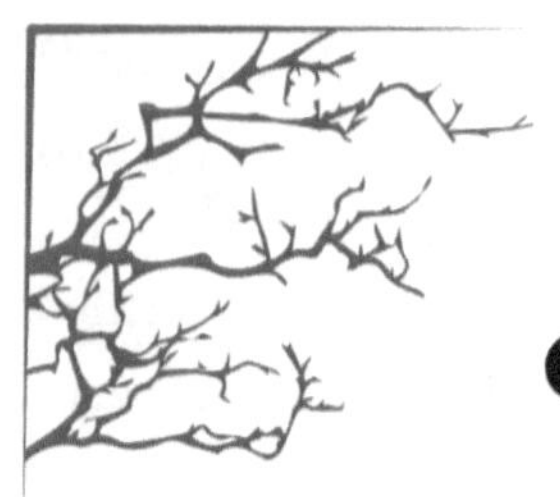

Chapter Eight

"Well?" Listening to his subordinate's excuses over the phone raised Hale's blood pressure with each uttered syllable. Reminding himself of how difficult it was to find good help didn't settle the seething frustration in his chest. Not only was the girl worth serious money with her long hair and fresh face, but she was also a witness they needed to take out of circulation.

"I had her. Then her boy toy showed up. Didn't know he was around."

"Yeah, let me get this straight. You failed to acquire the photographer, *and* you were identified by another?" In his mind, Hale pictured the dirtball's surprise when confronted with Caden's fury. Even two to one odds might not have overpowered the shutterbug's rescuer. Besides, getting involved on this level wasn't his responsibility.

"I don't think he saw my face." Hesitation communicated unspoken words. "How'd you know they swiped my mask?"

"Doesn't matter. Now they'll have your DNA, your identity. We have to move a little faster unless you fancy a lethal injection." Hale wondered if the bastard had used a condom when raping Ciera. He hadn't paid attention to that detail in the video. Chances were strong it'd been a bareback ride.

"They'll have no body. We moved the rich snatch."

"True, but don't you think a photographer who's had a look at your face, twice now, could draw a decent likeness? That plus any forensic evidence found will nail you." From the safety of his car,

Hale watched as red lights flashed in front of the small bungalow one street over. Maybe the snafu would prove advantageous.

"Shit. I'll get her tomorrow. One way or another."

"I prefer the girl alive. Now that she's spent time with Caden McAllister, we'll involve him, too. But not at the hospital."

"How'd you know—you're here? You watched this? Why didn't you lend a hand?"

"If you'd have handled one small girl properly, you wouldn't have faced the boyfriend. That incompetence is all on you. Watch the hospital and see where they go when they leave."

"It's time to kill this bitch, too." Hatred filled the predator's words.

"No. I want her alive. I have special plans for her." Despite further orders, Hale surmised the photographer's days were numbered. *Pity.*

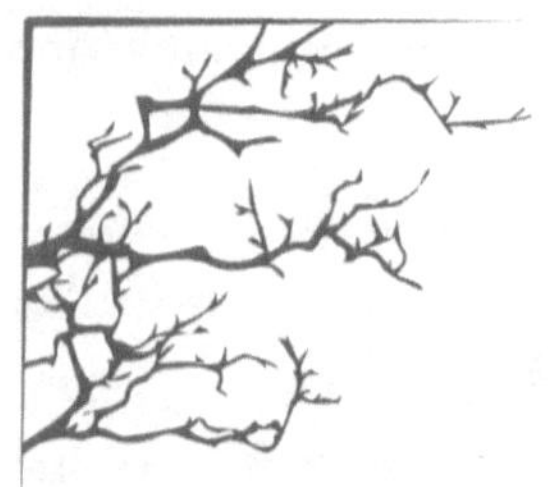

Chapter Nine

Consciousness crept forward in soft light overhead and muted sounds in the distance. Kaylee opened her eyes slowly, trying to orient herself to time and place. It came with an avalanche of pain and guilt.

Taking stock of injuries other than her wrist, she noted a swollen lip, her tongue swiping over the painful split, along with aches covering much of her body. Gingerly touching her face, she felt the swelling of her right cheek.

Utilitarian curtains framed the peacock range of colors during the sun's dip below the horizon. Sleeping most of the day had allowed her body to start healing but left her in a wash of muddled doubt.

The door, standing slightly ajar, ushered in routine hospital sounds. Distant beeps of IV pumps and heart monitors, patients admitted via stretchers, and the low hum of many conversations made up the normal ebb and flow in the corridor.

Caden's soft snore drew her attention to the chair by her bed. Several midnight locks had fallen across his face to cover his forehead and part of his nose. She grimaced when he jerked in his sleep as unseen demons held him hostage.

He'd survived his own hell yet retained the courage to reach out and help others. After Reese's death, she'd wanted to curl in a ball and never leave her bed.

When he fisted his hands and groaned, she wiped a single tear from her eye. How long would he suffer from the horrific event he openly mocked? When he jerked upright in his seat, his gaze searching for the threat of his nightmare, she reached for his hand then hesitated. His pride wouldn't stand for it.

As if feeling the weight of her stare, he zeroed in on her face. "How're you feeling?"

"Better. Hey, you didn't have to stay all day. I'm sure you have work to do. But I thank you. I didn't think I'd ever sleep again." Security derived from his proximity shielded and comforted in a way nothing else could.

"Not a problem. I figured the adrenaline washout would take you under and I love watching someone catching flies while asleep." His gaze shifted restlessly around the room.

"You're trying to avoid telling me something."

"Damn." He took a slow, deep breath. "I'm losing my touch. I've been hired to find your kidnappers."

"I'm a job?"

"No. You're my friend whom I want to protect. Now I have an excuse to tie you to me, at least temporarily."

She couldn't stop the heat sweeping up her face. "I could use a friend in this town."

"Since I'm part of a large family, you just inherited a bunch. 'Sides, once you reach out to old acquaintances, you'll have plenty more. And before you say anything, I understand you want to get settled first."

"So, have you spoken to my dad?" Fear of her father making the trip while recovering from his illness tightened her chest. Both parents would insist on her coming home.

"No, I wouldn't without your consent."

"Oh." Relief flooded her mind. After two scrapes with evil incarnate, she realized Caden's insight came with a price, stressing over privacy versus safety. An emotional tax every victim must pay.

"The doctor said you have a concussion and need to take it easy for the next couple weeks. Normal activities and exercise are good, overexertion, not so much." Caden leaned forward, resting his elbows on his knees. "I'm sorry for busting your door in like that. If I'd known you were right there, obviously I would've taken a different tack."

"Hey, you saved my life." Opening her hand, palm up, was a shift from her normal character, but for the last forty-eight hours, nothing in life resembled conventional routine.

Without skipping a beat, he took her good hand in both of his before pointing to her splint. "Hope you don't mind, I got bored."

Her spirits lifted at seeing the penciled, shepherd's head on the inside. "I love it. Thanks. Ya know, I was thinking I'd like to get a puppy when this is over."

"Sounds like a great idea. I have a friend who breeds long-coat shepherds. They've got a new litter on the ground."

The slow tease of his thumb over her knuckles incited a warmth in her belly.

"By the way, the doc confirmed nothing's broken. The splint is for support."

"I thought for sure that dirtball had smashed my wrist. I'll take a sprain over a fracture any day. At least it'll be back to normal sooner."

After updating her on the investigation, conversation drifted through mutual hobbies, from gradients they'd tackled to knee flipping their craft in white waters. Common ground rekindled a familiarity that comforted despite the surroundings.

A nurse who'd come in to monitor vital signs and check pupillary reactions assured all was normal. Nothing could have been further from the truth. Any assumption that *normal* would return with time and relocation now freewheeled through the cosmos heedless of her desperation and frustration.

Caden ate the dinner brought by staff, her stomach not able to handle the food. Soon after, a doctor made his evening rounds, suggesting she could go home if she wouldn't be alone for the next twenty-four hours.

As evening shadows crawled across the scrubbed linoleum floor, she chronicled her two terrifying encounters in hopes of remembering some new detail. "I'm sorry. Some of the specifics of last night's attack are still fuzzy."

Matt, Lucas, and Billy McAllister arrived during her retelling, each solemn, each resembling the mold that created them, yet so different in thought and action.

"I hope you're feeling better. You've had quite the unwelcoming party for your return to our city." Matt grimaced as his gaze roved over her face.

"Yeah, not what I was expecting, at all."

"So, did Caden break your wrist when he mowed you down?" Billy, another McAllister police officer, stood at the foot of her hospital bed.

She remembered Billy as the studious brother, logical, not as serious as the eldest and not as cautious.

"No. I was reaching for my gun—" Events of last night roared back to bring her current reality into focus.

"You were gonna shoot Caden? Damn." Shaking shoulders and the hand that failed to cover a smile betrayed Billy's mirth. "You really have converted to the dark side, bro."

Caden made a rude hand gesture then rubbed the back of his neck. "I was there because she'd called earlier and sounded a little off." A small flush shadowed his cheeks.

"When you wave, you should use all your fingers." Lucas snickered.

"C'mon guys. She's trying to concentrate. She doesn't need that kind of support now." Caden's commiseration spared her the embarrassment of a failed memory.

Kaylee continued her report in bits of stuttered flashbacks. "I heard the intruder come in the back door. It has a telltale squeak. At first, I thought I'd dreamed it but reached for my gun anyway. The prick was faster and slammed the drawer on my wrist."

"And *then* you managed to nail him anyway?" Billy asked. "Damn, you are as tough as I remember."

"Not tough enough to stay out of the hospital."

Caden picked up the thread of conversation. "When I'd arrived down the street, I'd parked and rolled down my window so the cool air would keep me awake. I heard her scream and ran for the house. A man howled, then something broke, probably the lamp."

"The prick caught up to me as I was trying to open the front door." The memory of her head slamming against the wall would surely repeat on a nightmarish reel. Last night, when she'd tried to explain what had happened, her memories wouldn't take shape. At least now, a coherent picture formed, even if it did scare the crap out of her.

"Do you have friends in the area you can stay with temporarily? Matt asked.

"And take this mess to someone else's door? No. I wouldn't jeopardize anyone else's safety. 'Sides, I was in middle school when we left. Who knows where my old friends are now."

Caden held her good hand, stroking his thumb over the sensitive flesh of her inner wrist. "We'll look up old acquaintances when the dust settles. You can stay with me in the meantime."

"I don't know if we have football gear her size, and thick enough to keep her safe." Lucas slapped a high five with Billy.

"Knock it off, guys. I have a spare room she can use until we sort this out."

Everything about Caden's actions spoke of a need to protect, something she'd only experienced around her parents and twin. Did it come naturally from family values or perhaps from his recent, dark, personal nightmare? "Do you always take in strays?"

With her hair a tangled mess, bruises marring her face, and pain in various muscles of her back and sides forcing a grimace, no wonder their expressions were so bleak. On the other hand, their banter seemed more a part of their normal interaction than an attempt to lift her spirits, though she appreciated the side benefit.

"Nah, he's just hoping you don't get your gun and shoot him for being so slow," Lucas quipped.

"Enough, you all need to leave so she can rest." Caden shooed them toward the door just as a couple entered. The man, obviously a McAllister by genetics, wore a black suit and escorted a striking brunette with a hand at her waist. The young woman's self-confidence flowed as naturally as the grin lifting the corners of her mouth.

"Hi, I'm Lexi." She held out her left hand in consideration of Kaylee's splint. "We've come to help. Well, actually, I've already started. I hope you don't mind, but I've gone ahead and pulled up your information to get things rolling." The smile directed at her escort embodied a warmth known only between lovers.

"Lexi, what about our little chat concerning citizens hacking police records." Matt's chastisement elicited chuckles from the men.

"That's why I left a trail back to Caden's ISP." Lexi brushed him off before turning her attention back to Kaylee. Each McAllister shook his head.

Watching Caden roll his eyes, Kaylee saw acceptance in his posture as he let out a deep sigh and dropped chin to chest. "Here we go again. Giving the captain yet another reason to hate me."

"Naw, bro. You did that all by yourself. Lexi's just adding the frosting," Ethan murmured.

"I saw that you produced a detailed rendering of your intruder." Lexi continued.

"She sure as hell did. As good as I could do." Caden's pride drew knowing smirks from his brothers.

"We're working with stick figures again? Really?" The grin slipped from Lucas' expression in the face of Caden's arched brow.

"That kind of incident pretty much stays in your mind, if you know what I mean. I wish I could say the second attack jarred an additional memory, a detail that might help. But I just don't have anything else to add."

"No worries. We'll track him. Meanwhile, you're in good hands." Lexi's genuine grace portrayed a warmth mixed with pain in her glance at Caden.

"Speaking of Caden's hands—" Billy murmured but halted under the oldest McAllister's throat clearing.

"Don't worry, she's not Caden's flavor of the week." Lucas grinned and stepped back with Caden's growl.

"Not with that sweet face and triple-digit IQ," Billy added.

"Jeez, guys, lighten up. They're friends." Lexi smiled at Caden, who nodded his head in gratitude.

"Huh, spoken by the woman who bonded with him over Himalayan tea and rats," Lucas murmured.

The macabre banter, having suddenly turned left at normality, converted Caden's easy smile to an obscure detachment. Tiny crinkles around his eyes and mouth conveyed a shared pain.

"Lexi was covered with peanut butter, tuna fish, and God alone knows what else by a psychopathic stalker. I kinda hung around in a fog after being poisoned." Caden grimaced at Lexi, the shared experience bringing his misery to the surface.

Tension in the atmosphere rose as Matt and Lucas looked at the floor, outside, or anywhere but Caden. Billy gripped Caden's shoulder and murmured something too low for Kaylee to hear before stepping away. Ethan pulled Lexi snug and kissed her hair.

"Back to business, guys," Matt redirected them all.

Kaylee's first impression of Ethan and Lexi entailed an empathetic and concerned couple. Now, she felt like she'd entered a strange dimension. Lexi was clearly *with* Ethan, who kept a protective arm about her shoulders. Yet the bond between Lexi and Caden, an obvious platonic one, appeared stronger than anything she'd ever witnessed.

Stay away from strange people.

Clearly, there was more than genetics and odd circumstances binding the group together. She recognized the strength of their commitment with Matt's affectionate squeeze of Caden's shoulder before Lucas' playful shoulder bump nudged her protector sideways. Another reminder of her missing sibling.

"Okay, you *all* need to leave. I'm taking Kaylee home and letting her rest. Lexi, I know you'll do your keyboard thing looking for the dipshit and keep us all in the loop. The rest of you have your own contacts and sources for information."

Caden banished them all amid reassuring back slaps and rude comments. As much as she'd normally enjoy their company, she needed time to digest current events in a quiet and secure environment. The snick of the door closing offered a cocooning effect to exclude the outside world.

"You okay?" Caden's concern vibrated between them like a discordant note struck on a piano keyboard. Her black and white world had upended with Reese's death, the sharp and blackened edges of reality interrupting the previously smooth cadence. She found no harmony, as if fate's conductor reveled in the deceptive dissonance of evil's aura and intended to lock her within it.

"Yeah, just ready to get out of here."

"All right. Let's ring for your nurse and see if the discharge orders are written yet. We'll stop by your house so you can pack a bag and collect your valuables."

The play of light and shadow had become Kaylee's world after delving into the sphere of photography, a place of wonder, speculation, and experimentation. She'd never been afraid of the dark. Now, she stood on her front porch while her keys slipped through trembling fingers. Shafts of moonlight danced along the floorboards as the night breeze sifted through the nearby oaks' overhanging branches, nature's eerie laugh ratcheting her anxiety.

Caden scooped up the keyring and nudged her aside. "Let me go in first, Gracie." A small click and the door opened. "I'm going to look around while you wait just inside the door."

"Gracie? Let me guess, Grace O'Malley, the female pirate?"

"I didn't take you for a historian. Good call." Silence spilled from the yawning dark interior, a hushed prediction that only the brave should enter.

"Reese and I used to love going through the caverns and caves near home after watching pirate movies."

"Isn't that redundant? Aren't they one and the same?"

"No. Most people think so, but they're not. I'll explain the differences over a cup of hot chocolate. You see me as a buccaneer?"

"Yeah. I kinda grew up on pirate tales, tunnels, and mysteries. You strike me as the same single-minded and high-spirited kid who'd face a rough-and-tumble gang, determined to win."

Striding back through the front door with borrowed courage fanned the spark of prior fortitude. The small but insistent inner voice of reality proclaimed it temporary, dependent on her rescuer's presence. Even after the kidnappers were caught, she wasn't sure she could return and live alone among the terrifying memories in the house.

Flipping the light switch flooded her mind with images of her intruder and the brutal attack. A blood smear contrasted the cream-colored wall near the doorjamb, a testament of her vulnerability. She gingerly touched the corner of her mouth, remembering the creep slamming her against the wallboard, the imprint a physical reminder of her near-death experience.

Lost in her thoughts, she jumped when Caden returned and lightly touched her shoulder.

"Sorry, Kaylee. I know the memories are scary, but it'll get better."

"Have yours gone away?"

"No, but they're not as bad with the passage of time."

Still, they haunted his dreams. An unwanted recollection of his body twitching in the hospital chair forewarned of tough nights ahead.

With his arm circling her shoulders, he led her back to the bedroom, stopping when she froze at the door. The sheets had been taken by forensics, and ceramic shards from the lamp peppered the hardwood floor. Sour glow from the overhead light gilded the bloody footprints silently narrating her desperate escape.

"I wonder where *she* is, if she's all right." Kaylee closed her eyes yet was unable to shut out the fact her body shook.

When Caden turned her to face him and pulled her in for a hug, she couldn't resist taking a slow, deep breath. The bone-deep weariness receded with the inhalation of his spicy aftershave. She breathed in security to expand her lungs, something taken for granted for so long. With nothing sexual in his touch, he simply held her, fortifying her reserves. When the moment passed, he released her but stayed close, somehow knowing she still needed his strength.

"It was a while before I could face my trauma and say *screw you* to the memories, even if I don't always win." Quiet words seemed to revive his own nightmare. "You'll do it too."

After his reaction in the tunnels with the squeaking, chattering rats and his brothers closing in beside him for support, she wondered how often PTSD slapped him upside the head with a *Hey Caden, let's schmooze for a while, I'm bored.*

"Thank you." Random thoughts flitted through her mind as she stuffed clothes from her dresser into the canvas bag retrieved from underneath her bed. The weather was warming, but nights were still cool, meaning a light sweater and corduroy pants were still in order. She used her body to block sight of all the lace panties and bras retrieved from the top dresser drawer. It didn't matter that she modeled them for no one. They made her feel attractive.

"Pack as much as you can."

"I have a suitcase in the closet. I—" A place, for some reason she couldn't face.

He would read her panic, knowing the thug had come in her door and hadn't lain in wait, but fear wasn't a rational beast that attacked head-on.

Once he opened the suitcase on her bed, she filled it with as much as it could hold, blushing as she tried to hide a sexy nightgown under blue jeans. *He doesn't miss a thing.*

She grabbed her laptop as he shouldered the duffle and picked up her suitcase.

"Hey. I carry my backup flash in this locket. When I was sitting at the café, I'd changed out the cards. So this one has all the pics I've taken since arriving."

"We'll look at them when we get home." Again, he glanced around, his lips set in a firm line. "All set?"

"Yeah. I just don't know if I can come back here."

"Give it time. We'll see."

"I know I'll have to return to regain my confidence."

"Priorities include you getting some rest." He paused as if unsure how to word his thoughts. "I'd rather leave your car here tonight. Since your intruder knew where you lived, it's conceivable he placed a tracker on it. I can check, but it's better to do it in daylight."

"That's why you took those weird routes from the hospital."

"I needed to make sure we weren't followed, just like I'll do when we leave here." A slight blush climbed his cheeks before adding, "If you have any perishables you want to bring, that's fine. I don't keep my fridge stocked, but we'll shop tomorrow."

"Hmm, a bachelor that doesn't cook?" He probably had to beat the women away. "I've got a few boxes in the closet we can use to carry the food. No need to let it go bad. And again, thanks." She sighed as she looked around. "Things like this don't happen to small-town girls like me."

Some anomaly embedded in her soul or cloaking her aura designated her as prey worthy of hunt and capture. The obvious vulnerability she'd fought so hard to beat since Reese's death now flourished with a vengeance. No amount of gazing in the mirror would reveal the thread of darkness wrapping her spirit in a blazing invitation only the dregs of humanity could see.

"Earth to Kaylee? Put both paddles in the water." Cade waved a hand in front of her face.

"Yeah, sorry. A lot's happening. Lucky for you, I'm a fairly good cook." Thinking of his experience as a PI and ex-cop, maybe she stood a chance at surviving when the thugs again tracked her down. *Eventually,* they would.

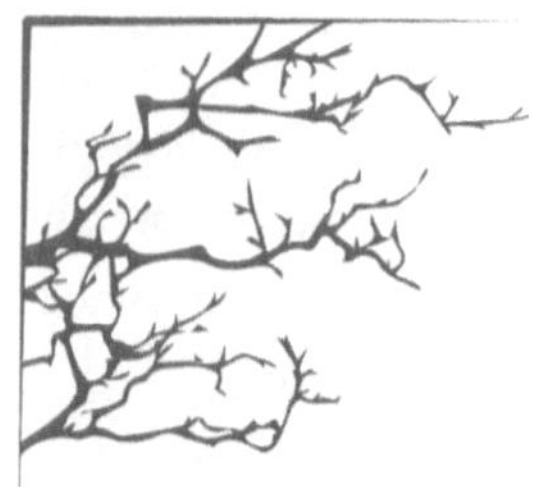

Chapter Ten

Caden filled the homeward ride with comfortable chitchat reminiscent of a Sunday afternoon on the porch with her parents and twin. As long as he didn't touch her or stand too close, she could see him as a friend, confidant, and shield against harm. Otherwise, her hormones soared into overdrive and blunted the edge of a normally sharp wit.

She'd expected to reconnect with old friends at some point, once logic and grit ruled emotion. Reese had been the popular one, the easygoing, handsome, and personable soul that drew others without effort. Without her other half, fear of rejection had set up camp and strived to control her actions. The unique and fragile license to rekindle friendship with Caden had sprung from desperation and insecurity yet calcified with shared experiences and mutual respect.

"You feel like calling them?" Spoken with the expectation she'd know to whom he referred.

"No, my father will flip out. I'm not ready to handle that. If we discussed the current situation, he'd be out here looking over everyone's shoulder and issuing commands. Trust me, you don't want to deal with him. He's a force to be reckoned with." Despite the knowledge he'd do it out of love, she didn't want her dad risking his health. Her parents had given her so much.

"You're a chip off the block."

"Hmm. They've always been supportive, even of my ambition for independence. When Reese died in the car accident, I didn't want to leave my dorm room. It was like the world caved in and I couldn't breathe." Small yet important details about her twin were slowly dimming, rejuvenating the pain of loss. "Gradually, I've surfaced and started rebuilding my life. We'd been planning on moving out here together."

"Ah, sorry I stirred bad memories."

"Not your fault. I'm learning to adjust." Initially, the internal buildup of pressure had grown exponentially like the vacuum of space where body fluids boiled and explosion was imminent.

Concrete sidewalks and city townhouses slid by before grass shoulders and deeper lawns with larger homes held sway. She could easily picture Caden in suburbia with room for family gatherings yet with enough privacy for the invariable long parade of women. Though he'd given no notice of the suggestive stares from the nursing staff, he was the type of man who tracked everything in his surroundings.

"In high school, I loved art but realized I'd never support myself with painting and drawing. Reese helped my parents pick out my Christmas present, a high-end camera, and I started taking photography more seriously. I was already addicted but hadn't thought of it as a career possibility. For my birthday, they gave me the software to manipulate the images, and from there it was a match made in heaven."

"I figured you had some type of computer background, considering your adeptness with my composite program."

She smiled. "At Syracuse, I majored in digital photography, loved looking at the world through a viewfinder as well as editing the images." At first, she'd felt lost at school, adrift from everyone and everything she'd loved but then threw herself into the study of shadows and light, technology, and the charm of New York. If not for her dedication to the craft, the tide of grief over Reese's passing would have pulled her under.

"I didn't take you for an extreme country boy, but it shouldn't surprise me." The farther they drove, exchanging developments for farmland and long stretches of dense woods, the more she realized the man had many sides, the most interesting were the ones he didn't show the world.

"I've always craved privacy, but now I'm not so sure. I just moved in recently, so fair warning. Boxes are everywhere." His gaze drifted out the side window where moonlight separated bare limbs reaching for the heavens in prayer. Gently rolling hills straddling the deserted highway created a surreal landscape worthy of a fiction writer's best efforts.

The narrow gravel path Caden navigated after turning off the state road bisected thick woods with early budding branches enclosing them in a darker world. A week ago, she would have viewed the scene as cozy and inviting, even romantic with little light penetrating from above, yet now she felt an ominous flare seething in the atmosphere. She wondered if the foreboding would evaporate with time and return her to a normal way of thinking when they caught the kidnappers.

A small audible exhalation escaped after rounding the next bend. A picturesque scene lay ahead, worthy of an old-world monastery. Graceful arches of hemlock and red alders dotted the front yard, allowing glimpses of the residence beyond.

She'd spent four years photographing sights and architecture in New York, a fondness deepening with each snap of her shutter. What she now saw personified aspects of Caden's character. Solid strength.

The house overhauled the concept of owning a cabin in the woods. The two-story contemporary with glass walls allowed an unobstructed view of the forest and boasted a twin-story, wraparound balcony. Rich, dark wood blended with the environment while the stone front encasing the glass extended the length of the verandah and completed the look. Recessed lighting brightened the downstairs while floodlights tucked under the eaves illuminated the surrounding area.

"Wow. It's beautiful. Looks like you could see everything from the balcony."

And an intruder standing there could watch you sleep, or undress.

"All the windows and sliders have one-way blinds that I use when I'm home. They still let in the light, but you can't see inside during the day. After dark, we can close the drapes." A glitter of steel flickered through his gaze before he cut the engine. "I always swore I'd have a cabin in the woods." His tone lacked the depth of conviction.

To redirect his thinking, she pondered aloud, "When I was little, I wanted to be a dog handler in the State Police." Popping the latch on her door, she glanced over before getting out.

"I almost went that route, but Matt beat me to it. I am, however, getting a pup soon. The litter I told you about is an American line of working German shepherds."

"Are they all spoken for yet? I'm definitely going to have a four-footed partner. He could go everywhere with me, especially when I'm out working." Her protector was a Good Samaritan and loved dogs. Damn.

The pro-Caden list gained momentum in her head. Not a good sign. She had no difficulty resisting mortal men but to find one with dominion over the average female with the growing list of attributes sent up a corps of red flags.

"No, not yet. We can make a call tomorrow. C'mon, I'll give you the grand tour. It's pretty quick." A ring of false enthusiasm corresponded with the smile that didn't reach his eyes.

He hadn't been joking when he said he had crates everywhere. From the brick walkway, she observed stacks of boxes behind a leather sofa and along the outer wall. Once inside, it appeared he hadn't unpacked anything. "You're not going to stay here are you?" It wasn't the stacked boxes that revealed his uncertainty but something deeper, darker, and unspoken.

A quick, soft inhale preceded the deer-in-the-headlights expression flashing across his face but gone in the next heartbeat. Each was long enough for guilt to slither into her conscience. "I'm sorry. I shouldn't have said that."

"No. No, it's all right. You're as insightful as my family and just as forthright." He pinched his bottom lip between his teeth before continuing. "I haven't resolved the issue one way or another. My brothers keep telling me to give it six months before deciding, afraid I'll regret a rash judgment. I am starting to warm up to the idea. Maybe with some modifications, it would be a good fit." After opening the door, he entered a code on his alarm system.

An open layout offered the vantage point of viewing more boxes stacked near a long kitchen island and underneath the open-tread stairway. Black granite countertops with white marbling reflected thin rays from the pendant lights. Dark, hardwood floors throughout might have encouraged a sense of gloom if not for the light flooding the space from all sides.

"This is absolutely incredible."

Standing in the middle of the open space, he held his arms wide. "And this nearly concludes the tour. Over to the left, there's a large office and a smaller den. There's three bedrooms upstairs. I'll grab your bags and bring them up before hauling in the food. You can freshen up while I put the edibles away."

Curiosity urged her to explore, yet recent experiences confined her to the open area where she'd be seen. The sound of the front door closing echoed in the massive space. It made sense that Caden's dark experience kept him from unpacking the boxes and turning off the lights, his subconscious warning him about the home's seclusion.

In stepping to the rear glass wall, she took in the breathtaking view at the back of the property. A stone patio extended from one of the rear sliding doors with a hot tub tucked in the nook near the attached garage. Considering his appearance and innate charm, he probably had to schedule the stream of women waiting to spend the night.

Except he didn't seem the snuggle-all-night type. In her mind's eye, she could visualize invisible waves of pheromones wafting from his body but concentrated and focused when his gaze narrowed on his next target. "Wow. This really is a bachelor's pad."

"Yeah, I guess it needs a bit of a feminine touch to avoid looking like a modern cave."

She hadn't heard him return. "No, not at all. Just need to unpack the boxes. I don't mind helping. It's the least I can do." Considering the number of cartons in her rental, she had to smile. At least it would keep her mind off the thugs who'd caged her like an animal.

"Sounds great." A slight tightness around the corners of his mouth cast an unspoken doubt.

She followed him upstairs and stepped into the bedroom on the east side. The view from the balcony was every bit as gorgeous as the rest of the house.

Floor-to-ceiling windows framed the sloping land falling away from the house and could showcase the most beautiful sunrise she'd ever witness. Perhaps tomorrow morning she'd drink coffee while sitting on the veranda and take some photos of the sun cresting over the treetops.

"This okay?" A thread of uncertainty underlay his concern. "We'll close the drapes now." The crawl of a metal slide in its tracks merged the heavy fabric to shroud the room in cozy luxury.

"Wow. This is fabulous. I've never slept in a king-sized bed. It's like your own personal island."

Or adult playpen.

Had she murmured those last words aloud? Her failed filter conjured the mental image of her and Caden spooning after hours of screaming orgasms. "Oh God."

His grin personified sexual athleticism, a taunt he probably didn't realize was broadcast with indifference.

His deliberate ramble forward granted the rich, appetizing scent clinging to him to entice her to lean against him. Only the seriousness of his expression kept her lips from parting to draw in air through a restricted trachea. Slowly, he cupped her jaw, searching her face for—something.

"You've had a rough couple days. Give yourself a break."

Only inches separated them and more than anything, she wanted to rise and touch his lips with her own, to absorb his heat, his passion. The unwelcome stirring both rankled and embarrassed while preventing her from meeting his gaze. She dropped her sight line to a safer zone, his chest.

The T-shirt stretched across the hard planes with each breath, outlining the thick bulges in his arms and expanding what she knew to be a perfectly solid wall of muscle. Each hard ridge defined in bold relief the form of his pecs, deltoids, and triceps. She nibbled her lower lip to contain the appreciative comments waiting to spill forth.

Without conscious thought, she found her hand resting lightly on the firm expanse while a slow curl of her fingers confirmed what the cotton couldn't hide, large, solid, and perfect. One flex of her fingers deserved another for confirmation while adding to the growing heat between her thighs.

She'd read about the anticlimactic backwash of hormones after extreme stress that heightened sexual drive and blamed her attraction on her body's natural responses. Her libido declared him addictive, like chocolate. Her inner voice likened him to a puffer fish with no known antidote.

With a quick shake of his head, he cleared his throat and dropped his hand, the warmth of his touch replaced by cool air. "The second bathroom is shared by the two spare bedrooms. It's right across the hall."

"I don't mind sharing a bath with you. Oh, I—I mean, I don't mind sharing a bathroom with a—another." *Crap.*

His grin betrayed the acceptance of his effect. "I know what you meant." Taking a step back, he added, "If you'd like to freshen up, I'll meet you in the kitchen and fix us something to eat. Any food allergies?"

"Sex." *Shit* "No, I mean, soy. I have a slight allergy. It gives me an itch." Heat engulfed her entire body. Clearing her throat was an excuse to cover a portion of her face. A light coat of perspiration dotted her brow. *I've got an itch all right, and he knows it.* "I think I took a solid hit to the noggin."

"Well, that's a relief. It'd be a shame for anyone to be allergic to sex." The teasing smirk should've ticked off anyone with a shred of pride.

She melted. He probably ranked sex above food and water.

"I've got an idea for tomorrow afternoon if you feel up to it."

Does it include a shovel and a very large hole in the ground?

If she survived this humiliation, she could take on the thugs single-handed. "Sure. I love surprises."

When he turned to leave, she couldn't help but admire the view completing the package, lean and strong, solid and sure. She could spend hours mapping the planes of his body with the play of light and shadow, purely from a photographer's viewpoint. At ease with his erotic masculinity, he wouldn't realize that compassion and a swoon-worthy protective streak rocketed him to demi-God status.

The classic cold shower would cool her body while her mind strayed to all the lovely male parts keeping her in a state of flux. She'd never thought of icy water as a cross-gender necessity and found that once in the spacious bathroom, she wouldn't need one, at least for the length of her stay.

On the counter lay half-empty bottles of expensive shampoo and crème rinse. A quick look under the sink yielded an open box of tampons. For heavy flow. The icy mist forming around her heart thickened and solidified with the realization, she was there to stay safe. *Lock down your granny panties, Kaylee. He's not for you.*

To complete the oddity of conflicting emotions, a cartoon figure nightlight in the socket glowed softly. Perhaps a preference from a previous guest if no more existed elsewhere. She hadn't noticed. A quick look around the bedroom revealed a different one by the door. Regardless of the short time they'd spent together, she knew it was *so* Caden.

Flirting was probably as natural to him as breathing, a habit he couldn't shed and survive, which loosened the band around her chest. She'd come to Portland to start a new life and unless she wanted to return with her tail tucked like a whipped dog, it was time to get her shit together. Friendship with Caden, despite his womanizing status, would be a welcome start.

She'd grown accustomed to inclusion as one of the guys until her brother's death. It was time to show her rescuer the resiliency of her backbone—if he didn't demolish her defenses first.

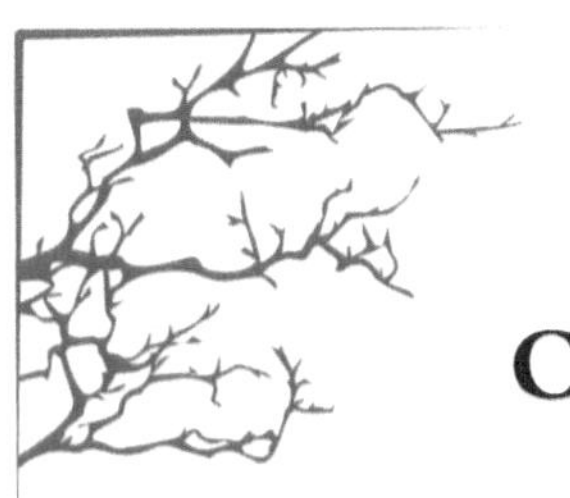

Chapter Eleven

"Looks like you're feeling better." Caden held his breath as Kaylee padded down the steps with an innate grace that glimmered despite shadows lingering beneath her eyes.

"Yep. A nice, hot shower and I'm good to go. Love the waterfall showerhead, by the way." A genuine smile showed perfect white teeth before she ducked her head.

She's self-conscious about the cuts and bruises. She had as much moxie as any cop he'd worked with during his stint in the department. No wonder Lucas had eyed her like a Christmas present, waiting for her to get her bearings before proving himself the man-whore his division proclaimed him. Damned if that was going to happen. "Hope you don't mind a breakfast-dinner. I'm not the best of cooks."

"Thanks, I just wasn't hungry in the hospital, but I am now."

Without hesitation, she padded to his side and took the spatula from his hand. "How about I take over this detail. You look a little unsure of what to do with it." After giving the implement a conspicuous once-over, she added, "You don't use this to swat flies or anything, do you?"

"Um, no. At least not recently." They fit together the same way his family did, unlike any other woman he'd met.

Two misses and she opened the silverware drawer to withdraw a fork. "I'll cook the bacon in the oven next time, see if you like it that way. Much healthier."

Normally it took a little time to learn someone's tells, but Kaylee's fidgeting proved a blatant sign that knocked him off kilter. Her strong character may have come naturally before moving to Oregon, but it now layered as a façade over a thick slab of insecurity. He'd always been one to call his friends and family on their bullshit. She'd be no different.

"Kaylee, you've had one hell of a twenty-four-hour period. How 'bout you sit at the counter and let me take care of you."

Her gaze slid farther away the closer he stepped. Each pace strengthened the tantalizing scent ensnaring his thoughts. "Bubblegum?"

"Yeah. Flavored toothpaste, a childhood habit Reese and I couldn't kick."

"Nice." Close enough to admire the golden specks in her storm-green eyes meant he also detected the uncertainty within. "You two were very close." Earlier descriptions gave depth to her pain and how much she missed her twin. Now she stood on new ground.

"I wish he were here. I thought a fresh start would help with the heartache, but it only made things worse." Tears jeweled her lashes before she angrily swiped them away.

The French braid of her wet hair prevented him from sliding his fingers through its rich, silky depths. *Not a good idea.* He merely wanted to offer comfort.

He'd hoped his close proximity would redirect her mind to a new focus, but it backfired. A slow deep breath helped steady his thoughts, until her fresh scent wrapped around his chest like a self-tightening strap, squeezing until he acknowledged her effect. One finger under her chin lifted her gaze. The merging of innocence and trust unified his body's reaction in a growing response he couldn't control. "Kaylee?"

"I'm fine. I moved back here to prove that I *can* take care of myself. I knew it would all feel different now, but hoped there'd be enough familiarity to help me start over." With a firm hand on his chest, she nudged him back until he sat on a stool. "I'll cook. You talk. I know you've contacted Matt, who seems to be the ringleader of your family. Any news?"

"Damn. I keep forgetting your father's a cop. Looks like he taught you well."

"Not good enough to avoid the kidnapper."

"Hey, anyone can get sucker punched. Happened to me."

"And you're avoiding my question."

"Double damn. You *are* a keeper, aren't you?"

If he hadn't been looking at her in that instant, he would have missed it. Some elusive emotion flickered through her gaze before she tucked it under a cool façade of arched brow and hand on hip.

"And you're good at avoidance—but not good enough."

"All right. Matt, Lucas, and Ethan are coming over to talk. I was thinking since you obviously didn't sleep much last night and nobody sleeps well in a hospital bed, you'd want to rest."

And isn't that the dumbest idea I've had recently. Ranks right up there with closing on a home you're not sure you still want.

After his own ordeal, he still couldn't stay abed all night, much less sleep for more than a few hours at a time.

"You've had no more rest than me. I. Am. Fine. I want to know what's going on. 'Sides, I want to go through my photos and see if anything pops."

"Sorry you lost your best camera."

"Yeah, it sucks." Disgust and sadness intertwined in her voice. "At least I'd switched SD cards when I sat at the café. I'd wanted to get a few more shots of the ships at sunset but had run out of room."

The likelihood of finding anything helpful on the card was slim, but action over inaction was preferable and would keep her thoughts moving forward. "All right. How 'bout we take a look after we eat."

With their initial direction set in motion, she finished the bacon and fixed chocolate-chip pancakes. If he'd ever met anyone who'd enjoyed the gift of gab, they couldn't compare to the chatterbox in his kitchen. After setting their plates and plopping in the chair beside him to eat, it was time to come clean.

"So, you gonna tell me what else is on your mind? The thing you've been avoiding." She cast him a sideways glance as they sat at the island eating.

Son of a bitch.

"You know, even my brothers can't read me that well."

She drummed her fingers on the counter. And waited.

"All right, all right. We have the identity of the girl in the tunnel." So good the moment before, the food now tasted like ash.

"And?"

"Shit. Okay. Her parents called and asked me to find her."

"So, you know them?"

"Jeez. You're like a dog with a bone."

"Tasty bone. Give."

"I used to—know her."

"As in the biblical *know* her?"

"Yeah. She'd had an abusive ex-boyfriend. I helped her get clear of him, then..."

"Yeah, I get the picture, hound dog."

"I haven't seen her in over a year. And hey, you can't come from my family and be a virgin at twenty-seven."

She sighed. "Like I hadn't figured that out?"

"How?"

"I didn't peg you for inventing unique uses for the tampons in the spare bathroom."

Heat crept up his neck with her imagined speculations. Her first impression would be difficult if not impossible to change.

"Hey, those are from when my sister visited."

"The one who lives just a few miles away?"

"Yeah, I went through a rough patch after discharge from the hospital. She's the proverbial mother hen."

"Really?" A thoughtful frown indicated she believed he might be telling the truth.

He couldn't give details of why Abagail spent a week as his guest. When the threat to his life had ended, his mind hadn't been able to get on board. Each of his brothers had anticipated his reactions and offered to stay for a bit, but his sister merely arrived with suitcase in hand.

Small thin scars lined his forearms and chest as a permanent reminder of the rodents' attack. Though Kaylee hadn't suffered the same scenario, she'd endured similar consequences, ones he knew well. Paying a good deed forward, he could help her through the current threat and demoralizing baggage.

By unspoken agreement, Kaylee let the topic drop, inherently knowing he wasn't ready to dredge up the past. Her restless mind urged her into action, clearing the table.

"Where's your dish towels?" She pulled on several drawers until finding one containing foil, baggies, and hot mitts. "Ah, here they are. At least you've unpacked your kitchen boxes.

"My sister set up the kitchen."

"An orderly kitchen comes from an organized mind. I don't remember her well, just that she had you all wrapped around her little finger." The glint in her eyes spelled trouble, like when Lucas hung most of his clothes in the surrounding trees not long after the hospital discharge, the not-so-gentle hint to get out of the house.

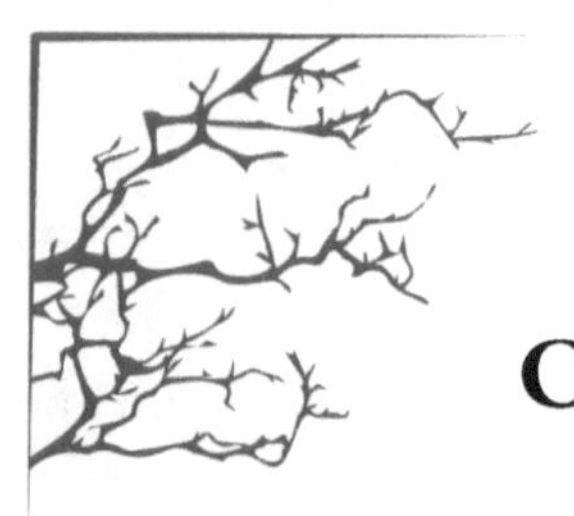

Chapter Twelve

Matt's arrival after they'd cleaned the kitchen also brought Lucas, Billy, Ethan, and Lexi. Once inside, Matt punched in the code on the alarm system and ignored his host's frustrated sigh. They each worked in different departments, but when it came to family, nothing banded them tighter than trouble.

At least they meant well.

"It's a nice day outside, mind if we open the house up a bit?" Lexi offered a confident smile as she set her bag on the kitchen island then removed her laptop. By way of agreement, each brother helped until a soft breeze provided cross-ventilation. "Hope you don't mind me sharing your new alarm code, Ca. It just makes sense to do so."

"Much better. We don't want your guest thinking you're a hermit." Lucas slapped Caden on the back before raiding the fridge. "Hmm, getting with the program, I see...Nice." Snagging an eight-pack of sodas, he placed them on the table.

"Also, I've put your security feeds on mine and your brothers' electronics." Lexi's casual explanation received chuckles while the soft hum of her computer went through its start-up process.

"Gee, thanks. I've always wanted to be popular. I figured you'd done that months ago after you saved both our asses." Caden's subdued revelation received a smile in return.

"Actually, well, I did. I just waited to tell you about it. And you're welcome." Nudging him aside and taking his seat at the counter, Lexi turned to Kaylee. "Caden said you're adept with CAD and photo editing software, so this shouldn't be difficult. I'm gonna show you how Caden set up his security system."

"Lexi..." Ethan glanced at Caden and hesitated.

"Hey, chicks before dicks. If she's gonna stay here, she needs to know how it works." Lexi pushed the laptop closer to Kaylee. "He can always change it later."

"It's all right, Ethan. The women have already closed ranks on us." Caden chuckled as Lexi pulled up the different menus and taught his guest the intricacies of the system, another sophisticated upgrade refuting the world as it was and shielding against those determined to destroy.

"Damn." Lucas grinned as they watched Kaylee on the keyboard. Only a few missteps slowed her progress.

"My dad's a cop, and I helped him install our system. It's a different one, but they share certain similarities."

The women held much in common concerning attitudes and perseverance. Lexi smiled as her protégé flipped through the different screens revealing different angles from the house.

"Okay, Matt, let's see what you've brought." Caden gestured Ethan, Billy, and Lucas to sit at the oak table, each solemn as their chairs slid soundlessly over the tile floor.

From his timeworn satchel, Matt retrieved three glossy photos of young girls, one blonde, two brunettes. Considered individually, one might think each teenager bore invisible bandages in a desperate attempt to prevent revelation of hideous scars. An all-too-familiar occurrence in an age of overindulgence and lack of self-discipline. As a group, they formed a pattern suggesting their hidden burdens outweighed the strength of their frames.

"Turns out that in the last six months, several other young women have gone missing. We didn't pick it up immediately since two were runaways believed to still be in the area but originating from out of state."

"So, what makes you believe the runaways are missing?" Kaylee's upper teeth worried her lower lip in a gesture marking her uncertainty.

Lucas closed his eyes and shook his head. "I have connections with some of the local shelters. The two girls helped Father McNally on a regular basis. He said they wouldn't have just up and left without telling him."

"So, what makes you think their disappearances are connected?" Caden studied each photo. "Ciera was far from being a runaway, same with Kaylee."

"We don't know for sure they *are* associated. Just a hunch," Matt replied.

"Kaylee, have a look and see if you recognize them. Maybe you've seen them in passing." Lucas moved so Kaylee could sit between him and Caden at the table while Ethan guided Lexi to sit on his lap.

"No. I don't recall seeing either. But I wasn't focused so much on people when I was shooting," Kaylee murmured as she studied first one, then the next picture.

"I pulled up footage from street cams around the Denelli shopping center taken the day before they nabbed Kaylee. I found Ciera Kirpatzel walking out of a shop; only she wasn't dressed like a spoiled debutante. She was wearing a baseball cap, flannel shirt and ripped jeans." Lexi pointed to one of the glossy pics, a girl who bore no resemblance to a socialite.

"Like maybe she's a runaway and not one of the affluent moving around incognito? But what about me? I don't fit that niche. I don't dress that way. And I don't remember seeing these girls, which doesn't mean I didn't photograph them. The shopping center was pretty busy."

"We haven't figured out how you come in, Kaylee," Lucas frowned as he tilted his head. "Probably because you're a new arrival."

"But they've definitely targeted you. We didn't find a tracking device on your car." Billy flipped open a notepad from his pocket.

"At least there's some good news. But when we identify the guy, it'll probably be an alias with an address pinpointing the middle of the Willamette River." Lexi added.

Kaylee fisted her hand against her jeans. Every gaze studied her as if she were a key that unlocked the mystery. An interactive moment where each seemed to silently search their inventory of experiences to lend clarity to the situation. And failed. "I'm usually the odd duck."

The smile, warm and sincere, didn't reach her eyes.

Caden smiled before offering his own interpretation. "In that case, you fit right in with this group." Slowly, he smoothed his hand across her shoulders and felt her strained muscles loosen.

The shudder which rippled under his touch sharpened his focus on her dilemma and warned him against fanning the sparks of their tenuous connection. Kidnap victim and home invasion survivor, newly arrived to the city, and now his guest. She was cut from sturdy cloth but human nonetheless.

She reacted every time he'd stood near, every time he touched her, even though she suspected him of chasing any skirt passing within striking distance. He didn't strive to create confusion in her mind, merely sought to protect and comfort. The fact her earlier demeanor warned of prank-like intentions hadn't slipped his notice, which meant they shared more traits or at least had shared them before encountering the darkness which tested their limits.

"Do you think they realize by now Ciera numbers among the social elite and she wasn't lying about having a rich family? I haven't seen her face splashed on the news." Matt's gaze zeroed in on Caden.

"I'm sure she enlightened them of her social position and informed them her parents would pay any amount of ransom." Caden knew Ciera would try to buy her freedom, and her folks would pay the price.

"She did. Now they might kill her *because* of her high profile." Kaylee voiced the truth their expressions revealed. "She saw their faces, and at least one of the bastards had raped her. They're not just going to let her go."

"And this is why all my brothers are here," Caden murmured.

"Captain formed a task force. He knows he's gonna have the media along with the city's upper crust breathing down his neck. Since Lexi's digital skills were instrumental in tracking down the psychopath three months ago, he put her on the payroll as a consultant, even though all contact is through Ethan. We don't get Lexi without her man. Hence he's also on the task force," Lucas added. "Captain's thinking this could also be drug related. When you were with her, wasn't Ciera into a little instant Zen?"

"Yeah. More than an occasional user." Regret pursed Caden's lips and tightened his chest. "Which explains Luc's placement."

"Maybe girls are exchanged for drugs." Billy's suggestion preceded a silence, the weight of which repressed further speculation in the same way an approaching tornado bears down on refugees huddled in a root cellar.

"We'll have to see where this takes us," Matt surmised.

"Crime lab turn up anything, yet?" Caden's flashbacks of Ciera, warm and wild in his bed less than a year ago, collided with images of the kidnapper raping her in the tunnel. He shuddered.

"No, and we went ahead and informed the captain about your, ah, previous association with one of the victims." Matt glanced at Kaylee apologetically.

"Gee, thanks, bro. Can we teleport into the future where this part of the conversation is over?"

"Hey, better coming from us than her husband. Though why she went back and married the prick, we'll never know." Ethan shook his head.

"Guess our little brother didn't set the bar high enough," Lucas taunted.

"Caden, just to follow procedure, we'll do your interview tonight." Matt's no-nonsense declaration stifled any argument. "I told the captain you were on surveillance the day Ciera disappeared. I assume you have time-stamped photos to back that up?"

"I do. Damn, Captain carries a long grudge. I wasn't *that* bad."

"You punched a guy in cuffs." Matt shook his head in the face of his siblings' grins.

"If I hadn't we'd have never found that girl, at least not alive. 'Sides, if I'd waited, you would've gotten to him first. What kind of example would that set?" Caden smirked at his eldest brother.

"Matt's the one with all the starch up his ass. And by the way, Abby says that if there's gonna be any further contact between you and the captain, she wants to be there." Lucas, the one who usually caused trouble, nodded to Matt.

"You said she's an attorney now?" Kaylee swallowed hard, guilt at involving Caden in her troubles etched in her furrowed brow.

"Yeah, big sis supervises Caden whenever he gets into trouble," Billy clarified, giving Caden a knowing smile.

"Knock it off, guys. Kaylee doesn't need to hear this shit." Turning to Kaylee, Caden asked, "You said you have the SD card from your camera. Why don't we take a look and see what's on it?"

"Sure. It's right here." A soft click of the clasp released the locket's flash card. Kaylee handed it to Lexi. "Sorry, but there's a ton of shots on here."

"No problem. Why don't we sit in the living room, and I can throw them up on the big screen." Without waiting, Lexi padded to the sofa and tossed the remote to Caden. "I'm not sure what misguided attempts you went through to set this up, so I'll let you put it on the right channel."

"You're kidding. Something electronic you haven't invaded?" Caden guided Kaylee to sit beside him. "I didn't think I had any privacy at all."

"You don't unless you use Morse code. I just wanted to make you feel good."

"She was probably afraid of confronting all the porn." Lucas jutted his chin at Lexi.

"We'll take a look before heading out. That is if you all can let up on Caden." Matt dropped into a wing chair. "We checked out the café, the last place you remember, Kaylee. We didn't find any trapdoors, secret passages, etc. Also, the owner and employees check out."

"If it's all right, I'll duplicate the file while I'm at it." Lexi's fingers danced over the keyboard in arrhythmic clicks.

"No problem. I was just taking random shots of the city. Getting a feel for the changes in layout and architecture, some of which is fascinating by the way. There was an old church being renovated out on Devlin Avenue. I'd stopped and talked with the contractor who let me go inside and photograph their progress."

"We used to go to that church, eons ago." Ethan smiled at Lexi's dropped jaw.

"You went to church?" Kaylee's voice was little more than a squeak. "And it's still standing?"

"Why do you think it needed repairs? Between Caden and Lucas, no physical sanctuary could withstand the force of their transgressions." Billy carried his soda over to the couch and sat.

"Enough of the past. Can we focus on the *now?*" Caden sighed his frustration.

One picture after another defined her path through the city. "Dad made me promise to send pics from the science museum and the Lan Su Chinese garden. It's spectacular with all the unusual plants. Most were brought over before the import ban."

"When did you start on this card, Kaylee?" Caden studied each picture yet nothing looked out of place, no one repeatedly appearing in her photos. At the same time, he admired her obvious appreciation of nature.

"It has two days' worth of photos. I started out at the Hoyt Arboretum and went from there. My brother and I used to love to hike, plus my family lived for camping. We're all nature freaks." A certain wistfulness crossed her expression as if remembering an experience she'd never repeat.

"Caden camps and hikes all the time." Billy nodded to his brother. "He's at home in the woods, but we're always afraid the squirrels will stash him in storage for the winter."

"Hey, that's in the Denelli shopping center." Caden nodded toward the screen.

"And how is it you recognize an upscale perfume shop?" Ethan's dropped jaw echoed his widened gaze.

"I know how to treat a lady, and it doesn't entail gifting them with soft, furry, little monsters." Caden's dig at referencing his shared bond with Lexi earned him a glare from Ethan.

"Let's see who's in the background. That man off to the right doesn't look like he's shopping for perfume." Matt leaned forward to get a better look. "Can you blow it up, Lexi?"

"No, Lucas is the explosive expert." Billy used his hands to mime a large explosion. "Almost cost the family the garage as a kid."

"I didn't know you'd added other chemicals to the mix. Bunch of heathens," Lucas grumbled.

"Figures. Here, I've enlarged it." Lexi snorted amid the siblings' guffaws.

"Oh my God." Kaylee gasped and recoiled.

Each man dropped all pretense of lightening the tension in favor of concentrating on the screen's image.

"Kaylee? Is it the man behind Ciera?" Caden dropped his arm from her shoulder to smooth his hand up and down her spine.

"No. No, see the man window-shopping? His shirt. I recognize it. And—the same greasy-looking hair, same size." Kaylee shuddered and leaned harder into Caden.

"Lexi, can you—" Matt began.

"Already on it." Lexi zoomed in on the window reflecting the man's face. "It'll be a little grainy until I can clean it up. I think he was in the process of turning, maybe trying to avoid Kaylee taking a direct picture."

"That's him! That's the man from the tunnel and who broke into my house. I remember the crazy eyes and greasy hair, like a combination of stoned, demented, and filthy, all rolled into one." Kaylee seized Caden's knee in a death grip.

"Lexi, can you send that to my office and also put it on a flash?" Matt reached for his cell.

"Already done. I've sent it to each of you guys at work."

"That's my girl." Ethan smirked as each of his brothers groaned. "What, you think she hasn't had electronic access to each of your computers since we met? Get real."

"Fine. I'll call this in. The sooner we find this creep, the better." Matt pushed to his feet and made the call from the kitchen.

"Speaking of finding someone—do you think he followed me after I took his picture?" Kaylee's hand on Caden's knee tightened.

"Probably," Lucas replied.

"Let's look through the rest of these. Though I suspect if anyone else kept tabs, they'd have done it from a greater distance."

"You said you thought one of them was female?" Matt asked.

"Yeah, but with a weird accent, unless the drugs muddled my thinking."

Through dozens of pictures of the Portland area and boats on the Columbia River, Caden hoped to see something stand out to his shutterbug, someone repeatedly cropping up in the background. Kaylee's body remained tight until his tactile reassurance reminded her to take a deep breath.

"Do you think they grabbed me *because* I got their picture?"

"Could be. But we won't know until we get more information," Lucas suggested. "If he knew you'd just arrived, that might've made you a target."

"How could he know?" Kaylee asked.

"You said you haven't contacted old friends since your arrival. Did you contact rental agencies about a place to stay or did you set that up before moving?" Lexi continued to surf through the photos. "Can you remember any specific conversations with clerks, maybe mentioning that you'd just arrived in town?"

"I found the house through an online ad and contacted the owners while still in Pennsylvania. But they're an older couple who've gone on vacation. I certainly wouldn't suspect them. And yeah, like a stupid kid, I wanted to get to know people. Several of the sales clerks were friendly. We chatted."

"We'll start with the clerks in the shopping center." Caden gave her arm a light squeeze before continuing. "Then we'll have a talk with the abusive husband."

"Considering your history, not a good idea, bro," Billy advised.

"Actually, it's perfect. I'll catch him at work. He'll be flustered enough that he'll be off guard, and there'll be witnesses should anything untoward happen." A smile curved Caden's lips at the thought of tripping the bastard up during an informal chat.

"Each of us can run this pic through our contacts. Lucas, you hit the streets. Billy, you run him through federal and contact NCB." Matt ticked off items, one at a time.

"NCB?" Kaylee glanced to Caden for clarification.

"Interpol. We don't know if these guys are taking girls overseas or keeping them local. Foreign accents might suggest the latter. If they're dealing internationally, Interpol might have a line on them. It would be nice to start connecting a few dots," Caden wondered about the size of the cesspool they'd found.

"Migrants and runaways, any marginalized group will add to the number of victims. Most are women and children, and there's a lot more of it within the states than you'd think," Ethan added.

"All right. Let's get to it." Matt gestured to Lexi. "If you come up with anything else on street cams, let me know."

"I'll dig in first thing in the morning." Spoken through her yawn, Lexi closed out her program in preparation to leave.

"I'll do Caden's interview while you guys close up for the night. We don't want him infecting the mosquito population." Matt nodded toward the bank of windows in the kitchen. Billy, Lucas, and Ethan closed the windows and curtains, each remarking about what a great spot he had for family gatherings.

Kaylee's tentative glance spoke volumes. "Um, I'm gonna go help close up."

"I won't be long, Gracie. It's just procedure."

Matt retrieved his tape recorder and began taking a formal statement. "Don't leave any of the day's details out. 'Cuz if anything else pops up, it won't be me asking the questions, and it won't be done here."

"Yeah, yeah. I know. But I haven't seen Ciera in the last year, not even from across the street."

"That's definitely in our favor."

"I'm kinda surprised the captain hasn't warned me off the case."

"He can't. Ciera's parents carry a lot of weight. And they want you searching."

"All right. Let's get this over with."

Chapter Thirteen

"Okay, folks. Thank you for dropping in. For future reference, a call ahead is always welcome." Caden stood, the abrupt coolness of Kaylee's absence felt bone deep. Having most of his family present during his recounting of the day's events when Ciera disappeared likened to time as a child, chastised by his parents while his brothers snickered.

"Yeah, we'd hate to walk in while you've got your nose stuck in a jar of hot sauce to open up your sinuses." Billy's eyes reflected the humor of his words.

Each sibling murmured farewell before shuffling out the door, a certain hesitancy in their steps. When the last of his guests had gone, Caden's sudden awkwardness manifested in blowing his cheeks out before slowly releasing the air.

Until facing his own mortality, the need to know another more intimately than a physical tie had never surfaced. Returning to the couch where Kaylee sat, he suggested, "You want to watch a movie or something?"

"Sure. Let's see what's on. I'm too wired to go to bed."

During his family meeting, small yet significant changes had crumbled the thin veneer of her emotional armor. A gaze she couldn't hold, slight rounding of her shoulders, and her most noticeable tell, nibbling her bottom lip between her teeth, all asserted her veil of conviction tarnished, her self-confidence deflating. She reached for the remote and flicked through the channels until finding a spy movie.

Caden rested his arm on the sofa's back. "You want a drink?"

"Nah, I'm good. Now, ya want to tell me why you're suddenly nervous around me?" A slight wobble in her voice belied the determination of her arms crossed over her chest.

The differences framing their viewpoints could fill an ocean; she dissected her choices, considered her options and weighed each one against a relentless well of practical experience before forming a plan. On the other hand, he'd always chosen whatever path suited him in that moment. "Listen, I know you think of me as a skirt chaser."

"So what? As your friend, I'd just want to make sure you carried plenty of protection and didn't tangle with the wrong kind of woman. You should probably own stock in the condom industry."

Nothing could stop his groan. "Okay. I *used* to be *that* guy. The one who'd nail a different girl every week." Closing his eyes in pain, he continued. "But I'm not like that anymore. I've seen too much, experienced too much, and want more from life than meaningless sex." Crossing one ankle over his other knee and bouncing it expended excess energy.

"Wow. All that before the age of thirty? And since when does a guy use meaningless and sex in the same sentence?" A minute of silence and a slightly furrowed brow registered her obvious understanding with a quiet inhale and open mouth. "Let me guess, your furry experience really did give you a different outlook?"

"It was a life-changing event." He knew before she opened her mouth what would come next. In divulging the details of his own nightmare, maybe he could lend assurance that surfacing on the other side of terror didn't make one weak.

But that's how I feel.

"Might help if you talk about it." With a hand on his ankle, she waggled his leg.

"Ahh, okay. I was supposed to be protecting Lexi from a psychopathic stalker. Turned out, he was right under our noses the whole time. He'd been working in digital forensics to manipulate evidence to hide his tracks."

"Holy shit. That's a sudden upcoming."

Caden swallowed hard and closed his eyes with the memories flooding his mind. "He showed up at Ethan's house, drugged us both and poisoned me. When I started to rouse, we were covered with enraged rats wanting to rip us to shreds." He pointed to the scars on his hands. "If not for Lexi, I would have died."

"Hence your close connection."

"Yeah, sometimes it drives Ethan crazy. Even though he knows I don't think of her in a sexual way. She's the sister I've adopted."

"And that turned you around?"

"*That* actually began when I started dating Ciera, after she'd left her abusive ex-boyfriend."

"But she was into drugs?"

"Not so much at first, or maybe I just didn't see the signs. It progressed. I can and have gotten into a lot of stupid things in my time, but drugs were never one of them."

"So now you want more out of life."

"I want a like-minded individual who stands on equal ground."

"So you're not the man-whore—"

"No, I'm not like Lucas. Not even close."

"When you retched down in the tunnels...I know *my* time down there will give me sleepless nights. Do you still have nightmares?"

"Not as frequently. Most nights, I just fall asleep on the couch instead of sleeping in my bed." *More like—every night.*

He hadn't realized he'd been caressing her shoulder until his fingers snagged in her braid. His absentminded search for comfort had led to contact with Kaylee. "Sorry."

"It's okay. It's relaxing." She leaned into him for long moments of contemplative silence before admitting. "I'm wondering if I'll ever stay in bed all night again." Spoken hesitantly, there existed a wealth of uncertainty in her words.

"It'll take time, but you will." He didn't tell her he slept on the couch because he didn't want to get too comfortable in his bed. Staying downstairs at night forced a lighter sleep and afforded the ability to see anything coming at him. With Kaylee's visit, he'd stay upstairs to be closer to her room, knowing she might wake up screaming.

A brief conversation with Ethan one day had revealed Lexi's suffering of the occasional aftereffect of their shared ordeal. Fortunately for her, nightmares weren't as often, and she was easily distracted with *exercise* or cuddling.

He couldn't bring himself to keep a woman for distraction. When faced with the brink of death, he'd grappled with an epiphany to discover what he'd been missing and the specifics needed to feel complete. His daily struggle with righting his world had precluded him from joining the dating pool. "We have a lot to do tomorrow, but I say we go have a bit of fun in the afternoon."

"Yeah, I'm ready to get my mind off all that's been happening."

A little squirm settled her solidly in the nook of his frame while the contagiousness of his yawn didn't dampen her obvious resolve to remain downstairs. He couldn't force himself to urge her to bed when her body molded to his side and centered his soul.

"I usually watch a streaming nature show at night." On the off chance the producers decided to showcase his nemeses, he kept the volume low, which also allowed his mind to regulate the sound to white noise and for a dozing rest to eventually come.

Other than his sister, he labeled few women as friends. They were either acquaintances or ex-girlfriends. Lexi was the exception, partly because of their shared past, and partly due to her being Ethan's soul mate.

"I love nature shows. Reese was studying to be a vet. He was gonna transfer out here to finish." As if seeking shelter from an encroaching enemy, Kaylee turned her face to his chest.

The pain in her voice tightened the knot in his throat. She'd endured so much yet didn't complain. Knowing she didn't want to be alone, he wrapped his arms around her shoulders, holding her tight for the mere purpose of offering whatever strength she would take.

Caden woke up to a warm body snuggled against him, soft and secure. The natural discomfort from the swelling against his fly presented an insignificant detail when compared to the peace and contentment insulating his soul. With his physical and spiritual forms at such odds, he had no choice but to forgo sleep in favor of holding her for the sheer pleasure of enjoying the new wonder. Several times, she stirred against him to adjust her position, each time squirming against his chest with a hand thrown over his heart or stomach. When her fingers drifted dangerously low, he gently repositioned them to a safer and less painful zone.

A glance at the digital clock in his kitchen warned him daybreak approached and the surreal interlude that animated his imagined, ephemeral connection would dissipate like morning mist. He snuggled her tighter. A brush of his lips over her hair imprinted her scent in his mind and on his heart. So naïve in many ways yet so strong, she embodied the warmth, humor, and character that called forth his baser instincts along with the need to keep her safe.

The arm slung across his waist began twitching before her body jerked at some subconscious threat. A low moan escaped her lips.

"Kaylee? Wake up, sweetheart." Gently, he touched her shoulder before smoothing his hand down her arm. Confusion retreated from the depth of her lethargic response, her luscious emerald eyes widening as she straightened.

"Um, sorry?"

"That you're human or that you're normal." Petting her hair, he snugged her tight with his other arm.

"I fell asleep."

"Looks like we both did. But I won't apologize. Wanna talk about it?"

"Not tonight. Can I go back to sleep—with you here?"

"Yeah. I'm comfortable too." The immediate relaxation of her body against him seemed to settle something deep within them both. It wasn't the first stirrings of infatuation or a tidal wave of lust that swept away rational thought. The soothing reassurance derived from like-minded individuals in sync rendered the atmosphere a zone of succor and serenity.

Nightmares were a natural process of recovering post trauma and would probably last for months if not years. Her pride in refusing to talk with a counselor reflected his own character after a man he'd considered his friend tried to kill him. Trust was an individual issue with each person, yet dark circumstances had formed a bond between them, a treasure he hadn't thought he'd share with another for a long time to come. The kid he'd rescued years ago now restored a portion of his faith even as he helped her through her own trials.

Predawn light filtering through a gap between curtains warmed his face yet didn't compare to the animated furnace in his arms.

Sometime during the night, they'd both shifted until he lay flat out on his couch with Kaylee's leg over his and her arm slung over his stomach. Warm, moist exhalations skating down his neck breathed life into a new future where he'd become the man he was meant to be.

Someone had marked Kaylee's back with the proverbial X, and it was only a matter of time before the kidnapper figured out she lay her head over his heart.

At that moment, she rested against his chest, cozy and secure, but for how long? When she no longer needed his protection, what new direction would her life take? Fate already sent the memo about his transient life yielding nothing of significance for his time on Earth. Now he'd found a woman who understood him down to the visceral level, he wanted to explore the possibility of a sincere and honest relationship.

In his mind's eye, Lucas chided him for breaking up the infamous McAllister duo known for competition in all things sexual.

"Hmm. So warm."

Kaylee rubbed her forehead against his pecs, much like a cat before settling in to snuggle again. The kiln-worthy heat of her arm drifting down his abdomen stopped with his hand on her wrist. When he relocated it to his opposite shoulder, she let it drift to his neck before twining her fingertips in his hair.

Jeez. That's so much better. The constant physical reminders that she was indeed a fully-grown woman had no place in their current relationship, but her fingers' gentle swirling at his nape kept him in a state of arousal. *Damn.* Nothing had ever felt better. "It's still early, go back to sleep, Gracie."

He had no expectancy of closing his eyes, not with the soft bundle squirming against his side and the increasing discomfort against his jeans. If he hadn't woken several moments ago, he might've powered through an intense release, something he hadn't done in years. In his defense, no one controlled subconscious urgings.

"I can't. Too comfortable," she murmured against his neck. She practically purred with each stroke of her hair.

His little pirate had a soft side begging for exploration. The thought of ruining his one relationship with an unattached female, not an ex, reordered his thoughts to more acceptable activities.

Contemplating saner endeavors filled his mind and offered a more vertical worldview. His sister would be proud of his progress.

"You know, there's a ton of trails crisscrossing through the woods. We should go hiking." It was a factor of country living he'd once craved before facing his own mortality.

"You're living in a strange sort of limbo, unable to move forward and unwilling to backtrack. But I've recently realized nothing in life is *safe and secure.* City life can be just as dangerous." She lightly tapped her fingers against his shoulder for emphasis.

"If not for the peace derived from sitting on the patio during a quiet evening, I wouldn't be sure which was the lesser of two evils."

Silent examination of his life led to two conclusions. After he'd resolved the threat to Kaylee and faced his own demons, he wanted what his parents enjoyed, a strong marriage, half a dozen kids and all the complications involved in raising them.

Already he could imagine his brothers' mocking comments but understood that an emotional bridge with a woman didn't make a man weak. On the contrary, observing Ethan and Lexi's bond, he realized they were stronger for it, not fragile as he'd once suspected. Each possessed qualities that when combined, formed something greater than their respective halves, a unique entity that presented a solidified wall against any challenge. Ethan and Lexi reminded him of a living contradiction, so different yet each supporting the other. It was their differences that locked them together.

"Caden, did you think Ciera was *the* one?"

"Hmm, at one time, I wasn't sure. I just knew she was different."

Was it the shared bond that wrapped Kaylee's essence around his chest and squeezed? She was the first non-McAllister woman to spend the night in his home. The fact he wanted to spend every night like this gave him pause. He had to remind himself she saw him as a security blanket, protection against a deadly threat. Despite his family's label as man-whore, he'd never been one to take advantage of a woman. He wouldn't start now.

Chapter Fourteen

Waking up snuggled against Caden's warmth with his fingers lightly stroking the length of her spine embodied everything warm, secure, and exciting as hell. She'd never again look at the couch as a mere piece of furniture. A long, slow inhale conveyed his woodsy, clean scent straight to her stirring libido to conjure images of them woven together in the age-old dance. With her arm draped over his chest and her leg resting atop his, she imitated a vine, wrapping around that which gave sustenance, if only for the soul.

"Morning." Her murmured greeting came out on a sigh. The steadily increasing beat of his heart rate under her fingers told her that his body stirred along with his mind. Instead of embarrassment, a profound satisfaction mingled with myriad tiny charges and heightened every sense. Very slowly, she flexed her fingers against the smattering of hair on his upper sternum, wanting to feel the first rumblings of morning vibrate under her touch.

"Morning. You get any sleep?" The deep rasp of his voice matched the heavy-lidded stare which accompanied a man accustomed to a robust morning appetite.

From his own special food group.

The slow glide of ephemeral fingers down and around her heating flesh kindled a dormant craving while his breath stirred her hair. Her full-body shudder instigated from the friction of her breasts rubbing against his solid wall of muscle elicited a soft moan. Underneath her hand, the deep rumble throbbing against her fingertips answered her primal urge to further their relationship. "Actually, quite well. You?"

"Pretty good. Right now, I'm hungry. How about I fix us breakfast?" The lazy drift of his fingers through her hair belied his desire to move.

"Breakfast sounds great." Try as she might, she couldn't reconcile the current sincerity and contented state with a skirt-chasing hound. Deep down, disappointment reigned when thinking others before her had enjoyed the same pleasure. Closing her eyes, she ducked her head as a heavy sigh escaped.

The gentle touch of his knuckle under her chin lifted her gaze to meet his stare. Within the indigo depths, his perceptiveness and compassion ruled the same hunger that gnawed at her belly.

"You're not ready, pirate."

"Wh—what?"

"I know you feel this connection, too. But you need time. And I'm not looking for a fling."

"You're not? But you—"

"Don't judge me by my past. I'm different now. Just like you."

Understanding on an elemental level came with the burning stroke of his finger down the bridge of her nose, across her cheek, and along her jaw. He wanted more than a casual alliance. She'd learned all too well in the random flings after Reese's death and her boyfriend's abandonment that sex as a stepping stone plunged the abuser into deep water.

"Does that go for you too? That you won't judge me?"

Parted lips and a frown accompanied the tilt of his head. "I wouldn't judge you. Regardless."

But you don't know what I've done.

"When Reese died on that snowy Pennsylvania interstate. My world imploded." Anguish and despair, the backlash of her grief, had cost her not only a large swath of dignity and mental stability but also her first solid relationship. "Then, grief pushed my boyfriend to arm's length. When I found his undeleted texts to another girl, I kinda cut loose, in every way imaginable." If not for the loving support of her parents, she would have done much more than six months of frequent, casual hookups. "It took me a while to get straight."

"I see vague uncertainty in your eyes. You'll see in time that I don't judge others. But right now, you're vulnerable, and I'll be damned if I'll take advantage."

"You want me?"

"You know I do. But this isn't the time. You're still in pain, still shook up over recent events, and still mourning your brother's death. You need time to clear your head."

"We were going to move out here and work together."

"A vet and a photographer. Nice combination."

"Until I met you, I hadn't talked about him."

"Maybe it's time. I'm a good listener."

"You are that, and I appreciate it."

"C'mon, let's grab a bite to eat, and you can tell me about your post-graduation plan."

It wasn't until she'd padded into the kitchen she realized how he'd steered her frustrated intentions into a healthier outlet. Conversation. Talking with Caden came naturally and surrounded her spirit with peace.

"I thought you couldn't cook." Watching him helped further change the direction of her thoughts. Brisk, no-nonsense efficiency saw him whisking eggs and cooking bacon like a seasoned chef. She set the table and poured their drinks. All the while, he continued to draw out particular aspects of her soul's clone she hadn't thought about in years.

"Breakfast. PB&J, and anything grilled, I can do." He hesitated before continuing, "Tell me more about him."

"Reese and I were really close. I guess it was a twin thing. The night he died, I felt it, a hundred miles away. Several minutes after he crashed, he called me, before EMS arrived. When his voice drifted off, it felt like something was crushing my chest. The last words he whispered, 'I love you,' still echoes in my mind." Long-awaited tears dotted her shirt and mingled with her hair. All these months, she'd held back the flood, afraid the rip current of grief would tow her under with a force she'd be unable to overcome.

"Jesus, Kaylee. That kind of pain would destroy anyone's world." Removing the skillet of eggs from the cooktop, he wrapped his arms around her shoulders, holding her tight and stroking her back.

For long moments, she stood there, locked to him, absorbing his strength and regaining her equilibrium. Quiet tears washed her face. "Dad arrived at an accident scene to find his son crushed, the last of his strength used to comfort me."

"I can't even imagine what that would feel like."

"For months afterward, when I finally got on my feet, I was kind of a wild child."

"Ah, grief takes many forms. Don't be hard on yourself. The important thing is to come out whole on the other side."

"I still feel lost—in a fog."

"You haven't talked about that night before, have you?"

"No. Only Dad knows everything that happened."

"Jesus."

When her tears dried, Caden guided her to sit at the counter while he prepared the plates then sat beside her.

"I don't remember too much about him." Sincerity and compassion radiated from a sad smile.

For the first time since the accident, she spoke of the bond that characterized their relationship. When Caden recounted some of his own stunts with his siblings, it dawned on her how much they had in common.

"I think I'm ready to call my parents now." Though she didn't know how to broach the subjects of both of her recent assaults and Reese's death, she knew the words would come.

Initially, they freaked. Kaylee took a deep breath then explained the steps she'd taken to stay out of the kidnapper's clutches. "Dad, you don't need to fly out here, and I don't need to come home. I'm fine. I'm safe. I've even met old friends. You remember the McAllister brothers?" The last seemed to upset them the most. Handing the phone to Caden was the only way to help her dad settle down.

The ensuing conversation included a lot of "Yes, sirs," and explanations of the McAllister family dynamics along with his assurance to keep her safe. When Caden handed the phone back, it equated to passing the nuclear football.

"See, Dad? I told you he's all right." The promise from Caden to provide frequent updates had altered their intention of immediately flying out. Chastisement over not informing them sooner had devolved into her mother's tears, her fear creating a tidal wave of emotion in dredging up old pain.

When she disconnected the call, a deep sigh fanned a lock of hair from her eyes. Catharsis came in many forms and varied ways. She knew this from a well-rounded slice of life but never expected to feel it so personally. "I need to feel the sun on my face, walk through a crowded restaurant, take some pictures, move forward the way Reese would've wanted." If she smiled enough, perhaps eventually, the vague enthusiasm would penetrate bone deep. "So. What's on today's agenda?"

"If you'd like to leave the legwork to my brothers, we can go hiking."

"No. There'll be time for that later. I need to face this mess head-on."

"Okay. Once we're cleaned up, we'll go speak with Ciera's parents and brother. Since they've asked me to see this through, I need to start at the beginning. After that, we'll talk to her husband before we retrace your steps using your photos as reference."

So much for normal.

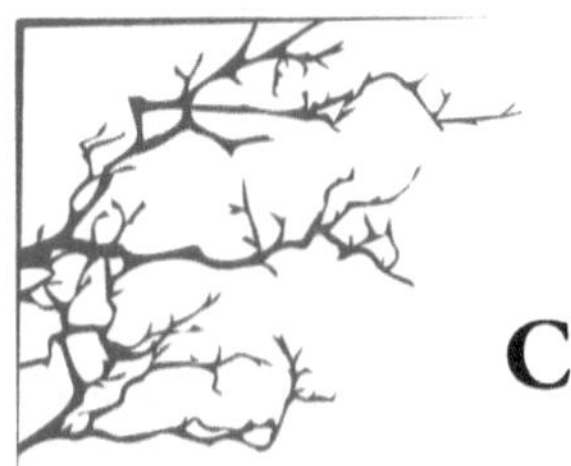

Chapter Fifteen

Caden hesitated before opening the passenger door for Kaylee. "If you'd rather not go—" He didn't want to subject her to more pain yet didn't want to leave her with one of his brothers.

"I'm in this up to my neck. 'Sides, I'm safer with you."

Morning sunshine filtering through budding oaks diffused the night's lingering doubts concerning his capability. No one would get to his charge. The fact his instincts had led him to her door in the middle of the night demonstrated his hunches were on target.

Rounding the hood gave him a minute to compose his answer. When seated, he hesitated before turning the key in the ignition. "Wariness is good until it hinders forward motion. We'll track them down, pirate. Don't worry."

"I don't doubt we'll find them if they don't find me first." The winding blacktop ribbon bisected the woods while the extended canopy overhead imparted stroboscopic light to reflect off the gear shift and into her face. With her spare camera nestled in her lap, she studied the play of light and shadow among the budding leaves and snarled briars. Wooded surrounds yielded to farmland and rolling hills to create pastoral views worthy of framing.

"To become completely invisible and go *off grid,* we'd have to make a ton of changes, which is easily enough done—but I don't think it's necessary. We'll have enough information to find them. We just need the time."

She snorted before explaining, "Sorry, the absurdity of you becoming invisible is ludicrous."

"Hey, people change, grow. You used to be this tenacious, obnoxious kid. Look at you now." He didn't get the chance to finish.

"With your looks, I initially figured you for a sports car kind of guy, not an SUV. But this fits you." Her gaze slid to the surrounding countryside, orchards that would bear a variety of apples, pears, and nuts, their first green leafy buds unfurling in the spring sunshine.

"Book, meet cover." He blew out a breath before adding. "In years past, you could've seen me flying low in a convertible, before I realized what I wanted out of life, realized what's important."

"Do you think she's still alive?" A note of finality infused her voice.

He understood but didn't want to whisper encouragement to fate's darker side. "I pray she's not only alive but hasn't been further harmed. Either way, you couldn't have altered her course." Reaching over the console, he linked their fingers and gave hers a light squeeze. "I'm going to introduce you as my assistant in training so they won't hammer you with questions. Okay?"

"Sounds good. So, I'll take notes?"

"No, I got it covered. I record conversations whenever I can. Since you've got a good eye for detail, just keep them open, and we'll talk after the interview."

"You think they had something to do with her disappearance?"

"No, not at all. But I want them as relaxed as possible considering the situation. During casual conversations, people frequently divulge tiny details they wouldn't think about when they're nervous, maybe an idiosyncrasy, preference, something about close friends, whatever. Sometimes it's those tiniest of details that help solve a case."

Fields prepared for spring planting ceded to a wealthy suburb with well-manicured lawns and artistically trimmed hedges. The lifestyle belonged to those cut from a different cloth. He and Ciera had existed as flame and dynamite, destined to terminate in a pile of ash. A sour wad of regret lodged in his chest with his failure to help her in the way she needed.

When he stopped before an ornamental gated drive with iron inlays of graceful deer and large black bear, Caden inwardly cringed at Kaylee's quiet gasp. Below the camera situated to view guests as they spoke into the attached mic, he pressed the button to announce his presence. More cameras on either side of the fenced yard monitored the vehicle and occupants.

"You dated a girl living in a palace?"

"For a while, yes. Huh, hard to imagine."

"Until you discovered she was into drugs?"

"That was one thing I just couldn't handle. Not even casually." A small shudder of remorse shook his confidence. Maybe if he'd been more patient with Ciera, she'd have cleaned up her act and still be alive.

"Caden McAllister?" The woman's voice, so strong a year ago, now held the hollow consistency of fear and regret. "Come in. We've been waiting to see you."

The ironwork structure that had dazzled him at one time, now rolled back smoothly in its channel, giving way to an even colder interior. "These people are good folks that care about Ciera, even if they don't show it on the surface."

"I'd rather grow up dirt poor than endure a family with flat emotions."

"I think my zany family is half of what Ciera couldn't resist. In many ways, we were so different."

"Sort of like Lexi and Ethan. Except in your brother's relationship, they share the same core values."

"On the nose, again."

The two-story, massive colonial continued its fancy façade with an arched portico supported by contemporary columns detailed to match the elaborate door's sidelights. Rounded stone steps welcomed all into the cold, formal interior.

"Maybe if she hadn't dressed like a homeless waif, she'd still be inside and safe. Even in the tunnel, I could tell she was refined, not used to a common life. She belongs here, in a place like this."

"Yeah, she was the darling socialite, groomed to take her place among society's elite. She believed we'd have a life together, but we just didn't feel *real*. Not in the way I wanted." *Not how I feel with you.* "Despite our differences, she taught me a bit about myself, and it shifted my priorities." Caden cut the engine, his solemn revelation like a bucket of ice water.

"To look for beauty on the inside versus only the outside?" Kaylee hesitated with her hand on the door's lever.

"Yeah, but men are handsome, not beautiful. Even a McAllister can evolve. Let's go see if we can learn a bit about Ciera's recent activities."

"If her family doesn't express their grief, it'll come out in anger or some other form, but it will surface in some way."

Bringing Kaylee along meant immersing her back into the nightmare, yet was the only way to ensure her safety. Her stride was steady until reaching the bottom of the brick steps. She faced another new situation, acting as his assistant, with a firm set of her shoulders. Caden linked their fingers and offered an encouraging smile.

"Think of it as field training."

"I've never aspired to be a detective, private or otherwise."

"Then think of it as part of your adventure," he murmured as he urged her up the steps.

He expected the tearful welcome from Ciera's mother and open animosity from her brother. As of a year ago, Nelson hadn't yet learned to keep his emotions in check when it came to family and would throw blame on the most convenient target for Ciera returning to the snake she married. If the younger man got out of hand, he'd lead Kaylee out and return later.

The formal living room could have come straight from a magazine with its deep-tufted sofas, aristocratic wingback chairs, and overstuffed ottomans. Rich, jewel-toned fabrics adorned the perfectly coordinated set and anchored expensive oriental rugs. The conventional seating area he'd once found imposing at first sight now held all three family members, who took note when he sat close to Kaylee, expressing their status without words.

Across from them, Mr. and Mrs. McFadden kept an austere façade. If not for the deep shadows under the older woman's eyes, one wouldn't suspect her world had been turned upside down. As usual, not a hair strayed out of place or a smudge of makeup could be seen.

"Thank you for coming, Caden. I know the police are working hard to find our daughter, but it helps to know you're looking, also. You probably know her better than anyone." Ciera's mother tugged a tissue from the pocket of her cardigan and blotted her nose.

"Before he dumped her and sent her back to that no-good louse she married." Spoken by the younger McFadden, Ciera's brother proceeded to hold nothing back in his viewpoint of his brother-in-law or Ciera's ex-boyfriend.

With his years on the police force and several more as an investigator, Caden understood the well of grief producing the mixed reception. He'd learned to read the convoluted culture even if he didn't want to be a part of it.

"Can you tell me a bit about the charities she's been working with lately along with anyone she might be tight with?" He'd never spent much time mingling with Ciera's friends.

Kaylee remained mute during the detailed analysis of Ciera's life, given in part by Nelson and in part by the grief-stricken mother.

"As the attorney for two of the charities, I oversaw expenditures, nothing out of the ordinary." Turning his analytical mind toward Kaylee, Nelson added, "You're not an investigator. You must be the other kidnap victim." Grief and anger shone from the younger man's gaze.

Kaylee's jaw opened and closed twice, but no words broke the silence. To be outed as such was unconscionable. They would not force her to relive the nightmare.

"I'm not a victim. I'm a survivor, and I've told the police everything I know."

Caden reached out and covered her hand with his own, suspecting Nelson was about to vent his spleen. Her pallor and slight tremble didn't prevent her from straightening her spine. If he took control of the conversation, he'd also undermine her self-confidence at a time when she needed it most.

"So you just left my sister down there in a cage?" A sneer detailed an obvious class difference while hostility emanated from his aura. Hands resting on his thigh clenched repeatedly.

"Enough, Nelson. Kaylee, why don't you wait in the car? I won't be but a few more minutes." She would not become a target or whipping post for the brother's grief.

"No." Her gaze met Nelson's with a universally understood determination. "I *couldn't* get her out. The crate had a heavy lock, and the thug was too big to overcome. Plus, there were two other men along with a woman down there, *and* I'd been drugged. If I had stayed, she'd still be there, and no one would have a clue where to look for her now."

"She was in a crate? Like a dog?" Mrs. McFadden gasped for breath, unable to maintain her composure.

Kaylee paled. Sweat erupted on her brow.

"Stop. Nelson, there was nothing, *nothing* Kaylee could've done to help Ciera. If she'd tried, we wouldn't have our present leads. As. In. Nothing."

"What did you get her involved in?" Nelson's approach, albeit from a different angle was equally inexcusable as he focused his venom on Kaylee.

"She's not *involved* in anything, Nelson. She just moved here less than a week ago." Steel edged Caden's warning. "In fact, the pictures she's taken as a *professional photographer* have given us yet another lead."

"Please, tell us she's okay." The mother's heartfelt plea spoke volumes in any universe. Each man turned to her, their expressions softening in desperation and compassion.

"I...I don't know. We're doing everything we can. There's already a task force working on this." Caden had difficulty holding the older woman's gaze.

As much as anyone would want to reassure a frantic mother, Kaylee sat mute, her mouth closed over lies that could lend false comfort. She didn't utter them.

"Do you know the identities of the kidnapper? We've not received any ransom demand." Hope infused the father's tone.

"No, but we have a visual likeness of one of them. From there, we'll get a name and be able to track him."

"I pray it's in time to help Ciera." Nelson's concession to logic helped ease tension.

"Ms. McFadden, has Ciera made any new friends lately?" Caden redirected Nelson's gaze if not attention.

The brother spoke up. "She's seeing someone on the side. The contractor who'd been working on the guest house." Nelson glanced away from his father's harsh glare before adding. "Not that I blamed her. That prick husband of hers has kept a woman on the side for months."

Ciera's mother gasped. "No. She wouldn't. Why would you say such a cruel thing, Nelson?"

"I caught them in flagrante several weeks ago while checking on his progress. It seemed to be taking an inordinate amount of time to make the upgrades and paint a few rooms."

"Jesus." The older gentleman spoke with the overwhelming grief and despair written in his face. "I suspected her husband was the type to play around and she was biding her time while gathering enough evidence for divorce."

"Had she hired someone yet or talked with her attorney?" As Caden watched, a new layer of solemnity overcame the parents, anger turned inward to form a guilt etching their faces.

"I referred her to the top divorce attorney in the state, but she wouldn't share the conversation." Soft drumming of Nelson's heel on the thick carpet punctuated his frustration.

After finalizing a few details, Caden suggested they look at Ciera's old room. In keeping with the rest of the house, elegance took the form of cream-colored walls, silk bedding, and hardwood floors. He searched each drawer then picked up a small laptop. "Mind if I borrow this? I'll bring it back in a day or so."

"Good luck. Everything's password protected." Nelson shook his head. "She carried that thing everywhere she went, which means she didn't want anyone else to see the files. She never used to care about electronics."

"Thanks. I have a friend who's a keyboard prodigy. I'll let you know what I find." Caden tucked the device under his arm.

Kaylee frowned when she walked into the bathroom, her reflection in the elegant wall mirror indicating she'd picked up something pertinent. In peering over her shoulder, various containers of blush, foundation, and other essentials filled a large lazy Susan on the vanity. Everything a woman could want for her daily makeup routine. Various bottles of shampoo and conditioner adorned the shower's shelf, seen through the glass enclosure.

"Why keep all this here when she lived just miles down the road? Unless she'd planned on staying." Kaylee turned a decorative container to view the label before glancing beyond at the massive closet. Only a few items resided in the built-ins.

Behind her, Ms. McFadden commented. "She kept clothes and makeup here for when she'd spend the night—occasionally. She hadn't said she was going to stay." In the mirror, her gaze slid away from Kaylee's, the telltale blush speaking volumes.

Again, guilt rode him hard. Caden thought back to Ciera's brief summary of her prior relationship and the embarrassment of hiding bruises when her ex's temper had taken physical form.

Back in the bedroom, each remained silent, steeping in private wells of guilt while unspoken words riddled the room with *what ifs.*

The things he'd done not three feet from where they now stood burned like fire in his brain. Ciera wearing his favorite hockey league T-shirt, then naked in his arms, screaming his name. Ciera wild and passionate in the shower, then sated and sleeping with her head on his chest.

After discovering her penchant for chemically induced fun, a long conversation had ended with her promise to clean up her act. He'd given her a pair of earrings, an intricate, inspirational twist of moon and stars to celebrate her decision.

Weeks later, discovering she hadn't kicked the habit had nearly broken him.

"She never told us the circumstances of your break-up." Mrs. McFadden's desperation to gather any information about her daughter could break the strongest man.

Ciera had begged him not to end their relationship, finally throwing the jewelry at him in a blind rage. He'd never retrieved the T-shirt. "We just weren't right for each other."

"You were never close to being in her league." Nelson's sneered words echoed in the quiet. "She probably realized you for a gigolo after you got her involved in drugs. Were you her supplier?"

"What?" With a hand flying to her blanching cheek and disbelieving gasp, Ciera's mother stumbled backward. "She'd never get involved in something that stupid. Nelson—"

"Enough." The elder McFadden laid a consoling hand on his son's shoulder. "Caden, I'm sorry my son's grief selected you as its recipient."

"I understand, but know this. I have never been involved with drugs." Matt warned Caden his Casanova ways would eventually catch up with him. To say anything more would cast aspersions on a soul not present, possibly not still breathing. Caden couldn't comment. "How about we take this back to the living room and finish up?"

After concluding the interview, they stepped outside where deep breaths failed to cleanse remorse and culpability from his chest.

"Wow, Caden. That was tough." Blinding rays of sun reflected off the SUV's hood as Kaylee hesitated before opening her door.

Once settled behind the wheel, he sighed. "You handled that well. I'm sorry Nelson verbally attacked you. He and Ciera are fairly close. I shouldn't have brought you here, but I didn't want to leave you alone."

"Hey, no problem. Reese would've been a lot worse."

"Everybody worries in their own way." Caden rounded the driveway and sped up, eager to leave the sordid memories behind.

"So, where to next?"

"Next stop, Conroy Kirpatzel, Ciera's husband and vice president of K&T Banking. I don't expect it to be a pleasant conversation so it might be wise if you stay in the truck. After that, I'd like to visit a few shops from your photos." Considering his past relationship with the missing victim, he'd normally be excluded from such an investigation. But the fact that Ciera's parents personally asked for his help carried significant weight.

"I should go in the bank with you, to act as a buffer and witness."

"You sure? He'll spew any filth that enters his mind."

"I can handle myself."

"You certainly can."

The trip to the city yielded minor traffic and less conversation. Warmer temperatures brought out young women pushing baby strollers and older couples walking hand in hand along sidewalks bordering perfectly manicured lawns. Opportunities Kaylee would have lost if not for fierce determination and inner strength.

Drafting his upcoming approach, Caden considered the risk to Kaylee if in fact, Ciera's husband orchestrated the abductions. Accumulated information pointed to Conroy being the ultimate hands-on type, preferring face-to-face confrontations to flaunt his superiority versus hiring street thugs. In the end, he decided it safer to publicize the fact Kaylee wouldn't be left alone.

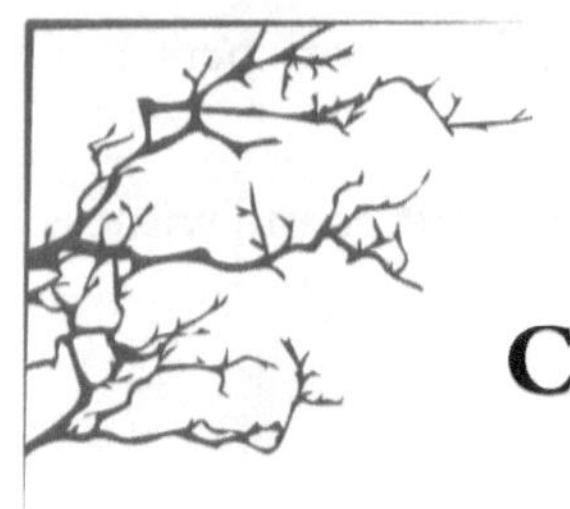

Chapter Sixteen

Passing storefronts boasted fancy spring dresses and an assortment of Easter paraphernalia, aspects of life Kaylee hadn't considered in some time. Her gaze lingered on a sophisticated, sexy halter dress when they stopped for a traffic light.

Fate was showing her different avenues of expression despite the weather bringing the urge to hike and camp as she'd done in previous years. It was time to shed her cocoon and fly, expand her horizons. She'd traveled across the country for a new start, not cultivate her dark persona.

It seemed she paralleled Caden's life after his own dark experience. Now she needed normal, any version of normal.

"Care to go rafting later?" Caden slowed to make the turn into the bank parking lot. "We can stay in calm waters, and I'll do the work. A little measure of nature might do you some good."

It seemed he read her thoughts with just a glance. The smile that could melt the ice between any woman's legs slid into place.

He. Just. Knows. Optimistic thoughts sliced through her brief wallow in self-pity. "Sure. I'd hoped to get a kayak and spend some time on the water and hiking trails. Rafting is even better. What class rapids?" She hesitated in unbuckling her safety belt, waiting to see how adventurous his streak ran.

"Let's start with the smaller waves and clearer channels until we find our rhythm. Then work our way up to the more fun stuff when you're ready."

"Okay, sounds good." Though years past would have seen her jumping right into deep churning waters, recent events instilled a new air of caution, especially when approaching a potential criminal. "Good idea to catch this guy when he's gonna have to concentrate on holding his temper."

"That's the plan. Since he's VP, he'll have a private space to conduct an interview. Plus, I don't want to give him a chance to think things through before answering." Caden escorted her inside where a receptionist directed them to Conroy's office.

Anger charged the air as soon as they entered. Beige-colored walls surrounded heavy oak furniture and thick, crimson carpet, perpetuating the feel of cold, artificial sophistication. Caden didn't bother to knock, merely strode in and sat in front of the desk. She took the seat beside him.

"Well, I figured you'd slither in here at some point." Even sitting, the man was built like a truck with a bull neck, wide shoulders, and thick chest. Sausage-like fingers shuffled several papers aside as he scrutinized first Caden, then Kaylee.

"How's the money biz, Conroy. Beating the hell out of things these days?" The reference to the abusive relationship earned a lip-biting glare.

"Staying out of the slums if that's what you mean. You should try it. Clean living that is. And go to hell."

"No thanks. I prefer internal plumbing...Look, let's get this over with. The sooner I find Ciera, the sooner she can serve you with divorce papers. Am I right?"

"We're perfectly happy. Not a marital cloud in sight."

"Really? Would you like another cup of ego? Perhaps decaffeinated? I heard she's seeing someone on the side, that she had a very friendly vagina." Caden's shoulders stiffened with the cost of goading the banker. How many times had he sliced his soul in the name of justice?

Purple mottled the banker's face as his eyes bulged and fists clenched. Though she understood the current tact, Caden wasn't the type to degrade women, under any circumstances.

"Piss-poor attempt, you inflamed boil on a pig's ass." Conroy spat through gritted teeth. "Now I know why you came to see me here instead of at my home."

Caden smiled. "When was the last time you saw her?" Caden kept his smile in place.

"Tuesday morning when I left for work. She said she was going shopping to pick up my favorite cigars before heading to her folk's house for a few days' visit." Conroy leaned forward, linking his fingers on his desk. Various framed degrees and awards dotted the wall behind him.

"Stay with her parents for days? The folks who live less than a half hour away? Really?"

"Hey, they're close. I was shocked when they called *me* asking where she'd gone." Directing his attention to Kaylee, he added, "Are you the street rat who lured my wife away?"

"And what would make you think of her in that way?" Caden reached over and squeezed her fingers.

"For some reason, Ciera was fascinated with the dregs of society. I assume that's why she briefly took up with you. She told me she'd dumped you when you coerced her into taking drugs."

"I'd like access to Ciera's personal belongings, take a look at her room." Caden ignored the defensive slights.

"First of all, no. You're not setting foot in *my* house. Second of all, I can't seem to locate her laptop."

"I've got her computer."

A flicker of some unidentified emotion, maybe alarm, passed through Conroy's changing expressions before recomposing his former stoic façade. "She took it to her parents' house? That hardware is mine, and I want it back. Now! Then I want you out of here."

"Um, no. Her parents gave *me* the laptop, so I'll return it to *them* once I'm finished."

"I'll have a court order by tomorrow." The banker's hands fisted before reaching for his phone.

"I'll have it cloned and deciphered by tonight." Caden grinned wide amid the banker's controlled bluster. With a wink at Kaylee, he stood and held out his hand. "C'mon, pirate. We have work to do now that we have our direction."

The irate rumblings of a man calling his attorney drifted through the closed door as they left. "That went about as expected." She could envision the arrogant snob boasting to his upper-crust friends how he kept his little wife in line, one fist at a time. She'd seen his type before but had never tangled with one before returning to Oregon.

Back in the vehicle, Caden called Lexi and explained the need for a rushed cyber snoop.

"I don't doubt the creep can get a court order for the laptop's return, and I don't want to miss anything. We'll drop off the hardware to Lexi before heading to the Denelli shopping center and talking to a few clerks."

"Maybe someone will remember something that'll help." Kaylee reached for the folder holding several key pictures she'd taken.

"After that, we'll grab a bite to eat before taking a break. The McKenzie River is a good place to blow off steam and relax. You can chill and enjoy a bit of nature."

"Both Ciera's brother and husband have blamed you for her getting into drugs. Even though it's bullshit, considering the circumstances, do they pull enough weight to cause you trouble?"

"No. With nothing linking us currently, it's all speculation. I'm fine."

Tense chitchat filled the ride despite Caden's attempt to lighten the day. A subconscious edginess tinted his aura with a constrained dangerous grace. No wonder several women at the bank eyed him like a piece of sweet meat. Between a smoking-hot body and a personality exuding confidence, the invisible pheromone trail ran nonstop.

"Sounds like a solid plan."

When they reached the shopping center, Kaylee's self-assurance slipped several cogs as she scrutinized the modern, sleek shop fronts. Someone could have followed her for hours without her knowledge.

The covert game of cat and mouse slithered from a world she'd never visited and didn't care to inhabit. Grabbing her spare camera from the back seat and slinging the strap around her neck instilled a false sense of security, the relationship between shutter speeds, apertures, and available light mimicking various renderings of her mood.

Myriad thoughts whirled through her mind yet couldn't hold her attention for long. Like the ball thrown counter to a roulette wheel's spin, her emotions were subject to her kidnapper's whim. He would strike again, and she needed to be ready.

"Does anything stand out in particular?" Caden stepped beside her, guiding with a hand at her waist.

"Since it was all new to me, everything does. I remember going into the fragrance shop at the other end to look for a hyacinth-scented shampoo. Reese used to buy it for me, said I was too tomboyish."

"Hmm, it does remind me of flowers that grow wild along the wood line each spring. I love it." Caden lifted a lock of her hair and breathed in its fragrance. "Yep. Love it. You want to start here and work our way down?"

"Sure." Relief flooded her that he didn't suggest splitting up to cover two shops at a time. The distance, though small, equaled miles in her mind.

"Anytime."

Caden's easy smile and sex appeal assured a warm reception from each shopkeeper they interviewed. None recalled serving a man matching the composite she'd drawn. More often than not, women proprietors asked for his business card in case they remembered a significant detail. None asked for a photo of the thug.

"You must have to beat women away with a stick."

"I *could* say the same about you with men. But I don't judge."

"Sorry. I get it. New leaf and all that."

"I'm no longer controlled by my joystick. Too many women make a game of it."

Each time Caden spoke to an overeager manager or sales clerk, Kaylee watched him maneuver the conversation away from personal queries. Years of experience had equipped him with *basic survival tools* yet didn't chip away at his patience.

When they approached the perfume shop, nervous tension coiled her body tighter. Not only did she associate the fragrances inside with Reese, but her mind also held the image of her kidnapper caught in the window's reflection to ratchet up her anxiety. Her protector's light touch grazing down her spine then back to her neck induced a shiver while redirecting her focus.

"Thought that would distract you."

"Beast."

His chuckle thawed the icy shards knotting her belly. He well understood his effect yet didn't use it to *his* advantage.

Glass shelves bore elaborate bottles of cologne in all shapes and sizes. Each section of the horseshoe-shaped glass cases boasted *Try me* testers and colorful displays. Caden spoke with the manager while she drew the cordial clerk aside for a discreet conversation. The young woman, dressed in upscale linen slacks and knit sweater, remembered the visit, and remarked on her new camera. They hadn't previously discussed any particulars of photography. Both her rigs were the same brand and looked identical to the untrained eye. It seemed a peculiar detail to notice. Before she could ask further questions, Caden interrupted.

"Hey, sweetheart, time for us to head out. We don't want to be late." Caden's silent steps had transported him directly behind her using an athletic grace that drew the clerk's attention.

When he slid his arms around her waist and hugged her to his chest, her breath lodged in her chest. *He's doing it again.* That knowledge didn't stop her from leaning back into his embrace, a small smirk hiking up one side of her mouth. He used the back of his knuckles to graze her cheek, her eyes closing of their own volition.

"I hate being late." Her thoughts failed to focus on anything other than his touch.

"Then we'd better get to it. Did you find something you like? You always smell so good." Giving action to thought, he nuzzled her hair and inhaled deeply. "If not, we really do need to get going."

"I'm ready." Her low groan preceded his nuzzle against her ear and the *mhmm* of approval, the slight rumble from his chest against her back providing more fodder for her overactive imagination.

"I suspect so."

His words delved deeper than the warmth spreading through her limbs, the encumbered response alluding to wild nights of ecstasy a given.

Then, the reality check.

Her pride prayed for the earth to swallow her whole after her imagination finished playing mythical goddess of the earth to his Dionysus, God of wine, pleasure, and festivity. Sudden coolness created by his withdrawal and low chuckle exposed a dichotomy of emotion and reaction. The backlash heated her skin to volcanic temperatures while the words replayed in her head. The deeper he delved into her heart, the greater his control. More importantly, the more it would hurt when she saw him with another woman.

In the meantime, she could do naught but follow his lead. Always the gentleman, he held the door, then twined their fingers together before leading her to his vehicle.

"Hope you didn't mind a little misdirection, but your new friend acted a little twitchy, and I didn't want her to think you were alone."

"I got the same impression. Her nervousness stemmed from more than your presence."

He rolled his eyes. "I want to do a little research before taking another run at her."

"She noticed I had a different camera but didn't know how to adjust F-stops and ASAs. It was an odd conversation."

"We'll look into her."

The ride home offered time to contemplate her assumptions regarding the entire confusing ordeal. "Do you think Ciera was planning on staying with her parents and not returning? If so, it would've been difficult for the husband to track her, considering how she was dressed. He didn't seem the type to *hire out*. 'Sides, she would've been wary, and looked for him over her shoulder."

"I hope we'll find more details when we get into her digital files. Lexi's going to come over after she's finished digging into them."

A half hour later saw them standing beside Caden's kitchen counter making homemade subs. "You know, that clerk really made me nervous. Few people not in the profession can recognize minor differences in cameras. Usually it's the length of the lens or maybe an attached shade. Something else about that clerk bothered me, too. She didn't visually undress you like other women do—more like—she was cautious."

"Gee thanks. I don't feel objectified. Nope, not at all." His grin deepened the dimple in his right cheek. "How about we eat these subs on the patio."

Being in Caden's proximity stimulated her love of nature and the need to rekindle something she thought long neglected. Once again, she could imagine herself hiking, rafting, and camping, at least with company.

It was a beautiful home in a woodland setting and he appeared more relaxed since talking about his ordeal. Maybe the catharsis allowed room for his life to forge ahead, if only a bit.

"How different are your cameras? And length is very important, so I hear."

His teasing grin, as much as his words, brought another furious blush to her face. "My backup is still an SLR but doesn't offer the clarity, the autofocus isn't as advanced."

Caden shook his head before answering, "Focus *is* important."

Chapter Seventeen

Cleaning up the dishes lent an air of quiet intimacy to the scene. In her mind, she realized that without Caden's help, she wouldn't have experienced any of the day's routine events, something as simple as sitting on a patio and watching squirrels flit from tree to tree, or the birds building their nests. Still, the chill coursing through her veins wouldn't ease until they found Ciera.

Minutes later, a low buzz announced the front door breach. A cool gust of wind ushered in Lexi with a satchel strapped across her chest, Ethan, and a large dog. Lexi reset the code. "Hi, guys. Meet Hoover." Hearing her name, the mixed-breed bounded forward and greeted first Caden, then Kaylee, with tail wags and curious sniffing.

"She's beautiful." Kaylee grinned at Caden. "Yep. I'm definitely getting a puppy."

"Great, Hoover will gain another playmate. She'll love it." Ethan plopped several grocery bags on the kitchen counter. "We brought you some edibles, so Kaylee doesn't have to suffer your cooking." Ethan smiled at Caden.

"As long as they're store bought and not homemade. I don't want to bite into deviled eggs and find buttercream frosting."

"Hey, you were a skinny kid. Matt said you needed to eat more calories." Ethan shrugged a shoulder. "Seemed like a good idea."

"New aftershave?" Ethan pulled his lips between his teeth as his shoulders shook.

"I like it. Kinda creeps out to leave a subtle scent." Lexi's eyes twinkled with devilment."

"So do skunks." Ethan replied.

The shuffle of removing Lexi's laptop signaled her eagerness to begin. The computer's soft *whir* echoed the seriousness of her demeanor while the air of concentration etched in her face rivaled a champion chess player. From hearing Ethan's descriptions of her digital prowess, Lexi had blown through firewalls and dissected the contents within minutes.

"Caden, I hope you don't mind. I went ahead and copied the hard drive so I can cull through the rest of the files at home."

"Like anyone could stop you?" Ethan chuckled as they sat at the kitchen table.

"Hey, at least I'm asking." Lexi's smile turned a little feral, a little scary.

Minutes later, Lexi thrust her fist in the air. "Okay, I'm in the private social media account. The one she obviously didn't want others to see. I've already looked at the one she used for family and public use but didn't find anything that stood out. I'll write down the passwords for those and the email accounts, Caden, so you can look at everything later."

"Anything interesting?" Ethan asked.

"Hmm, yeah, she says here she found a receipt in her husband's coat pocket, for condoms, yet she and her husband don't use them."

"Maybe the girlfriend's afraid of catching something she can't scrub off." Eyes narrowed and nose wrinkled, Caden leaned back in his chair. "Anything else interesting?"

"Not that I've found yet." Lexi's tapping foot betrayed her annoyance.

"What's new on your front, Ethan?" Kaylee asked.

"Thanks to facial recognition, we have the name of your assailant. Ning Klinefeld, no known address, no known employment or associates, no tax records." Ethan replied before adding. "We've put out feelers to all our contacts for more information. Plus, Matt and Lucas are going to interview Ciera's friends."

"We talked with Ciera's parents. Her brother recommended a divorce attorney *and* they knew dear hubby had a girlfriend. If we find her—" Caden began.

"Both Nelson and Conroy blame Caden for Ciera's drug usage." The thought of Caden getting roped in as a suspect gave Kaylee chills.

"I'm digging," Lexi added. "I've got emails from his personal account to—"

"Don't tell us how you got the information. We don't have a court order yet." Ethan groaned and shook his head.

"What, like you stand a chance of keeping up with her?" Caden regarded Lexi, then turned to Ethan. "The captain knows she's gonna hack her way through any and all obstacles. He needs answers, fast, so he's not going to ask how she gets it as long as it doesn't have to go to court."

"Look, speaking of El Capitan. He got an irate call from Ciera's husband. The threats and finger pointing are worthless, but still, Conroy carries weight and is great at acting the panicked husband. They reached an agreement to let the rest of us handle interviews." Ethan held up a placating hand before Caden could speak. "I know you're not going to stop. I'm just saying—why not take a break? Kaylee could probably use one."

"Yeah, all right. We were gonna take a few hours later this afternoon anyway."

"Good. As soon as she's finished, Lexi and I will head out and leave you to it," Ethan said.

"While you're at it, look at the clerk at Lush Fragrances. She knew Kaylee had a different camera yet didn't seem to know one end from the other." Caden prompted.

"All right. I'll dig up her records before Ethan has a chat." Lexi's gaze narrowed with an increased flurry of keyboard tapping.

"I'm glad you're on my side," Kaylee murmured when Lexi chuckled.

"Caden, I sent the passwords and access codes to your printer. I'll let you guys know what else I find when we come by tonight." Lexi began packing up her gear while adding in a tentative voice. "Caden, the weather's turning nice. How about we have Sunday dinner here?" Sympathy softened her tone as her not-so-subtle push to see Caden expand his horizons in the new home earned a frustrated sigh. "Your free-loading brothers want to break in your house, and probably some furniture, a few lamps, and dishes. You don't have any stains on the floors or sofas. They can fix that, too."

Ethan squeezed his brother's shoulder in a show of support. "It's time, bro. We're all behind you."

"All right. Next Sunday. I've wanted to unpack my chess board and whip your ass."

"Told you he'd say yes now." Lexi grinned wide and gave Kaylee a thumbs up before turning to leave.

"Hey, just for the manipulation, you can give us a ride later. We're gonna hit the rapids this afternoon. We'll need a ride back to the car. I'll call you with a meeting point."

"Kaylee, are you up for that?" Ethan glanced from Kaylee to Caden.

"She's fine. We'll keep it calm and simple." Sunlight had chased the shadows from the room by the time Caden escorted his guests to the door.

A cold sweat dotted Kaylee's brow with progressive clicks of the mouse in Ciera's social media account. In older photos, a decidedly exuberant, fun loving, young woman laughed and partied with her friends, presided over social functions with her brother, and crowded in for a family photo at a holiday dinner. Later photos revealed a more somber woman with shadows under her eyes and a pasted-on smile while standing next to her husband at a banquet.

Surfing through the files of a woman who'd accused her of abandonment, Kaylee fought the overwhelming guilt but persisted in hopes of spotting something, anything that could help. Caden sat beside her on the sofa as she opened each digital folder to examine its contents. "If Conroy was still abusing her, and I can't imagine that stopping, then she might have spoken in code, so to speak, about any information or conversations she wanted to hide. But her family didn't mention it. She had to have been connecting with someone."

"Let's take a look at her private account and email. As soon as Lexi identifies the recipient detailing Ciera's discovery of the condoms, we'll know a lot more." Caden rested his arm on her shoulders.

"All right." Kaylee opened the first digital mailbox. "Do you recognize any names in the sender's list?" Clicking on the *from* column organized the names alphabetically.

Caden frowned as he scanned the messages. "Yeah, most of these people, I do. Let's open a few of these." Caden pointed to several that listed dates for fund-raising events.

"It looks like she keeps both her inbox and sent folders pretty clean. I'm thinking she deleted any her husband wouldn't approve of due to the nature of the exchange or the recipient." Kaylee blew out a long breath.

"Not a problem. Depending on the setup, Lexi can still retrieve them. As with other files, just because you hit delete doesn't make the information disappear. Those chunks of data are set aside, waiting to be overwritten. If anyone can resurrect it, Lexi can."

The remaining folders failed to give a clue or insight of Ciera's secret life where drugs played an integral part.

"She wasn't paranoid by nature, but I suspect she grew adept at hiding things. I remember when she called me after we broke up, said she was seeing the prick again, and that it would be different." Caden shook his head. "Most of the pictures included immediate family. I'm thinking she hated her social life even though they haven't been married long."

"I'd really hoped to learn more about her. Something that might give us a clue. I wonder how long she's had the street persona. Seeing her in those ragged clothes in the cage and then these pictures is kind of a sudden uptake. She could have tons of friends we'll never identify."

"When I learned of her involvement with the seamier side, she tried to drag me into it. When I wouldn't budge, we cut ties. I don't even know how she came by her stash."

"The family's going to eventually learn so much, things they won't forget. I feel sorry for her mom."

"Damn. Yeah, it always comes out in the end. We'll protect her as much as we can." Caden closed the laptop and moved it to the end table. "How about we take a break and hit the rapids?"

"Sounds like a good idea."

"Great. I'll grab the gear after updating Matt. You pack us some goodies to eat. We'll talk safety procedures on the way."

"You have waterproof cases for your cell and food?"

"Yep. Got it covered. It's gonna be a carefree afternoon of peace and tranquility."

Chapter Eighteen

"Wow. I haven't had so much fun in a long time. By the way, nice rubber." Kaylee's eyes sparkled with devilment. "Maybe next time we can tackle something a little rougher. A higher class?"

The McKenzie River's lower gradient presented less difficulty in navigating the bars, boulder fans, and other obstacles commonly found. It was the second time Caden had guided them to an eddy to assess Kaylee's energy reserves. Though he and his brothers had soared down Class IV smokers, he wouldn't risk taking her in choppier waters until assured she was ready and her wrist completely healed. "Sure. I just wanted to make sure we weren't pushing the envelope. Here's where we hop off. Up ahead, it gets pretty rough."

"I'm fine. Not even a slight headache, and my wrist is fine."

"Your foresight and agility are impressive. I wasn't sure you'd see the rooster tail." He rested his paddle over his knees. He should have realized she'd insist on paddling, too.

Her not-so-innocent comment referencing his raft and their sexual undercurrent made him smile. She obviously took great delight in verbal taunting yet never followed through with a come-hither smile. If he closed his eyes and concentrated on the surroundings, he could imagine himself hanging out with the guys.

"Hey, I watch for changes in flow, and that water plume probably came from a sizable underwater obstacle." Her grin epitomized delight and a slight weariness from activity.

"You sore? We've been at it for an hour, and I hadn't counted on your participation. I just wanted to give you a change of scenery." He nodded to the left bank. "There's a rest area over there where Ethan will pick us up."

I'm just a little tight. It's been a while since I've done this, but I'm ready for more." Rolling one shoulder up and forward conveyed her meaning as she dipped her single-bladed paddle in the water, playing with the small eddies.

"We'll come back in a few days."

The soft breeze wrapping her in nature's soothing aromas, the sun's warmth on her upturned face, and the anticipation of the next leg of their journey, must've called forth the enthusiasm of previous trips taken with her twin. Tranquility encompassed her expression when she took in the beautiful scenery of the wilds bordering the river, inhaling deep, as if renewing both her senses and determination to live the life she'd planned.

It was one of those idyllic moments remembered fondly at the end of the day.

The thin whine of a rifle's shot echoed off the low canyon walls at the same time Kaylee's body bucked forward at an angle. Her paddle flipped to the floor. A second shot ricocheted off the rock inches from her head.

"Damn!" A crimson stain bloomed on the back of her sleeve. She grabbed her arm with her other hand.

"Down!" Snatching her vest, he urged her to the floor before shifting and pushing off the surrounding rock and into the current. "Keep your head down."

Without a weapon and no cover, he paddled into the faster current and hoped they could round the bend before taking another hit.

By using downstream angles, avoiding eddies, and remaining in the stronger jet of the current, he made better time. Searching for the shooter was impossible, sparing a backward glance in the increasing fury of the river could be just as deadly as taking a bullet. Twice more, the telltale sigh of a slug's passage whispered confusion in his day. Each time, a corresponding jolt underneath him foreshadowed the shooter's intent. If he couldn't zero in on Kaylee, he'd sink the craft in the increasingly violent waters.

Seconds later, he felt the easing of passage created by Kaylee's paddle cutting through the water.

"Rock garden ahead. River right." Another shot fired. Instead of searing pain in his back, he felt another punch to the raft. Over his shoulder, Kaylee's eyes rounded with understanding, but her determination persevered.

"Effing bad aim, prick." Her voice shook underneath the bravado.

Praying her experience was on par with the current portion of the river, Caden maneuvered them right while remaining in the faster-rushing current. Beneath and around them, the raft softened each time one of its chamber took a hit. The roar of the water overshadowed its hiss from air loss. *Maybe not such a bad aim.*

What felt like hours took place in a fraction of the time. The next shot ricocheted off an adjacent boulder as they rounded a broad tongue of land. They'd have cover from bullets but not the watery disaster fast approaching. The craft wobbled underneath.

"Right bank. We need to get ashore before the next run out." Though he'd topped off before leaving, the raft's death-throe writhing was as dangerous as the river in which they traveled. They wouldn't make it to shore. Shock stalled his heart when Kaylee's paddle bounced up and down in the water to his left, jetting downstream ahead of them. Instinct swiveled his gaze back to see her face contorted in anger. She didn't appear to have suffered further injury.

"Hell! Sorry, Caden." The bloodstain blossoming on her right arm trailed down her shirt.

"We've got to bail out. Can you still swim?"

The raft's softening floor created a more immediate problem. The decision of when to jump vanished when the craft folded in half, the middle rising up and throwing Kaylee under water.

Either instinct or experience urged her body into a *lawn chair* position when she surfaced, her arms moving in sync to guide her toward the bank. Toes up meant she could use her feet to push off rocks and her boots wouldn't snag on natural hidden traps below the surface, holding her body while water rushed overhead and filled her lungs with water. Shock of the cold engulfing her thin frame would quickly lead to hypothermia. She didn't have enough fat to insulate her against the frigid temperature for long.

Having twisted to the side, Caden entered the cold flow an instant later, using his greater strength to swim toward her and the shore. Each time her head bobbed below the water line, panic drummed a louder beat in his ears. Her helmet would protect her head from injury but not from drowning. They were thirty yards from the bank.

Aligning himself to cut across the eddy line at a ninety-degree angle, he maneuvered to the top where it wasn't as wide. Never in his life had he been so glad to get his hands on another person. Latching onto her vest and hauling her close, he angled her body over his hip then used his other arm to swim toward shore. Kaylee used her outstretched arms to paddle and help guide them. Once again, they were in sync.

"We're in shallow water now. Once I'm past these rocks, we can catch our breath, and I can check your wound." The last thing he wanted to do was let her go. Twice, he lost his footing in the violent tempest yet managed to keep her tight in his arms.

Rocky shore yielded to grass. For once, nature didn't collude with fate and send him crashing onto the boulders with his precious burden.

Violent shivers and tightly clenched eyes drafted a likely scenario if he couldn't raise her body temperature. Gently, he sat her on a thickened knoll of grass and kneeled beside her.

The slice in her sleeve widened with a quick tug to reveal the wound. Blood continued to trickle from a shallow slash where the bullet had grazed the back of her upper arm. If the water had been less turbulent, the shooter could have killed her.

"Looks like he nicked you pretty good. I'm gonna tie my handkerchief around it to stop the bleeding." Further examination yielded no other wounds. "Jesus. What a miracle. Does anything else hurt?" As if unable to wait through her self-assessment, he lifted the back of her vest and shirt to examine for injury.

"I'm okay. It barely hurts. Do you think he's still coming for us?"

"Don't know. Can you walk?" Helping her stand, he assessed her both mentally and physically.

"Yeah. Did your phone survive the trip?" Checking the pocket of her vest, she added, "Mine didn't."

"Mine's good, but we lost the food."

"Not hungry, just want to get out of here."

"Unless he swims across, which is highly unlikely, there isn't a bridge for several miles. The trees and brush are thick enough to give us cover." *The bastards just keep coming.* The current fiasco pointed to either a large group or one that was well organized.

Caden retrieved his cell from its waterproof container to call Ethan, who should have been closest to their present position. A decidedly clipped response followed the first ring.

"What's wrong? I didn't expect you to bother me for hours."

"Shooter. Pick us up at Brody's shop."

"Intact?"

"Yeah, Kaylee's injured, but we're good." Caden ended the call abruptly amid Ethan's verbal relay and Lexi's background string of curses.

Nothing made sense. Some elusive thread foiled his attempt to ferret out how the shooter had known where to set up. They hadn't been followed. To place a tracker on his vehicle while parked at the shopping center constituted a very desperate or preplanned move. He prayed for the former.

"How far are we from the main road?" A little color returned to her cheeks after a few steadying breaths. She'd tucked her hands in her wet, vest pockets.

So I don't see them shaking.

"Several miles. You up for a hike?" The aftermath of their narrow escape left an overload of adrenaline flooding his system to leave his emotions in a swirling whirlpool of relief, worry, and anger. Before he hoofed it out, his mind and heart needed affirmation she was emotionally fortified. Gently, he pulled her into his arms, holding her close to his chest. "God, I'm so sorry, Kaylee. I thought this would be a break from the stress."

"Hmm, it is now."

Her softer body parts molded to his larger, harder frame in such a way he knew they'd be a perfect fit. The pressure of her hands at the small of his back provoked its own response despite their chilled trembling. When he started to step back, she pulled him tighter, her entire body shaking. He couldn't deny her what they both needed. Affirmation of life.

"We're going to be okay, sweetheart."

"I know. But I've learned the hard way to appreciate what I have when I can. And you're distracting me again."

"Yeah. Kinda."

"Scalawag."

His grin created like in kind and preceded the moan felt against his chest. "You're still shivering." While observing for thickened speech, decreased coordination, and blue-tinged skin among others—he slid his fingers to the measured beat throbbing in her neck.

"I'm fine, Caden. Exercise will warm me up."

Under different circumstances, he'd suggest the perfect exercise. *And what in the hell is wrong with me?*

Understanding the phenomena of survival-mode frenetic lust didn't excuse his thoughts. He was a rational man, evolved.

Precious seconds passed. When she pulled back, he led the way through nature's joke of a path. Deer trails crisscrossed at various angles leading from the water's edge while occasional mumbled curses about spurs and stickers drifted forward. Several times, he stopped to free her from the countryside's grasping thorns.

"At least our vests afford us some protection from the briars. We're lucky the underbrush isn't thicker in these parts, yet it's enough to block the brunt of the wind." Guilt twined with anxiety for putting her at risk.

"How did they know we'd be here today?" Kaylee stumbled over a log, her misstep sending her plowing into Caden's back.

"Careful, pirate." He stopped to let her catch her breath. "We'll check, but someone could've put a tracker on my truck while parked at the shopping center or could've heard us talking while we were there. I know for sure we weren't followed."

Each time he stopped along the trail to listen for signs of pursuit, he noted how she'd scrutinize her surroundings, wary of the hunter.

He'd hoped to erase at least some of her anxiety today but succeeded only in multiplying it exponentially.

After climbing out of a steep ravine, he urged her to rest on the stump of a large oak. She swiped at the perspiration dotting her brow without uttering a complaint. Exhaustion didn't detract from the determination in her gaze.

"Why are you smiling, Caden?"

"Your stubbornness is—"

"If you say cute, I'll dropkick you into next week."

"I was going to say endearing, but I think I'll change that to admirable."

"Good call." She pulled at some thorns attached to her vest.

"Sun's setting, but we should be meeting up with Ethan in a few minutes."

"How'd you know where we are?"

"I grew up rafting this river. My brothers and I have been through here a number of times. There's a small mom-and-pop store about a half mile ahead. Ethan's gonna meet us there."

It took another thirty minutes to forge their way to the small convenience store where three familiar vehicles parked next to his own, each bearing a brother leaning against the hood, tapping their fingers, or clenching a jaw on admonitions waiting to spill.

"Sure know how to show a girl a good time, Ca." Billy smirked as Caden wrapped his left arm around Kaylee.

"Hey, if it weren't for him, I'd be dead, twice." Kaylee matched Caden's step and snuggled closer.

Ethan and Lexi greeted them with warm blankets and spare clothes. To wrap his charge in the soft warmth of the thick pile throw and reduce her shivering appeased a small portion of guilt.

After changing in the restroom and re-checking Kaylee's wound, Caden related their near-death experience. Matt and Billy each eyed her as if wanting to cross-examine to draw out more details. Each refrained with Caden's glare.

"Billy and I'll take Damien to the other side and see if we can pick up the shooter's scent. He'll be long gone since there'd be no advantage in hanging around, but maybe we'll get lucky and find a shell casing or something he dropped." Matt held the kidnapper's mask in an evidence bag. "I wanted to see for myself that you two were okay."

"Ethan and Lexi brought your SUV after searching it for spyware. Found a puck attached to the frame. We've bagged it and will trace it as far as we can." The corner of Billy's mouth twitched. "You can drive Kaylee to the ER, and we'll meet up later."

"Don't say it, man. The hospital has *plenty* of beds."

"Knock it off. Both of you. No bitching." Matt shook his head. "Stubborn as hell. Match made in heaven."

"I don't mind, Caden. 'Sides, you'll get to see that nurse who drools every time you walk by."

Caden couldn't help but shake his head at Kaylee's attempted peacekeeping. Her hand resting gently on his forearm might as well have employed a steel grip. He could refuse her nothing.

"If you weren't already on a first-name basis with the ER doc, I'd feel like some type of jinx." Kaylee hummed her appreciation when the blast of heat from the floor vent rushed over her feet. "This feels great."

"Two of the docs have been there since we were teenagers and know us well." Caden grimaced at the thought of returning with yet another injury to the woman he was tasked with protecting. Ribbing from his brothers would be endless and brutal.

Ninety minutes later, Kaylee sat on the same stretcher, receiving four stitches from her deadly encounter. "I'm ready to go home and play cards or something equally low key." With the second injury requiring stitches in short succession, Kaylee hadn't flinched during the doctor's ministrations.

The familiar doc harrumphed while tossing the soiled drape in the trash. "Caden, these need to come out in ten days, and I'd rather not see her again before then. The nurse will be back in a minute with discharge instructions, which you could probably recite by rote."

Kaylee chuckled as the doctor left. Exhaustion weighed heavy on her shoulders.

"Huh, had enough excitement for one day? I thought you were game for any adventure. After all, you did say you loved my rubber." Watching her flush bright crimson was worth the embarrassment of a nurse walking in mid-conversation. "Ah, we were discussing the differences between rafts, canoes, and kayaks."

"Sounds to me like rafts would be the easiest choice since you have enough hot air to blow 'em up." The nurse smiled after calling him on his bullshit. Turning to Kaylee, she added, "I have your discharge instructions. We'll go over them, but I'm assuming if you've spent any time with this one, you're accustomed to this type of thing. Believe me, I know." Her chuckle insinuated experiencing similar situations.

"Thanks, Marissa, like she really needs to hear that. How've you been?" Remorse colored his tone despite his teasing grin.

"I'm good. How about you? Been in a coma? Haven't seen you for a while."

Her open, honest expression revealed a concern of shared experiences and more than a passing friendship. It seemed his past haunted him at every turn. How was Kaylee supposed to believe he was a different man when his ex-girlfriends appeared around every corner?

"Uh, kind of re-structuring my life a bit. Staying under the radar."

"Hmm, I think you need to duck a little lower." Her speculative gaze swung to Kaylee then back to Caden. It spoke of good times passed in great company and with much excitement. "Take care of this one. I'd say she's a keeper since she's still with you."

You have no idea. "Absolutely."

Lights over the automatic doors kept shadows at bay when they left the hospital. Caden had kept in contact with Matt to stay up to date. The eldest McAllister kept them abreast of the grand picture in an evolving array of puzzle pieces where no two seemed to fit.

"Well, what's the latest?" Kaylee reached for his hand before crossing the parking lot.

"Okay, what we figure so far is this. Today's shooter and the kidnapper whose head you clobbered are one and the same. Matt parked his car on the shoulder of the road then hiked it through the woods until Damien alerted and picked up the trail using the kidnapper's mask. They got impressions from the thug's boots and tire tracks." Witnessing the hope expressed in her eyes nearly broke his heart. All she wanted was to be left alone and live her life. When he opened the car door for her, she leaned into him before slipping inside.

"That's progress. Thanks for sticking with me through all this. You don't know how grateful I am."

Which makes me a heel when I can't control my damn lust. "Unfortunately, the prick must've policed his brass at the river."

Each remained quiet for the ride home, the suburbs he'd shunned at one time passed in a blur before the bucolic scenes and rolling hills echoed the shadows of doubt chipping away at his self-confidence. Even inept goons might launch an effective strike against them in his secluded digs. He imagined Kaylee's thoughts ran along the same vein.

Chapter Nineteen

"How about a nice quiet evening with a half-gallon of chunky monkey smothered in chocolate syrup and crushed pineapple?" Kaylee's speech drifted off as she hesitated at the front door. The thought of the shooter lurking inside and awaiting her return fashioned future nightmares for her subconscious to keep her entertained.

"Sounds like a plan. Let's throw some hot dogs on the grill after I check my security feeds." Caden entered and keyed in his alarm code. "We're good, Pirate. C'mon in."

"Sorry, I'm a bit antsy." Stepping over the threshold, she realized nothing looked out of place.

"No problem. If you want to grab a shower, I can cover your bandage with plastic wrap to keep your wound dry."

"I can do it. I'll meet you in ten." Kaylee's gaze fixed on the stairway, her feet growing roots, sending down invisible tendrils to hold her in place.

"What kind of host would I be if I didn't escort my injured pirate to her door and carry her things?"

The fact that he played the gallant card and didn't mock her fear warmed her heart. "Reese would've told me to tote my own crap."

"Ah, but doesn't the beast eventually woo the beauty? Gotta practice so I don't blow it when the time comes."

Compassion radiated from the gentle touch grazing her hair. When he pulled her in for a hug, she didn't resist, instead claiming that small space in time to thrive under his soft caress.

"Hmm, you need to try harder." *Because I'm still in a solid state and not a puddle on the floor.*

His chuckle radiated through her chest, the vibration instigating a tingling sensation spreading throughout her extremities. The extreme carnal emotions fluttering in her heart created enough heat to power the city for a week.

In response, he molded her closer, their perfect fit another example of how fate and nature played the odds. Any heterosexual woman would react to the woods and spice scent combined with the strength to make her want the whole package. However, destiny had sent her in the wrong direction, again. Caden surfed the waters outside her league with his easy charm and highly social nature, which meant nothing between them could last.

It doesn't mean I can't enjoy the feeling of security.

He waited, simply holding her until she pulled away, understanding her on an elemental level.

Hot water melted the tension in her limbs while sluicing down her frame to carry away immediate worries.

This is what normal feels like.

Something she desperately wanted.

Once downstairs, Caden's calm self-possession supplemented her sense of serenity. Despite his reported lack of skill in the kitchen, he proved self-assured with the grill. A meal of hot dogs and warmed baked beans waited on the small table. Arched retaining wall blocks surrounded the blazing fire, the crackle and snap of dry timber adding to the cozy refuge. The casual cookout reminded her of home, family, and peace of mind. Nature surrounded them on all sides in all its forms.

"I love the way your patio is so sheltered. We used to have cookouts all the time. We'd make up ridiculous stories while we ate."

"Yeah? Let's hear it."

"Mhmm. Reese wanted to get into vet school. He'd entertain us using the animals we'd see. We'd all have binoculars, and he'd tell us details about all his woodland friends."

"Like?"

Kaylee nodded toward the tree line. "Looks like your squirrel tree is ripe. I remember one night after Reese had domesticated a family of the little critters. They'd come right up and eat from his hand while he made up wild yarns about their family squabbles." She smiled at the chattering, bushy-tailed critters flitting from limb to limb. To watch several scamper up the tree while others played among the branches provided nature's version of comic relief in a world of chaos. Remembering the details brought her twin's countenance more firmly into mind.

"I put food out for them but don't try to otherwise tame them. I don't want them getting too relaxed around people in their traipsing about or approaching a hunter and getting shot. There's quite a few to entertain you on quiet evenings. They're kind of cool to watch over time. Some of them have markings that change seasonally. They're active little buggers, year-round."

The vibration of his cell interrupted their quiet communion with nature. "Looks like we have company." His lips tightened into a straight line.

Kaylee leaned over to view the screen. "Ethan, Lexi—and someone else. Think they have news?" As much as she wanted the kidnappers caught, the thought of going back to her home filled her with dread. She couldn't imagine feeling safe when alone.

"Hope so. Sit tight. They'll find us."

Minutes later, Hoover bounded through the back slider with Lexi and Ethan trailing. Kaylee didn't recognize the man with them, but shined boots, TAC pants, and polo shirt, pinned him as an officer.

"Hi Ca. 'Bout time you changed the code on your alarm, don't you think?" Glancing at Kaylee, Lexi added. "Looks like you're feeling better." Crinkles around her eyes and mouth belied the tension in her voice.

"I'm fine." Kaylee didn't miss Ethan's slight roll of his shoulders. "Judging by the company, this is a business call."

"Um, yeah, it is. I was just granted the courtesy of a ride along. You remember Detective Saunders?" Ethan dropped down on the cushioned loveseat beside Lexi. His frown and haggard appearance presaged unpleasant news.

Saunders, standing off to the side, nodded to Kaylee before addressing Caden with a sly grin. "We've found a woman's body. It was Ciera Kirpatzel."

"Where?" Caden's low murmur held the pain of loss.

"In a shallow grave just inside the wildlife refuge. She was dressed in a familiar red, white, and black, hockey T-shirt." Ethan's apologetic gaze regarded Kaylee before returning to his brother. "Less than a mile from your insertion point."

"What the hell!" Caden paled as he jumped to his feet. Pacing to the edge of the patio and back, his fists clenched and relaxed before turning back to Ethan. "They're trying to frame me."

"Either that or remove the obstacle protecting Kaylee," Lexi suggested in a calm tone.

"When we were in cages, she was dressed in torn blue jeans and an old flannel shirt." Kaylee's anger flared, spreading heat up her neck to encompass her face.

"Kaylee's accounting is partly why we're allowed this courtesy." Ethan tugged at his earlobe, his hesitance to continue filling the room with apprehension. "Her interview was conducted *before* Ciera was murdered."

"Jesus. This is a tangled nightmare." Caden's gaze darted to Saunders as if an invisible noose closed about his neck.

"Also, the husband is spouting off about how you two had a fling and that you went ballistic when she ended it. Not to mention pointing at you as her supplier. There were traces of drugs found on the body."

"That's not how it happened! And you know I've never touched that shit." Caden's jaw opened and closed several times before Ethan continued.

"Hey! I've been within three feet of him since I escaped." Kaylee's indignation didn't alter Saunders' stance.

"*We* know that—which is why we explained the shirt to the captain before forensics identifies your DNA. But they want you to go in and give a statement, just to clear the air," Ethan shuffled his feet in a rare show of uncertainty. "Abagail is on her way to the station now. I told her we'd meet her there. You talk to no one until you've spoken with her. Got it?"

"Yeah, let's get this shit over with."

Caden drummed his fingers on the metal table, waiting for his sister to enter and read him the riot act. It wasn't the first time he'd been on the wrong side of an interrogation table but prayed it was the last. At least two of his brothers would be observing on the other side of the one-way mirror.

A whoosh of cooler air brushed his brow when Abby opened the door. Dressed in a slim black suit and heels, her hair in a neat bun, she was all business. It wasn't that long ago he'd wanted to break another detective's jaw for the reference of femme fatale.

Settling her briefcase on the table across from him, she sat, releasing a long sigh. "Jeez, Ca. Who'd you piss off this time?" A folder with several sheets of paper kept her attention as she read one report after another.

"Conroy Kirpatzel."

"The banking magnate? Go big or go home?"

"C'mon Abs. You know how that went down with Ciera." To see his sister so serious spelled more trouble than he wanted to contemplate.

"Yeah, I know. But two years ago, after you punched that creep to get information, you shot any credibility you had here to shit. Here's what's gonna happen. We're gonna spend the next hour going over every detail I can pick out. Then, the not-so-nice detective is going to come in and ask questions." She paused for effect, "You're not going to open your mouth except to answer *my* questions. Got it?"

"Yes, ma'am. Understood."

"By the way, Kaylee is bending the captain's ear concerning your innocence. That's after she called her father, who, as you may or may not know, has no clout here whatsoever but doesn't stop him from issuing *suggestions*."

"Damn."

"Don't worry about her. Feel sorry for the captain, at this point. She certainly is one determined young lady. Speaking of which, I also need to know the extent of your relationship."

"Look, all this shit is circumstantial. Yeah, I'd left my T-shirt at Ciera's house when we broke up. Hell, her brother blames me for her returning to the abusive prick *and* getting her into drugs."

"Yeah, the drugs are one thing the brother and husband agree on, which doesn't look good at all."

"Shit. This doesn't even make sense. I was *with* Kaylee when she was shot. And I was here in the station when she first stumbled in."

"First, you have no alibi for the hours she was in the tunnels. Second, per her statement, there are at least two men." Abby held up her hand to staunch Caden's denial. "They can't charge you yet. At least not until the DNA results come back."

"And you know Saunders will put a rush on *that*."

"It's well known that he hates you. You beat him on promotional exams. But, the captain is fair."

"All right. Let's start from the beginning. I want to know *everything.*"

After obtaining pertinent facts, Abigail narrowed her focus on Caden's eyes. Now, for the final and most important questions. "At what point did they tell you that you're under arrest?"

"They haven't."

"What? Has anyone read you Miranda rights?"

"No."

"Then why did you come? You know this drill." The same shark's smile had forced many opposing attorneys to cringe. "You don't speak to anyone, and I do mean no one but me about your previous relationship with Ciera. Got it?

"Yep."

"I've already laid into Matt, Billy, Ethan, and Lucas. If they even hint at a question of your past dealings with any of the McFaddens or Kirpatzel, I will flay them alive. Understood?"

"Yep."

"Good. Now let's get the hell out of here and go home. I'll deal with Saunders tomorrow."

Caden felt sorry for Saunders.

Chapter Twenty

"Saunders is an asshole." Caden grumbled.

"We all know that," Lexi, sitting in the front passenger seat, agreed.

Sitting in the back of Ethan's SUV, Kaylee reached for Caden's hand, taking a deep breath when he relaxed and linked their fingers. "Yes, and now he's gonna look like a fool. I think your sister's gonna rip him a new one."

"Always the bright side, huh?" He nodded his chin toward a group of girls walking out of the movie theatre as they passed. "You should be enjoying life like them, not spending your nights at the police station. I hear you gave the captain a run for his money, though. Kudos to you."

"Combined with your father calling, it put him on the defensive." Lexi swiveled in her seat to see Kaylee face to face. "I thought a united front of McAllisters was a force to be reckoned with, but it sounded like your dad ranks right up there with them."

Ethan caught Caden's gaze in the rearview mirror and nodded his head before adding. "It became quickly obvious that Mr. Tate has put stock in your assurances of Kaylee's safety. It seems he's put faith in you already. How'd you swing that?"

"Maybe because I'm competent."

Once home, Ethan and Lexi followed Caden and Kaylee through the kitchen to the patio. Lexi had pulled out a half-gallon of ice cream en route. Hoover padded behind, obviously expecting a treat.

"I've got spoons and laptop." Kaylee appreciated like-mindedness.

Each sat at the patio table while Lexi booted up her computer.

"I've gone through Ciera's files, pics, and social media. One man I identified, as recently as two months ago, is a contractor, Basil Millen. He popped up in several photos taken at parties and charity functions, so I went into his media pages and email as well. Quite a few messages were detailing their private, um, meetings." Lexi turned the screen to face Kaylee. "Do you recognize him?"

"Yes! He was the guy I told you about—at the church. Is he in any other photos I took? I wasn't paying much attention to people."

"No. I've already checked." Lexi pointed her spoon at Kaylee for emphasis. "You did say that *you* approached *him*, right?"

"Yes. I stumbled across the church he's renovating and took some pics while they were working. He was standing out front talking to one of the crew, so I went up to ask a few questions and get permission to take some pics inside, too."

"I dug deeper and found his emails referring to their future together. Ciera was going to divorce her husband and take up with Basil. She also described a woman, Vasilisa Sokolov, as her husband's whore. It was easy to track *her* down, she's here on a student visa studying computer science, also employed as a personal assistant at Janson's Import Export. *And* she's living way beyond her means."

Lexi frowned before continuing. "Since it'd make no sense for Ciera's boyfriend to hurt her, we need to look at the husband and *his* girlfriend." Lexi leaned back in her chair. "I see where Janson's has been under investigation for questionable practices in the past. Another strike against the husband if he's involved with them, though I haven't found those ties yet."

"Well, weren't you a busy little bee while at the station." Caden shook his head.

"Ciera was supposed to meet Basil the evening after she went home, but she disappeared first." Lexi's time line drew a more puzzled frown from everyone present. "Which doesn't tell us how the husband knew where she was—especially considering how she was dressed."

"Do you think the husband knew about his wife's lover? What I saw of his temper, combined with motive and his impulsive behavior..." Kaylee glanced at Caden, trying to read his expression. He'd locked down his emotions.

"Definitely possible," Lexi replied, "but I can't find proof." Ethan rubbed Lexi's shoulder, who couldn't mask the shudder shifting her weight.

"Ciera's brother put us in touch with her attorney, who confirmed she'd begun proceedings for divorce," Ethan added. "We've not found evidence proving the husband knew it was coming. Two members of the task force are searching his home as we speak." Ethan opened the bag of marshmallows left on the table and picked up a skewer from the stacked stone surrounds. After sitting and threading several of the gooey treats on the rod, he held it over the open flame. "Jeez, we used to love these as kids."

"What about the clerk at Lush Fragrances?" Kaylee asked.

"The only thing we've dug up is that her father is an amateur photographer, which might be how she knew you had a different camera with a sketchy knowledge of the equipment," Ethan said. "He also has a short sheet for accepting stolen merchandise. We don't have enough for a search warrant. If they are involved or have received your camera, they wouldn't be stupid enough to use it in public."

"How did Ciera die?" Caden's monotone pain lanced the subdued atmosphere.

"Strangled." Ethan shook his head. "A poacher's dog found her during a quail hunt."

"When are you gonna talk with the boyfriend, Basil? Maybe he'll shed more light on the marital relationship or the husband's girlfriend." At the wood's edge, a robin's sad trill echoed other songsters, giving voice to the anguish in Caden's expression.

"Billy's gone to interview him." Ethan's fist repeatedly clenched on the skewer holding marshmallows. The McAllisters stood united.

Quiet details of the investigation filled the gaps as Kaylee's thoughts went to Ciera. The sight of her begging for freedom would haunt her nights for years to come. As if reading her mind, Caden stepped behind her, massaging the knots forming in her shoulders and neck.

The absentminded gesture continued as he spoke about the case. She couldn't help but wonder how much Ciera had meant to him. He'd once thought of her as his new beginning. In earlier conversations, he'd described them as distant friends after breaking off their relationship.

"All right. We've got to get going." Ethan handed the last marshmallow to Lexi. "We'll be back on Sunday for a proper meal."

"That includes graham crackers and chocolate, dude." Lexi stood and gave Caden a hug.

"We'll lock up on our way out." Ethan smiled at Kaylee before adding. "We're closing in on at least one of them. Once we have him, we'll get the rest."

Meant as comfort, his words reminded her she was the only surviving witness to killers on her trail.

"Peace and quiet once again, but it's starting to cool off a bit. How about we take this inside." Caden rubbed the back of his neck before offering his hand. "I appreciate you believing in me."

"Seriously? Anyone with a single working synapse can see they're framing you. The kidnappers murdered Ciera. Now they'll be highly motivated to eliminate any witnesses." Her thoughtful gaze took in her surroundings, the darkness of the woods, quiet and deep.

Kaylee wrapped her arms about herself yet couldn't smother the full-body shiver. "I hope they catch him soon. Poor Ciera. She begged me not to leave her, and I ran like a coward."

Caden loosened the grip of her hands and wrapped his own about her waist. "You took the only viable option. You have to know that." Slipping a finger under her chin, he stroked the soft under-curve of her neck. "You survived, Kaylee. In that situation, it was the *only* way possible. At least now, we can get justice for her.

"She was pretty bruised up, but I couldn't tell if it was from the kidnapper or her husband. I guess we'll never know."

"We'll figure it out, sweetheart." Holding her in his arms generated a satisfaction threaded with exhilaration he couldn't deny. His brothers' teasing words about the parade of women he'd previously enjoyed and Ethan's warning that one day he'd grow bored and want a deeper connection drifted through his thoughts. Lexi's appearance in Ethan's life had irrevocably changed him for the better. Would it be the same with Kaylee? The responses she stirred in him were as much psychological as physical.

"Would you like a nightcap?" The sudden disconnect when she'd padded toward the house set him adrift in a wash of uncertainty.

"Nah, I'm good. I just want to unwind."

Her body softened with his touch, every time. Still, doubt remained whether their obvious chemistry comprised the lion's share of their relationship, or, more likely, the culmination of grief over losing her twin, kidnapping followed by the attack, and her injuries, all swirled her emotions into a confusing maelstrom of unchartered territory she'd never untangle. He'd man up and keep things platonic. After all, he and Lexi were merely friends.

They spent the rest of the evening in quiet conversation. The fact she snuggled against him on the sofa as they debated the merits of cave exploration over trail hiking added fuel to his existence in the friend zone. After everything she'd been through, she seemed to take things in stride, as if expecting life's torrent of bombs to continually batter her consciousness yet determined to persevere anyway. All things considered, his new sidekick showed more spine and courage than any woman he'd ever known.

It wasn't until he woke to predawn light filtering through the curtain's gap that he realized they'd fallen asleep on the couch. They both lay full out, with his body spooning hers and his arm slung over her waist. Never in his life had he slept with a woman all night.

Hell, and we're supposed to be just friends.

His brain below the belt hadn't received the memo. The thought caught in his mind like the cog in a misshapen wheel that rhythmically hitched with each rotation.

When she rolled over and snuggled on his shoulder with her breath warm on his arm, he didn't mind the fact his hand had gone to sleep. It was worth every tingly, shooting discharge. Very gently, he stroked her waist and flank then let his caress drift up her back. Her hair held the hyacinth scent that begged him to nuzzle ever so lightly. The little squirm, her response, provided a painful reminder that they were platonic. If she'd felt the evidence of his desire, she disregarded it. *Another new experience.*

Ignoring the prodding of his libido, he let his thoughts drift in a profusion of hope and uncertainty until his cell phone rang.

"Lucas, what's up? Kind of early for you to have your eyes open, much less thoughts clear enough to operate heavy equipment."

"Dumbass. While you've been playing house, I've been working. We got her kidnapper a few hours ago. Stupid shit was catching the ferry to Victoria."

Caden smothered a groan when Kaylee sat upright and stretched, arched her back, and yawned. Her T-shirt stretched snug over perfect breasts, soft mounds he'd vowed not to touch until she was safe.

"Good. Did he give up his accomplice?" Caden readjusted himself before leaning up.

"No. Says he doesn't have a name, just called his partner, butt-rot. The guy's not smart enough to set this up. Watch your back till we catch the prick."

"Anything from forensics on Ciera?" Caden closed his eyes against an image of the killer strangling the terrified socialite, once so filled with energy and enthusiasm for all life had to offer.

Kaylee's show of nonchalance didn't fool him. She may crave the coffee she now prepared, but the new firmness of her jaw, neck, and shoulders, screamed stress and a need for current information.

"Yeah, they got fluids off her body. It'll take some time to see who we match." A slight hesitation warned of Lucas' concern. "I was thinking, why don't I come over and help you set up some trail cameras. I know you have a video system around your house, but this guy we caught—he had gun residue on his clothes but not his hands. He might've stood beside your shooter, but he probably didn't pull the trigger. It'd be nice to have an earlier warning system."

"Nah, I can set them up. It'll get me out of the house this morning."

"All right. Oh, and don't be surprised if Matt drops by. I think he wants to touch base with your girl again."

"Did you check the husband's alibi?" Caden asked as he watched Kaylee still while tossing the empty bacon wrapper in the trash.

"Yeah, he was out of town."

"All right. Keep me updated. I'll catch you later." With his gaze focused on Kaylee, it took him two tries to disconnect the call.

She padded over and sat beside him, nudging him with her shoulder after setting his coffee on the table. "Well, what's the verdict?"

"Hmm, first of all, thanks for the coffee. Secondly, you're going to help me set up trail cameras today." After taking a drink, he asked, "How's your arm and wrist feeling?"

"Fine."

"Good. Okay, here it is in a nutshell. Lucas said they caught one kidnapper heading north. They have forensics working on his clothes now, but he's probably not our trigger man. Both the husband and boyfriend have solid alibis. We still don't know how and where the husband's girlfriend fits in all this."

"Figures, but we didn't peg the boyfriend for being involved anyway." Concentration furrowed her brow as she took another sip of coffee.

"What do they know about the girlfriend?"

"Lucas says the damn feds have a file on her, but they're not sharing." Caden's coffee cup landed with a heavy thump on the end table. The small lip of the coaster contained the sloshed contents.

"So, she's a dead end?"

"Only legally." A feral smile tilted the corners of his mouth. "Lexi will let us know what she finds."

"Handy talent."

"Yep. Plus, they'll break the creep in custody and hunt down the partner. Let's think about better things, shall we? How about I finish cooking breakfast. I can dazzle you with my amazing skills."

"Pancakes that can double as *chakrams*?"

"How do you know about Indian weapons?" Caden asked, wondering what other surprises she had in store.

"Had a friend in college that was into exotic, martial arts stuff."

"All right, then. Watch while I cook phenomenal pancakes without turning them black or deadly."

Working in companionable silence then eating at the kitchen counter, Caden marveled at Kaylee's stoicism. Afterward, urging her to call her parents again and check on them, he realized keeping them in the loop was a necessity. Even from across the country, they bolstered her spirits. Like before, he explained in detail the day's events and how he'd avoid another catastrophe before her father would let him go.

"Do you think the other kidnapper is on the run now?" Kaylee's shrewd gaze didn't miss a beat. Scrutinizing with a sharp intellect had become natural.

"Most likely. But we'll stay alert, just the same." Quiet, efficient movements cleared the table and allowed him to study her surreptitiously. Her slight frame had lost some of the earlier tension, yet the weight of guilt still burdened her shoulders.

The soft purr of a truck's engine overshadowed the start of the dishwasher. "Sounds like Matt's here." Lucas' forewarning had sounded a little off but lacked specifics.

Soft chimes designated the coming visit abnormal. For Matt to ring instead of barging in signified either loss of key or a prime example of, *Oh shit, now what?*

Caden's back stiffened while checking his phone's screen, hooked into his surveillance setup. His brother's plastic smile hid an agenda only time would reveal.

"Maybe he's got more news." Kaylee trailed him to the door.

"Hmm, but using the doorbell's got to be a first. Maybe he's confused about its purpose."

"Hey, at least he cares enough to visit. Sounds like he brought Damien. Cool." Kaylee's excitement bubbled up in a smile and hum of approval.

Soft woofing muffled by the door ended with an excited bark. Morning sunshine spilled through the open doorway before Matt's shepherd forged ahead to greet Kaylee. Caden had received a light nudge.

"Bro, what's up with the formality? You've never bothered before." Caden peered inside the duffle bag shoved into his hands.

"You've never had a house guest." Smiling at Kaylee, Matt continued, "It would seem you're a good influence. Congrats."

"What's all this? Lucas said you wanted to talk with Kaylee." Either behind the eight ball or playing catch up summed up his life.

"I've got a new K-9 handler to train. Can you watch Damien for a couple weeks? I brought enough food and toys."

"Seriously? You're just gonna dump a dog—" Soft cooing and snuffing between Kaylee and the shepherd cut off Caden's words.

Matt grinned. "See? Match made in heaven. Thanks, man." Matt slapped Caden on the back. "Lucas said you were gonna put up trail cameras. Need any help?"

"No." Despite Caden's recent near-death experience and the small freak-out in the tunnels, and because the brothers had always read each other so well, Matt wouldn't emasculate his brother by suggesting they move to a safe house. In his way, he still protected those he loved while helping in any way *he* saw fit. Still, the insinuation that he couldn't protect Kaylee stung.

"Matt, I don't think now's a good time." *From dropping off his dog to setting up trail cameras, Matt and Lucas discussed this before arriving.*

"Oh. I've always wanted a shepherd. He's beautiful. You don't mind, do you, Caden? If it's too much, I can take him—"

"No. The dog can stay. At least *he* knows his place." Caden scrubbed a hand over his morning scruff. He should have seen this coming.

"Good. Let's sit for a while and talk. You got any more coffee, bro?" Matt made himself comfortable on the sofa while Kaylee sat on the raised hearth to be at eye level with the dog.

"Sure. Make yourself at home." Ambling to the kitchen, Caden realized Matt wouldn't leave until finishing his assessment. The fact his brother took a seat and acted as a guest instead of pillaging through the kitchen spoke volumes. "Any news?"

"Yeah, Ciera's parents' are offering a huge reward for the capture of the kidnapper's partner—dead or alive."

"I expected they would. How are they holding up?" Cups clinked when Caden took one from the cupboard.

"As best they can. Abby went and spoke to the McFadden's. The brother wanted to apologize for mouthing off to you—and about you. I told him I'd pass it along."

"Shit. With all they're dealing with, that shouldn't even register."

Matt turned his attention to Kaylee. "Caden says you're a decent shot and you own a pistol. Are you a hunter?" Unpacking the duffle and tossing Damien a tug toy added a false air of nonchalance.

"I don't hunt, but I love to trap shoot."

"Ah, passed down from a police officer to his kid?"

"Yep. My brother and I used to shoot registered targets, but it's been a while since I've practiced."

"Well, I've got some extra time. Why don't we set up some plastic jugs out back? I'd love to watch you embarrass Caden with your skill." A wide grin revealed his eagerness to test her ability.

Chapter Twenty-One

"You're stressed, Caden." Kaylee winced when she handed him a trail cam. His smile never reached his eyes. "Are you upset that I handle a gun with ease?"

"What? Hell no. Actually, it's kind of sexy. You were a real badass, this morning. Your dad taught you well."

"Still not as good as you. And before you ask, no, I didn't hold back." Kaylee sifted her fingers through Damien's soft fur as she watched Caden check the box's settings.

"Yeah, I knew you'd want to kick my ass. Thank God you didn't because my brothers would *never* let me live that down."

"Maybe next time."

During Matt's persistence in appraising her marksmanship and evaluating her ability to assess various situations, Caden's teeth grinding and heavy sighs had provided a constant distraction. It didn't take a genius to realize Matt was assessing them both. Explanations detailing how the aftermath of harrowing experiences could cause hesitation or loss of focus during intense situations was aimed at Caden. Barely heard comments defined what might constitute Matt's future and what he should do in the meantime.

Now that they were alone and hiking the trails around the property, Caden relaxed into his former self-assured persona.

Damien padded by her side, navigating the steep hills and ravines, sniffing curiously every few feet.

When Caden held out his hand to help her navigate a rough incline, she accepted, not because she needed the aid, but because she needed his warmth. Each time his thumb brushed over her knuckles, a simultaneous thrill arced along the distant threads of her nerves.

They shared many traits in the way they related to each other, reminding her of the easy comradery of family. The only exception, when he stood close. Then, pure instinct took over, a soul-deep yearning to merge to one spiritual being.

"Hold still, I want to take a pic of you against that backdrop." Maneuvering her camera into position and adjusting the field of view, she opened the aperture to narrow the depth of field so he'd stand out against a blurred background. Several clicks later, they continued down the trail.

A moment of apprehension followed when she stopped to push aside thick vines concealing a darkened, wide-mouth entrance to a cave. The stiffening of Caden's frame was the only outward indication he didn't want to enter. Damien sniffed several times but displayed no evidence of a perceived threat.

"It's small, not very deep. When I first inspected the property, I thought it was great—now it's kind of a security nightmare. There's a bunch on the property."

No sounds emanated from within, lending a creepy atmosphere that would surface again in her dreams as the backdrop for another round of terror-induced hell. "I get that. I do. I also need to face my fears. Not today, but soon. Will you take a pic of me in front of it after I take yours? It'll be a visual goal for me. Kind of like hanging a pair of skinny jeans on the bathroom hook to badger my conscience into sensible eating." Once framed, the picture would be a symbolic reminder of all they'd conquered.

"Just so you don't use software to draw a crown of daisies or a tiara on my head." His frown alluded to an understanding that pride would never voice.

Standing with her back to the cave, she waited for him to manipulate the settings for the desired effect. In her mind, subjugating the cave to a vague blur gave her a sense of power over fear. A small step in the right direction. When she finished and stepped away, the incremental confidence boost lightened her step.

Cresting a small hill, Kaylee sat on a small rock outcropping to rest. Damien rubbed against her thigh while wagging his tail, demanding his due of attention. "It's beautiful here."

"Yeah, this place has everything I'd wanted in a home."

The pensiveness in his voice and distant look in his eyes squeezed her heart. She pushed to her feet to stand eye to eye, the best way to interpret nonverbal. "What?"

"You read me too accurately. It's a little unnerving. Only my brothers can do that."

"I speak two languages fluently, English and body."

"You've learned well."

"And you're stalling. Whatever's churning in your mind and gut, spit it out."

"This stalker. I'm not sure of the best way to keep you safe."

"First, that's my problem. Second, I feel safer with you than anywhere else. If I'd been alone on the river, well, I'd be dead now. I dropped my paddle, remember? I wouldn't have made it around the bend or to shore."

His answer was part smile, part grimace. She didn't know how to respond, so she turned away and smoothed her hand through Damien's soft fur when he sniffed then pawed at the ground before whining. "What's up boy?"

Frowning, Caden set the duffle aside and kneeled by the dog. "He's found a scent that doesn't meet with his approval. Matt said he doesn't like bobcats. Maybe we've crossed paths with one. There're quite a few in the area."

The shepherd barked and cocked his head to the side before giving the ground and small rock base a final sniff.

"These woods are ripe with all kinds of game. I've seen tons of tracks. It'll be interesting to see what my trail cams pick up."

"I assume you've already updated the firmware and these have GPS chips?" Kaylee noted the camera's distinct demarcation in several spots.

"Let me guess, your dad?"

"No, Reese. He used them to study yarding behavior in deer. In wintertime, they shift to areas that better sustain them—hence we tracked their movements. Initially, we had some equipment stolen. If you yank the batteries out, it can't notify you of tampering, though if you have it set up on a feed, you might get a pic of your thief first."

"At least with the way I'm attaching them, we won't lose the feed due to vegetative growth. Hold on while I fix one atop this ridge. We can capture anything on the path without it being easily spotted." Navigating off the trail a short distance and scrambling up a steep slope, Caden climbed a moderate-sized white oak before attaching the device with a locking cable snugged tight.

"When the trees bud out more, I'll probably have to move this one, but at least the height and cable will deter theft."

"Not many poachers or scumbags slinking through the woods are gonna look up." Kaylee swatted at a buzzing fly while tracking Caden's progress.

Free fall facilitated his return when a smaller branch snapped underfoot. His deft tuck and roll ended with him standing near the tree's base. "Nice that we can face it north and still capture two trails without worrying about exposure blow-out."

"You're like a giant cat, grace and all."

"Yep. Unfortunately, I think I've used up most of my lives. What's up, pirate? You have that *look*."

"Not sure. Just feel like someone's watching us. Scratching the back of her neck didn't relieve the itch between her shoulder blades blooming into a blaring premonition.

"Yeah, I do to at times. But you've got me and Damien to watch over you." The confidence in his words matched his expression.

Shadows crept along the forest floor, growing, and fusing to form monstrous figures with moving parts, each threatening her wavering stability. "I guess it's just the sun's setting that's giving me the creeps." She'd never been one to ignore her instincts.

"Are you getting flashbacks of the tunnels?"

"Sometimes. Maybe the earthy smell kinda takes me back. Last night I dreamed about the accomplice. He was arguing with someone else, his accent was worse with stress. I couldn't hear the other voice well enough to discern anything about it. The thing is I don't know if the accent was real or just my imagination. Plus, the tunnels distort sounds. I guess we both have cause not to like them."

"All the more reason to go down there again at some point."

"Jeez, to think fascination with the area's history brought me back here."

"Obviously I'm sorry a crimp got ahold of you, but I'm not sorry you're back. Are you going to stay once this is over?" A furrow of concentration lined his brow as he spoke.

"I don't know. I'd surely never find another Caden to see me through a similar adventure." Whether he referred to her leaving his home or the area didn't matter. Both enticed her to make the area her stomping ground. Bad things could and would happen no matter where she went, making it crucial to focus on the good. *Caden is an adventure unto himself.*

"Considering you're nearly as good a shot and have a greater wariness, I don't think you'll need one."

Ah, but I do. A very specific one.

Despite the comforting words, she was glad he'd kept his shoulder harness on for their walk. Technology, medical advances, transportation, and many other things had changed over time, yet humanity couldn't weed out greed, cruelty, and aggression. *That creep* will *be coming for me.* "I'm beginning to wonder if there's such a thing as a safe place."

"C'mere, pirate. We're going to get through this."

Comfort derived from close proximity could never be duplicated with anything else. Contact from shoulder to knee meant she could absorb his heat as well as his strength. The light rumble of satisfaction emanating from his chest and feather-light graze down her back created emotions she couldn't hope to suppress. Nor would he miss the shudder.

"Cold?" A low chuckle filled the air.

"Nah, just right." Therein lay the problem. He *did* fit and felt too perfect, too comfortable, unlike anything she'd ever experienced. The longer she remained in his presence, the harder it would be when another woman took her place.

Even if he wanted her to stay, she couldn't. She'd always wonder if it was because of her feelings for Caden or fear of being alone. She had to stand by herself again to know.

He molded her closer, the invisible threads connecting them thickening to undermine her will.

When she inched back, she had to tilt her head back to meet his gaze. "Thanks. You always know how to make me feel better."

"I want you to stay."

Knowing he was going to kiss her didn't prepare her for the tidal wave of heat washing through her body. Like the endless flow of lava from an unseen well, the blazing inferno created by Caden's lips brushing across hers multiplied to the point of pleasure-pain. Heaven in one stroke. When he settled them lightly over her own, the rush of lust surging through her frame crested in her chest and broke any remaining thoughts of a platonic relationship. She wanted him, for however long and however much he'd give. In the past year, she'd learned to grab whatever happiness fate sent her way. Now Caden spoon-fed it in short spurts that made her hunger for more.

The light sweep of his tongue along the seam of her lips preceded him delving inside to twine and explore. Weakening muscles were no concern when he tightened his hold and supported her weight.

Nothing in her life compared to that moment in time when nothing could hurt them, a split second in the vast universe that remained sacred and invulnerable. Her groan answered the growl rumbling under her fingers while the steady rise and fall of his chest created a tantalizing friction against her breasts. Evidence of his growing desire pressed against her belly to augment her hip's natural inclination to tilt into his length. The result brought a slight twist of his hips that was her undoing. It was no longer a matter of if they would join, but when. Air became a precious commodity taken in short gasps as the volcanic heat from their contact tightened the muscles around her core.

Her thin mewl was answered with his fingers tightening on her ass, pulling her snug while massaging the muscle with his large hand. Her breaths came shorter, faster, spiraling her toward a bliss where nothing existed outside of a natural wonder that would consume her from the inside. Caden's harsh breath stirred her hair before he nuzzled her neck. The light nip of her earlobe brought a pleasure-pain that rocketed her senses near the point of no return.

When he ripped paradise from the natural world and loosened his hold, she opened her eyes to see his cocky grin.

"How many times have you done that to a girl?"

"What? Supported her weight so she didn't fall?"

"Yeah, that."

"Never like this, Kaylee. Believe me, never like this. If we weren't up to our necks in this mess…but I won't take chances with your safety. We can't do this while there's a killer on the loose."

As if understanding she needed a minute to regain her senses, he supported her with hands at her waist until she took a small step back.

"You sure know how to take a girl back to nature."

"Hmm, why don't we finish setting up these cameras and head back? A late lunch and a little relaxation in the hot tub sounds good."

She couldn't stop the groan. "Beast."

He grinned before leaning in and whispering in her ear. "Soon, Kaylee. Soon."

"I don't have a suit. You won't mind if I go in naked?"

"Ha. Now who's the beast?"

"Hey, I give as good as I get."

"Can't wait to test *that* theory."

Damn, what a kiss. A fog of bliss swirled through her thoughts for the duration of their hike. Caden set the cameras at strategic locations, explaining the angles he used and the easiest ways to access his property from the surrounding woods along with what lay beyond in each direction. In such a remote area, his few neighbors were a good distance away.

The trek home passed quickly with images of Caden in swim trunks flitting through her mental catalog of top pics. Each gave new definition to the memory of substantial ropes and ridges of muscles her fingers had defined. He'd shunned a brief sexual encounter in his desire for a deeper relationship yet wouldn't take advantage while she was in danger.

Admirable.

Damien whined while visually searching the path ahead.

"Has he ever had a grudge against deer or other wildlife?" Kaylee inched closer to Caden's side, keeping her gaze trained ahead along the trail.

"Not that I know about."

Near the edge of the tree line adjacent to his home, Damien growled low in his throat. His hard-eyed gaze locked onto the house. Chuffs morphed into a threatening rumble. Caden urged her behind him. "Stay back, Kaylee. I'm gonna let Damien go first to see if he can track the scent."

Using the garage to shield their approach, he scanned the area. She hadn't heard the telltale slide of metal over leather, but he'd palmed his gun, its shadow against a large oak reminding her that Caden's darker side would compel him to shoot an intruder. Matt's earlier words rang true. Shooting a person was a lot different than paper targets. She didn't know if the same conviction ran in her veins.

No noise warned of danger, yet icy fingers of dread increased her pulse and breathing. She expected the sharp bite of a bullet in crossing the open yard.

Rounding the corner of the garage, Caden's soft expletives spoke volumes. "Back slider's ajar."

The shepherd growled.

"Search, Damien." With his tail out straight and nose low to the ground, the dog bolted, tracking an invisible route into the house. Glass walls gave them a bird's eye view of his progress until disappearing in the den.

Caden glanced over his shoulder and frowned as if undecided on what to do with her. She didn't have a gun and weighed all of a buck ten when soaking wet.

She took the options off the table without tact or diplomacy. "I'm going with you."

"Yeah, figures. Stay close but leave me room to maneuver."

"You set the alarm before we left."

"Yeah, but it didn't sound—and I didn't get an SMS text message."

She'd known the killer would eventually track her down but didn't expect it so soon. Each time death or capture came for her, she'd escaped. No doubt, Ciera had felt the same way, that she'd cheat the reaper's best effort.

With Caden between her and the house, she wouldn't see a frontal threat until it was too late. Keeping an eye out to make sure no one circled around behind them was the best help she could offer.

Minutes earlier, she'd locked her body in a timeless embrace, praying for more passion, more intimacy, and more security. Now, she just wanted to survive the next ten minutes, then the next hour. Over Caden's shoulder, Damien padded down the stairs at a uniform pace, sniffing side to side with each step.

In a frantic bid for normalcy, her mind tabulated various factors to bring logic back into the equation. The time line of the puzzle pieces coming together narrowed their suspects to Ciera's husband, the proprietors and clerks in the Denelli shopping center, along with anyone who'd happened to be nearby and shopping that day. *Great.*

Her father had bragged about her analytical mind—which now failed to filter the vague evidence to come up with a plan. Her location at the time of the abduction pointed to a shop owner, probably close to the café. *But how'd they know where I was staying?* She'd paid cash for her few purchases.

Caden's shadow form and shadow gun advanced along the garage wall, followed by a small, trembling, pretender. Phantom branches from a nearby oak shook with laughter, slapping them both soundly for their intention to outsmart destiny.

Caden led her through the kitchen, watchful of his surroundings. Damien sat by the front door, excited breaths and quiet snuffling marking his enthusiasm and their intruder's absence.

"Looks like our uninvited guest has left. Stay with me while I clear the rooms."

Looking around, she noticed Ciera's computer was gone, and the security panel by the door was open, the cover hanging by one hinge. *Figures.* Was the killer somewhere in the woods even now trying to track them down to finish what he'd started? Thinking back to the tunnel, her assailant didn't appear to have the intelligence to disable an alarm without triggering it.

After they'd swept the rest of the house and returned to the kitchen, Caden called Matt. Soft profanities heard through the connection reminded her how much the brothers had in common.

When he hung up, all she wanted to do was run.

"Don't touch anything. The gang will be out shortly to see if we can lift any prints. Damn these bastards are quick." Running a hand through his hair, he continued, "Let's go to the office. I want to check the security feeds and see if they picked up anything that might help."

Chapter Twenty-Two

Déjà vu. Two months ago, he hadn't protected Lexi from a cyber stalker who'd hidden in plain sight.

History will not repeat itself.

In the study, he guided Kaylee to sit on the deep-tufted sofa. Though pale with stress lines about her mouth, she mimicked determination with a stiff posture and steady gaze. It wasn't until he delved within her contemplative regard that the façade she presented proved paper thin. Rapid deterioration of her resolve produced beads of sweat above her lip, pallid skin, and a slight tremble of her chin. Her fertile imagination probably superimposed her face on a mental snapshot of Ciera's body.

Once at his desk, a figurative anchor fell heavy in his stomach, its flukes embedding in the lining. "Son of a bitch." Tiny screws sat in a pile on the calendar. The side of his tower slid off its mooring with the push of a finger. Inside, the hard drive had been removed.

Kaylee hovered over his shoulder. "Jeez, why take your hard drive to prevent us from collecting evidence. Wouldn't it be easier to wear a mask?"

"Yeah, but body height and shape is a little harder to conceal. Point by point analysis would've given us at least something."

"You thinking maybe the husband's girlfriend? Maybe she's connected to all this. She is studying computers."

"Could be. I pegged Conroy for a bully and a coward, but not a killer. Much as I hate to say it, it's possible the girlfriend is connected to the thugs and wanted Ciera out of the way. In taking the hard drives, maybe they figure they've cut all connections with you."

"Both mine and Ciera's computers are missing. At least he didn't get my backup camera."

"Maybe this was a reconnaissance and recovery mission. I'm sorry about losing your work. We'll get you a new laptop. At least Lexi copied the hard drives. My brothers will be camping outside after this charade."

"They love you and want to see you safe. I'll bet anything we get invites to visit with them."

Part of him wanted to whisk Kaylee off to a secluded location—yet that meant hiding—something he'd never done and went against every basic instinct declaring him a man. He'd spent months in the isolated home, not facing his past and reluctant to forge a path ahead. Bringing a vulnerable young woman into his intended fortress and life had made him want to be a better man, one capable of protecting those in his care. In his heart, he knew she dominated increasingly larger portions of his soul, a blending of spirits he couldn't detach, nor would he try.

"No, that's why Matt left Damien. He knew I wouldn't accept anything else. We'll be fine. But it's time to step up our game and take these bastards out."

"Why didn't they stay and ambush us when we came in?"

"Maybe it was the girlfriend, and she just wanted to retrieve evidence."

Matt's brisk arrival preceded Lucas and Billy's striding through the doorway, each bearing equipment from the department. They hadn't gone two steps before demanding all pertinent information.

"Thanks, guys." Caden realized their unspoken show of solidarity and support stemmed from a long history of stubborn awareness and insight.

"No problem. Lucas was on his way over anyway, wanted to bum lunch and hang out for a bit. If Kaylee can't cook, he covered that angle, too. You'd all starve otherwise." Billy quipped.

"He'll bring more food, preprepared or steaks, got you covered regardless of who's fixing the meal." Lucas gave Billy a shoulder nudge before adding. "It's enough for Sunday lunch. *I'll* cook since I'm the only male in the family that can."

"No, Ethan is better. His meals don't taste like roadkill," Billy retorted.

"I'm gonna take Damien out and see what we can pick up, though I don't expect much since your intruder probably wore gloves and we have no scenting object like we did with the first bastard." Matt clipped on the dog leash before heading out the front.

"Let's retrace your steps and make a list of the shop owners you've interviewed and places you've gone." Billy took a seat at the kitchen table.

Caden had already begun. "Either the prick was well-informed or was in a big hurry. They could've waited for our return."

"Maybe they know you're armed and you have a dog." Lucas moved to kneel by Kaylee. "How you holding up, hon?"

"I'm good. Glad the prick at the river wasn't a better shot."

"I'd offer you sanctuary in my home, but Caden would probably release his inner gryphon and slash me to bits. 'Sides, he's one of the best at what he does." Glancing over his shoulder, Lucas added, "You gonna stay here?"

"Yeah. If they found us this fast, they're well organized. At this point, trying to hide would be useless." Caden took in the set of Kaylee's jaw and stiffness of her shoulders. He would keep her safe, regardless of the measures it took.

"All right then," Billy murmured. "Here's an update. Forensics matched DNA on Ciera's T-shirt to you, Caden. But fluids on Ciera matched her husband along with the thug we caught. Her spouse claimed they'd made love the morning before she left, hence we have nothing on him. Looks like the killer raped and strangled her, then dumped her body. Ethan spoke with the family this morning, told them we have one of the shits in custody."

"Are they gonna arrest me?" Caden expected Saunders to stride through the door at any moment.

"Not after tying Vasilisa Sokolov to organized crime and Kirpatzel. The feds are more interested in her for the moment."

"So, we have no DNA on the other perp."

"Not yet. He's been pretty careful so far. We don't know if he's even in the system," Billy looked around as if missing pertinent clues. "There had to be something important on the laptops to want them that bad."

"Maybe they were afraid Ciera found out about Vasilisa?" Kaylee looked to Caden for his opinion.

Lucas stood and ambled to the window overlooking a deep ravine bordering the side yard. "We can ask Lexi to track Ciera's computer. No doubt she planted something amid the software when dubbing the hard drive."

"Her standard protocol." Billy snorted before turning back to Caden.

Further conversation defined their options and highlighted their vulnerabilities. Each decided Kaylee was safest with Caden.

"One more thing." Lucas frowned as he pinched his bottom lip between his teeth. "The first kidnapper died in his cell last night."

"What? How? You didn't think that important enough to share before now?" Caden drew in a slow calming inhalation to combat the rising tide of frustration.

"Don't know how yet, no visible evidence. We figured with the connection to Kaylee broken, they'd no longer be interested in you two."

"Makes sense for them to go after the one we caught. It's overkill to go after a witness who doesn't have further pertinent information...personal even." Caden moved to stand behind Kaylee's chair to gently rub her shoulders. If only he could remove the stain of fear from her aura, evidenced in her hunched posture and shifting gaze.

"Sounds like it. I'm surprised someone didn't use a shiv from a bed's framework." Billy's report received nods from those present.

"Better than honing a petrified ass apple." Lucas' quip received a glare from his brothers.

"He also had a female visitor late last evening," Billy added.

"Gross." Kaylee looked away in disgust. "Do you know if the woman was the banker's girlfriend?"

"No identification yet. Either the lead dog wanted to close ranks, or the kidnapper made a quick enemy. Either is possible," Billy shrugged then added, "Maybe they figured Kaylee is too much trouble since she couldn't identify any others and they'd close ranks on the other end. Maybe they just wanted the computers to see what we had." Conversation drifted through the possibilities of various scenarios.

When Matt returned, he held up a small evidence bag containing a piece of black cloth. "Can't say who it belongs to just yet, but Damien found this." The shepherd, now off lead, padded to Kaylee and sat by her feet. Immediately, she tunneled her fingers through the thick fur.

"Good. We'll see what comes of it." Lucas took the evidence bag and placed it in his case.

"I'd like to think they've given up on me, but the best way to find out and end this is to—" Kaylee turned to look up at Caden.

"Kaylee, do *not* finish that sentence. You are not going to set yourself up as bait." Dread coiled inside Caden's chest, squeezing painfully.

She's already done that by staying with me.

"It would work." Her insistence earned hard stares from each sibling.

"It might also get you killed. We don't know who we're up against. The only reason the feds haven't posted a detail here is because we're family and standing united." Matt's gaze shifted to Caden. "Let us know if you need anything. I want regular updates. Like when Ethan had a problem, the rest of us will be taking turns keeping an eye on the place."

Caden sighed. "Let me show you the coordinates for the trail cams so you can share them with the others." Doubt and reluctance shadowed his thoughts in pursuing his current course. He'd learned long ago that when he didn't know who he was up against, he didn't know which way to run. At least he secured home turf advantage.

For the first time since buying the home, Caden didn't feel paranoid about using the drapes.

Kaylee heaved a quiet sigh after his brothers left, her expression somewhat resigned. "I'm trying to remember what a normal life felt like."

I know just how to distract her.

"We've had a rough day. How about I throw some steaks in the oven, then we can cuddle on the couch and stream a movie."

"Sure. How about a romantic comedy?"

How about an ice pack for my jeans? The more space she took up in his heart, the harder it was to view her as a friend. Speculating on the timing of the next attack, knowing there would be one, kept a lid on his libido.

Chapter Twenty-Three

"Morning." Kaylee yawned and stretched, arching against Caden on the couch. Waking up snuggled against him had become a habit she didn't want to break, although continuance in that comfortable vein wouldn't restore her self-confidence.

Two weeks had passed since the break-in, yet the first stirrings of cabin fever failed to hover among her thoughts. It seemed the bastards who'd hunted her, had given up. Until they'd uncovered more of the conspirators, the brothers had taken turns staking out the house.

"Mhmm." Caden tugged her back against his chest.

Mutual nonverbal agreement declared neither one willing to give up the contact at night and sleep in their own beds. Despite her frustration, he declared them friends until they'd ended the threat. Unfortunately, he took great delight in taunting her with his addictive masculinity and powerful sexuality.

"I'll let Damien out." Not that she wanted to move, at all, but the longer she remained, the harder it was to get up.

Upon hearing his name, the shepherd padded over from his bed in the corner and proceeded to lick her face. "Hmm, yes, boy. I love you too. Let's go."

"Damn. Wish I was a dog."

"According to your brothers, you were the one in high school voted most likely to *not* die while *jacking da stick*."

"Hey, those days are behind me. How about I let the dog out, and you cook breakfast." Caden cracked his finger joints as he moved to stand.

"Sure. You mind if I grab a quick shower first?"

"Help yourself. I'll call Matt and get an update."

A narrowed gaze, crooked grin, and the way his teeth nibbled his lower lip warmed her all the way up the steps and into the cool, man-made waterfall.

The fact he'd woken with morning wood reminded her of the cost of his restraint. That knowledge plus the feel of the hard planes of his chest against her back had fueled her need to take the next step, but his resolve was unshakeable. To exist as the object of his intensely masculine focus, even for a few minutes, softened her determination to move forward with her life when the time came.

He'd declared her on the menu as soon as their threat was over, the interim weeks spent in constant contact solidifying their odd if as yet undefined relationship.

Old habits usually proved hard to break, and his desire for more than just sex might not withstand the test of time. Difficult as Caden was to resist, being discarded when he no longer lusted after her waffled the line over which she couldn't return.

On the other hand, his arms surrounding her during the night had prevented nightmares while his warmth against her body supplemented her dreams. Yes, dreams were a safe zone where she could enjoy all the aspects of his sensual overflow without compromise. For the time being, she needed to switch gears.

Breakfast consisted of French toast, sausage, and steaming, hot coffee. Satisfaction and contentment went hand in hand with the food, allowing them to slip into a companionable silence. Yet Caden's heel gently tapping the tile suggested he withheld something significant.

"Did Matt have any news?" Her father would have chuckled at her impatience.

"Yeah. Lexi digitally tracked the computers to a construction site just west of Portland. The dipshit buried it under the sand but didn't remove the battery, and they recovered it before the workers poured concrete. Looks like someone took a hammer to it instead of reformatting the hard drive."

"Energetically expensive as well as futile. You can't fix stupid." Kaylee removed their dishes and began cleanup.

"No, but you can give it a court date, or a grave marker." In sync as if they'd been together for years, Caden wiped the counters and put away the condiments.

"So it obviously *wasn't* the girlfriend who took it—or she got what she wanted then handed it off to a lackey for disposal." Kaylee tried to fathom the fit of missing threads in her new and confusing life.

"Maybe she disabled the alarm then surfed the computer files before handing stuff over to the shooter, who was slow in disposing of it."

"Unless the thug's *training* has been very specific or perhaps more than one intruder, each with a specific job. As a PI, you have very specific knowledge of computers, yet still go to Lexi for specific searches."

"Forensics matched DNA from the underground prison to another missing girl. The department is reaching out to other agencies to find out more."

"Do you think they intended to sell us into slavery?" Kaylee's stomach churned with the thought of enduring such a fate.

"You may have fallen into the flesh for drugs trade." Caden snagged their empty plates and rinsed them off.

"Jesus, a life for a few highs."

"The man who broke into your rental and died in prison—his autopsy showed signs of long-term drug use. Also, he died from Gelsemium poisoning, AKA heartbreak grass. It only grows in Asia."

"You think Vasilisa is probably involved. Maybe she wanted to cut ties before running. Where is she now?"

"I'm thinking you're right. Apparently, she's vanished without a trace." Caden said.

"Maybe I'm in the clear now?"

"Possibly. The cloth Matt found gave up more evidence. It seems our intruder, or one of them, got snagged by some briars out there. The cloth had dried blood on it—revealed a liver problem. Probably hepatitis B. Trace DNA matched him to a smuggler in the NCIC database."

"Seriously?" Kaylee marveled at the advances in forensic science.

"Yep. We have a name, if not his current alias. We also have some known contacts. By tapping into medical records, they found his liver disease is chronic, and he's taking meds. He's also suffering from mild diabetes. I didn't know those ailments were common among that ethnic population."

"So, they're gonna stake out all the drug stores? How's that gonna work?"

"By limiting the list to those drugstores dispensing particular *combinations* of those medications to a male of that lineage, we narrow the field of possibilities. Regardless of what name he uses presently, it's just a matter of time before we catch him, even if he's running." Caden sat beside her again, taking both her hands within his own.

"So, we just have to wait him out. I can do that." Kaylee let out the breath she hadn't realized she'd held.

"Of course *we* can.

"What makes you think he's using an alias?"

"Matt said there's nothing registered to him as far as license, vehicle, home address, etc. He has zero social media presence despite known associates popping up on several sites."

"So, he might be messaging his buddies using publicly available search engines under a different identity. Wow." Kaylee shivered as Caden gently rubbed her arms.

"Since the investigation stepped into the sphere of a larger authority, we'll have less in the way of updates now—plus the fact you'll be interviewed again by federal agents. I'll be with you."

"Thanks. If my shooter used friends to communicate with my kidnapper after he was caught heading north, they could've relayed messages about your involvement and figured I'd be hiding out here." She couldn't stop the shiver instigated by the memory of being slammed against the wall.

"For all we know, the second guy could've noticed my car with the door hanging open the night his cohort broke into your house. We don't know yet."

"Jeez, what a mess."

"We're gonna get through this, sweetheart. For now, enough talk. Wanna get out of here? We could go visit family or—"

"Actually, I'd love a day to just chill with my sketch pad and veg out on comfort food." She needed a day that screamed normal.

"A day of chilling on the couch it is then."

"What about you? Aren't you missing work?"

"I'm okay for a bit. I also got a call from Ciera's parents—said they were sorry for not calling sooner. Can you believe it? With all they're going through? At least they have closure after the shock of losing their daughter."

"They expected you to find her—alive."

"They did. But now they want the partner. They felt guilty over their son pointing fingers at me. I don't think anyone in that situation can understand such senseless violence. But we wouldn't have any information if not for you. You've been the key to it all."

It was a moment where she searched to clarify a situation comprising myriad and muddied fragments. Failure came at the hands of too many facets, viewable from infinite angles where each one led to equally ludicrous conclusions.

"She meant a lot to you. Ciera." Had Caden and Ciera shared the depth of connection she now relished?

"Yes, at one time. But we never related on a deep emotional level. We were both fun loving and adventurous. I think she was a little brasher and rougher around the edges."

"You and I have a bond I've never shared with another person. Why?"

"A combination of circumstances, history, and chemistry. I was in the right place at the right time, and we reconnected. I've never thought of a woman as a partner—until I met you. You're fiercely protective of those you care about, loyal, strong-willed, all the things that push my buttons."

Indomitable intensity swelled within his gaze. Beneath the cultivated message delivered, he withheld a deeper, illusive implication. One that promised she'd never be the same and leave her heart as ash in the wind.

Passion simmered in his heavy-lidded gaze, flaring with the cadence of his words and each soft step closer. Inches apart, separated by worlds as his warm breath fanned over her cheek. His look, so intense, she startled when his fingers traced a line over her forehead and down the bridge of her nose, a gesture which accompanied his look of awe.

A lock of inky-black hair fell over his forehead. She couldn't help but brush it out of the way, leaving the crystal-blue stare to delve into the depths of her soul, searching, dissecting her emotions. The slow rasp of his lowered voice raked her smoldering libido until she thought she might climax from his slightest touch.

"You're dangerous." Her unchecked utterance filtered back through her mind to strangle the tattered remnants of her equanimity.

When he moved closer and molded her body to his, she couldn't find the strength to step away. The atmosphere's slightest micro currents whispered across her neck and dissolved any hesitation with the intent written in the curving of his body around hers, the light grazing of his touch down her spine before his large hand molded her ass. She closed her eyes and let her head tilt back with the touch of his finger under her chin.

"I can't wait any longer. I've tried." He brushed his lips across her forehead before nuzzling the erogenous zone behind her ear.

The colossal sensitivity weakened her knees. Those words were as much forewarning as he'd give, advance notice that he'd ravage her mind, body, and soul. Self-preservation should have forced her to step away. In time, she might look back with regret.

To conjure rational thought with his warm breath fanning over her face rivaled an exercise in futility. She'd scale this mountain that was Caden McAllister and scream her pleasure from the peak, regardless of how far she'd fall.

Hot and cold, wet and dry, safe and forbidding, all that and more brought her thoughts to a stuttering halt. Instinct took over, accepting his advances and upping the ante with her fingers raking down his back.

"Tell me to stop." His voice grated through her body and the tender flesh of her thighs as if searing them with his volcanic touch.

"I can't." Raw, primal, sheet-clawing need ripped through her chest.

The thought of tearing off his shirt, listening to the buttons plink to the floor, then exploring the broad expanse of his muscled chest gave rise to a wave of heat spreading from her belly outward.

"Caden." She couldn't manage more before he sealed his mouth over hers, his tongue delving inside to twine with hers and explore the recesses and reactions. Weakening legs bred embarrassment until he lifted her up with a gravelly mandate. "Lock your legs around my waist."

Answering his command generated more heat as he ground himself against her. How could he be self-possessed when she was melting under his burning advance?

She moaned.

He growled.

"I want you to be sure, Kaylee."

She merely nodded before he bent to take her lips once more. The melding of flesh to flesh, spirit to spirit, and soul to soul, sculpted a new unseen entity where she would never experience uncertainty in his desire or intention. The potency of his gaze declared he was playing for keeps.

Everything in her body tightened, responding to his knowledgeable touch, the master of her emotions that owned every aspect of her being.

The button-down he wore took too long to open. Desperation provided the impetus to rip the plastic discs from their moorings and scatter them abroad. His chuckle only inflamed her lust.

Somewhere between laying her flat and covering her body with his own, their clothes lay scattered on the floor. Insignificant details blurred in favor of concentrating on the calloused pads of his fingers scraping over sensitized skin, inflaming her hunger to the point of pain.

"Please, Caden. Now." She let her hands drift over the bunching muscles in his shoulders, the ripples as he moved heightening her need for exploration over his sweat-dampened skin.

"Aw, darlin', we have a long way to go. Settle in and enjoy." The rip of a foil packed flagged his attention to detail.

She didn't know whether to laugh or scream, deciding instead on a groan when his fingers feathered along her lower curls. Despite the burning need inside, she wanted to feel him in her hand, stroke him to a fevered pitch before succumbing to what she knew would be the ultimate, mind-blowing release. When her touch slid down his flank and homed in on her destination, he simply slid down her body.

"Not yet, sweetheart."

Warm, moist breath heated her chest and bathed her nipples before his strong suckle arched her back in pleasure. Breath came in quiet gasps, quickening as he moved from one peak to the other. His fingers negated cool air from encompassing her breasts as he molded with one hand while suckling the other needy peak. Her hips took up the rhythm of his tongue, imagination supplying the missing sensations he'd create in her sheath.

His gaze held her immobile as he retrieved a foil from his wallet on the floor. In that split second, an epiphany rocked her soul. He didn't just want to *send* her to paradise and take his release, he wanted their joint exploration to be synchronous, a sharing of Nirvana. The bond they'd formed delved deeper, excising pain and replacing it with passion and devotion, tenderness, and respect. All the things she couldn't voice radiated from him in waves that encompassed them, cocooning her mind and soothing her fears.

He'd give her the ultimate release, an experience she'd never regret, yet hold tight in the recesses of her mind for eternity. His strength, his passion, his commitment was written in his gaze.

When her heart rate slowed and she could breathe again, words failed to pass her parched throat.

After several long seconds, his incredible mass of spent muscle and masculinity relaxed into her, drained of energy. Every part of her body tingled. Every muscle ached in a way she knew she'd forever crave.

"Wow," she whispered against his neck.

"Back at ya, sweetheart."

He raised up to grin at her. Underneath the passion, their bond flared, stronger, tangible with the lightest graze of his lips on her forehead.

"You could end me doing that." She'd never felt such peace. No words existed to convey the depth of her feelings. If she never again reached that pinnacle above all peaks, she would still remember it as the one experience that couldn't be topped. The peace and serenity etched in his expression declared the same.

"Hmm. I can't think of a better way to go, but I think we can get away with a lot more of this before we have to worry about heart failure."

"You don't hold back, do you?"

"Nope. Matter of fact—How about a shower?"

"How about a jump start?"

The deep-seated tranquility which followed could never be duplicated. There was only one *first time* with a man. The ensuing cuddle time cemented her heart's desire. She would forever want and need Caden in her life, in whatever capacity he'd afford.

"Next time, I want you in bed." His declaration carried the promise of a man with insatiable appetites.

"Next time, I want an energy bar beforehand."

Chapter Twenty-Four

The only thing better than waking up with Kaylee in his bed would be waking up with Kaylee snuggled against him minus the whining dog crushing the moment's sense of perfection. Each morning for the past three days, he'd roused her for some morning delight, captivated by her enthusiasm for lovemaking. For in his heart, he was falling for her with a finality that declared there could be no other to reach his soul, soothe with a look, or burn him to embers with a touch.

"What's going on? It's not even light out." With one arm slung across his chest and her head on his shoulder, she huffed a warm sigh across his neck.

Predawn light had not yet slipped around the curtain's edges. Maybe the timing wasn't inconvenient after all. *She's up, I'm up. Might as well make the best use of the moment.*

As he reached for his cell to check the time, Damien bounded out the door and raced down the hall. Low snarls and threatening growls morphed into angry barking as his toenails clicked down the hardwood. At the same time, the insistent buzz of his security alarm sounded.

"Kaylee, up and dressed, now. We've got uninvited company." Caden surged to his feet while snatching up the phone. "Don't turn on the lights. It'll mess up your night vision."

"Got it." Fear and anxiety twined in her tremulous voice. Behind her, a nightlight backlit her jerky preparation for trouble.

Lucas' face appeared on the now-bright screen, the dramatic ring tone mocking the current situation. "Lucas? Where are you?" If not for the curtains covering most of two walls in the room, they'd be as fish in an aquarium.

"Fifty yards north, on the ridge. You've got incoming. Count unknown. I've seen two, one on a trail cam. I rolled one down the ravine in plastic cuffs. Backup's on the way."

"Shit. We'll stay upstairs for the best vantage point. Don't come inside. Kaylee's armed too."

"Right. If you have to leave, head toward the road. Ethan will be waiting."

After disconnecting, Caden punched in the emergency number on the digital keypad by the door to silence the alarm. A glance down the hall afforded him the view of the open staircase. Anyone ascending could be easily picked off. The open area was clear.

Despite Kaylee's proof of marksmanship, he wouldn't risk a sibling or officer stepping into her line of fire. Panic altered one's aim. Glancing back, he noted her dressed and opening the gun case after snatching it from under the bed. Though her hands shook, a stiffened frame declared her ready if not capable.

From his closet, he fumbled before yanking out his old Kevlar vest. "Here, put this on." He sensed her quick jerky movements, not surprised with her inefficiency or grumbled answer.

"What about you? Do you have another?" Soft swearing filled the room with her frustration.

"No. I'm not their target. We've got at least two intruders, probably more. We'll stay holed up here until reinforcements arrive." Caden pulled on his clothes while keeping an eye on the door.

"How long?

"Lucas is outside, the rest, probably fifteen minutes." The sound of glass shattering below flagged the first intruder's entrance. The hallway upstairs was clear, giving him a bird's eye view of the kitchen and part of the great room. A rock used to break the glass of his back door thudded against the kitchen island before the invader's gloved hand pushed past the curtain to thumb the lock open.

As Damien lunged at the fingers groping for the knob, Caden placed two rounds where he expected to hit center mass. *Pay dirt.* The arm jerked back accompanied by a bellow of pain.

A thin whine next to him swiveled his abbreviated gaze to his charge. Sweat dotted Kaylee's brow, but her gun hand was steady. She'd proven herself a survivor and able to fight back. He prayed she'd withstand the current mental pressure.

"I'll watch the stairway. Stay behind me and keep an eye on the curtains. Shoot any shadow that moves. They won't be friendlies."

Few young women faced circumstances necessitating fighting for their lives. He'd no doubt she'd pull the trigger. Consequences would come later.

"Damien, come. Now!" The dog obeyed yet snarled his displeasure up the steps.

Once in the room, Kaylee gripped the dog's collar to hold him in place. Damien's rigid stance, snarling, and exposed teeth, expressed unmitigated anger.

From somewhere downstairs, more glass shattered. Damien barked.

"Sounds like they're coming in from the office. They'll probably enter from the back, too. Watch the curtains."

A minute passed, lights flooded the downstairs. The thugs remained under the balcony and unseen. *Why would they turn on the lights? What are they waiting for?*

"Send the little bitch out, and I won't burn down your house, Caden. You got two minutes." Grit and a steadfast resolve laced the heavily accented ultimatum. "The only reason you're not already burning is cuz I want that cunt alive. She's cost me both a partner and valuable merchandise."

The voice didn't ring any bells of recognition. The dipshit had done his homework in approaching from a blind corner that negated the possibility of a shot. The only hope included stalling for time until reinforcements arrived.

"Walk away from this. She hasn't seen your face."

"I don't leave loose ends. Send her down or die with her. Your choice, for the next sixty seconds."

"Is that why you had your partner killed?" Amid the threat and attempted stall, Caden needed to obtain information to follow the criminal food chain. The prick had no reason to lie.

"He was too stupid to survive. Would've talked eventually."

"Interpol already has a line on your ass. You're wasting time here when you should be running."

"You're full of shit and stalling. They got nothing on me. And your time's up."

The silence was deafening.

Movement to his side snapped his gaze to Kaylee.

"I'm gonna check to see if the balcony's clear." Kaylee's grip in the dog's fur diminished her shake.

She'd taken one step before he grasped her upper arm and hauled her back. "No. They'll be looking for that. Stay here."

He'd do anything to wipe the fear from her gaze. Like oil floating on water, her layers ran deep, separate, and complex. There were no words of assurance. He couldn't lie. Their chance of survival diminished with each frantic heartbeat.

The connection they'd formed allowed him into her deepest motivations, understanding her need to protect as well as assert dominance over her life. Kidnappers had stripped her confidence then murdered a stranger she'd promised to help. Now, in her eyes, a need for revenge surged. Retaliation wasn't justice and would stain her soul. He briefly mourned the loss of innocence.

Stealthy movements downstairs defied definition as he tried to form a mental picture of their furtive actions. Compelling them to talk at least gave him their location.

"We got your DNA from your last visit in the woods. Only a matter of time before you're nailed. Give it up now and save yourself a bullet in the head."

More glass shards hitting the floor defined another angle of entry from below. Another approach he wouldn't see coming until they stepped farther into the great room or to the stairway. "How's the stomach feeling? Bet you're tired and achy." A friend who'd suffered through hepatitis had complained of those symptoms.

The subsequent sounds propelled a sour wad of dread to his throat. He met Kaylee's gaze and saw stark terror. Sloshing. Someone poured a liquid.

"You smell that? It's gas. They're gonna burn us alive." Tears tracked down her cheeks. "There's no reason for us both to die. They must have at least one man posted at the corner of the house to keep us from getting out. They've waited weeks to plan this." After laying her gun down, she stood, searching his eyes for either permission or strength to do what she felt right.

"Hell, no. Not gonna happen." Caden wrapped one arm around her waist and pulled her tight, his grip letting her know she wasn't going anywhere.

The sound of breaking glass behind him coupled with the pop of gunfire from the stairway didn't alarm him as much as the faint smell of smoke wafting up from the first floor. Instead of poking holes in the glass with bullets, the intruder on the balcony had used something solid to break it.

Kaylee wrenched free and scooped up her gun, aiming toward the side wall of windows and glass doors. Thick shades obscured all but the outline of her target yet didn't stop her from firing. "Screwy bastards. You may get me, but I'll take at least one of you along for the ride."

Caden hurled his own leaded response down the stairs.

"I think I got him." Frenetic shaking of her gun hand defied the prospect of a true aim. Within seconds, her entire body shook.

Wood splintering by his head snapped his attention to the hallway. The hiss of the bullet's passing kicked his adrenaline rush into overdrive. He traded shots with a masked man taking cover behind the stairs. His own bullet thudded in the stair tread. Matt's verbal lashing circled his thoughts.

Calm and concentrate.

He'd just taken aim when the intruder pivoted with the simultaneous bark from a pistol, his body bucking forward into the spindles then falling to the floor. The crimson stain blooming on his back would soon coagulate from the growing heat.

Lucas was on the back porch.

Faint tendrils of flame licked along the hardwood downstairs, gaining height and speed with every heartbeat. In minutes, it would climb the stairs. Air filled with toxic chemicals and particulate matter, expanding, rising to the cathedral ceiling and flowing like a menacing cloud. Visibility would soon be nil while smoke and carbon monoxide stole precious oxygen.

"There's one down, Caden, but I can't put out the fire. It has you blocked off from the front. Go out the back or side." Lucas sacrificed his position to deliver the warning. Thickening smoke decreased visibility and obscured the origins from subsequent rounds fired.

Knowing his brother would circle around to add cover fire, Caden focused on retreat. Glass defined one wall of the room while shards littered the floor between supports on the other. Kaylee's shooter's stance remained rigid as she waited for a target to appear from behind the billowing curtains. "I think I hit one but don't know if he's dead or even on the balcony.

"We don't have time to wait. We have to go." Nudging her weapon down and Kaylee behind him, Caden opened fire to mark a horizontal strafe along the remaining glass. Loud crackling preceded large chunks crunching to the balcony floor. He reloaded and pocketed an extra magazine from the bedside table.

A brisk wind had kicked up and blew the curtains inside, waving from nature's blown raspberry. With no visual confirmation of a hit, he had no idea if he was about to step out and inherit targeted lead or just a light breeze. Damien's growled warning mixed with intermittent whining mimicked his concern.

"We should separate, each take a side." Kaylee pulled her T-shirt over her mouth and nose to filter smoke.

"No. You follow me. We stay together." Gripping her hand, he added. "Be ready to fire but watch what you're shooting. Lucas is out there and circling around to us. I don't know how much company we've attracted. By my count, there's at least two more."

Flames already crept along the south decking when he peered out in search of immediate threats. Extreme heat and smoke choked his thoughts and cut off one avenue of escape.

The staccato beat of firecrackers below confused him until realizing the blaze had found his stored ammunition. Multiple mini-explosions cloaked any shots fired by the enemy. Though the assassins wouldn't have stayed inside the burning inferno, they might've been in range to take a hit. His brother should realize the need to steer clear.

Friendly fire will kill just as fast.

Vague movement off the home's north corner snapped his gaze to a black-clad form running for the wood line.

Lucas? Distance and a hunched posture defied identification. *Damn!*

If he jumped directly off the balcony, he'd risk taking a stray shot from his own ammo supply, not knowing if fire had finished consuming both gun cabinets. Shifting their jump-off point toward the corner of the house might leave them more exposed to remaining gunmen and risked the balcony floor giving way beneath them.

"After you land, keep low and behind me. I'm gonna jump first with Damien. You stay to my right. Nail anything that fires at me." Using his body was the only protection he could offer. Sweat glazed both their faces with second-story visibility narrowing to mere inches.

"I'll cover your back." Kaylee stepped out from behind him.

Knowing they had minutes to escape, he couldn't take time to clear the way. The floor under his feet shook, the ominous creaking a forewarning of imminent disaster. Thick clouds of smoke engulfed the entire structure, which denied visibility between himself and the tree line. Gunfire from killers or his own store of ammunition exploded rapid-fire as he visualized flames spreading through his den. He was out of options.

Tucking his gun in his waistband, Caden scooped Damien up in his arms and threw one leg over the balcony. "Climb up, Kaylee. Tuck and roll when you land, then head to the trees for cover. Don't hesitate and don't look back." He didn't need to tell her to have gun in hand, or that she'd land among glass and burning embers.

Caden waited until she'd straddled the wooden railing before leaping as far as he could. Damien's violent struggle against his hold hindered a controlled landing as his bulk negated flexibility. A combination of whine and growl erupted from the dog's throat.

Heat seared Caden's back and head with the flames shooting through the cleared space of the once-spacious windows.

Free fall and a prayer.

A second of panic.

Pain shot through his right ankle and up his leg on landing. Twisting his body to the side to not land on Damien yielded more searing pain along his left shoulder from glass shards and burning debris. A gasp imported smoke to seize his lungs in a coughing fit.

The dog yelped as it scrambled for balance and away from the living wall of fire. Visibility increased slightly but night vision was shit between the smoke irritating his eyes and the ever-increasing flames engulfing his home.

Beside him, Kaylee's landing manifested in a thin cry before she rolled to her feet and snatched her gun from her back waistband. "You okay?"

"Yeah, just rolled over something hot. I think—" Before she could finish, her body bucked forward from the force of a shot. The angle of impact indicated the dirtball fired from the north.

"Kaylee!"

Her legs crumpled even as her arms grasped for his shoulders. Sweat and pain glazed her eyes, both heightened by the burning inferno.

Damien growled his rage, bolting north through the glass and smoking debris. A stream of yelps indicated his acknowledgment of painful footing.

Scooping her up, he couldn't risk assessing the damage until finding cover. Even retrieving her gun would cost precious seconds he couldn't afford. Time a shooter could use to end them both. He prayed the vest took the hit and would leave her with only a bruise or broken rib.

Flying embers danced in the breeze flowing toward the road, a dazzling display of chaos. Ash covered the ground while cinders died out after contacting dew-laden grass. Despite moisture on the ground, hundreds of acres of forest would be razed if the fire departments didn't respond quickly.

Damien's fury roared above the fire. Smoke would obliterate his tracking ability and make him more vulnerable.

Another shot kicked up dirt as Caden raced for the woods. He'd never been a man of prayer, but with Kaylee's life at stake, he offered a silent supplication in their bid for safety.

An exchange of bullets with none striking his vicinity indicated a second shooter had joined the fight. *Lucas providing cover.*

"Damien, come!" Distant snarling growls gained volume as the shepherd returned and kept pace beside them. Behind a large oak, he took refuge while praying Kaylee's body armor bore the lead intended to snuff out her life.

Kneeling down, he laid her out on a thick carpet of leaves. The fact she stirred against him and was regaining consciousness bolstered his spirits. Her groan preceded a frantic, uncoordinated effort to gain her feet. "Let me up. I can run. Vest shot."

"Hold a sec and catch your bearings. I have an exit strategy." Within seconds, his searching yielded the smashed bullet wedged in the material. An inch lower and he might have been saying goodbye.

Now the vest was weakened and might not protect her from another hit. "We're gonna slip through the woods a short distance then run for the gulley. It lies perpendicular to the road and will gives us some cover, but we'll have to climb out about two-thirds the way down. There's a bunch of brush piled up. We can hightail it through the woods till we come to the end of the lane. Ethan will be waiting for us."

"They won't be expecting us to do that?"

"Doubtful. Even if they do, they won't expect us to climb out before the end unless they've thoroughly scouted the property." Caden scanned the surroundings before continuing. "The wooded area extends for miles and offers more refuge. Unfortunately, we don't know how many of the shits are here nor their whereabouts."

Chapter Twenty-Five

The roar and heat of the fire had diminished with distance, but smoke permeated everything. Ambient light highlighted the evidence of their struggle in dirt smudging her face and the smoky aroma worn like a halo.

As expected, she rolled to all fours then stood while gingerly twisting side to side in testing for injury. "I'm good to go." Her wince when stretching to the right cited minor damage. Protection from a bullet's penetration didn't equate lack of pain. At the very least, she'd have some bruising.

Lucas knew they'd head toward the road, but understanding his older brother wouldn't give up the fight weighed heavy on his mind. There was a time to engage an enemy and a time to step back and assess. Lucas rarely knew where to draw the line.

A few hours ago, he'd lain sated with Kaylee in his arms. Now, with each heartbeat, he expected a bullet to drop them in their race for survival. "Hunch over when you run for the ditch. You'll make a smaller target."

The wild mass of hair swirling around her face gave the appearance of an avenging angel, but its movement in the breeze would act as a beacon. Gently, he finger-combed it to remove bits of glass and debris. Lightly twisting it into a rope, he tucked it under her vest. "There's a lot of briars in here."

Caden turned and peered through the murky shadows, avoiding the pull to survey his once-beautiful home. A glance in that direction would cost him precious night vision.

With the support of his hand at her elbow, he urged her through the thick brush. They had about thirty yards to go before breaking cover in a run for the ravine. Thorns tore at their shirts and jeans. Twice, he stopped to listen then assess Kaylee's stamina.

Until several months ago, he'd never contemplated his own death. Flashes of Ciera's lifeless body resting in a shallow grave urged him to move faster.

When in open ground once more, he resisted the urge to carry his greatest treasure. Expecting the biggest threat to come from his right, he kept Kaylee on his left, using his body as a barrier.

At the edge of the ravine, he helped her down, each sliding among the leaf litter, twigs, and other debris. Twenty yards at a steep angle passed quickly but sheltered them from anyone waiting farther ahead in the woods.

"Listen, this gulley is a bit rough traveling. Step carefully, there's lots of holes. It also shallows out in places so stay low. These bastards will probably have someone waiting close to the end. When we near the pile of limbs and a fallen tree, we'll climb out on the other side. From there, we'll cut across toward the lane." It was the best impromptu plan he could devise. "Close your eyes while you catch your breath. It'll help you adapt to the lower light quicker."

"I'm good. Let's move. I'll follow." Her words came out in a harsh whisper.

Years of playing cops and robbers with four siblings followed by years in the department supported his assumption of how and from where his other brothers would converge. For now, he needed to get Kaylee to safety.

The roar of the fire receded with their steady pace along the ravine's bottom while small rocks and fallen branches granted treacherous footing. With his gun in one hand, he scanned the ridges ahead on both sides. The orange inferno prevented him from assessing the rear, but the probability of thugs hanging around after their initial attempt to capture Kaylee seemed unlikely.

Scattered clouds filtered patchy moonlight to give him glimpses of their path while jagged terrain graded downhill until they reached a small patch of marshy ground. When he'd first walked the property before purchasing, there'd been a small pool of water from melted snow. Beyond it, piled limbs provided a home and limited protection for a family of woodrats.

When he stopped, Kaylee bumped into him.

"Sorry," she whispered.

"It's okay. From here, we go up the other side. Once we reach the tree line, the wooded path we'll take is thick with briars, but there's a few deer trails that'll make it easier going."

Shadows covered her face, but her emotions radiated loud and clear. He could have lost her in the fire or to some prick's bullet to the head, yet here she stood, next to him, determined to do whatever necessary to survive.

"Caden, I..."

Like minds came together as they closed the distance and his lips covered hers. Insanity surrounded them in the distant roar of the blaze and the uncertainty of their future, but he claimed that minute in time, giving and taking with a hunger he'd never quench. Background sounds were little more than a nuisance as they each conveyed without words, what roiled inside them.

When she pulled back and opened her eyes, he knew in that instant what he'd always lacked in a relationship. A union that could bind for eternity and withstand a nuclear explosion. All they had to do was persevere and outmaneuver the bastards after them.

Her petite hand cupping his cheek held him in thrall. How could one small woman capture his heart in such a short time?

"Thank you...for everything."

Two souls merged as one, the bridge forged by tragedy, determination, and a fervent desire for healing, then fortified by trust and mutual attraction. It was all etched in the touch of her hand and the depth of love in her gaze.

"Once we're on the trail, we'll head east. Stay close. We'll keep Damien tight, but with all the smoke in the air, I don't know how effective he'll be."

She nodded. "I'm ready."

Climbing out proved a more difficult endeavor with a steeper angle and little to use for hand or footholds. Twice he sensed her slip yet scramble faster to keep up.

Near the top, he took a minute to survey the surrounding area for any movement, anything out of place before they broke cover.

Once she caught her breath, they'd run the short distance to the woods, then a few minutes of trails until reaching the road and Ethan. Cool air skimmed his forehead while the moon's luminescence revealed what he sought.

Their path would take them back to the road adjoining his driveway. With all that Kaylee had been through, he prayed she'd hold up long enough to clear their current predicament. The few seconds taken for her to rest allowed him to again scan for movement, danger. To his right, Damien whined his confusion. Whether from the threat already faced or a new one couldn't be determined.

Meager light painted targets on their backs while he scouted their path. Thirty yards to the woods seemed infinite. When Kaylee signaled her readiness, he pointed to their destination. "See the two tallest oaks ahead? That's where we're going. Once inside the woods—follow me and keep low. If Damien starts a racket, you drop to the ground and stay there."

Again, she nodded.

In the distance, headlights from two vehicles slewing around the last curve to the house bolstered his confidence. Crowding trees made a strobe of their lights. *Matt and Billy. Lucas will update them. Ethan should be at the end of the lane.*

Setting his gun aside, he cupped his hands and imitated the song of a whip-poor-will. After several repetitions, an answering song behind them signaled Lucas was safe.

Ethan would be combing the edge of the woods by the road, and like himself, unaware of who or how many might be waiting. Again, he cupped his hands and imitated a birdsong. Seconds later and from the road's direction, another answer.

"That's Ethan. He knows we're here and he's in the woods."

"How do you know it's Ethan?" Kaylee's doubt rode her furrowed brow.

"Four calls, four brothers. 'Sides, he can't carry a tune any better than he can fix a car."

Sirens in the distance signaled the approach of emergency vehicles, which meant his shooters would probably cut and run. Still, he wouldn't take the chance they'd wait close by for Kaylee's return until emergency personnel flooded the area. Ethan would have parked on the road not far from his lane, a better gamble.

A thunderous noise from behind signaled the roof of his home crashing down. A crueler twist of fate would have yielded himself and Kaylee's charred remains buried there.

With his gun in one hand and Kaylee's shaking fingers in the other, they raced for the woods. Each step equaled a lifetime of dread where some unknown bastard permanently ripped Kaylee from his grasp.

Sudden movement in the shadows ahead outlined a large male form stepping clear of low lying brush. Caden's worldview narrowed to focus on the man squaring off with his feet shoulder width apart, thin shafts of moon glow glinting off a gun barrel. It seemed fate wasn't finished jerking them around.

Halfway there and caught in the open, he skidded to a stop. Kaylee stumbled to a halt then froze. Damien's barking began as a throaty growl then morphed into a menacing threat.

"Damien, stay." Caden's command was obeyed, grudgingly.

Fifteen yards to the relative safety of the woods. Fifteen. Freaking. Yards.

Instinct aimed his barrel at the intruder's chest. Beside him, Kaylee's thin whine was barely audible.

Dressed in black, the barrel-chested asshole wearing a mask and gloves, chuckled. "I'd hate to shoot a dog, but I will have my due. Now drop your weapon." If bravado and contempt held human form, the thug would be its shell. His harsh laughter ended with a *tsk, tsk*.

"Damien, quiet." Caden could end the prick, but not prevent him from killing Kaylee in that split second it took to pull the trigger. Panic swelled when Kaylee's grip relaxed, and she tugged her hand free. Instinctively, he grasped her arm, knowing her intentions when she took a deep breath.

She twisted free, leaving Caden to grasp thin air.

"Kaylee, no." He didn't need to see the tears trailing her cheeks to comprehend their presence.

"I won't see you or Damien hurt because of me." She widened the distance between them. Turning to the gunman, she added, "I don't recognize your voice."

"No matter. You'll soon learn to recognize all of me." White teeth contrasted the surrounding black mask, the killer's grin bearing nothing but malice. "I've waited a long time for this. You've cost me the entire setup here. Relocating is gonna be expensive. Lucky I'll have a pretty little puss to keep my dick warm." Sneering at Caden, he added. "I heard you'd be trouble but didn't realize how much. I can't find two of my buddies, though I heard your brother shout that one's dead."

Damien's initial ruckus might bring backup if heard over the fire's commotion. *But not in time.* Caden would rather die than know Kaylee suffered Ciera's fate. "So, you've done your homework." Caden sidestepped toward Kaylee only to have her move toward the killer and block his shot. *She's trying to protect me.*

"C'mon bitch. I've got a car stashed, and we have a ways to travel. I was beginning to think I wouldn't get you alive, but this *is* a bonus for work well done."

When she stood within arm's reach, he fisted his hand in her hair and jerked her forward. Turning her around, he leered down and gave Caden a show of what lay in her future. Several tugs loosened the hook-and-loop straps securing her bulletproof vest. A harsh yank and he tossed it to the ground.

Skimming a hand over her shirt, he gave a deep hum of pleasure. Kaylee's knees buckling resulted in her captor tightening his hold. She cried out as the ham-sized fist squeezed her breast. It must've cost the last of her reserves not to struggle.

Leaning down, he spoke in her ear loud enough for Caden to hear the details of his plan. Her gaze dropped to the ground in defeat while starlight highlighted the tears on her face.

In reversed circumstances, Caden would shoot the dog to prevent tracking. Once inside the obscurity of the woods, chances were fair they wouldn't be found.

As if thought brought action, the killer's gun swung toward Damien.

Simultaneous events occurred. Kaylee twisted her hips to the side and slammed her fist into the scum's groin. Contact brought an instant buckling and loosened grip around her chest along with his pain-filled howl. Her enraged shriek coincided with her twisting down and to the left.

Caden fired. The first shot bit into the bastard's shoulder, the second struck him in the face. His body flew backward, dead before hitting the ground.

Kaylee stumbled forward and dry-heaved.

The negligible interval between one heartbeat and the next in getting to her side was eternal. Had their timing been off or any of a hundred other factors occurred, he could have lost her forever.

He did his best to hold loose strands of hair back while supporting her shoulders until short gasping breaths slowed and sobs quieted. She turned into his embrace.

"You okay? We can't stay here in the open like this. There may be more pricks lurking about." Precious seconds passed while he held her, smoothing his hands over her trembling frame before she quieted.

"I'm good to go."

Her body shook so hard she'd never walk the distance to the car, and he couldn't carry her through the narrow briar-filled paths quietly. With more first responders filling the yard around his home, his best option was to return. "In the gully and back to the house. We've got reinforcements." As he spoke, another fire truck and squad car cut the night with their stroboscopic red and blue lights. His driveway and front yard would be full.

There'd be no salvaging the house, yet his priorities remained intact while he protected the most important treasure of his home. Kaylee. Helping her descend the moderate chasm rendered a loosening of the vice gripping his chest. At least they had cover.

His next bird sound imitated the quark of a night heron. Only those combing the edge of the woods might hear him. "They'll know it's us coming." His brothers were careful, but announcing his return meant they'd warn other officers of his approach.

Helping her retrace their steps, he kept the pace slow, despite the urgent need to check on his siblings. Regardless of her inner strength, every woman had her limit. Kaylee had surpassed hers. Dirt-smudged tears and shoulder-drooping weariness revealed the heaviness in her heart branching out to encompass her aura.

"I'm sorry, Caden. I have no words—" She stopped and scanned the blaze ahead. Only the upper portion of the burning inferno manifested above the gully's ridge. Bright plumes of smoke and leaping jagged flames shot skyward in a choreographed sequence befitting a pyromaniac's wet dream. The hard slope of earth blocked the full-shock value while the aftereffects, flame, smoke, and soaring embers remained visible from their viewpoint.

Her body shook as he stopped and turned to face her. "Hey, we're not going there. Ever. Got it? You're safe. I'm safe. Damien's safe." He hadn't heard from Lucas and prayed his brother was unscathed.

"But you've lost everything."

"No. I *have* everything in my hands. As we speak." Slowly, he framed her face with his palms and bent to kiss her forehead, then her closed eyes, before nibbling at her lips, slow and thorough. Her tears mingled with the sweet taste of Kaylee, soft and warm against him.

The feel of her arms circling his waist and holding him tight was all he needed in that split second of time. The strength derived therein would bolster their depleted reserves. He should have been better prepared, maybe taken her out of state. He knew how to hide a witness. Stubborn pride had almost cost them both their lives.

Even with other possible gunmen unaccounted for, Caden had no choice but to tuck his gun in his waistband to carry her back. He doubted any surviving thugs would hang around with so many cops present, hence taking the time to pick his path along the treacherous bottom presented small risk. Ahead, thick clouds of orange smoke surged into the sky as a reminder of what he *almost* lost. Once he reached a point of climbing the slope, Kaylee tapped his shoulder.

"I'm okay now. I can scramble up the side." Squirming to get down, she straightened her shirt and wiped her face with a dirty sleeve. Adorably smudged was a sexy look.

The full ramifications of their situation struck like a lightning bolt once he stood on the ridge. All his memories, pictures, every precious item that had remained boxed—gone.

The remoteness of his location increased the fire department's response time and assured the total destruction of his possessions. With so much glass, all blown out in the fire's early stages, flames both inside and out received plenty of oxygen for fuel. Containment was the goal, protecting the surrounding environment.

Even so, they'd done what they had to do to survive. The rest—he could replace, rebuild, or cherish in his memories.

Ahead, several silhouettes stood in bold relief beside one of the fire trucks. Recognizable despite his limp, Lucas broke off his conversation with a fireman and headed toward them. "Where the hell have you been? I figured you'd cross paths with Ethan, Matt, or Billy. They're searching for more of your obnoxious guests." A wad of cloth banded his thigh.

"You all right?"

"Yeah, fine. Just a scratch." Lucas made a vague hand gesture indicating his leg.

"We ran across the Asian. He's dead. There's at least one more on the loose. I think he was wounded and headed for the woods." Caden tried to extract any details from his chaotic thoughts that might aid in identification.

"No, Billy and Matt rounded him up. Uniforms are escorting him to the hospital. I'm guessing you didn't think to grab your phone?" Lucas stepped closer to Kaylee, visually inspecting her for signs of injury. "You okay, hon?"

"Must've lost it when I jumped. And she's fine." Caden wrapped a protective arm around her shoulders.

"Thank God. It's finally over. We're free." Her small sob was the beginning of the storm of tears she'd held back.

Waving Lucas away, Caden turned her flush against his chest and held her tight. "It's okay, sweetheart. We're safe. I've got ya." Tears dampened his shirt, yet her warmth filled his soul.

Time ceased to matter. He held everything within his grasp. The comfort of her embrace evoked images of something he'd never wanted, a wife and kids, with all the trials and tribulations involved. She'd gone through tremendous heartache and had yet to gain her feet. Convincing her not to pull up stakes again in search of safer ground might be difficult.

Minutes later, Matt strode toward them, his gaze locking on and assessing. Ethan and Billy flanked him. Damien whined as he padded over and sat at Matt's feet.

"Everybody in one piece?" The first tentative rays of sunlight streamed over Matt's shoulder as he reached to brush Kaylee's arm.

Determination and pride turned her gaze to meet him. "We're good."

"She's fine. Just shaken and a little banged up." Caden stroked Kaylee's hair.

"Amazing, considering she probably had to protect your sorry ass. That's gotta get tiring." Lucas smiled at his brother before adding. "If he ever gets to be too much work, sweetheart, you just give me a ring."

"Coming from the man voted most likely to succumb during an orgy, I think she should pass." After losing everything he owned, Caden was surprised he could joke.

"I wasn't sure you all would remember the bird calls."

"Sounded like a bunch of tomcats fighting to me." Billy snickered when Ethan gave him a shove.

"I wasn't sure whether you were trying to tell me all clear or you were under attack by zombies." Lucas' lips twitched as he spoke.

Flames engulfed the atmosphere, having crept down the north corner of jumbled debris in the completion of its deadly mission. The walls had long since caved. Black smoke capped and contrasted the yellow and orange inferno reaching for the heavens before expanding and dissipating in the morning breeze.

Had he grown into a different man owning a more common house closer to civilization, perhaps firemen could have vented the roof to reduce back draft and flash over and salvaged at least part of what had burned. Yet that wasn't who he'd grown to be and still wanted to become. Moving here had been the right decision. In his mind's eye, he looked forward to rebuilding, with certain modifications.

The first time Caden had walked the property, he'd known it was the perfect setting. The house, beautiful, open and spacious, ticked off each of his must-haves. After his entanglement with death and facing his own mortality, confusion and doubt prevented him from settling in emotionally. Kaylee's explosion into his life had changed his worldview.

Her mere presence cultivated a distinct and improved version of what he'd considered a rough draft of himself. He knew *what* he wanted, *and* whom and why and for how long. They were peanut butter and jelly, beer and a campfire, Wyatt Earp and Doc Holiday all rolled into one. Every part of each one fit a specific niche for the other.

Convincing her to stay by his side might be an issue in light of the loss she'd suffered, the notion keeping him wary. Would she erect a thicker armor than before? Time was one thing he held in spades, patience was another. They had a lot to sort.

Chapter Twenty-Six

"Seriously?" Kaylee took in Caden's somber demeanor before continuing. "You want our first purchase to be a camera? We need clothes, groceries, bedding, among other things." Heat engulfed her face and choked her voice on the last word.

His brothers' chuckles heightened her embarrassment as they stood in a semicircle on the restaurant's sidewalk.

"He'd be fine with cedar chips and a wool blanket out in the woods." Lucas caught Caden's wad of paper tossed at his head.

Odd looks from the older couple entering the restaurant turned her face into Caden's chest. Lexi punched Lucas in the arm while Caden's sharp look toned the laughter down to muffled snickers. The words priorities and combining all three brought guffaws.

"My brothers are freaking philistines." Caden palmed Kaylee's face, narrowing her vision to the sincerity and compassion in his gaze.

"Hey, they love you." Callouses brushing her cheek set off a chain reaction worthy of a nuclear reactor.

The previous day had blurred into endless accountings and written statements before scrubbing her skin to lose the fresh-roasted scent. After the day's harrowing events and exhaustion, she'd snuggled next to Caden on the couch at Lucas' house. It wasn't until early in the evening when she woke to Caden's brother cooking dinner she realized she hadn't eaten. Sleep had been the priority.

They'd talked late into the night, then woke to coffee percolating as the sun chased shadows across the floor. The soothing aroma offset smoke's pungent odor inundating her hair. It'd be a miracle if her sinuses ever filled with anything else.

Warm breath fanning across her cheeks brought her back to morning sunshine and the sweeping comfort of family.

"Sweetheart. We can send Lucas for bedding, Ethan and Lexi for groceries, and Matt for kitchen stuff. *We* are going to buy you a new camera, then go for clothes. That way, we can all meet at the cabin for dinner while they help us get settled. You'll love the setting. Abagail is there now doing a little cleaning."

"I've totally demolished your life, uprooting you..."

Resting his forehead against her brow, his murmured words were meant for her alone. "No, Kaylee. You've given me back something I never thought to recover. Staying at the cabin will give us time to plan how to rebuild. Besides, my parents used to take us all to the lake for getaways. It's familiar, and it'll be perfect. Those cabins are where we all got our love of the great outdoors."

"I'm grateful for your family's help." During the planning over breakfast, discussing options, and sorting priorities, no one mentioned her returning to the rental house.

Acceptance had eased her mind and filled her with a sense of belonging she hadn't felt since Reese's death. The nightmare was over, which meant the long-overdue call to her folks would require patience and repeated explanations. If her luck held, they wouldn't visit until the following week, after she and Caden had settled.

Living in a secluded cabin wouldn't be possible without Caden's presence. His assumption that she'd stay with him lent a comfort all its own. Four other rentals spaced a good distance apart would make it a great location to enjoy nature yet have the security of others nearby. Lucas and Billy had rented two of the other lodges, claiming they needed a vacation after the past several week's madness of watching over the baby of the family. Her sixth sense declared something amiss, but Caden wouldn't budge with an explanation.

"Do you know how much a good camera costs? You don't know when your insurance company will reimburse you for your losses."

"I figure if you're looking for a nonproprietary, high-end megapixel pro camera with all the bells and whistles along with a backup DSLR—I'd think this would more than cover the cost." Caden retrieved a check from his wallet. Snapping it open, he held it up for her to see.

"Where'd you get this?" She didn't recognize the business name written on the paper's corner.

His expression sobered as he explained. "The reward for finding Ciera's abductors. Her parents refused to take no for an answer." Tucking the check back in his pocket, he couldn't hide the guilt over Ciera's fate.

"How'd they physically tie the Asian to the case? I never saw his face."

"They found his digs. He had information on others, all of which has been turned over to federal authorities."

"The nightmare really is over." Stepping into his embrace, she inhaled his unique scent. All Caden.

"Yeah, sweetheart. It's finished."

When she pulled back, the others had dispersed, leaving her cocooned by his potent strength. Nearby traffic faded to a distant hubbub under the fast, erratic beat of her heart. Need washed through her, the tsunami drowning any qualms about public displays of affection. "I want you."

"I can't wait to get you alone. Speaking of which, we *could* make a stop before shopping..." Each murmured word was an aphrodisiac, filled with a promise only he could satisfy utilizing the vast components of his specialized skill set.

"It seems we took a step back in cuddling on the couch last night, but I didn't want to sleep alone in the guest room." Close proximity to Caden was an addiction.

"Like I wouldn't have joined you?" Lust branded his words.

"Yeah, but I can't be quiet, and Lucas would've set up a tape recorder outside the door. I can hear it now as he played it back at a family dinner or barbecue. I have a good grasp of your family's dynamics. *They* would laugh. My parents wouldn't."

Caden leaned in to kiss her, gently, slowly, thoroughly.

It wasn't the bone-gnawing, back-clawing, urgency that made her want to scream for more. This sweet invasion began with a nibbling at the corner of her mouth then evolved when his tongue invaded and twined with hers to ignite a passion growing from the delicious infiltration. She could no longer deny her feelings.

Nothing else mattered more than his hand sifting through her hair, the taste of him on her lips, or the warmth he imparted with his nearness. He ended the kiss and rested his forehead against hers, their alliance remaining strong with unspoken words. The soft stroke of his fingers up and down her arms stilled while their breathing came under control and she regained her composure.

A young man smiled in passing as his female companion harrumphed and mumbled about inappropriate exhibitions.

When he lifted his head, and ran his tongue along his bottom lip, she groaned.

"You did that on purpose. You sidetrack my thoughts to insert your will."

"Looks like it worked. C'mon. Let's go, pirate." Taking her hand, he tugged her toward the parking lot.

Sunset on the lake, grilling hamburgers on the screened back porch of their cabin, and surrounded by her surrogate family, Kaylee enjoyed a sense of calm and belonging reminiscent of years past.

Caden's assumption that she'd stay with him, which should have equaled the culmination of her dreams, brought both pain and pleasure. To regain her self-confidence, she had to face her fears, realized after standing in the clutches of a killer. That achievement entailed living on her own and regaining her independence. The length of time depended on how long it took to obtain her figurative balance. Yet she'd had a taste of sleeping in his arms and the thought of a cold bed felt like punishment—not a path to rejuvenating her self-esteem.

"Dinner with your family was fun. I've always dreamed of having lots of brothers and sisters."

"Huh, you've entered the madhouse where Matt is the warden."

Caden sat in the chaise lounge chair beside her, stroking his thumb over the back of her hand. The serenity of sinking into the thick cushion and watching the molten ball of sun settle below the horizon didn't negate the doubt niggling the back of her mind. It seemed the pall of her past hung like a cloud around her.

"He's very protective of you all, despite his comments. Must be because he's your oldest brother."

"Hmm, he's got a social security number of one...They can be a pain in the butt sometimes, but when you need them, all you have to do is look around. They'll be waiting."

"Why are Billy and Lucas staying close? You said the connection with the kidnapping ring was broken when they caught the third man."

"It is broken. The feds tossed his apartment and are piecing things together, following the money trail up the ladder. Still, they didn't find any information on you among the notes of the other girls. We figure you were taken because of the incidental photos and being a new arrival. It's just that—despite Ciera dressing like a street urchin, she wasn't. Those bastards had done their homework on the other girls, but we found nothing on Ciera. They haven't figured that out yet."

"Maybe they took her on impulse and because of her looks. She was beautiful."

"We might never know." Caden shook his head, the weight of the world heavy on his shoulders.

"Which makes me a footnote."

"No. You're the lynchpin that brought down their entire house of cards. If not for you, there'd have been no chance of recovering the other girls *or* preventing more women being sold into sexual slavery."

"So, the abusive husband is just an asshole. What about his girlfriend, Vasilisa?" She had no more excuses, no justification for delaying assembly of her life's shattered pieces.

"Matt said they haven't found her yet. Looks like the banker was just a sadistic prick used by a scheming bitch. They found deposits in her bank coinciding with withdrawals from the husband. She used him, then maybe decided Ciera was in the way. Now, she has vanished, which isn't surprising."

"Speaking of this monstrous situation, I've kinda come to a conclusion." Her gaze slid away from the depth of his passion, unable to maintain their link while uttering the words she knew would bring him pain. She had to combine the right syllables and sounds to make him understand she wasn't rejecting *him* yet had to do this to restore her soul.

Caden held his breath, unable to focus. He'd known the time would come. After surviving his own ordeal, he still hadn't come to terms with his specific demons. Kaylee hadn't even had time to catch her breath, much less excise the cankerous succubus siphoning her confidence.

He'd saved her life, but the psychological and spiritual wounds remained, a subliminal bleep that would surface when least expected and derail her intended course. The fact she'd revived and repaired parts of his soul previously unreachable wasn't the bait that framed his desire and bound them together. Their bond came from something deeper, more primal. "Sounds serious."

"Well, I want you to understand. I want you. With every fiber of my being, I need you. I always will. And I don't want our relationship to change per se."

"But you're leaving." The burgeoning mass of icy apprehension slid along his neural pathways to leave him frozen and unable to contemplate rejection. No one had ever set him aside.

"Not exactly. I need to know and need you to realize that I'm with you because I *want* to be with you. Not because I'm afraid to be alone."

"You're going back to the rental house?"

"No. I'm not ready to spend the night there. I'm going to rent an apartment. Someplace my parents can visit and see that I'm in one piece, mind and body." A cool breeze lifted her hair as she moved to straddle his lap. "I don't want anything else to change. I just need my own space for a while to regain my self-confidence."

"I get that, more than you realize. I think that's why I hadn't unpacked most of my stuff." The instant stirring against his jeans would let her know the subtext flowing through his thoughts. Unpacking his jeans vaulted to foremost in his mind, anything to wipe away the tension of her impending departure.

Slowly, he let his touch flow over her hips, flanks, and under the curve of her breasts. Beyond the porch, darkness reigned, the normal night sounds filling the air along with the scent of night-blooming flowers.

In his arms, the first blush of desire tinted her cheeks, her aura shimmered with heat as she stretched languidly, her gaze promising Heaven on Earth.

"Are you going to rebuild on the same spot?" Her eyelids fluttered closed as she tilted her head back on a groan.

"Yeah. I will—but with a design more to my specifications. I don't want to live in a house of glass. There are always changes we make after traumatic experiences. This'll give me the opportunity I need to finally adjust." Understanding her predicament on a visceral level dissolved the gelatinous lump forming in the back of his mouth. The concept he struggled to voice, given full volume after reflecting on her circumstances, relegated his current desperation to the back burner. *This is what she needs to feel whole. Give it to her. Help her from the background.*

A small wiggle brushed her hair aside.

"Glass half-full, got it. I also want to learn more self-defense moves. Will you teach me?" A slight twist of her hips ground her against him while deft fingers unbuttoned his shirt. Thin bars of illumination spilled through kitchen blinds to paint channels of light across her face. The play of shadow mimicked their time together.

"I'm not a black belt, but I've learned techniques from a good street fighter."

"So much the better. Speaking of belts, this one looks too tight." Giving thought to action, she slid the leather free of its loops and tossed it to the cement floor. "Ya know, after all we've been through, I can still find comfort in the dark. It doesn't scare me." On a deep sigh, she gazed out at the trees surrounding their yard, their grasping shadows falling short of the cabin. "Maybe I'm more whole than I thought. But right now, I want you."

For the first time in his life, the soul-jarring demand to join with a woman issued from a source that required baring his spirit, his heart. "You own my soul, Kaylee." Gently, he coaxed her to lay back on the lounge chair, showing her with the softness of his touch and the devotion in his gaze exactly what she meant to him.

Their lovemaking was slow, enriched by a mutual need to pleasure before igniting a fire neither could fully quench. The unspoken command to hold his gaze allowed him to delve underneath her invisible shields and strengthen their bond with each slow-burning glide.

When her warm breaths became short pants, his energized pace quickened until her nails raked his back and her scream, muffled by his kiss, filled his mind. No other woman had ever consumed his thoughts or driven him to such heights of ecstasy. The slow drift down to Earth deepened his need to keep her close.

Only when her body shivered under him did he realize the night had cooled. "How about we take this inside?" When her sheath released its grip and their bodies unlocked, the bone-deep completion he'd felt faded to an insidious hunger.

"On the sheets with cartoon winged avengers and spider silk?"

"That was Luc's idea of a joke. I think he failed to hit the mark on that one." Soft shafts of moonbeams highlighted the contentment written in her expression. A moment he'd love to capture on film.

"Hey, at least it isn't a princess theme."

"Wrap your legs around my waist." With all the graceless aplomb of a sated lover, Caden stood and started for the back door. He understood her fear in explaining the need for space and time to regain her mental footing. He'd answered her unspoken concerns with his body, letting her know they'd remain together regardless of the distance between them.

"What about our clothes?" Shirts and slacks lay strewn around the chaise.

"Not going anywhere. We'll get 'em later."

Cold seeping from the cement floor urged him to hurry as much as the chill breeze across his bare ass, but the benefits of the air currents on Kaylee's breasts outweighed his discomfort. "What a wonderful beginning to our night."

"Son. Of. A. Bitch!" From the cabin's side, the deep voice threatened epic violence with four choked words.

Oh hell no. Lack of recognition declared the speaker an instant enemy while nudity betrayed an uncharacteristic vulnerability. A mental tally of possible weapons contributed nothing harsher than a slingshot condom.

"Oh God." Kaylee unlinked her ankles and dropped her legs. The fact she ducked behind him should've been a clue. She'd proven fearless when facing a gunman.

"Who the hell are you?" Caden's roar didn't faze the intruder. The trembling in Kaylee's fingers at his waist stirred a rage he'd unleash regardless of his nakedness. Spreading his feet shoulder width gave him a fighter's stance and a cold breeze on parts not meant to feel it.

Behind him, Kaylee's continued mantra of, "Oh God", set off a different type of alarm. He sensed her gathering their clothes and shoving jeans at his clenched fists before the rustle of fabric indicated her dressing.

Mere yards from the house, a tall stranger dressed in jeans and flannel shirt bore an equally enraged expression. "Who the hell are *you?*"

Lights from the next cabin filtered through pine trees separating the yards before the back door slamming preceded pine branches slung aside. Lucas appeared, gun in hand. "What the hell's going on?" Dropped jaw and slumping shoulders defined his brother's shock.

Caden stuffed his legs into his jeans while keeping an eye on the bull-necked man with murder in his gaze.

"That's what I'd like to know!" The stranger's dark hair cut high and tight along with a braced stance bore the semblance of a man with a long military experience. "And thanks for the visual."

Or police experience. "Oh shit." The resemblance hit him like a club. The same eyes, same turn of the mouth, about the right age.

From the other side of the yard, Billy's voice provided more humiliation. "Don't move." The quiet metallic draw of a pistol's slide drawing a round into its chamber drew the stranger's attention.

"Except for you, Caden. You might feel a little exposed." Billy wasn't usually the smart-ass.

The intruder glanced at Lucas then over his shoulder at Billy but gave no indication of fear or uncertainty. His bulk overshadowed Lucas despite their equal height.

"Daddy, what are you doing here?"

"Did you call him daddy? Oh, damn." Caden's mouth dried as he briefly closed his eyes.

"No, not yours. Though from what I've seen, I think that might be how you should address me—and very soon."

Lucas chuckled, lowering his gun, and holding out his hand. "Hello, Mr. Tate. It's a pleasure to finally meet you, despite the, ah, particular circumstances." Throwing a look over his shoulder, he added, "You'll have to forgive my brother. He seems to lack social graces."

Muffled guffaws behind him induced prayers Billy hadn't pulled out his cell and started filming the scene.

Glowering at Caden, the older man added, "Not to mention pants. I imagine you'd like to dispose of your *funsock* and clean up while I talk to *my daughter*."

Caden's normally glib tongue failed as pieces of desiccated thoughts filtered through his mind. He merely nodded while tugging on his shirt then realized it lacked a few buttons.

Billy took a step back, shaking his head while no doubt reviewing how and to whom he'd recount the events. "I'll catch you later, bro. Have a good evening." Murmured words resembling, "Antarctica" and "nice place to visit", filtered back on the suddenly frigid atmosphere.

"Caden, if you need me to bring some food or drink for your guest or contact your friends, let me know. I realize how busy you've been." Murmured names all included the precedent *father*.

Jesus. It's an avalanche of smart-asses. "Go away, Billy. I don't need any *help*."

"So I've heard." The muffled reply ended with a snort.

Kaylee stepped forward, now fully dressed. "I'll meet you inside, Dad. Where's Mom?" Her deer-in-the-headlights look faded slightly.

"In the car, thank God. Nobody answered the door. I called the station after our bloody plane landed, and your brother Matt gave me the address. Go on over, he says. Make yourself at home."

"It's um, nice to meet you, sir." Caden swallowed hard, silently vowing to disembowel his oldest brother. "Why don't you and your wife come around front?"

A low growl answered his question.

Without another word and a cloud of rage surrounding him, the older man stalked around the side. Muttered words promised death and dismemberment.

"Sorry, Caden. He said he wouldn't drop in, but I should've guessed Mom would push until he did."

His siblings' chuckles drifted on the breeze before the distant slamming of cabin doors resounded in the awkward silence.

Chapter Twenty-Seven

It wasn't the first time Caden had faced an angry father, but it was the first time he'd cared deeply about the parents' regard. Stilted conversation had given way to Kaylee's reliving the details of her kidnapping, assault, and harrowing experiences, depleting her reserves. Despite her subdued tone, she'd stood her ground in defending their relationship. It hadn't taken long to win Mrs. Tate's approval. The elder Tate continued to scowl and grumble, the vein at his right temple bulging every time Kaylee smiled at or reached for Caden.

Staunch opposition continued through the next morning as the elder Tates joined the hunt for a suitable apartment. It was Caden's turn to grind his teeth.

"I really think the duplex on Kenworth Avenue would be great. It's already furnished, close to the lake, and far enough away from the city that I won't hear traffic all night." Kaylee's exuberance had grown with each passing minute.

"They need to trim their shrubbery. It's a security hazard." An oversight Markam Tate vehemently pointed out to the landlord. "At least it's a monthly lease. If you change your mind and want to come home, you're not on the hook for a year."

Returning to the rental house to collect the rest of her belongings and settle into her new digs took the rest of the afternoon.

Once comfortable, they offered to stay a few days to visit. Watching their interactions had lent Caden a deeper understanding of the family's dynamics.

Despite Caden's assurance that Kaylee equaled more than a fling, her father hardened his jaw with every kiss or show of affection. On the other hand, their presence in her life seemed to bolster her confidence, which meant he'd encourage them to stay while enduring the steadfast censure.

"I love evenings by the lake. It reminds me of the cabin in the mountains we visited each fall." Kaylee filled evening conversations with memories of grand adventures and good times. Her parents provided supplemental stories to heal longtime wounds and gave further insight into their shared past.

"Speaking of landmarks, how about we visit the International Rose Test Garden tomorrow?" Caden offered. His knowledge of the city and its attractions made him the perfect guide. Since Kaylee refused to let him back off in her parents' presence, he figured he'd make himself useful. The end result included Markam's tight expressions and monosyllabic responses. Maybe determination would eventually wear down the animosity. Offering the father a dental guard came to mind.

"Sounds like a great time in the making," Markam grumbled through gritted teeth.

Caden's mouth twitched, but in the act of self-preservation, he withheld comment.

Each night, the elder Tate insisted on escorting Caden to his car before striding back into Kaylee's house. The obvious design to put distance between the two lovers clear.

To buffer the stifling crosscurrents of the father's attitudes, Kaylee insisted Caden barbeque chicken for the coming Sunday's get-together, inviting his brothers over to fill the awkward silences.

Grudging truce transformed into wary acceptance after a three a.m. conversation in front of Kaylee's duplex. Like the previous nights, Caden sat in his SUV, maintaining surveillance a short distance down the street.

He straightened in his seat when the elder man padded down the middle of the road bearing hot coffee and a small paper bag. Mentally girding his loins, Caden rehearsed his speech, devised ahead, in preparation for the present scenario.

Instead of approaching the driver's window, the elder Tate simply opened the passenger door and dropped in to talk.

"The first two nights, I thought you were waiting to sneak inside. Then I realized you're maintaining surveillance. Talk."

With little hope of deceiving a seasoned detective and father, Caden laid his cards on the table. "The whole thing just doesn't feel right. Matt got word the feds are working with Interpol and tracking down the ringleaders involved, but something is off. I feel it."

"Like the night she was attacked in her bed?" He nodded his agreement. "You think it's not over. My gut says the same. Why in the hell are you out here where you can only see two sides of the house?"

An interesting conversation ensued. When faint tongues of gray light crawled over the horizon, they'd finished their food and reached an understanding, if not mutual respect.

Sunday breakfast consisted of a large meal followed by strong coffee on Kaylee's back porch. Relaxed conversation marked the transition from previous tension during their encounters.

"You a fan of hiking?" Mr. Tate's gaze took in the lake with a skiff tied off at the end of a community dock.

"Absolutely. There's some wonderful trails through these parts. I spent a lot of time near here as a kid."

"Wouldn't be a bad area to settle down." An arched brow and hopeful smile accompanied Mrs. Tate's comment.

"We used to hike quite a bit." Color crept up Kaylee's cheeks. "Well, before—"

"Before we lost Reese," Her dad finished.

"Well, you men seem to be hitting it off now." Mrs. Tate canted her head to the side, examining their expressions.

"We've reached an understanding." The older man's nod in Caden's direction spoke volumes.

Her mom's answer spoke for them all. "Finally, a cease-fire. We can all take a deep breath." A smile softened her words.

Caden thanked Providence for smoothing the way. Appreciating the underlying and familiar interactions of the Tates hadn't established his foothold in their good graces until they fully understood his commitment.

"We'll be heading home this evening. I assume I can count on you to watch over my girl?" The older man's tone intertwined demand with an interrogative.

"To my last breath." Meeting her father's gaze head-on, Caden understood the worry. It echoed in his own gut.

"Then it's settled." A poignant heartache settled in his aura. Every parent knew there came a time to let go and trust. Instilling confidence in offspring came with a cost. Fear of the unknown.

Matt and the rest of the McAllisters joined Kaylee and her parents Sunday afternoon at Caden's cabin. Barbecue, chess matches, sports games on TV, and discussions involving anything of interest kept the conversation lively. It was too much to hope—and think—they'd behave in front of his woman's parents. They'd started in soon after arrival.

"Nice to see you invested in plates that don't soak up the sauce then fall apart. Damn, bro. Kaylee's a real keeper." Lucas began the torment that would last for hours.

"Yeah, and these cups won't melt with coffee," Billy murmured. "I feel like I'm living high on the hog."

Jesus, guys. Not now, they're just starting to warm up to me.

"Matt bought non-breakable when he got the coffee pot," Ethan said, before tapping the princess themed plate. "And it's all matchy-matchy in pastel colors."

Lucas' insistence in giving a tour of the cabin ended with the master bedroom, where the cartoon character bedspread and curtains would have completed the visual painting of a scary resident if previous conversations hadn't established Caden as a solid individual. When the retired policeman returned amid his brothers' guffaws and Caden's murmured threats, the older man's slap on the back ensured the comical impression would never fade. Shared beliefs and character gave them much in common.

Regardless of the lively banter and clever jabs from his brothers, Kaylee's father had injected his own subtle inquisition to flesh out his perception of his only child's boyfriend. If fate had reversed their situations, Caden would have done the same, minus the subtlety.

"Well, I guess it's time to head out. Our plane leaves in a couple hours." Mrs. Tate's eyes brimmed with tears. "I wish we could stay longer."

Her dad's knitted brow echoed his body's tension. "Call me with any questions or problems." The generalized command held an edge born of frustration and concern.

Kaylee promised to call daily for the next week, her posture relaxing with her mom's tears and an invitation for Caden to visit them on the East Coast. It didn't surprise him when her father asked for one of his cards. Caden wrote his number on the back, knowing it would be used—frequently.

"You must think it's ridiculous for me to keep the apartment when we'll spend nights at your cabin."

"Well, since you have more age-appropriate bedding, we could spend some nights there if you like." Putting an end to the abstinence curse brought on by her family's presence had derailed other thoughts after his siblings left.

"No, I'm comfortable right here. I actually love this couch, even better 'cause we're not sleeping on it. But I'm up and out early tomorrow. Lexi and I are shopping in the morning." Her warm breath lifted the fine hairs on his chest when she leaned over to nuzzle his neck.

"Sounds like fun. I have a meeting with the architect but should be finished by noon. I think the floor plan we sketched out is gonna suit us perfectly."

"I can't wait to see it built. I'll have to thank Lexi tomorrow for the extra software on our new laptops. She has a great CAD program."

Developing a floor plan specific to his current viewpoint in life solidified his objective to move forward. Tapping into Kaylee's ideas for exterior hardscaping provided new and fresh ideas he couldn't wait see come to fruition. Her remarkable perspective and experience in photography came into play while exploring her photos, repopulated on her new computer. With a little tweaking by the right mind, their dream would become reality.

"You know, all this time I'd been living out in the country and wondering if it was the right place for me. Now I realize it was the right choice, just the wrong style home." It'd taken one evening at Kaylee's apartment to realize he craved the open space.

"I've come to the same conclusion. I'd rather have foxes, squirrels, and deer, for neighbors. They're quieter and more entertaining."

"And soon you shall. Nobody to bang on your ceiling if you make too much noise." He'd snickered when the duplex's other tenants had blasted loud music after Kaylee got particularly vocal during their early evening delight.

He hadn't addressed his biggest concern, convincing her to move in with him and drop her lease. There was a time and place for every conversation. They'd climb that mountain when she was ready.

In the back of his mind, the nagging thought the nightmare wasn't over surged forward. If she insisted on spending a few nights alone to prove she'd vanquished her demons, he'd stake out her place at a discreet distance. The fire had destroyed his inventory of surveillance equipment, but replacements he'd ordered would allow visual access to all sides of the building.

"You're thinking too much." Her smile could thaw an entire iceberg.

The slow glide of her fingers over his bare chest stirred the same heat building in her gaze. The side effects culminated in a dry mouth and intense pressure against his fly. He'd use his body to reinforce what they both felt, making words trivial.

Chapter Twenty-Eight

The previous night rivaled the best she'd ever experienced. Moving to Caden's rhythm had sent her into new realms of pleasure where nothing could intrude. It hadn't been the instinctive reaction to surviving an adrenaline-producing event. Last night's merging cemented the bond originating from circumstances that had shaped an indestructible barricade against any force, natural or contrived. "I've found a new set of muscles." Agile as she'd always been, she hadn't known she could manage those positions.

"Here, roll over. I'll work the knots out for you."

Within seconds, he'd put words to action, massaging her sore back and thighs with deep, strong strokes.

"This isn't fair. You know Lexi's coming over in another hour." She made no pretense of trying to resist.

"Better sated than frustrated. By the way, I want you to model your new lingerie tonight."

"And what makes you think that's on my list?"

"Let's call it wishful thinking."

Again, his loving was tortuously slow and nail-scrapingly thorough. She'd never achieved such heights or even imagined they existed. Only in Caden's arms did they become reality.

When her breathing and heart rate slowed, the realization of how close she'd come to losing everything, not once but three times brought a new awareness. Life found balance between dark and light, good and evil, dangerous undertakings and the serenity of leisure.

"Now, you're the one lost in thought. I must not be up to par." His chuckle filled her heart.

"It just occurred to me—how trite and unfounded my stubborn pride has been. My strength has been there all along. I've survived."

"*We've* survived."

"And thrived."

"Good girl. I was hoping that insight would come. Maybe a few more orgasms will enlighten you to just how good we are together."

"Seriously? *That* would send me to the hospital. Forget kidnappers, snipers, and thugs trying to burn us alive."

"Your arm, wrist, and scalp have healed nicely, but I'd rather not see Dr. Henly again so soon."

"Now all I need is the strength to keep up with Lexi this morning."

"She does have an abundance of energy. But she's also world savvy. She grew up on the streets and could teach us both a few things."

"She seemed kind of protective of her past, like maybe she's embarrassed?"

"Just careful about preserving her privacy. She'll open up once she knows you better."

"She said she'd help us train a puppy."

"No doubt about that. You'll like her teaching methods, always positive reinforcement. The litter I referred to earlier is old enough for us to take a look at tomorrow, if you want. I helped the owner a few years back, and he's offering us first pick."

"Yes! That would be wonderful!"

"We'll train him together. I know your independent streak means you need your own space, at least for a while, but we're good together. Stay with me and see where this adventure takes us." Blue eyes darkened with the earnestness and intensity of his gaze.

He wasn't asking for marriage, yet his words, as well as the possession radiating from every aspect of his body, demanded so much more. He'd staked his claim on her heart, craving that which bridged the physical and the spiritual. After his own horrific experiences, nature had urged him to grow and flourish from a world of casual hookups and careless disregard. Even in the short span of time she'd known him, she saw the extent of his growth.

"I can't imagine being anywhere else."

"Good. It's settled—and you're gonna be late. You hit the shower while I fix breakfast. Tell Lexi I'll meet you girls for lunch at Sutter Joe's. They have great cheesesteak subs."

The day turned out seasonably warm with a light breeze sifting through ornamental trees dotting the edge of the mall's sidewalk. Kaylee inhaled deeply, enjoying a newfound sense of freedom while trying to keep pace with her friend.

"Hey, how about we park it for a bit. Looks like you could use a break." Lexi asked, her air of subtle mystery entwined with hard-shelled self-assurance softened with her expression.

"Love to. I hadn't realized how energy sapping shopping could be. Thanks for coming with me today. I appreciate it." Taking a short break after stowing their bags in Lexi's car, Kaylee smiled at the thought of Caden's reaction to her purchases. It was going to be a fun night after she bragged about sitting near the table where she'd been previously abducted.

Building confidence.

"Hey, shopping with any man is a waste of time when it comes to clothes. They only want to see stuff made of lace and scraps of satin."

A grin tempered her admonishment. "Not that they don't have their place. But a girl needs other things as well."

Crisp, clean air carried the tang of the nearby river, pungent on the soft breeze driving a food wrapper across the sidewalk. Revisiting the same shopping center instilled a sense of power, like the last piece of a puzzle making sense of the whole picture.

Kaylee stretched her legs and yawned. The next time she went shopping with Lexi, Caden would have to give her a few more hours of sleep. Still, it felt good to sit and relieve her sore muscles while watching other women carry their new finds, eating a bagel from the bakery, or simply chatting with a friend in passing. "This morning has helped me regain a sense of normalcy I wasn't sure I'd feel again. Like an old part of me has resurfaced. Thank you."

"Hey, I understand where you're coming from. Plus, I've seen firsthand how much you've helped Caden, despite your own losses."

"Thank you." Kaylee smiled with the warm acceptance. Her life had finally turned around. Even the barista who'd prepared their favorite drinks seemed to nourish an inner glow, judging by the smile tilting her lips. Savoring the caramel latte and listening to music as the base beat resonated within her heart topped off the experience.

"You've never lost all your clothes in one fell swoop, and even though you bought a few necessities the other day, men usually focus on small details."

Kaylee's ungraceful snort of agreement sloshed hot liquid over the side of her cup. "If Ethan's the same way as Caden, they'd have us parading around in bikinis whenever outside and naked when inside." She laughed at Caden's wish voiced earlier while in bed. "What time's it getting to be? I promised Caden we'd meet him for lunch." Sticky fingers wiped on a napkin left a paper residue.

"We've got a few minutes yet." An awkward glance at the river preceded Lexi's next words, a foreshadowing of internal conflict.

"I'm glad you and Caden have hit it off so well. He deserves to have someone good in his life."

"Thanks. I never thought I'd have a chance with him." *Understatement.* The warmth of his encouragement had infused confidence to face her fears and enter the same stores she'd visited the day of her abduction—without him by her side. The morning's solid conviction that she could peruse the shops hadn't faded with his absence.

"He's something, all right." Lexi nibbled her bottom lip, a *tell* that she wanted to impart something but wasn't sure how to approach.

"You mean handsome, heart-poundingly sexy, and protective." Kaylee waited for a beat, waiting for Lexi to flesh out the concept her unvoiced thoughts had developed.

"Yeah, he and Ethan have that in common with the rest of the McAllisters. But it's more than that. He's a changed man, despite the teasing about running a grind train through his house."

"I'm still waiting for women to throw their bras and thongs at him when he walks by." When Caden first helped her retrace her steps after the kidnapping, she'd counted at least half a dozen women who'd specifically asked him for his business card and personal contact information.

"I know what you mean. It's funny though, all the brothers seem immune, except Lucas, not that he's shallow, just always horny, I guess."

"Huh, I think Lucas just assigns numbers instead of taking names."

"Good morning, ladies. I thought I recognized you." Tall and swarthy, the gentleman smiled, his shadow arcing across their bodies as he stood in front of them, directing his gaze at Kaylee. "Mind if I join you for a minute?" A veiled tension filled the air, due in part to the grin which never reached his eyes.

"You're the contractor rehabbing the Methodist church on Devlin Avenue." Twisting to gauge Lexi's reaction, she added, "I stopped to ask a few questions and take some pics."

Lexi's shoulders tightened almost imperceptibly as she sat straighter, yet there appeared to be no viable threat. The guy was obviously *slick,* but they were in full view of many pedestrians. Ingrained curiosity dictated she solve the conundrum.

"How's the renovation going?" Remembering Caden detailing her friend's street savvy, Kaylee still didn't perceive any threat. The guy maintained an affable if slippery persona.

"We still have a ways to go, but the outside entrance is done if you'd care to see it." Extending his hand toward Lexi, he added, "Hi, I'm Basil Millen. I don't believe we've met."

Instead of taking the proffered hand, Lexi picked up her drink and took a sip before answering. "I'm her friend." Monotone flat.

If anyone could form ice balls in hell, Lexi was the prime candidate. The smile plastered on her face wouldn't fool a soul. Her instant dislike pulsed in the air like a foul smell.

Okay, the guy's a shark, that's evident. But why snub him so abruptly? "Um, we'll stop by and take a look in the next day or so. Thanks," Kaylee replied. *Not likely.* If this creep set Lexi's sixth sense into orbit that fast, there was no way in hell there'd be further contact. A vague acceptance and avoiding confrontation was better than a public pissing match, especially when she didn't understand the variables in play.

"Come on, Kaylee. We have a meeting to get to." Lexi stood, the hard edge of her voice as clear as the threat settled in her expression.

Instinct urged Kaylee to her feet, her napkin sliding from her lap and skidding against the bench's leg. "O—okay. I'm set." *I can pick up the trash later.*

"I think we'll take a little detour." Basil sidestepped to block their paths, latching onto Kaylee's elbow. An exaggerated motion of his hand in his jacket pocket formed the outline of a gun barrel.

Kaylee gasped.

"At least this time I haven't had to go to the trouble of drugging you, then explaining why my girlfriend is drunk this early in the day."

Lexi grumbled a threat too low to discern.

"Yes, it is, and no, I won't hesitate. With the silencer in place, it won't even be heard." The shark's grin widened with the cold, clipped threat. "Now, we're going to take a little walk. First, you're gonna throw away your cups and cell phones. No one's gonna track us, either the two or four-legged hounds."

"Our men will find you. Count on it." Lexi's gaze canvassed the area.

"If you don't move it, you won't be alive to find out. Though I am curious about what tipped you off."

Lexi sneered as her gaze raked him from head to toe. "It's Monday morning. You say you've been working in construction, yet you're wearing two-hundred dollar loafers. Plus, the likelihood of just running into us is a little too much coincidence."

Fear yielded to anger despite the horrific images of Ciera's lifeless body surging forefront in Kaylee's thoughts. If she didn't come up with a plan, she and Lexi would vanish without a trace. From previous experience, she knew surveillance cameras would yield nothing in their disappearance. If they were forced into a car, chances were slim they'd be found. In counterpoint, if they were forced through a deadfall or trapdoor in a nearby shop, she stood a chance of leaving a trail.

The moment's mental standoff allowed a weak plan to form. One where she and her friend didn't end up in a harem of unwashed, desperate women. Fear granted strength to jab her nails deeper into her palm. She kept her hands down and by her side, determining the creep was more interested in keeping an eye on Lexi than the ground behind them.

When she felt the telltale warmth dribble over her clenched knuckle, a slight flick of her right wrist sent the organic beacon behind them. Instead of breadcrumbs, she'd leave drops of blood to delineate her path into another realm of hell.

Basil kept to Kaylee's left side, guiding her while keeping Lexi in his sights. Wooden movements carried them forward, their gazes firm, steely, and cold.

Lexi's street skills were useless without close proximity to the dirtball holding the weapon.

If Kaylee passed out, he might decide they were not worth the trouble and shoot them. Despite the light breeze, sweat dotted her brow and dampened her back. Blood thundered a violent beat in her ears while a heaviness grew in her limbs. Nausea accompanied the mental images of Ciera's dead body.

"Where're you taking us?" Lexi's question grated through clenched teeth.

"Back to the tunnels. Think of it as a blind date. Yep, I know all about how you came back to find the rich bitch. But you were too late. We'll even take the same route, with you girls side by side. At least this time you'll remember it for the rest of your life, however long I decide that to be."

"Why? The police found no links between you and the Asian." Kaylee's gaze desperately searched the shoppers on the sidewalk. Happy times for many, a few intermittent tense conversations, but none with the terror which reigned within her mind.

She released another drop of blood. Alternate clenching and releasing ensured the wound wouldn't clot.

"Let's just call this insurance for future employment and a penalty for your boyfriend. He's cost me an entire business network unless I can deliver you as promised."

Months ago, she'd studied the architecture of the tunnels and deadfalls leading to them. She'd never expected someone to force her through one. *Certainly not twice.* A glance at Lexi communicated the nonverbal, *this bullshit's not gonna happen.* The same conviction filled her own mind.

Shoppers milling about and flitting from one store to the next had no idea of the tragedy unfolding. Smiles and greetings from people contradicted the fact that no one would remember two women accompanied by a man dressed in casual slacks and a polo shirt.

No one would solve the puzzle of how the thugs had whisked her away without a trace unless Matt brought Damien. When they came to a sign suspended in the covered walkway advertising vitamins and supplements, Basil guided them to the door. It was a few scant yards from the café where she'd first enjoyed a sunset.

Another drop of blood.

"I see the wheels turning in both your heads. Forget it."

Kaylee's thoughts whirled with possibilities and wondered what plan Lexi conjured. The hard glint in her gaze detailed a fighter when the opportunity arrived. Every scenario had a weakness for exploitation if recognized. *Keep your eyes open.*

"What better place to take someone who's feeling under the weather than to a health and nutrition store?" Basil smiled and nodded to the male clerk behind the counter. No other patrons were present as the younger man stepped forward and turned the sign hanging on the door to, *Closed for lunch. Be back soon.*

The click of the door locking equaled the sound of a casket closing.

Chapter Twenty-Nine

Caden stood nose to nose with Joe, owner of the cozy café. "What do you mean you haven't seen them? They were supposed to be here ten minutes ago. They wouldn't be late intentionally." Caden's fear and anger warred for dominance as he suppressed the urge to shake Joe by the collar.

"Caden, I haven't seen them all morning." Annoyance overshadowed the patience encompassing the older man. "And women shopping are ten minutes late? I wouldn't think it's time to call out the National Guard just yet."

Several ladies sitting at a nearby table had shown no recognition of Kaylee's picture on his cell phone.

Without another word, Caden pivoted and headed for the door. His gut told him Kaylee and Lexi had found trouble in some form or another. Restless energy hummed through his neural passages in a forewarning he couldn't ignore.

Matt answered on the first ring.

"The girls are missing. Never made it to Joe's. I'll find Lexi's car and ring you. Bring Damien." Growled expletives mimicked his own thoughts. Precious minutes passed, his heart beating a staccato rhythm to match his steps. A prickling sensation began in his stomach before acid seared the back of his throat. He should never have let Kaylee out of his sight.

All during his meetings, he'd worried about them but knew Lexi would stay close, and safety lay in numbers. *Then where the hell are they?*

Midday sun blazed down and glared off the parking lot's hoods and windshields. Rows and rows of assorted steel, rubber, and glass behemoths held their master's treasures and waited to transport them in cool luxury at the touch of a button. Lexi's small sedan wouldn't stand out.

Rather than race down each row, Caden vaulted up on a patio table to gain a better perspective. Disparaging remarks from nearby diners equaled a radio's squelch in the background.

From his vantage point, he could view the bulk of the lot. Scanning each line until spotting Lexi's car close to the end of the third row, he knew in his gut something horrendous had taken place.

Grumbles and admonishments trailed him through the crowd when he took to the pavement. Scrutinizing both the lot and the shoppers, he found no sign of the women. Air became a commodity secondary to his need for Kaylee.

She'd suffered so much yet refused to break. Would this be the final straw? She'd declared death preferable over enslavement.

Lexi's car remained locked with packages piled on the back seat. The time taken to retrieve a lock jock from his SUV would waste precious minutes. Minutes that could take the women out of his reach.

His brother had remarked on several occasions how a jacket made a good buffer, He wrapped his windbreaker around his fist before smashing the back window. Several bystanders gasped and retrieved their cell phones.

Just what I need, my face featured on the evening news.

With shaking fingers, he yanked the bags from the seat and spread them over the car's trunk. Looking back at the shops, he took note of the names, coordinating each bag with the store's physical location. Several bags contained receipts with date and time stamp. When he finally had them in chronological order, he knew where they'd shopped last and their direction.

Skidding tires snapped his attention to Matt and Ethan's vehicles halting behind him. Unadulterated rage manifested in Ethan's flushed skin and clenched fist holding one of Lexi's scarves. Bystanders, watching the scene unfold gave him a wide berth.

"Update." Matt's clipped command echoed Caden's anger. Excited chuffs marked Damien's exit, picking up his master's anxiety and ready to work.

Difficulty breathing and a roiling stomach combined with Caden's grinding teeth to make it difficult to articulate his thoughts. "Last known shop they visited—Sheer Delights, the lingerie shop. Time stamp is less than a half hour ago. Joe hasn't seen them."

"Neither one is answering their phone and reception here is good. They both know better than to ignore it." Ethan scanned the shopping center's walkway.

"Billy and Lucas are heading to the tunnel exit where Kaylee came out." Matt tightened his hold on Damien's leash.

"I checked in with Kaylee about an hour ago, everything was fine." Caden's hands shook while replacing the bags.

"There's only a few stores between. Let's start with their last known location. Get your vests on." Ethan tossed Lexi's scarf to Matt. "Scenting material."

Caden snatched Kaylee's jacket from the back seat and handed it to Matt. "Will two scenting objects confuse him?"

"No. And unless someone carried the women or forced them into another car, Damien should pick them up." After giving the command, Matt allowed the dog to sniff the garment.

"Jesus, I shouldn't have let them go alone." Caden raked furrows through his hair. Desperation squeezed his chest.

"Not like you could stop them. Lexi's as single-minded as your woman." Ethan stopped to show some bystanders Lexi's picture. Several girls recalled seeing her but had no other information.

Damien's sudden pull toward the coffee shop altered their course. Matt gave his charge extra lead.

With his nose in the air, Damien zeroed in on his invisible goal. When he reached a bench and began sniffing the supporting legs, the two ladies resting there *harrumphed* and left amid comments of, "What the hell?"

"Kaylee must've dropped the napkin." Ethan sheathed his hand in a glove and picked up the discarded trash.

Chuffing and pulling at his lead marked Damien's desire to move. With his nose to the ground, he stopped and sniffed at a stain on the pavement.

"Looks like blood." Caden crouched on the other side of the dog. "Shit. It is." A cold sweat broke out over his body while a low buzzing sounded in his head.

"Caden, get a sample. Ethan, go grab our gear. We might be headed through a deadfall. We'll need flashlights." Matt reached over and squeezed Caden's shoulder. "It's just a drop. We're in broad daylight and surrounded by lots of people. Maybe she left it—intentionally—for us."

"Yeah, but either way, they've got her. We don't even know who *they* are." Caden spat the words through gritted teeth.

"No, not the same now. This time there's two women. It won't be as easy to control them both. Plus, I doubt either is drugged since it would draw too much attention. Chances are—considering the time stamps on the receipts, the girls still have their wits about them." Matt's hardened jaw and deep frown betrayed his emotion's undercurrent.

Caden fumbled, then gently folded the gauze and placed it in the paper bag Matt provided. "This has to belong to one of the girls. It's fresh."

"Damien seems to think so." Matt nodded to Ethan, carrying a duffle, as the dog pulled them along. "Let's go find our girls."

"I promised Kaylee's dad I'd call him with any news or updates. Christ. He thinks I've taken advantage of his little girl."

"Actually, he *caught* you taking advantage. At least that's the way Lucas told it." Matt's attempt at keeping Caden from going ballistic didn't help.

Damien's chuffing, nose-to-the-ground gait led them to a storefront with a *Closed for lunch* sign hanging in the door. Floor-to-ceiling glass allowed potential customers to view the health supplements and vitamins on display.

"Closed during the busiest time of day? I don't think so," Ethan growled.

Caden centered himself to the door to shatter the glass with a well-placed kick.

"No, Caden." Matt pulled Damien away. "We have no evidence."

"I see blood on the floor inside," Caden said, almost snarling. "And I'm going in—now."

Behind him, Ethan grumbled his agreement after dropping his gear bag.

"The floor is black tile. How can you possibly see a drop of blood?" Matt cupped his hand around his temple to block the glare while peering through the glass. Damien scratched at the glass door.

"Yep, he's right, bro. I see it too." Ethan backed his younger brother despite his stance three feet behind them both. Over his shoulder, Caden saw his sibling's need to find Lexi etched in fear and desperation. Several bystanders stopped to witness and murmur their curiosity of observing three men and a dog peering in a health store.

"Probable cause. But let's be smart about this. Caden, help me hoist the trash can over here. A kick won't work and will probably just break a bone." Ethan yanked the metal barrel sideways, his feral grin matching Caden's sentiments.

Matt stepped back with his dog to address the few onlookers. His calm, authoritative tone preceded dropped jaws and more phones recording the event.

Caden grunted with the effort to lift the can. "What do they put in these things?"

"They weight the bottoms to keep 'em from blowing over when empty."

A loud crash preceded crunching glass shards hitting the concrete outside and the black tile floor inside. Shocked gasps from the gathering crowd turned to low murmurs when Matt issued a short statement about police emergency, holding up his badge and warning others to stay out of the shop.

"Grab the bag, Ethan." Caden swallowed the lump in his throat. No doubt the blood trail would lead them underground, a place he'd wished to never revisit. Tension held him immobile like a negligible element in the eye of a hurricane. Time would sweep away what he loved most if he couldn't stand strong and grow a pair.

Ethan crossed the sharp fragments glistening like diamonds littering the tile before Matt carried Damien over the broken menace.

The thought of losing Kaylee surged through Caden's blood, pulsing with desperate need. He would kill anyone who threatened her. The crunch underfoot barely registered.

"There's got to be a deadfall here somewhere." Just hours before, he'd had Kaylee teetering on the edge of collapse, exhaustion written in every line of her sated body. She'd be running on emotional fumes now when some bastard thought to extinguish the light he held most dear. *Hell if that's gonna happen.*

The shepherd's quickened snuffling and pulling at his lead jerked Matt along as they followed the blood trail, taking them through an open doorway to the storeroom beyond. Shining tile gave way to old wooden floorboards, weathered from years of scuffing feet. No hollow sounds denoted a hollow area where a deluded crimp could squirrel away unwary captives.

Caden and Ethan visually searched for a hidden doorway while Damien sniffed around the floor. It seemed the trail ended without a clue. Air redolent of rotting vegetation and incense didn't slow their frantic search.

"I just thought shopping was a good way for her to get out of the house. A small measure of independence." Caden opened a small door, the interior illuminated with backlighting from behind him. A small mop and bucket, one broom, and various cleaning chemicals, comprised the small space. Efficient movements saw the bucket tossed aside in favor of stomping the floorboards.

"Now's not the time for a tantrum, dude," Ethan admonished.

"Shut up and listen for a hollow sound," Caden retorted as his boots' thudding echoed in the small space.

Damien stopped at the far corner of the back room, scratching at the floor and whining. "Over here." Matt pulled the dog back to test the floorboards. "Doesn't sound any different. Let's see if these shelves are hiding a door."

"Look, there's a slight arc worn in the floorboard." Caden kneeled and fingered the slightly discolored curve scratched in the wide planks.

"Okay. Somehow these shelves slide out." Matt pulled on one shelf after another. Nothing budged.

"Maybe a hidden lever?" Ethan nudged his way in and shoved the contents of the upper shelves aside. Glass jars of supplements, plastic tubs of protein pills, and vitamins of various types all clinked together.

Caden started on the bottom shelf, swiping everything to the floor.

"Hey, what the hell, Caden?" Matt, searching through the middle shelves, stepped aside.

"I got it." Caden shoved on the rough backing, a savage grin curving his lips when rewarded with the screech and release of the hidden entry.

Backlighting marked the front portion of the small cubicle's interior, four feet square with no shelving, no furniture, and no apparent purpose.

Caden squeezed through and stamped his foot in several places, eliciting a hollowed sound in the center of the space. The floorboards gave slightly with each strike. "This is it, but I don't see how to open it."

"No drag marks. The girls were still under their own steam. They'll have their wits about them. That's to our advantage." Ethan's logical thinking imparted through a clenched jaw characterized strength under pressure.

Caden's heart seized with the cold surge of terror. He prayed she'd have the strength to fight if and when the opportunity presented itself. His grip on the makeshift doorjamb disengaged with Ethan's not-so-gentle nudge.

"Here, there's a perpendicular seam across these boards. See that small hole? Step out so I can see if it—" Ethan knelt and scrabbled at the surface. "Here. Help me get this open, Ca."

Not waiting for assistance, Ethan struggled to open the trapdoor. A weathered, crude wooden ladder disappeared in the infernal void beneath them, an endless black abyss. "We need light. Caden, grab my bag and see if you can find another flashlight. They must keep some on hand since they're using this tunnel."

Figuring the owners had no reason to hide something as innocuous as a flashlight and with none visible in the back storeroom, Caden surged back into the store proper to check under the sales counter.

Several drawers held various notebooks and papers, all slinging forward with the force of his search. "Found some!" Two flashlights gave weight to his words. I'll grab the bag and vests." Matt's duffel would contain first aid supplies and a blanket. Hopefully, they wouldn't need either.

When he'd returned, Matt was settling Damien around his broad shoulders to descend the ladder. Ethan's key chain penlight highlighted the bottom from below.

"Thanks. Drop it down, I'll catch." Ethan's disembodied voice drifted up from the new hell.

Caden used one of the flashlights to search below before dropping the duffle to his brother. Liquid chain saws shredding his stomach lining wasn't a new sensation. His body produced the same mind-numbing anarchy the last time he went in the tunnels. Again, his worn boots spewed forth tendrils of ephemeral roots that corkscrewed into the floorboards and kept him immobile while a whirlwind of turbulence battered his mind.

His brother's throat clearing snapped him from a remembered horror of crazed rats in a feeding frenzy. A thin film of clammy perspiration covered his body while the buzzing in his ears grew until it overshadowed all but his tunneling vision. Down there. A deep, dark, and dank environment rife with the beady-eyed bastards of his worst nightmares awaited his arrival.

"Caden, hand me the flashlights and coordinate things topside. Matt and I will track from this end." Ethan's voice sounded distant, tinny, his face covered in shadows that moved in time with Ethan's tiny light.

"Screw you. I'm going after my woman." Tucking away the emotional baggage, he set one tremulous foot on the top wooden rung. It creaked under his weight.

"There's the man who can fart Christmas tunes in key." Matt sniggered.

"I was twelve." Caden's descent into hell brought acid to his mouth.

"Still are, with fifteen years of experience." Matt's hand on his shoulder when at the bottom of the steps remained tight and communicated more than words could convey. "Let's go." He wouldn't say more.

Damien's snuffling in the dirt segued into a thin whine of impatience while Caden distributed the flashlights and swallowed his anxiety. The scent of something foul, more than the rodent carcasses forced him to briefly close his eyes. *Ciera wasn't found down here.* Yet the smell persisted on micro currents created by the open trapdoor.

Damien whined before pawing the dirt. On closer inspection, a significant size of dark crimson sand and scuffling furrows indicated a fight and bloodshed. The dog's reaction wasn't an expected response to finding what he sought. Instead, he sniffed then continued to pull them farther into the tunnel.

"We don't know it's one of the girls, Caden." Ethan's grip indicated a need for support as well as unleashing anxiety.

If the ground split open and spewed forth a horned demon with a long, forked tail, Caden's fury would strike it down and send it back. Impotent rage seethed in his soul with no outlet. "Let's go." His chest ached in fear for Kaylee's life. The warp and woof of emotions staggered his mind and step.

The canine led them through sections of the tunnels they'd not marked as kids. Using their old system to leave a trail in the dirt near the wall's edge at every bifurcation assured a return trip. Occasional, furtive scurrying marked their passage. Ethan kept pace beside him, one hand on his shoulder.

Flashbacks, both of recent events and long ago sifted through Caden's thoughts. His little pirate was strong, and Lexi had street smarts. A deadly combination. They wouldn't go easily, and both knew their men would track them to the ends of the earth.

The weight of the air rounded his shoulders, further hindering his ability to breathe and reminiscent of sucking air through his shirt during the fire. Now, instead of heat and smoke obstructing his windpipe, stale, moist air might as well have been aspirated through a sponge.

Intermittent chittering took his mind back to when he'd sworn to protect Lexi. Instead, he'd been poisoned and left to a horde of trained, aggressive rats intent on scraping every bit of flesh and muscle from his bones. Those nightmares had decreased since Kaylee entered his realm. In return for restoring his life, he'd failed to protect the woman in his care.

Time stalled in the somber oblivion where three beams of light sliced the air in the hope of finding further visible evidence of a struggle in the underground's arteries. He breathed a little easier when they came upon one of their old markings. They couldn't determine exactly where they were, but they had a starting point to draw a mental map.

Checking his watch, Caden realized they'd traveled underground far too long. They should have found some indication of the girls' state of being. Damien followed his invisible trail but didn't appear interested in the bloody drops clumping loose dirt.

All three froze when his pirate's scream echoed through the tunnels. Sheer terror gripped Caden, his stumble-shuffle step ending with a dropped flashlight to brace himself against the wall.

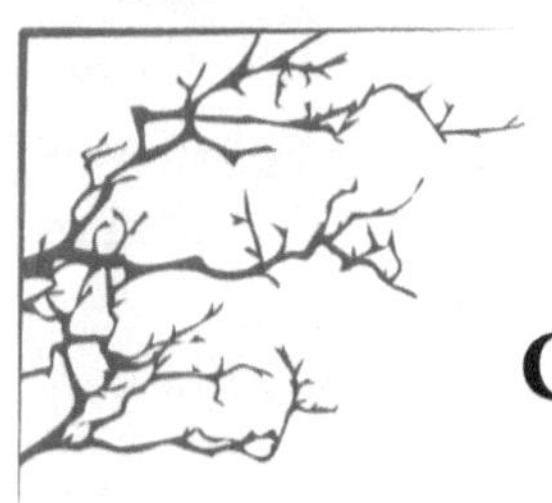

Chapter Thirty

Immediately, Matt gave Damien a "quiet" order, obeyed with a low grumble. The dog's excited sniffing grew exponentially as did the foul odor.

As much as Caden wanted to bolt forward, Matt's grip on his arm preceded the whispered words that brought back a small piece of sanity. "That was rage, not pain. She's alive."

Douse your light. I'll use my pen light so we can edge a little closer. Zip your jacket to cover your Kevlar." Ethan's low drawl added weight to the plan unfurling.

The air's salty tang announced their closer proximity to the tunnel's end, but the scent of death breathed fire and ice through Caden's veins. Every vile inhalation increased the rage toward anyone who'd kidnap, rape, and sell another human into sexual slavery. His mind couldn't face an aftermath of Kaylee meeting Ciera's fate. All light would cease to exist in a world without his pirate.

"What the hell's wrong with you?" Kaylee's broken speech hissed through the now-dark tunnel after Matt extinguished his light. Lexi's condemnation followed in less-than-eloquent epithets.

They inched forward until ambient light slashed across the ground mere yards from their feet.

"What kind of sick bastard does that to a man?" Lexi's fury lashed out at her kidnapper. "You stabbed him, then forced him through the tunnels before you eviscerated him? Who does that?"

"The same kind who does it to rich, helpless women. I couldn't let him stink up the tunnels, now could I? Now that I've solved my bitch problem, I might decide to use these passages again."

The male's voice held no recognition with Caden, but Ethan grabbed his arm and pulled him close to whisper in his ear.

"I know him. Lucas and I interviewed the prick. That's Basil, the contractor Ciera fooled around with in the pool house," Ethan murmured.

Damien pulled forward but dropped his butt to the ground with Matt's hand signal. "We don't know how many dipshits are out there. Spreading out is the best chance to take them. Ethan, you stay here with Damien while we assess the situation. You're the ace in the hole."

Caden took several slow breaths, listening for any clue to aid his assessment. A false start or wrong move could see either woman dead.

"C'mon bitches, either get in the boat or die with the bloke whose weighted carcass won't be found after I drag it into the river."

"How did you come to work *with* Ciera's husband? Why didn't he kill you for touching what he considered his property?" Lexi's voice didn't cover the sound of Kaylee retching.

"I was just her supplier, with benefits. When she told me she was going to divorce her husband and clean up her act, well, I had no further use for the rich twat. Dear hubby found out about us 'round the same time, but couldn't kill me for fear of evidence I'd left behind coming to light. We hatched a plan. Instead of divorce, he got his wife's money and the knowledge of her complete humiliation. I got money from selling her to upper management after eliminating Vasilisa. Win, win situation with all loopholes closed."

Kaylee's enraged gasp followed the sound of flesh striking flesh. "Prick."

"You think you're gonna get away with that? Effing bitch."

"Ahh," Kaylee sobbed.

The sound of Kaylee's thin cry nearly made Caden bolt blindly into the open.

"You, bitch, threw a monkey wrench in the whole works. When you escaped, I had to kill the whore to tie up loose ends, but Conroy wasn't happy with just his wife's money. No, he wanted Caden to suffer, too. Hence, you came back into play after he saw you two together at the bank."

"You missed her, both at the river and Caden's house." Steel-edged anger burned in Lexi's voice.

"I thought the river would drown you when my new partner said he'd shot then sent you overboard. The Asian bungled the house fire, too. If you want something done right..." Basil's grunt followed Kaylee's thin mewl.

"Then why kill Ciera's husband?" Lexi asked.

"Because he was a loose end—just like you. He bitched about not wanting her dead, just out of the way and degraded. Started grumbling about botched deals."

Hell no. Caden stepped out into the bright light, temporarily blinded to the unfolding scene. To his relief, only one gunman held the women hostage. Basil faced his boat while holding Kaylee tight to his chest, his hand fisted in her hair.

The short, floating dock on which they stood swayed in time with the wavelets' lazy slide to shore. In front of Kaylee, Lexi assumed a rigid stance, her gaze on the gunman's face.

A glance to his right revealed Conroy Kirpatzel's body, partially eviscerated. Blood and bowel contents coated his lower abdomen, having soaked through and stained his rumpled pants. He now collected a long-overdue tariff for dealing out pain and misery.

Recognition lit the contractor's eyes. "Ah, Caden, now you get to stand by helplessly as you lose a second woman. Or perhaps I should shoot you first." Basil's sneer turned sly. "Decisions, decisions."

"In that case, I better move closer, so you won't miss. Your aim is probably as inept as the help you hired." Caden sensed rather than heard Matt exiting the tunnel.

Basil's eyes widened with recognition. "Hmm, apples in a barrel."

On the dock, Lexi and Kaylee stood beside a sleek white, fiberglass cruiser with a below-deck compartment, no doubt intended to store the women. If Basil got Kaylee and Lexi on the boat, they'd never be seen again.

"Hmm, I have more than one McAllister to play with. Never shot a cop before. Now I get a cop and a PI. Isn't this interesting." The barrel of Basil's gun weaved a path from one McAllister to the other. "Oh, by the way, I didn't shoot her at the river. *I wouldn't* have missed. And the dead asshole behind you couldn't flow with the plan. Hence, I spilled his guts literally before he could do it figuratively." Basil imitated the slicing motion that disemboweled the banker.

Caden kept his gaze trained on the grinning psycho with each step down the sandy incline until reaching the first wooden plank. When the gun's barrel swung wide in Matt's direction, a glimpse to the side revealed a steeper sloping ground.

Matt advanced slowly. "So, you're the brains behind all this? I don't think so. From what I gather, you piss a bit of your brains away with drugs every day."

"I'm the new go-between, money for women."

"How's that working out for you? You've got what, five people killed so far?" Caden taunted. "And how many women have you taken?"

"Ciera and two others were *my* first acquisitions. Ciera was the cost of changing management. The Asian and his partners were incompetent." The shark's smile suggested a fond memory. "I contacted the source and renegotiated our agreement, women instead of drugs. I'm tired of supplying quick fixes to the rich snobs of Portland. This is much cleaner, not to mention more profitable and fun."

"But Kaylee threw a glitch in the works when she inadvertently took your *employee's* picture. She must have inadvertently gotten a photo of Conroy's girlfriend." Caden took another step forward. "You had to have that back to clean up your mess."

"Huh, the foreign whore wanted to stay stateside, had grown to fancy the banker. To make matters worse, Conroy's whining grew tiresome." Basil motioned for Caden to stop. "Then, when your little whore escaped, I decided it was time to change things up." His gaze flicked between brothers. "Close enough. Can't miss putting a hole in your heart from here."

"So where is Conroy's girlfriend?" Matt redirected the gunman's attention to himself.

"At the bottom of the river. I didn't need her anymore."

No force on Earth could prevent Caden's feet from moving him forward.

"No, Caden. Stay back." The pain in Kaylee's plea ripped through his gut. Twenty yards equaled the interplanetary distance between Earth and the sun with Kaylee being the richest source of electromagnetic energy, her aura emitting the invisible rays that sustained life. His life.

He closed half the distance, close enough to see the beads of sweat on her forehead and tears jeweling her lashes.

The bastard twisted her head until they locked gazes. "My new little whore is right. We don't want blood spatter on the boat." To emphasize his authority, he pushed the gun barrel to her temple, causing her to cry out.

Every muscle in Caden's body locked tight with the icy fist squeezing his lungs. In his peripheral vision, Matt stood five yards back and to the side with hands out in surrender. Caden had wanted to extract as much information as possible to give them time to develop a plan.

Their time was up.

"I do love instant obedience." He risked a quick glance at Lexi. "Okay, bitch. On the boat you go, but if I hear that motor start, your girlfriend dies along with your friends."

"Hey, dirtball." Ethan's voice and Damien's fierce barking snapped attention to the charging shepherd from the mouth of the tunnel.

Simultaneous events blurred definition.

Lexi leaped into the low-slung boat then pivoted to rock the floating dock. Basil's balance faltered with uneven footing as Kaylee's elbow struck his gut. Caden charged forward. Matt and Ethan rushed the dock.

Basil's first shot spun Caden around and into the water. Pain in his chest and the cold depths closing over his head kept him conscious. The bullet hit him center mass with his vest preventing penetration but not the monstrous burn spreading throughout his chest. He fought to remain coherent.

Muffled screams from above indicated the ongoing struggle as he gathered his senses and swam forward and under the boat to surface behind the struggling trio. Breath burned in his lungs.

In breaking the surface beside the dock, he heard two more shots in quick succession. Damien yelped before a loud thud indicated something heavy hitting the deck.

Shock filled him at seeing Lexi and Kaylee struggling with a downed Basil, his gun dropping to the plank. Matt buckled to the platform, his hand clutching his shoulder.

Basil's fist crashed into Kaylee's cheek. Ethan snatched her back before another belt rendered her unconscious. In a maelstrom of flying fists and disordered actions, Kaylee struck out blindly, seldom connecting with her target. Lexi struggled against Basil trying to confine both her wrists in one of his hands. Her foot connecting with his groin produced a howl of rage and pain.

The deadly scene continued to unfold with the contractor struggling to right himself despite Lexi's determination to keep him down. As Caden heaved himself up, Basil recovered his gun and shoved it in Lexi's face. Quick reflexes saw Lexi's arm come up and her head duck to the side at the same time Ethan latched onto Basil's gun hand.

The shot went wide.

From behind, Caden gripped Basil in a reverse chin-lock at the same time Ethan snatched the gun away. The bastard had tried to kill everything precious in his life and deserved what he'd now receive. The choke hold tightened until the shit's gasping sounds weakened, but Caden didn't soften his grip.

Matt wheezed a breath while holding pressure on his wounded shoulder, his gaze assessing the situation. "Caden, enough—"

Voices continued to buzz like annoying insects yet made little sense. Nothing mattered other than stopping the dirtball's next breath. Cold seeped into his bones, just as death approached the sadistic thug within his grasp. It wasn't enough.

A warm hand scrabbled at his upper arm while a familiar softness cupped his cheek. The cherished heat thawed the ice surrounding his heart and limbs.

"No, Caden. Don't. Please." Kaylee's glazed eyes pleaded her cause.

The contradicting rush of adrenaline urged him to snap the weakening neck in his grasp.

An eternity passed in those few heartbeats of time. Two futures, one where she carried guilt over him killing her kidnapper, and another where her soul filled to bursting, remained connected to him on a spiritually equal field.

Matt's tirade began cutting through the haze. "Caden. Stop. I'd rather see bruises on his face than lilies on his chest." Sitting up with his brother's help, Matt looked to his shepherd. "Ethan, help Lexi with Damien."

The heat of Kaylee's body pressing against him as she sidled closer thawed his icy resolve. Slowly, her touch drifted down his arms to cover his wrists, gently prying them away. With no other anchor in his panicked world, he scooted sideways and wrapped his arms around her melting form. Basil slumped unconscious to the dock.

"It's Damien's shoulder. Someone's gonna have to carry him." Lexi examined the shepherd, his plaintiff whine filling the air. Lexi looked to Ethan. "I can help Matt if you can carry Damien."

After checking on the dog, Ethan hauled Lexi to her feet and held her tight, his lips slanting over hers. It was a long moment before either came up for air.

"Matt, you okay?" Caden stared at the carnage wrought. All for greed.

"Yeah. Thanks, everybody, for asking. I'll be fine, but I need to get to the hospital. And we might need to get a garden hose to separate these two. How about you?" Matt's face contorted in pain with movement.

"I think the impact broke a rib, but I'm in one piece and not leaking."

Ethan stepped back while Lexi helped Matt to his feet, supporting him with her shoulder.

Kneeling up offered Caden thigh to shoulder contact with Kaylee. To absorb her soft scent after burying his face against her neck and taking her very essence into his soul, restored his sense of the world. "Don't you ever do this shit to me again. Got it?" The thought of not gazing into her eyes and connecting with her spirit spiraled his thoughts to a dark and foreboding place.

As if sensing his deteriorating mood, she pulled his head down for a kiss. His compliance was immediate, sealing his lips over hers, demanding entry and taking everything she offered, giving equally of himself.

"Great. Now we need a fire hose," Matt muttered.

When Caden lifted his head, Kaylee's love and assurance reflected back. The unspoken truth and certainty in her eyes spoke of the future of which he'd dreamed.

If he'd been seconds later, he could have lost her forever. If the bastard had been a better shot or turned his gun on her instead of him, she wouldn't be soft and loving in his arms. So many ways fate could have screwed them. *Yet here she is, safe and warm in my arms.*

"Check. Avoid sadistic kidnappers at the top of my to-do list. Got it." Her sassy grin spoke of pranks yet to come.

"Pirate, I oughta warm your ass."

"Right now, other parts are warming just fine." Her seductive smile presaged a new beginning, free of constant tension, fear, and uncertainty.

She knew damn well he couldn't make good on their volcanic attraction right then, yet her grin denoted knowledge of her effect as she squirmed against him.

He'd settle for kissing her senseless, loving the dazed look, softening body, and wobbling knees. It only took seconds to achieve.

"Guys? C'mon. What the hell are you doing?" Matt complained.

"I've got neither the time nor the crayons to explain, Matt, but you'll figure it out someday. I promise." Caden grinned against Kaylee's lips before pulling back.

"Hey. It's bad enough when Ethan and Lexi stay lip-locked long enough to challenge any free diver, but, Caden, you don't need to compete."

Kaylee swiped a lock of wet hair from his face. "Let's see if he's got some blankets stored in the boat."

"Well, at least we have convenient transportation." Caden helped Kaylee up before securing the prisoner.

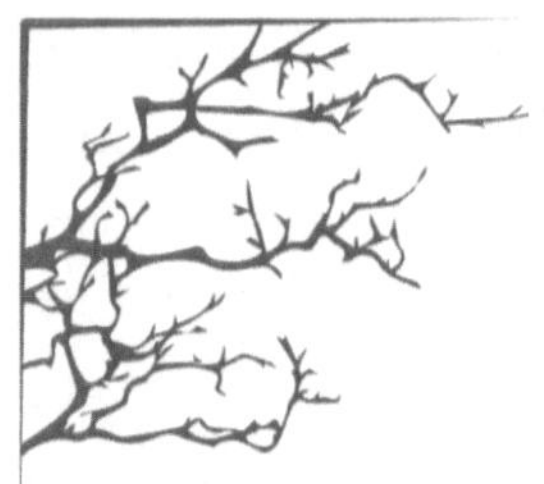

Epilogue

Soft, warm, furry pups scampered over Kaylee's legs as she sat amid the roaming, scrambling furballs. For the past half hour, she'd sat and cooed over each one that tried to climb her chest to reach her face. The rough rasp of moist tongues on her cheeks were memories to treasure.

It'd taken two weeks before her life began to settle into a normal rhythm. Days at the cabin were relaxing and soothing with short hikes and long conversations while evenings with Caden's family brought the folksy and humorous wit that characterized their relationships. Plans for the future evolved during nights in her soul mate's arms.

Caden crouched beside her, visually evaluating each pup. "Kaylee, there's eight here. We can only take one." He snorted when she turned pouty lips in his direction.

"But look at them. This one's nestled on my lap and her brother is giving me a tongue bath." She smiled, knowing what went through his thoughts. His gaze showed it in spades.

"Yep. Only one, babe."

"But then that one would be lonely. She'd cry over the loss of *all* her brothers and sisters. You can imagine what that feels like after Matt was shot." The fact they'd emerged from her nightmare with everyone intact was a miracle.

"Hon…"

"Matt said that if you have two, they keep each other company." Last night's campfire with all the McAllisters present rekindled long-ago feelings before Reese's death, a time when she'd taken family gatherings for granted. Matt had inadvertently dropped the idea of them each having a dog. Kaylee immediately adopted it as a foregone conclusion.

"Matt was just trying to make my life hell because I didn't listen to him at the dock."

"He doesn't blame you for getting him shot. He just wanted to harass you."

"Changing the subject won't change the outcome." The grin twitching at the corner of his lips betrayed his intention.

Cahill, the breeder, turned to Caden. "Dude, you lost this battle before you even arrived. It's easier just to give in."

Caden sighed, ignoring the obvious. "Sweetheart, if you get two, it'd have to be one male and one female. Otherwise, we run the risk of them fighting when they're older and alone in the house. And *that* means you'd have to have one spayed or neutered. Which means surgery and pain. You wouldn't want to put your best friend through that, would you?"

She gasped. "I would never consider doing that to you!"

Cahill laughed. "Man, you oughta quit while you're ahead. Know what I mean?"

"We'll figure something out. Please?" She knew she had him. He was just drawing out the scene for his own purpose, for which he'd take great delight in obtaining compensation once they were alone.

In the SUV, her eyes burned with unspent tears at the pups' pitiful howls. Each one clawed at the crate's metal spindles. She sat on the back seat between them, slipping her fingers through the bars and stroking their fur. "They don't seem to notice the T-shirt with their mother's scent."

"They'll be fine once we get back to the cabin. We've got all the time in the world to acclimate them to their new environment."

Freshly tilled farms gave way to gently rolling hills, the morning sun spilling over their crests. Caden's gaze returned to the rearview mirror before he shook his head. Even in his softhearted moments, he radiated a focused masculinity that knocked her socks off. Instead of fading over time, it had gained momentum.

"Can we take them to the construction site after the workmen are gone?"

"Yup, they go where we go. However, they gotta wear a harness whenever they're outside or away from home. By the way, I got a call from the contractor. The extra trees have been cleared out, and he received the approved permits to start."

"Wow. It's really happening. We've got all the muck and nonsense behind us. Now we can finally take a deep breath and move forward." In her mind's eye, she saw their home finished, their children playing in the backyard with the shepherds under their parents' watchful gazes. From the ashes of Reese's death and her own tragedy, she would emerge to fulfill her dreams.

She had her fresh start.

Lexi and Kaylee's stories continue in Inconclusive Evidence where lines between predator and prey blur. Wade through the intricate waters where polymer microchips and nanotechnology can change alter mankind's history through surgical techniques. Read further for an excerpt.

Inconclusive Evidence

Death In Degrees

Jackie Milburn didn't do fear.

The late-night walk to her car had never provoked an accelerated heart rate. Tonight, however, a bone-deep foreboding arose from vestiges of instinctual awareness, all merging to question her mission's strategy. If she failed, millions would suffer and life as anyone knew it, would end.

Indistinct shadows granted a cozy ambience where she often lurked, but dingy light filtering through overhead branches mocked her bravado. Shadow limbs shook with laughter as Fate's sense of humor conspired with nature to saturate creation's mindset with malice.

Regardless of destiny's intentions, she squared her shoulders while scanning the deserted parking lot, alert to any threat. A sense of relief had washed through her after depositing the damning evidence in the USPS blue box. The evil shits would never expect an investigative reporter to mail the sophisticated mechanisms across country. Precautions taken with the dispatch ensured no one could trace the recipient. *Always have a backup plan.*

This was the biggest scoop of her career and would spotlight one of Delaware's billion-dollar companies as a collection of hi-tech, sociopathic thugs.

It wouldn't take CSV Pharmaceuticals long to discover crucial evidence missing and ferret out their traitor. As corporations went, they were as paranoid as any. She prayed Dr. Sorenson made it out of the country alive, and not as shark chum. Paranoia had compelled her to refuse him the number to her newest burner phone. Intuition saw the last one tossed in the Willamette River after tapping out a quick message to her old college roommate. Jackie survived by instincts and prayed they would serve her well—one more time.

Making the last stop to pick up her go-bag would supply the necessary items to disappear until her story broke. The finishing touches included copies of lab reports and communication between the Delaware scientists and a company on the West Coast, ClickChip.

Various colored and styled wigs, plain lens glasses, makeup, and diverse fashion ensembles would allow her to blend with any crowd, but wouldn't prevent CCTVs and facial recognition programs from pinpointing her location. Planning ahead, she had a well-stocked safe house outside city limits.

Trembling fingers failed to punch the unlock button on her key fob. Instead, her headlights cut a swath through the misty ground cover, a beacon to any waiting goon. *Shit.* The subsequent knocking of heart against ribs rivaled the best hammer drill while sweat coated her palms and face despite her warmed exhalations sending puffed smoke signals in the frosty air.

A slow, deep breath reclaimed her sense of calm and allowed the subtle scent from emerging camellia blossoms drifting on the night's currents to settle her spirit. *There. This is who I am.* For visual affirmation of her feelings, she glanced at her reflection in the driver's side window.

The sudden thrust of a phantom arm emerging from the dark pinned her against a hard chest. The steely limb angled and applied pressure to tilt her head back as if she were a rag doll.

"Oomph." Collision forced air from her lungs while shock produced a gasp that inhaled a sickly sweet odor from the cloth rammed over her mouth and nose.

"Wanna play?" Malice drew out each syllable in a parody of innocent sport.

Momentary panic barred all reason. Instinctive reaction initiated clawing at the viselike grip. Subsequent kicking and twisting of her body yielded no compromise in her position.

In her periphery, she caught sight of a malevolent smile and glinting dark eyes under a black fedora. *The boogeyman does exist.*

Lethargy and disorientation. Another breath or pass out from hypoxia. No more pain. All her muscles relaxed against her will. The invading blackness closed in from the margins.

NO! An enraged cry died in her throat.

Thank you for reading <u>*BOUND BY SHADOWS*</u> Independent authors rely on support to spread the word of their work. If you enjoyed the story and have the time, I'd really appreciate a brief review.

Sign up for my newsletter[1] for the first peek at new books, exclusive giveaways, and sales.

---

1.   https://reilygarrett.com

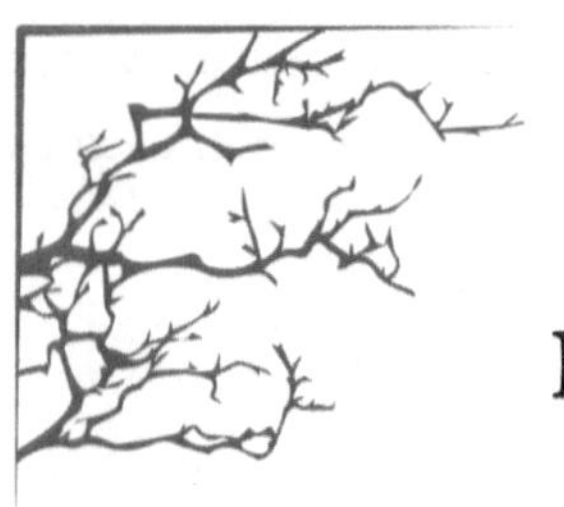

Reily's Books

Romantic Thrillers

McAllister Justice Series
Tender Echoes
Digital Velocity
Bound By Shadows
Inconclusive Evidence
Carbon Replacements
Shattered Reflections
Remnants of Evil

Moonlight and Murder Series
Shifting Targets
A Critical Tangent
Pivotal Decisions
Seeds of Murder
An Unlikely Grave
Deadly Interception
Love You To Death

Psychic Thrillers

Mind Stalkers Series
Bending Fate
Silent Depths
Shadow Guard
Whispers After Death
Mind Hunters

Guardian Series

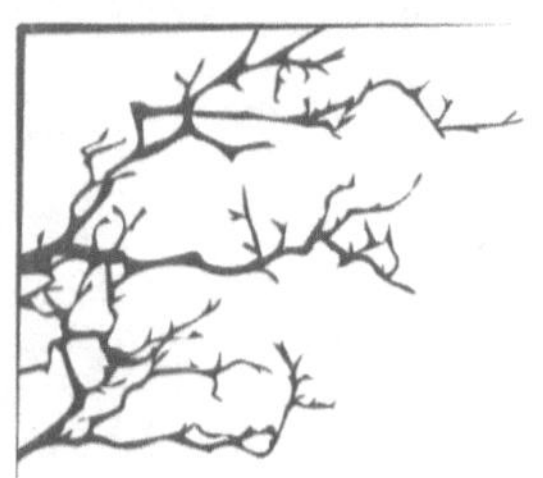

Copyright

All rights reserved. No part of this book may be reproduced or transmitted in any form or by any means, electronic or mechanical, including photocopying, recording, or by any information storage and retrieval system without the written permission of the author, and where permitted by law. Reviewers may quote brief passages in a review.

This book is a work of fiction. Names, characters, places, and incidents either are products of the author's imagination or used fictitiously. Any resemblance to actual persons living or dead, business establishments, events, or locales is entirely coincidental.

BOUND BY SHADOWS

Copyright © 2017 Reily Garrett

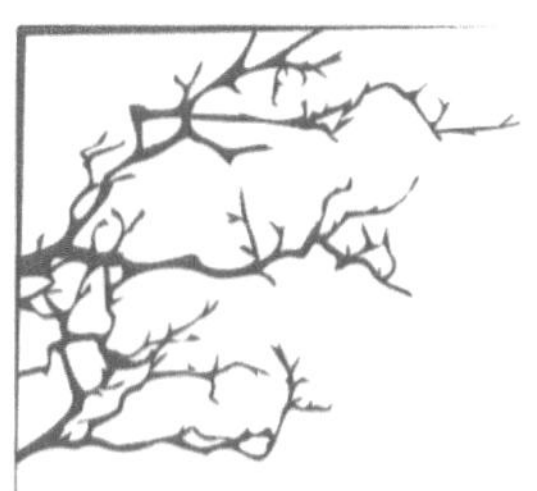

About Reily

Reily Garrett is a writer, mother, and companion to three long coat German shepherds. When not working with her dogs, she's sitting at her desk with her fur kids by her side.

Author of chilling suspense and snarky romance, her stories span the distance of romantic thrillers, paranormal romance, and erotic romance. Regardless of genre, each book delves into a dark and twisted imagination yet is tempered with romance and a touch of humor.

Reviews by Kirkus Reviews, San Francisco Bay Review, and BestThrillers.com best describe her work:

"This could be James Patterson, Lee Child, and Tess Gerritsen rolled into one, but the dark, twisted methods used by the serial killer could surprise even those readers..." - San Francisco Bay Review

"...steamy, seductive police procedural..." - BestThrillers.com

"...well-researched thriller that remains romantically genuine throughout." - Kirkus Review

Prior experience in the Military Police, private investigations, and as an ICU nurse gives her fiction a real-world flavor. Find Reily below.

Website[1] Facebook[2] BookBub[3] Amazon[4] Goodreads[5]

---

1. http://www.reilygarrett.com/

2. https://www.facebook.com/reilygarrett/?modal=admin_todo_tour

3. https://bit.ly/2mSSOap

4. https://www.amazon.com/Reily-Garrett/e/
B00SXK3WEU?ref=sr_ntt_srch_lnk_1&qid=1554734223&sr=8-1

5. https://www.goodreads.com/author/show/11126619.Reily_Garrett

www.ingramcontent.com/pod-product-compliance
Lightning Source LLC
Chambersburg PA
CBHW031445160726
47994CB00005B/1881